TALES FROM ZUID HORN:

The New Apprentice

Michael Weber

Ten 16

www.ten16press.com - Waukesha, WI

The New Apprentice
Copyrighted © 2023 Michael Weber
ISBN HC: 9781645387176
ISBN PB: 9781645387190

The New Apprentice
by Michael Weber

For information, please contact:

www.ten16press.com
Waukesha, WI

Editor: Jenna Zerbel
Art Director: Kaeley Dunteman
Cover & Interior Layout Designer: Jayden Shambeau
Illustrator: Michael Weber
Photographer: Scott Curty

For my friends and family.

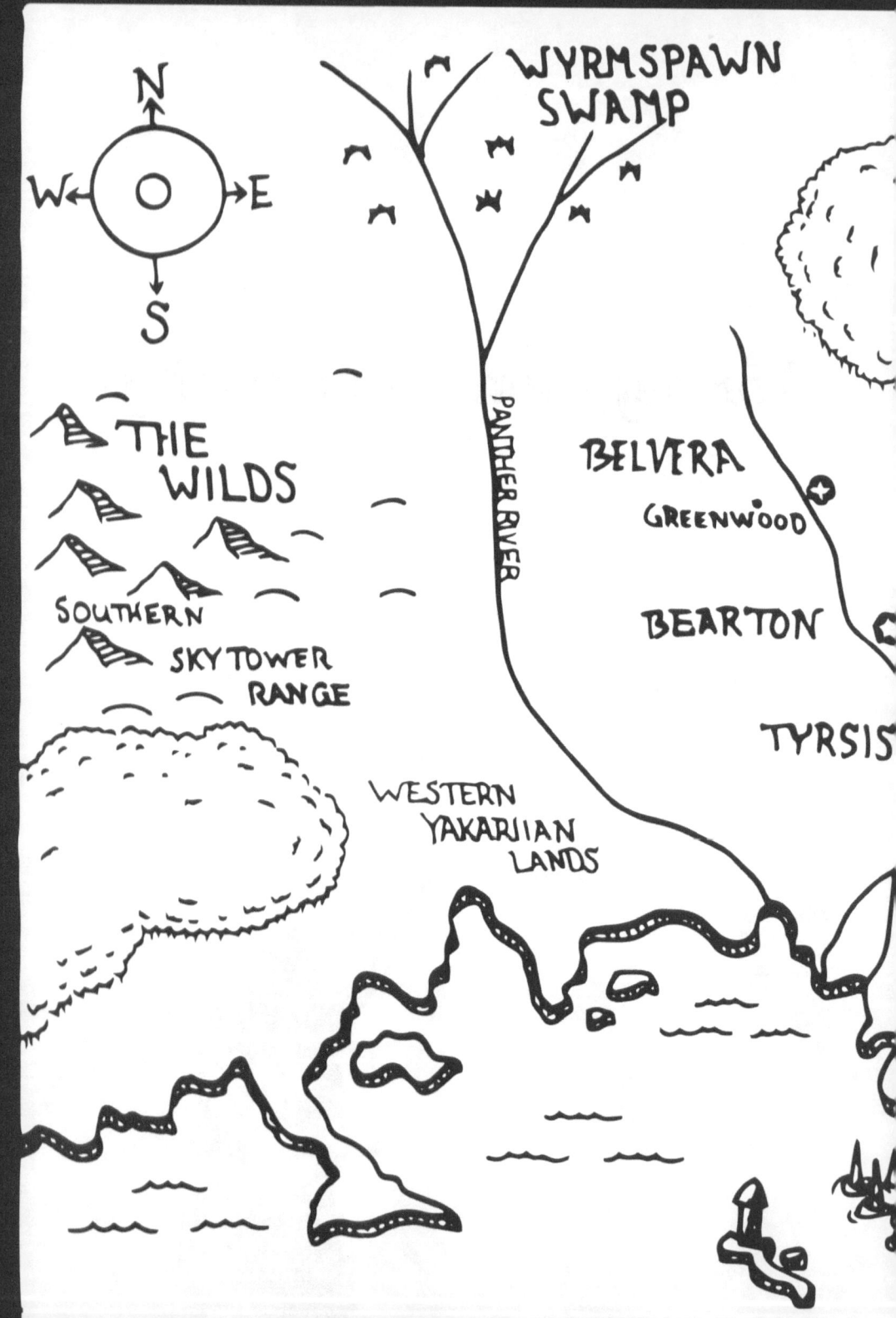

ISBANDIA
MISTWALL MOUNTAINS
Onyx Castle
CARDOSA
Tonásul
OASIS RIVER
To BENGAZII
SHADIZAR
DESERT SEA
COASTLAND
BREECH WOOD FOREST
ZUID HORN
THE MAW

TABLE OF CONTENTS

1

Derek almost Drowns
in Zuid Horn

isten.

This is how the city of Zuid Horn was destroyed.

First, there was the explosion that rocked Derek Fulstarter and his family from their beds. The blast echoed across the famous city of foundries, reverberated off the eighty-foot walls surrounding the city, and rumbled over Zuid Horn like the grumbling forest giants that worked loading and unloading ships docked on Ploughman's Wharf.

Derek and his family stared wide-eyed into the dark of the sleeping loft over their fletchery shop. Mum didn't even get a candle lit before the second explosion shook their house and sent shelves of arrows tumbling to the ground.

"Hammer and Anvils," Da swore. He limped across the loft and swung his game leg over the ladder to their first-floor kitchen. "What the devil is going on?"

"Is it Gilgameth Tuft?" Derek's youngest sister, Sarah, whispered.

She would think that, Derek scowled. *But then again, maybe she's right.*

"Shush, girl," Mum hissed. "Don't say his name out loud." And then, in case the wizard was listening, she added, "If it is, he's protecting Zuid Horn, not destroying it."

Mum's candle flickered to life. His sisters rubbed their eyes and squinted into the dark. Derek hurried over to the edge of the loft and hopped on the ladder. "Da! Wait for me."

"No, I'll be right back," Da muttered as he passed the coals still flickering in the oven. "You stay here." Then he was through the kitchen doorway and into their arrow-making shop.

But Derek was in no mood to listen. He had to know. What was going on out there? He scurried down the ladder, slipped through the kitchen, and followed his father.

Da's shop was dark. The pine scent of resin, the woody smell of freshly split ironwood, and the cool ting of blue steel arrowheads filled the air as it had for generations of Fulstarters. They were fletchers, after all, who for generations had been one of the best arrow-making families in Zuid Horn, and this was their home. Derek ran his hand along the smooth countertop of the nearest workbench to help find his way to the door. Another explosion hammered the night. Derek jumped and hurried to catch up with Da.

A dim light from the oil streetlamps shone through cracks in the walls and around the frame of the double door leading to Gillman's Way, the street in front of their shop. Derek peered into the shadows. Da grunted and muttered and dragged his game leg past the silhouettes of workbenches, barrels, and racks of working tools. Derek crept quietly behind in the dark, waiting for his father to unlock the doors. While he waited, a fourth explosion lit up the night. Bright, orange light streamed through the planked walls. For a moment, the light was so bright Derek couldn't see. His vision came back just in time to see Da throw open the doors and step into the street.

An orange ball of fire mushroomed into the clear, moonless night above the Gladstone Foundry. Even though the foundry was a half-mile away, the explosion hit Derek like a hard slap to the face. Three plumes of flame roared into the starry sky. Derek stumbled through the shop toward Gillman's Way. "The foundries!" he shouted, pointing at the tumbling rivers of smoke and ash rolling across the heavens.

Da shook his shaggy head. "I told you to stay with your sisters."

Derek ignored him. "What's happening?"

The light of the burning foundries flickered in Da's black eyes. "I don't know."

Screams rose from the city's center. Derek heard men yelling for help and the deep roars of forest giants calling for water.

Three more explosions shook their shop's rafters, and three more foundries burst into flames. "This is bad," Da whispered. "This is really bad."

Up and down Gillman's Way, people poured into the street. Still dressed in their sleeping britches, Derek's neighbors stared and pointed at the rivers of sparks and ash tumbling higher and higher with the wind. A pair of ten-foot-tall ogre porters thundered past with huge packs thrown over their shoulders. Their eyes were wide and rolling with fear. Da pulled Derek back to avoid being trampled.

"Watch where you're going!" he shouted at the beasts, but they ignored him and kept running. Da shook his head. "You know it's bad when even the ogres are scared."

Derek nodded but held his tongue.

In the distance, the clang of fire bells and din of people shouting filled gaps between explosions. Over it all was the roar of a growing fire and the nose-stinging stink of burning pitch.

"Derek!" His good friend and neighbor, Peter, the carpenter's son, ran up to him. "What's going on?"

Derek shrugged. "I don't know. We just got out here."

"I'll tell you what's going on," Da said, the dark curls of his beard and mane shining in the light of the fires. "Zuid Horn is burning. If someone doesn't get this under control, the entire city is going to be ashes by morning."

The metallic clanking of armored boots on the march drew their attention down Gillman's Way. A unit of twenty guardsmen,

fully outfitted in steel armor, longswords, and shields, trudged in unison toward them. These were members of the Iron Guard, Zuid Horn's famous warriors who had defended the city for generations. The best warriors from around the realms had always rushed to Zuid Horn to sign on with this famous band, protecting the realm's wealthiest city from enemies, disorder, and now an unexpected fire at the city's industrial heart.

"Thank the Forge." Derek drew the tips of his fingers across his forehead and then over his upper chest, a sign of reverence for Zuid Horn's chief deity. "The Iron Guard will know what to do."

"Maybe," Da muttered, his mouth a tight line.

"At least they'll keep the humanoids in line."

Da grunted. "Let's hope."

The captain at the front of the unit had his visor up. "All families should prepare for fire defense!" he cried above the din. "Douse your rooftop, wet blankets to put out falling ash, and fill all the buckets you can. We must work together to save Zuid Horn!"

Derek, Peter, and Da watched the unit thunder past. "You had better go home," Da said to Peter. "Your parents are going to need your help."

Peter nodded. "I think you're right, Mr. Fulstarter. I'll see you later, Derek," Peter said, and then hurried away.

Da put his hand on Derek's shoulder. "Go tell your mother what is going on. Tell her to pack a bag and make it quick. We're leaving."

"But the Iron Guard said to get water ready."

Another explosion lit the sky. Derek and his father instinctively crouched low. Da grabbed Derek by the shoulders. "Water isn't going to put out these fires, boy. Smell that? That's foundry fuel. Too hot for a bucket of water to do anything."

"But the shop!"

Da shook his head. "I'll see to that. You just get inside and tell your mother what's going on."

"But I want to help you!"

"Hammer and Anvils, boy! You *will* help me if you stop arguing and get to your mother."

Derek ground his teeth. His jaw was so tense it felt like his teeth were going to crack. But he had disobeyed his father before, too recently, and knew better than to tempt Da's patience when tensions were high. Derek rubbed the fresh scar on his chest through his shirt. No, in situations like this, Da usually knew best.

He was about to turn back to the shop when a deep boom pulsed over Zuid Horn and silenced the city. This was not the crackling quick explosions taking out the foundries one by one. This was something deeper, something lower, something unnatural. It made Derek's bowels tighten and twist like hungry serpents. Derek and Da looked at one another with the calm of people who know they are about to witness something terrible, and then together turned their gazes toward the Tower of High Sorcery, the home of Gilgameth Tuft.

Black and ominous, the tower loomed over Zuid Horn. The night air around the wizard's stronghold shimmered as though it radiated an awful heat, but no flames danced over its obsidian walls. Fear's cold talons gripped Derek's guts. The tower boomed and pulsed again. When the ocean answered from a mile away, Derek almost wet himself. He licked his suddenly dry lips.

Da's voice rattled him. "I said, get to your mother. Now!"

This time, Derek didn't argue.

He dashed through the shop and burst into the kitchen, almost running straight into Mum. "Whoa, whoa, careful, Derek. What's going on out there?" She looked over his shoulder, trying to see into the street.

"No time to explain," he said, all in a rush. "Get a bag packed. I'll grab Liza and Sarah. We have to go."

"What's going on?" Liza, Derek's other sister, poked her head over the loft's railing. Her long, black hair was still tangled from sleep. "What's all the booming about?"

"You don't want to know," Derek muttered, climbing the ladder to the loft two rungs at a time. "Get a bag packed. Quickly."

"Why?" Sarah asked. "What's wrong?"

Derek wanted to scream. "Just do it," he said, trying to sound as calm as possible. "You'll see as soon as you get packed."

The girls threw a blanket on the loft's floor and began tossing clothing and necessities into the middle. He nodded. "Good. Tie that into a bundle when you're done. Don't bring too much. We have to move fast."

"Why?" Mum asked from below.

Derek checked on the girls one last time and then hurried down the ladder. "Zuid Horn is burning," he whispered. "And the wizards, they're up to something."

Mum's mouth tightened and her eyes grew still, calculating. "Tell your father we'll be right out. I'll help the girls, and then we'll be down." She turned and scaled the ladder to the loft without waiting for an answer.

Derek started back toward his father but froze in his steps. What was that sound? A deep growl rose from the city's chest, getting closer and closer, and with it came a curtain of screams from the Warehouse District. He was standing stock still, trying to decipher the sounds, when his father burst through the doorway.

"Forget packing," Da said, loud enough for the whole family to hear. "We need to go. Now." Da's face was ashen.

"What's that sound?" Derek asked.

Da ignored him. "Nadetta," he called to Derek's mother, "we need to go."

Mum looked over the railing. "What's going on?"

"Just grab the girls."

Derek took a step toward the ladder to help his mother with his sisters. He knew how they *had* to ask questions, *had* to know what was going on, especially when the family needed to move quickly. And if they ever had to move quickly, it was now.

But it was too late.

The rumble of destruction was upon them, barreling down Gillman's Way. It burst into their shop with a roar, and then, somehow, the sea was upon them.

Chill black water smashed through the front door, smothered the smoldering cooking coals with an angry hiss, knocked Mum's leek stew off the stove, and then plowed across the rough plank floor. Thick tongues of dark water poured through the door and windows.

Derek and his father sloshed through the quickly flooding kitchen. Da snatched Derek by a thin shoulder and limped against the powerful current to the lashed ladder leading to the sleeping loft. Trapped in the loft above them, the girls screamed for their father.

Da pushed Derek up the ladder and followed quickly after his son. "Hurry, boy! The water's rising."

Derek scrambled up the ladder and tumbled into his mother and sisters. Mum lifted a lone candle. "Bryton! Through the roof!" She glanced over the railing at the sea filling their kitchen. The lines around her chocolate eyes tightened like a spider's fists. "The water is still rising!"

Da nodded grimly and climbed the last rungs of the ladder, grunting each time he bent his bum knee. Droplets of floodwater glistened in the dark curls of his bushy beard. He pointed toward an oaken barrel stuffed with ironwood arrows they had just finished fletching for the Ranger Outpost that afternoon.

"Help me grab that," he grunted at Derek, and the two of them dragged the barrel across the loft to the lowest point of the pitched roof. "Up and through the roof on three," Da said. "One, two," they swung the barrel back, "three!" Together, father and son smashed the solid barrel through the roof. A shower of freshly fletched arrows and thin shingles rained down around them. Bryton hurriedly brushed them aside and gestured to Derek. "Grab your sisters. Don't worry about your mother and me."

Derek helped his sisters through the hole in the roof then offered a hand to his mother, but Da grabbed Derek around the

waist and pushed him toward the hole. "No time for us. Just get your sisters up."

A sharp crack split the night, and the western wall of their house gave away. The roof dropped drunkenly, and his sisters slipped down the wet slope. "Get them!" his father screamed. "The house is about to go!" Derek scrambled through the hole and onto the roof.

He spun in a quick circle to assess his surroundings. The sky over Zuid Horn was clear and moonless, but mountains of smoke billowed from the city's center, where thirteen foundries lined both sides of the Black River. The towers of smoke, lit by the burning foundries, rose over the city like frowning giants. Derek tried to step closer to the street, but his sisters' screaming snapped him back to the present.

Water boiled past the house, almost up to the edge of the roof. The raging river battered the street side of the building with debris and drowning people. They screamed and waved at Derek and then were gone in an instant. There was nothing he could do to help. A great roaring came from up the way. He watched in horror as a great cow of a minotaur swept past. It tossed its horns and bellowed before the torrent drank it up. Derek took a step closer to the edge. Were those giant rats swimming in the flood? Flushed from the sewers no doubt.

"Derek!" Liza cried. "Get over here!"

Liza and Sarah clung to the roof, slick with flood spray. "Mum! Da!" Sarah screamed.

Derek rushed over and stuck an arm through the hole in the roof. "Mum! Give me your hand!" She reached for him, and their fingers touched. Another crack and the loft collapsed, dropping under his parents' feet. They disappeared beneath the dark tide. Derek leaned into the hole. "Mum! Da!"

Da broke through the surface. There was fear behind the scowl. Derek could see it. "Where's Mum?" Derek asked.

Da spit and splashed in the flood to keep afloat. "Damn it, boy. Get your sisters to the peak. I'll find your mother." He gave his son a final look, and then he disappeared beneath the roiling waves.

For an instant, Derek froze. His parents were gone. How could it all go so wrong, so fast? Then, his father's words cut through the fog, *Get your sisters to the peak.* He scrambled toward the girls on hands and knees and toes over the wooden shingles, slick with wet moss. He grabbed his sisters by the elbows and hauled them to the peak, where they all collapsed, gasping for breath.

The black water was rising fast. It rushed through the streets, carrying bits of buildings, benches, a drowned dog, and there, a boy's corpse. "Derek!" Liza shouted, pointing at the dead boy. "It's Peter!" Liza clutched the edge of their roof and screamed. "Peter! Peter!"

Peter.

Derek stared at the body as it rolled over and over in the current. It couldn't be Peter. They were just talking with Da in the street. How could someone be alive one instant and dead the next? He wanted to go to his friend, drag him out of that torrent, but he knew the current would pull him down as well, and Derek would end up among the corpses rushing past. Something in his heart turned off.

Peter.

Derek felt his face harden. If he was going to survive, if he was going to help his sisters survive, he couldn't mourn now.

Sarah looked up at him and tugged his arm. "Where's Mum? Where's Da?"

The fletcher's son grimaced. Water lapped at the hole in the roof now, its creep constant. "They're coming. Just hold tight," he said and hoped it wasn't a lie.

Sarah nodded and dug her tiny fingers under the shingles. Liza sobbed and moaned at the edge of the roof. "Peter," she muttered.

Derek crawled over the shingles toward her. "Liza, he's gone. Come away from the edge."

Liza reached toward the dead boy's body, now almost out of sight as the waters tumbled past. She didn't fight Derek, though, not like she normally would have, and she let herself be led to the roof's peak, where they clutched the top of their tattered home.

A burst like a thousand thunderbolts ripped through the night. Bright yellows, oranges, and whites lit the sky over Zuid Horn, illuminating the silhouettes of the foundries. Derek rose on shaky feet to see better. The roof jerked and pitched beneath him, but he needed to know what was going on. From his vantage point, Derek could see that most of the foundries were in flames. Tendrils of orange and blue snapped into the night sky. Derek's house was a good half mile from Zuid Horn's industrial center, but the fire was so strong he could feel the heat on his face.

Derek shook his head. "We have to get out of the city."

Liza wiped her eyes and stood next to him. "But how?"

A deep rumble brought their attention back to the water swirling about the house. The roof jerked, and more of their home broke away. Derek called for his parents again. "Mum! Da!"

No answer.

A gust of wind howled and kicked up a spray of salty mist. The roof rocked, and his sisters screamed. The support beams groaned under the pressure of the rushing water. Soon, the house would give way, and the roof would be sent spinning like a drunk down Gillman's Way. Derek searched the swirling waters and prayed he wouldn't find his parents among the gray faces floating by.

He raised an arm against the breeze and peered into the night. The wind had shifted, bringing with it the acrid stench of foundry fuel. Hot ash from the fires nipped at his eyes and face, forcing him to squint if he wanted to see into the distance.

Rising through the ash and flame, Gilgameth Tuft's tower soared without blemish above the water and the smoke. Doorless and windowless except for a balcony ringing the uppermost floor, it seemed impervious to the destruction below.

Something moved on the balcony. Blue flecks like dancing sparks flew from the tower into the murky flood waters. Then a groan issued forth and rolled across the city. The water in the streets groaned in response and surged inland. What was left of

their house caught the current and jerked hard toward Gillman's Way once, twice, and a third time. Derek wobbled back and forth. He tried to keep his footing but thought better of it and dropped to his hands and knees. There was a hard snap, and the roof broke loose and spun into the rushing torrent.

Liza and Sarah screamed and held on to one another. Derek scrambled over and wrapped his shivering arms around them, pinning his sisters to the floating chunk of rooftop. Together, they spun in dizzy circles, careening off neighboring houses and businesses. There went Mr. Martin's meadery. That was Beru's natural remedies shop. They bounced off the Clayton tannery, twirled across the watery way, and smashed halfway through the second-floor windows of The Forgeshine Inn. The shattered roof serving as their makeshift raft shivered against the hungry current but held fast.

"Derek!" a voice shouted from the rooftop. "Up here!"

It was Augie, Derek's best friend in the world, besides Peter. Augie's parents, Karl and Sasha Innskeep, owned the inn into which Derek and his sisters had just crashed. They appeared next to Augie on the roof. "Get up here, Derek!" Mr. Innskeep yelled. He reached out his hand as far as he could. "Your raft is about to tear free!"

"Sorry about the windows," Derek said.

"By the Forge, boy! Don't worry about that. Get your sisters up here before you all drown!"

Derek squatted low on the floating rooftop to keep his balance and grabbed Sarah around the waist. "What are you doing?" she screeched.

"Quit squirming. You're going up." Derek lifted his sister into the air and took a step toward the roof of the inn, but the raft dipped hard to the left when he stepped. Wood cracked, and bits of broken glass dropped into the black waters. Their raft shivered against the current. Derek risked a quick look and saw the only thing keeping their raft in place was a few thin lattice boards.

"Look out!" Augie yelled. "You're breaking yourself free!"

"He's right," Mr. Innskeep shouted. "Throw the girls. Sarah first." He got down on his knees and reached for her. "Come on, now!"

Derek grunted and got back on his feet. "Ready?" he asked Sarah and grabbed her around the waist again.

"What?" she said, struggling to get away. "No! What if you miss?"

"No time to argue," Derek said and tossed his sister to Mr. Innskeep.

Derek's breath caught in his throat while Sarah flew through the air. Mr. Innskeep caught her by the armpits and hoisted her onto the roof with Augie's help. No sooner was she on the roof than Mr. Innskeep was back at the edge, reaching his arms as far as he could. "Liza, you're next."

Derek turned to Liza, whose eyes were wide. "No way. I'm too heavy."

"Liza! It's our only choice!"

"But what about you?"

A solid thump yanked the raft farther to the left. Derek and Liza stumbled but kept their balance. Derek looked to see what had hit them, just in time to see the hulking back of a drowned yakariian warrior rolling over in the dank waters. The thing must have towered well over seven feet tall when it had been alive, but now it was little more than a floating slab of beef.

"No time to argue," Derek said, his face tight. "You're going now!" He grabbed Liza by the upper arm with one hand and about the waist with the other. He spun in a tight arc and hurled her to Mr. Innskeep.

Augie's father, perhaps not ready for the quick toss, missed Liza with one hand but snatched her with the second. "Gotcha!" he yelled.

Derek pumped his fist. "Yes!" he shouted. He smiled at Augie, who was waving for Derek to hurry onto the roof.

Something moved in the dark behind Augie. An explosion in the distance lit the sky long enough for Derek to see four hulking

figures towering behind his best living friend in the world. "Look out behind you!"

Augie whirled and screamed. Derek took a step to help his friend, and that was when his luck ran out. The raft dipped deep beneath Derek's weight, breaking the last of the lattice holding the roof-raft against the inn. The raft spun and pitched Derek hard to the side. He windmilled his arms to catch his balance, but he was too far gone. He managed a quick, "Help!" before he dropped over the side, and the flood drank him with a cold gulp.

2

Derek Finds a New Face

Thirty days before Zuid Horn was gutted by fire and swallowed by the sea, Derek Fulstarter started his morning like any other, and that meant preparing to get a good tongue lashing from his father well before breakfast. Derek was in the kitchen behind the family shop with his mother and sisters when Da bellowed. "Boy! Get out here!"

Derek grunted in irritation. He was halfway through peeling the burdock roots for lunch. Now, Da would have some stupid errand for him, lunch would be late, and Derek would get yelled at. Again.

He wiped his paring knife on his apron and stomped out of the kitchen and into the shop, the burdock root clutched in his fist.

Da had the shop's double doors flung open to the street. Gillman's Way was stuffed with venders pushing carts of sizzling meats, potions and tinctures, and bolts of woven wool. Across the way, an ogre had an iron chest slung across its back, while its master chatted with a merchant. A pair of shifty plains goblins darted through the crowd. Derek scowled at them. He was about to tell his father to keep a close eye on their wares when Da barked from the front of the shop. "Where have you been? We have a customer."

Derek dragged his feet to stand before his father. "Sorry," he muttered. "Mum had me doing something."

A tall man in a deep chocolate-colored cloak stood just inside the doors, his back to the street. The man was a good head taller than Bryton Fulstarter, but nowhere near as wide. Derek's father had the build of the north, with heavily muscled shoulders and forearms, and thighs like the mighty ironwood trees of Breechwood Forest. At sixteen, Derek had his father's height, but he was years from thickening up.

Derek glanced at Da who, as usual, was frowning. Derek prayed his father wouldn't embarrass him in front of a stranger, but Derek knew what that look meant. Da pointed at Derek's apron and burdock roots. "What's that you're carrying?"

Derek looked at his hands and held them up for his father to see. "Lunch."

Da shook his head. His dark curls and thick beard waved like irritated smoke. "Give that to your sister. I have man's work for you."

Derek sighed and half-turned back toward the kitchen, where his sisters were helping their mother with breakfast. "Liza, come here," he shouted, trying to keep his voice as deep as possible.

There was a pattering of feet, and dark-haired Liza appeared in the doorway between the kitchen and the shop. The morning sun sliced through an open window, and when Liza ran through it, the sunlight highlighted her cheekbones and the new curves that had shown up over the winter. She was fourteen now, just a couple of years away from her presenting at the Coming-of-Age Festival. Neighborhood boys were already sniffing around. The thought of their leering eyes on his sister made him want to punch something. He scowled like Da instead.

Liza ran up the aisle between tall barrels of arrows and tables littered with tools. When she saw Da had a customer, she slowed to a stroll and studied the handsome man with the closely trimmed beard. Without taking her eyes from the customer, she asked Derek, "What?"

"Here," Derek said, pushing the unwashed burdock root into her hands. "Take these to the well and wash them. Peel them, dice them, and let them soak in cold water for a while. Then cook them with some butter, salt, and garlic. That will be our lunch."

Liza finally turned her attention to Derek. She looked at the burdock and frowned. "We don't even have breakfast ready yet."

Derek ground his teeth and cleared his throat. "I know. But if we want burdock for lunch, it has to soak first."

"I don't want burdock for lunch."

Derek's jaw tightened, and the back of his scalp tingled. "It's what we have."

"Doesn't mean I have to like it."

There was a muffled chuckle from the front of the shop. Derek turned to see the customer covering his mouth with a fine leather glove. He felt his face beginning to burn. "Just do it."

Liza's eyes flashed. "Do it yourself. I'm too busy helping Mum." She tossed the bundle of roots back to Derek.

The borders of Derek's vision boiled. "By the Forge, Liza," Derek growled and stormed toward his sister.

Suddenly, Da's voice boomed over the shop. "Derek! Grow up and knock it off."

Derek wheeled around. "But Da!"

"No buts." Da glared and balled his fists on his hips.

Liza snickered behind Derek, and it was all he could do not to scream at her. Derek threw an arm in Liza's direction and shouted at his father. "Do you see this?"

Da didn't budge. His eyes moved between his children and finally settled on Liza. "Go help your mother, girl."

Liza smirked at Derek and then lifted a rosy smile to her father. "Of course, Da. Breakfast is almost ready." She skipped out of the shop and back to the kitchen.

Derek wanted to throw the burdock roots at her back, but he swallowed his anger and turned back to his father, who was talking to the tall man. "Sorry about that," Da said to the man, and then to Derek he said, "Come here."

Derek came to stand next to his father, away from the customer. His face was still burning, and it was all he could do to keep his hands from shaking. Derek kept his eyes down, not wanting to let the customer see how angry he really was. That was when he saw the paring knife still in his hand. Derek had carried it all the way from the kitchen and had forgotten about it in his fight with Liza. The blade shook with Derek's simmering temper. He slipped his paring knife into a sheath on his belt and wiped his hands on his apron. When he looked back up, the customer was studying him.

"You're wearing an apron."

"Yes, sir." Derek dropped his gaze again. He knew his father wouldn't want him looking a customer in the eye. Customers were above Derek's station. He was only sixteen, after all, and barely making it as his father's apprentice.

Da took a deep breath. "Apologies. The boy fancies himself a cook."

"A cook?" the man said, raising a robust hedge of bristling eyebrows over his dark brown eyes. "With hands that size and his reach, I would be surprised if the Iron Guard didn't come calling for him."

Derek felt his chest swell with the man's praise. "Thank you," he mumbled, slightly embarrassed.

Da snorted. "The Iron Guard? We'll see about that. The boy says he likes cooking too much."

"Is he any good?" the man asked, resting his hands on the pommel of a slim rapier hanging from his belt.

Surprised a stranger would take so much interest in him, Derek ignored his manners and took a moment to study the customer. He was tall, Derek saw, and smiling. His face was kind and framed by a trimmed beard of black and silver. The man wore a worn leather jerkin, a pair of battered bracers, crimson pants, tall deer hide boots, a pair of woodman's gloves, a steel cap, and a khaki cloak thrown over it all. From the look of him, Derek guessed he was one of the rangers who roamed Breechwood Forest and came into Zuid Horn occasionally to trade for supplies.

"Watch your manners, boy," Da rumbled and smacked the back of Derek's head.

Derek felt his face burn. He didn't drop his eyes from the customer but turned his attention to his father.

Da scratched his beard. "Any good? At cooking? What does it matter? He's going to be a fletcher if I have anything to say about it."

The man chuckled. "Is that so? And what do you say about that, Derek?"

Derek opened his mouth to say something, but then he stopped. How did the man know Derek's name? Da had just been calling him "boy" like he always did. Had they been talking about him? Da cleared his throat and whacked Derek on the shoulder. "Answer the man, boy."

"Sorry. Yes, sir. I'm going to be a fletcher."

The man crossed his arms over his chest. "So, you want to take over the family business?"

The back of Derek's neck tingled, and he blurted, "I'd rather be a cook than a fletcher."

Da blew out a quick breath and rolled his eyes. "A cook? What kind of living could you make as a cook?"

"I could do it. I'm a good cook."

"Bah," Da growled.

The customer ran his fingers over his moustache. "Learned from your mother, did you?"

"I guess so," Derek said with a shrug. And then, because his blood was still hot from his argument with Liza, he muttered, "I'm practically a slave around here."

This won him another cuffing from Da. "Watch your mouth, boy. You do what you're told and little more. When I was your

age, my father had me working from dawn to dusk. You live a life of leisure compared to how I had it when Baba first brought us to Zuid Horn."

Derek rolled his eyes. How many times was he going to have to hear this story? But the customer seemed interested. "Your family is from Bearton, correct?"

Da nodded. "My father brought us along the Coastlands just as the Alliance Wars were wrapping up. He was banking on fletching for the wars to the east. That was long before Valis and the uprising in Shadizar."

The customer nodded. "Well, you'll always have work in Zuid Horn. Generals have been buying weaponry and armor here for centuries. And besides that, with Breechwood Forest surrounding us on two sides, the rangers will always need arrows." The tall man untied a coin purse from his belt and drew out two shimmering silver coins. "Which is what brings me in today. The Ranger Outpost needs fifty score arrows and quivers for every score. Can you fill the order in two weeks?"

Da let out a low whistle. "Two weeks? That's short notice, and I have other orders to fill."

The tall man smiled and leaned closer. "Well, I wasn't supposed to say anything, but maybe this will sweeten the deal for you. The Ranger Outpost is looking to lock down a fletcher as our exclusive supplier. We have a couple of other bids out just to be safe, but I heard Captain Gier saying he hoped you would win the contract."

Derek glanced at Da, who was looking over the meadery across Gillman's Way toward the black spires lining Zuid Horn's famous steel-reinforced walls. Derek followed Da's gaze to the black and green pendants snapping in the breeze off the spires. Fifty score arrows? A thousand arrows? That would mean almost nonstop fletching for the two of them. With their other orders — the hunters of Breechwood, the Iron Guard bowmen on the city wall, not to mention the Shadizarian sailors on warships anchored in the harbor — there was no way they could get it all done. But when

Derek turned away from the Zuid Hornian flags flying proudly over the city and looked at Da, he knew what his father was about to say.

"We'd be honored to fulfill your order," Da said, hands on hips, feet braced wide. "You can always count on a Fulstarter to get the job done."

The tall man smiled. "That's what I thought you'd say, Bryton. You've got a solid reputation in this city, my friend. I knew you wouldn't let us down."

They shook hands on the deal, and Da laughed. "It will be hard, but it's too good an offer to pass up."

The man handed Da the coin purse full of silver. "This is half the silver as a down payment. I'll be back in a week to see how you're doing."

Da took the silver and tucked it into his belt. They shook hands again and exchanged a few last pleasantries before the man left. Father and son watched him go, and then Da turned to Derek. "Alright boy, do you know what this means?"

Derek's shoulders drooped under the weight of his answer. "I'm not going anywhere for the next two weeks?"

Da grunted, a sound just short of a laugh. "Almost." He took out the silver the man had just handed him, poured half into his thick palm, and handed the remaining silver and purse to Derek. "I need you to get feathers from the goose yard, resin and ironwood from the mill, and steel arrowheads from the foundry. You know where to go."

"Yes, sir," Derek said, and he tied the coin purse tightly to his belt.

He was hurrying out of the shop when Da called after him, "And don't dawdle. We'll need to get started right away if we are going to meet this order."

Derek stopped in his tracks and looked back at his father. "Why don't we just use some of the silver to hire extra help? We could get the order done in no time with a few more hands."

Da shook his head. "Wouldn't be Fulstarter arrows, then, would they?" Derek opened his mouth to protest, but Da silenced him

with a look. "Our family name means something, Derek. Someday, you'll understand that. Now get going."

Derek wanted to argue that his sisters could help get the job done faster, but a shadow fell over him. He wheeled about to find a seven-foot-tall monster standing behind him. The thing was massive, with a head like a hammerhead shark and broad shoulders made broader by the battered leather armor it wore. Heavily muscled arms dangled at its side. It was a yakariian scout. A warlike breed, the yakarii were raised on battle and blood. City states around the realm used them as shock troops in their wars against one another.

Derek looked at the black talons that sprang from its fingertips and shuddered. Why Zuid Horn let nonhumans inside the city walls was beyond him. Who could trust those beasts anyway? He agreed with the merchants who sipped wine at the street carts on Ploughman's Wharf. Without the Iron Guard, these monsters would overrun Zuid Horn in a day.

Da crossed his arms over his thick chest and grunted. "Back so soon, Yak'cha?"

Yak'cha grunted. "Lots of game north of the city."

Da looked at the scout's side. "Your purse looks empty. Did my arrows fail you?"

"Your arrows are fine. It's my aim that's the problem."

They shared a laugh. "What can I do for you?" Da asked.

Yak'cha held up two silver coins and pointed at the barrels full of arrows. "How many will this get me?"

Da shook his head. "With your aim, maybe enough arrows for a rabbit?"

They laughed again, and then Yak'cha thrust his chin at Derek. "Who's this?"

"This is my son." Then, Da scowled at Derek. "Where are you supposed to be?"

"Getting supplies."

"Then get there."

Da turned away from Derek and back to Yak'cha the yak-ariian scout.

Derek grumbled and stalked down the street. He was glad his father's shop was competing for the Ranger Outpost's contract, but winning the contract meant two weeks of solid work for Derek. That meant no time for his friends and no time for fun.

Derek was passing Beru's remedy shop, with its bundles of herbs drying in the open window, when he spotted Augie and Peter just down the street in front of The Forgeshine Inn. Peter looked up and waved Derek over. Derek peeked over his shoulder to make sure Da wasn't watching. When he saw Da was still busy with the yakariian scout, Derek scuttled down the street to meet up with his friends.

Peter and Augie were rubbing finishing wax onto a new table as Derek arrived. Peter looked up and patted the top of the table. "What do you think? We just finished it up."

Derek ran his hand over the smooth wood. "You guys made this?"

"Yep," Peter said, his face beaming. "My dad's got me on tables now. When Augie's mom said she needed a new table for that back guest room, I got my first order."

"You didn't do it yourself," Augie protested. "I helped."

Peter shrugged. "True enough." Then, Peter looked up at Derek. "What are you so *scowly* about?"

"Nothing," Derek began. But when his friends both raised their eyebrows, he said, "It's my stupid dad. We just got a huge contract, and I'll be busy for the next two weeks."

"We could help you," Augie cut in.

"I'll work for free," Peter said, a little too eagerly.

Derek rolled his eyes. "By the Forge, Peter. You're not going to impress my sister working in the shop. She's not even interested in you."

"That's not what she told me at the Moon Festival on the Black River last week."

Derek's jaw tightened. "What are you talking about? You didn't see Liza there."

Peter's eyes sparkled. "Are you sure?"

"You were with me and Augie the whole time."

Peter and Augie exchanged a quick glance. Augie smiled knowingly. "Actually," Augie cut in, "remember when you and me were at the hatchet throwing booth and Peter went to get us some honey sticks?"

Derek's felt his face slide into a frown. "Yeah."

Augie cleared his throat and shrugged. "Well," and that was all he said.

Derek looked back and forth between his friends. "Well, what?"

Peter and Augie held their tongues, and suddenly the truth dawned on Derek. "Wait, you snuck over to see Liza?"

Augie punched Peter in the shoulder, and the carpenter's son grinned. "Maybe," he said.

Derek's hands balled into tight fists. "Blazing Forges, Peter. That's my sister." He grabbed the table so hard his knuckles turned white.

"I know," Peter said. "She's cute."

"Why you..." Derek started and lunged for Peter, but the smaller boy danced out of Derek's long reach.

Augie and Peter burst into laughter. "Wait, wait," Augie said, getting between his friends. "We're just giving you a hard time."

Derek stood there, huffing with his fists at his sides. "You better be."

"Lighten up, Derek," Peter said. "Liza's going to grow up one day, and she'll have plenty of suitors stopping by the shop to court her. How long until her presenting ceremony?"

Derek scowled. "The Coming-of-Age Ball? Too soon."

"Well," Peter continued, "there you go. And don't think there aren't lots of guys around here waiting for that glorious day. Would you rather have some weasel courting your sister or one of your best friends?"

Derek scoffed. "Who said you two weren't weasels?"

"Fair enough," Peter conceded. He lifted his chin at Derek. "So, where are you off to?"

"Getting stuff for this new contract," Derek said with a sigh. "Feather, resin, broadheads." He kicked the street. "I can't believe I'm locked up for two weeks."

Peter smirked. "Well, I'll stop over as often as I can. If Liza is giving you a hard time, I'll get her out of the shop so you can have some peace."

"Whatever," Derek muttered as he waved and turned away. "I have to get going."

"Bye, Derek," Peter called. "Tell Liza I said, 'Hi.'"

Derek grumbled as he left Augie's. Why did he always let his friends get to him like that? Normally, their teasing didn't bother him, but after Liza's taunting in front of the customer and Da making Derek's plans for the next two weeks, Derek felt like he was about to explode.

He was down Gillman's Way, about to turn onto Miller Street, when someone slapped him hard on the back. Derek stumbled forward a couple of steps. He flailed his lanky arms to keep balance. A brash round of barking laughs broke out behind him. Derek felt his stomach twist into a nervous knot. He didn't need to look to know who it was, but he turned around anyway. "Hi, Conrad."

Three raggedy boys — bare feet stained black all the way to their knobby ankles — stood together in a clutch, pointing and laughing at Derek. He recognized them immediately. *Street rats* is what the orphans of Zuid Horn were called, and these were some of the dirtiest in the bunch. They had been giving Derek grief on and off his entire life.

"Hi, Conrad," the smallest one mocked in a sing-song voice. "You're such a girl."

"Shut up, Lars." Derek balled his fists.

"Loser," the one named Jenkins said with a laugh.

Conrad — not the tallest of the three, nor the biggest, but definitely the one with the sharpest eyes — smacked Lars Underfoot

on the back of the head. "Is that how you treat the *lord* of Gillman's Way? With slaps and taunts?"

Derek cocked his head. "Lord of Gillman's Way?"

Conrad sneered. "You know what we're talking about. The way you strut around here, acting all high and mighty just because your daddy is so famous."

Derek felt his face burn. "My dad's not famous. He just makes arrows."

Conrad spit at the ground by Derek's feet. "Yeah? Then how come he's got rangers from Breechwood coming to him?"

Derek froze for a second, unsure if Conrad was really that stupid or if it was a setup. "Rangers need arrows for hunting." And then, as an afterthought, "You idiot."

If Derek had been hoping to avoid a fight, that chance was gone now. Conrad's face blazed pink and then red. The boys on either side of him chuckled nervously, waiting for Conrad's orders. The boy's mean eyes tightened and turned a dark gray. His mouth bent into a thin, red smear. "You're going to pay for that," he hissed, and then they were on Derek at the same time.

Conrad's friends took Derek high, while Conrad himself went for Derek's waist. Derek hit the ground with a grunt and tried to roll over, but the three boys pinned him to the dust. A pair of women in loose, gray smocks shouted at the boys to not knock over the apple stalls they were setting out. The ball of brawling boys somehow obeyed and rolled toward the street, away from the stall but into the path of a clanking coal wagon heading to one of the foundries.

Derek saw the cart coming and tried to get out of the way, but the three boys attacking him held him fast. Fists pummeled Derek's arms and face. Knuckles hammered at his arms. Derek let a whimper slip from his lips. Conrad's buddies laughed. "Listen to the baby," Lars taunted. "Can't live up to his daddy's legend."

Then, something in Derek snapped. His vision closed in from the sides until all he could see was a vertical line of white in front of him. His scalp tingled, and his jaw tightened. Hot strength pulsed through his limbs, and suddenly, Derek was ready to fight. "Don't you ever talk about my da," he growled.

Jenkins tried to gouge a finger into Derek's eye, but the fletcher's son chomped down on it with all his might and almost bit the thing off. That's when Conrad caught Derek with a hard left hook to the jaw, freeing Jenkins' finger. Derek ended up spitting out a mouthful of skin and blood. Jenkins let go his hold and plopped down in the street. He held his hand to his chest and howled like a scolded puppy.

Conrad, seeing he was down a man, unleashed a torrent of blows into Derek's soft underbelly. But Derek was mad now. He flexed down hard against Conrad's fists. He ignored Lars, who was trying to twist Derek's ears off his head, and instead grabbed two handfuls of Conrad's hair and yanked until the leader of the pack squealed. "I quit!" Conrad hollered. "I quit!"

Lars, stunned by Conrad's sudden defeat, let loose his hold on Derek's ears and backed away. Derek still had Conrad by the hair when his vision began to clear. He was standing over the boy, twisting tight knots of the bully's hair in his fingers, when he realized they weren't alone in the streets.

Not only were the merchants and locals watching them, but all of Gillman's Way had come to a dead stop when the coal wagon clattered into oncoming traffic to avoid hitting the boys. Passersby bobbed their curious heads on chicken necks to watch the fight. Worst of all, a line of twelve guardsmen — clad in gleaming plate mail with silver helmets and long, steel swords in their belts — stood silently witnessing the street brawl. Derek felt his stomach drop. The Iron Guard! The uncompromising enforcers of Zuid Horn's justice.

Before he had a chance to move, two of the guards swooped in and snatched up Derek and Conrad in their mailed fists. Another two guards grabbed Conrad's orphan friends before they could slip into the gathering crowd. One of the Iron Guardsmen clanked up and raised his visor.

His dark eyes studied the boys for a moment, and then he raised his voice for all to hear. "I am Captain Gier of the Wharf District Guard. You have been found guilty of disturbing the public peace. You are hereby arrested and sentenced to two days in the stocks on Ploughman's Wharf."

Conrad squealed again and tried to break free, but Derek knew better. This was the Iron Guard. Their word was law in Zuid Horn. The guardsmen yanked the boys to their feet and dragged them toward the piers on the city's southern edge.

The jeering crowd parted before them, many taking advantage of the chance to mock an artisan's son. Derek's face burned with shame. He'd been in fights before, but he'd never been caught. And to be caught now, just as his father needed him most! As bad as the stocks would be, facing Da's wrath would be even worse.

Suddenly, Peter and Augie appeared next to him from out of the crowd. Derek freed an arm long enough to grab the purse of Da's silver. He tossed it to Peter. "Get that to my da," he said.

The Iron Guardsman grabbed Derek's arm again and barked at the boys. "Stay back."

Peter and Augie threw their hands up. The purse of silver jingled in Peter's fist. "Yes, sir. We're just looking." Then, to Derek, he whispered, "Don't worry! We'll get your dad!" And before Derek could thank them, they disappeared into the crowd.

Another guardsman came forward carrying several burlap sacks. He came to the boys and slipped a sack over each head. Just before the bag went over Derek's head, he locked eyes with someone in the crowd. Someone whose eyes twinkled as if they knew something. Then, the bag was closed tight, and Derek was left alone with the dust in the bag and one burning question.

Why was the tall man from Da's shop laughing at Derek as he was being hauled away?

3

A Dark Night Grows Darker

Caught in a whirlpool that spun him around and around under Augie's inn, Derek raised his arms to protect his head as the undertow beat him against the front of the building. He fought and fought, but the current was simply too strong.

Worse, he was not alone beneath the icy flood.

Things, disgusting things, tumbled in the salty waters. Bodies of the dead — his neighbors, night walkers, and merchants — rolled round and round in the whirlpool. Their ghastly arms and fingers dragged over him, weighed on him, kept him from the surface. Derek strained against the flailing dead, their limp limbs a horrid web. And rats, some as big as small dogs, dipped like sleek otters through the debris. Flushed from the sewers, they clambered over Derek and pushed his head down. His lungs burned for breath, and his head thundered. Derek wanted to scream at the madness of it. He flailed, and then he was free.

He broke the surface and managed a sparse mouthful of air before the dank waters swallowed him again. The current sucked at his legs, and the dead clutched at his clothes. He wanted to scream, but if he opened his mouth, the Forge only knew what would rush down his throat.

Derek refused to die. He made a desperate grab for the inn and found the frames of the smashed dining room windows, now underwater. He clung to the frames for all he was worth, the broken glass slicing his palms. Bodies crashed into him, along with broken bits of tables, boards from storefronts, sides of street carts, and melons. Fighting the rush, Derek climbed the jagged frame hand over hand. The broken glass bit deep, but Derek would not let go. He was almost to the surface when the window frame snapped in his hands. He flew back into the torrent and went down again.

Derek bounced hard off the cobblestone street, now the bed of a raging river. He twisted over, planted his feet before the current could tear him away, and leapt for the surface. His lungs howled, and his throat throbbed. Derek pumped and kicked for his life.

He broke above the water and drank in a great gulp of air. A table spun in the whirlpool next to him. Derek gave a cry and lunged for it. His desperate fingers clawed over the slick wood and caught the edge. He scrambled on top spread eagle and held on with everything he had left. Round and round he spun in the whirlpool next to Augie's inn. Cool air rushed down his lungs, and for a moment, Derek was just thankful to be alive.

Then his sister screamed.

Derek looked to the roof. Liza, Sarah, Augie, and Augie's parents cowered against the edge, facing four hulking shadows. "Stay back!" Mrs. Innskeep shouted.

Derek didn't need another explosion to light up the night sky. He had already seen what was on the roof with the Innskeeps and his sister.

Yakariian warriors.

Glimmering water ran in rivulets over their pasty skin. They had stripped themselves of armor and weapons and were practically naked save for the dirty loincloths they wore as underclothes. Even without armor, the yakarii were formidable beasts. Towering between seven and eight feet tall, these creatures sported maws filled with rows of razor-sharp teeth, natural boney crests that

protected their heads, and terrible talons at the end of enormous hands. They looked at the trembling humans and laughed. "Grab the old man," one of them said. "He'll make a fine dinner tonight."

"Too tough," complained another. "Let's eat one of the girls."

"Quiet, fool," the first ordered. "The master wants young ones for the mines. This old man won't last a week. Let's eat him while there's anything left of him."

"No!" Mrs. Innskeep screamed and clutched at her husband.

The yakarii laughed. One of them came forward, snatched Mrs. Innskeep by the arm, and yanked her away from her husband. It tossed her to the side where she collapsed in a heap. Mr. Innskeep stumbled to her. "Are you alright?" When she nodded, he turned to the yakarii. "The merchants were right. We never should have let your kind into the city."

The yakarii stopped laughing and lunged at the Innskeeps in a powerful rush, grabbing them by the arms and lifting them into the air. The Innskeeps screamed and struggled, but what could they do while their feet dangled? The other yakarii moved in and snatched up Augie and Derek's sisters. The beasts tossed the children over their broad shoulders, chortled at the children's cries, and then carried them away over the rooftops.

Derek clenched his jaw. He had to do something, but what? He was caught in this cursed whirlpool with no escape in sight. His hands were shredded, and he had no weapons. Another explosion lit the night. It was brief, but in that quick flash, Derek saw something that gave him hope. A bent piece of wood shaped like a hook, perhaps a decoration from a merchant's wagon, floated in the water next to him. He snatched it out of the flood and examined it. The board was a little longer than his arm and light like driftwood. That was good because driftwood was strong. Derek did a test swing and smirked. A perfect club.

When the whirlpool brought Derek and his tabletop around again, he swung the club at the inn's wall as hard as he could. The wooden head punched through the plaster and caught like an anchor. Derek's tabletop slipped out from beneath him, and he let it go. The club was all he needed, so he put his energy into making sure he didn't lose it.

Hand over hand, he climbed up the club until he was almost out of the water. Derek kept a firm grip on his club with one hand and lurched for the roof's lip with the other. His fingers found the edge, and he pulled himself up. He spun on his belly and tore his club free. Then, with weapon in hand, he scanned the darkness for his sisters. He spotted them several rooftops away.

"Hammer and Anvils," Derek swore and dashed across the roof, careful to look for thin spots where he could fall through.

He closed the gap quickly. The yakarii were massive creatures, and the beams of the roofs squawked in protest under their weight. They moved slowly over the thin roofs, so in no time at all, Derek trailed them from only one rooftop away. He crouched low and scurried from peak to peak, knowing the yakarii had excellent night vision. Even from a rooftop away, he could hear them arguing. "I'm starving. Let's eat the old man right now."

Mrs. Innskeep battered her fists against her captor's back, and the yakarii carrying her growled. "Quit your griping, or we'll eat you as well, master be hanged."

This only made the Innskeeps howl even more. "Enough!" the leader barked. "Nobody's eating anything until we get out of this city. Gods only know when the water's going down, and I want to be long gone when that happens."

"We better get paid well for this," another grumbled.

"You'll do as you're told and no less," the leader growled.

"How much longer do we have to carry them? Can't we just tie them up and make them walk?"

The leader roared in frustration. "Do you see any rope around here?"

"I haven't really been looking," the complainer admitted.

"There was some back in that shop we looted," another added.

"Did you grab any?" the complainer asked.

"No."

"Well, we're not going back now," the leader said. "The master will be expecting loot tonight, and there's nothing he loves better than fresh slaves."

They fell silent as they worked their way over a gap between buildings. Once they made the crossing, Derek had to wait while they moved over a flat rooftop with no cover. By the time he caught up to them, they had struck up their conversation again.

"How the devil should I know?" the leader asked.

The complainer shrugged, bouncing Liza on his shoulder. She yelped, and the yakarii growled. "Quiet there." Then, to the leader he said, "I don't know. I just thought maybe the master might have said something."

"The master don't tell us grunts nothing," the leader said, "especially about things like this."

"I don't know," another butted in. "I would've liked a little warning."

"That's what I'm saying," the complainer agreed. "Who destroys a city but doesn't warn his troops?"

"How many times do I have to tell you?" the leader asked. "The master didn't have nothing to do with this. We just got to keep our eyes open for opportunities when they come up, and here one is."

"I don't know," the complainer whined. "I hate water."

"Yeah, should have said something at least."

The leader roared. "That's it! You're driving me crazy. I can't march with you two anymore. Ku'da," he said to the yakarii carrying Augie. "Bring that boy and come with me. You two," it said to the two yakarii carrying Liza and Sarah, "can meet us at McGoodin's trading post."

"What? That's a three-day march," the complainer carrying Liza whined.

"That's three days not listening to your trap flapping," the leader said. "Find your own way. Ku'da, let's go."

The two yakarii watched their leader and Ku'da disappear with the entire Innskeep family. When their leader clambered over a wall separating the Artisan District from the merchants' estates, the complainer spit into the floodwaters. "Glad he's gone."

"I'll say. Nothing but, 'Do this,' and, 'Carry that.'" The yakarii carrying Sarah puffed up its chest and marched around, imitating the leader. "'Look at me. I'm so important.'"

Their laughter sounded like rocks rattling in a sack. When it died down, the complainer said, "I'm still hungry."

"Me too."

The complainer held Sarah up by the arm and poked at her thin ribs. She cried and tried to kick the thing in the face, but its arms were too long. "Not much here. I'll bet the master wouldn't even notice if a bit of her were missing."

"That's the kind of thinking I like to hear," its companion said. It looked from side to side and leaned in. "What if we ate 'em both and just said they died on the way?"

The girls squealed, and Derek's gut tightened. He scrambled across the roof and ducked behind a roof garden of green peppers. He leaned in closer to hear more.

The complainer's maw broke into a toothy grin. "Nobody'd know."

"That's what I'm saying."

"Oh, he'd know," Liza said suddenly.

"Who?" the complainer asked.

"The master," Liza said. "Who else?"

"How? Who'd tell him?" the friend asked.

Liza scoffed. "You know how it is. Every time you think you can get away with something, there's some snitch waiting to rat you out."

The complainer and its friend sighed. "True enough," the complainer said, eyeing its companion.

"How come you know so much?" the friend asked.

Liza shook her head. "I've got an older brother. Gets me in trouble all the time."

Derek ground his teeth. Liza was doing her best to distract the yakarii. If he was going to save his sisters, he needed to act fast. Liza couldn't distract them forever.

Derek tightened his grip on his makeshift club. His mind raced for a plan. All he could think of was to sneak in from behind, take out their knees, and make up the rest from there. He would get no better chance to save his sisters before they were hauled off to the salt mines up the coast.

He crouched low and was just about to cross the wide roof when he heard the creak of wood behind him. The hair went up on the back of Derek's neck. Another yakarii? He knew yakariian scouts were stealthy, but he had barely heard anything! He whirled to face his attacker and then almost cried out.

Creeping over the edge of the roof was not one yakariian scout, but four.

4

Derek Takes a New Path

The sun beat down on Ploughman's Wharf and baked Derek's skin until it was as red as a tomato. Greasy sweat beaded his forehead and dribbled down his face and neck. It stung his eyes and made his ears itch. As bad as the sun was, the hecklers were worse.

As soon as the Iron Guardsmen slapped the stocks closed on the brawling boys, the dockworkers descended like flies. Tossing rotten fruits and vegetables, the workers made side bets on which of the boys would cry first. A well-placed cabbage to Lars's face brought the first gush of tears and won five coppers for a pair of Shadizarian oarsmen on shore leave. When several rotten cabbages failed to win any tears from Derek, the bystanders heckled him. When that failed, they paid a barefoot street urchin a copper to find out more about Derek.

Derek scowled at the dockworkers, which only earned him more heckling from the dockworkers. "Oh, look at the little boy! Is baby having a bad day?" Several of them wailed like babies and rubbed their eyes.

Derek's neck burned, and he fought against the stockade holding his ankles. "Hammer and Anvils," he swore. "I hope they choke."

The jingle of bells drew Derek's attention. A group of men dressed in flowing robes of copper and gold pushed through the gathered masses. One of the men led the way, holding aloft a staff adorned with a yellow, wooden sun. He stroked his neatly plaited black beard as he came to stand before Derek and Conrad. Several men in similar dress took up spots behind the man. Derek recognized the group immediately—sun cultists from Shadizar. Zuid Horn's port was open to all, and that included minions of the Sun King, Victor Folio. "Repent!" the man called, loud enough for the crowd to hear. "The end is near!" He smiled a smile that didn't reach his rheumy eyes.

Derek's vision crackled with fuzz. "I've got nothing to repent."

The man lifted a neatly groomed eyebrow. "Really? Your situation states otherwise."

"I shouldn't be locked up." He tilted his head at Conrad, who was standing in a stockade to his right. "This idiot and his friends jumped me. I was just fighting them off."

The cultist snorted. "Who among us is truly innocent?" Derek tried to come up with a quick-witted response, but the cultist held up a leathery hand. "Ponder your fate child, under Ra's watchful eye." The cultist lifted a palm to the simmering Zuid Hornian sun. "Perhaps, if you have your wits about you, you will glean some scrap of wisdom from this affair. Seek me out if you wish to grow in the way. But don't dally. Remember, the end is at hand!" The cultist opened his arms and dipped his head, a Shadizarian mockery of a bow. Then, lifting his sun staff, he led his flock down the pier.

Derek and the crowd watched them go. Derek spit. "Foreigners."

This seemed to earn a grain of respect from the dockworkers. "Watch yourself with that lot, boy," one of them growled. "I've heard stories."

"Don't worry about me," Derek replied. "I've no love for Shadizarians."

With that, the dockworkers left, and the crowd died down enough to let Derek take in his surroundings. They were locked into a row of stocks about a hundred paces long. The stocks paralleled Zuid Horn's main pier, Ploughman's Wharf. Ships from all over the realm docked here — black hulled triremes from Shadizar, bulky cogs from Belvera and Bearton, even some long ships from the yakariian warlords far to the west of civilized lands. All these sailors and tradesmen had to pass the stocks on their way into Zuid Horn.

A little farther down the pier was a row of gibbets, displaying the decaying bodies of those being punished for offenses more serious than children brawling in the street. All races and species were punished equally on the dock. Just a few prisoners down on Derek's right was a hulking ogre sleeping off a night of drinking. Farther down yet were two plains goblins totally at home under the tropical sun, content to munch on the rotten vegetables littering the dock. When the stocks and gibbets were full, the message to newcomers was clear. All are welcome in Zuid Horn, but if you disturb the peace, justice will be fierce and swift.

Derek sat in the stocks, his legs stretched out straight before him and his feet almost a full foot from the ground. His bare ankles chafed against the stock's rough wood and creosote preservative. Derek wanted to bend his knees to relieve the downward pressure, but every time he tried, the stocks ground into his raw ankles even more.

He scratched at the blood crusted on his forehead and mouth and then inspected his fists. His knuckles were dark with Conrad's blood. Derek glanced at his nemesis and felt the disgust rising in his throat. Conrad, unlike Derek, had been forced into the standing stocks. Derek smirked and snorted. The standing stocks were usually reserved for the instigator of a disturbance. Someone in the street must have clued the Iron Guard onto who the real problem was.

Fat, green flies buzzed around Conrad's blood-matted hair. When he heard Derek snort, Conrad turned a swollen, baleful eye on him. "What are you looking at?"

"An idiot."

Conrad shook his head. "You're lucky the Iron Guard came along."

Derek's laugh was more of a dry bark. "Whatever."

"Don't forget, we're only in these stocks for two days. As soon as we're out, my boys and me are coming for you again."

"And I'll send you home, crying to your mommy again." A mean spark flickered inside Derek and flared to life. "Oh, wait, you don't have a mommy."

As soon as he said it, Derek wished he hadn't. Conrad and the others were bullies, for sure, but even they didn't deserve that.

Conrad tried to spit at Derek but only managed to dribble down his chin. "You think you're so great, the son of a famous craftsman," Conrad scoffed. "What did you do to earn your way? Nothing. How much skill does it take to get born into the right family? None. What can you do that I can't? Nothing. You're trash, Derek Fulstarter. Trash walking around in fancy clothes. Everyone knows it."

Surprisingly, Conrad's words didn't ignite Derek's temper. Instead, his heart sank in his chest. He wasn't the kind of person to insult an orphan. Was he? And what Conrad said, was that what people really thought of him? Derek opened his mouth to apologize, but just then, a shadow blocked out the sun. "I send you for supplies, and this is where I find you?" Derek squinted into the blazing, Zuid Hornian sun. Da was standing with his legs braced wide, his fists firmly on his hips. Derek raised a hand against the blinding light. "Da, I'm sorry."

Da just shook his head. "I'll say. The biggest order of our lives, for the Breechwood rangers no less. I need you, Derek, and this is what you pull?"

Conrad sniggered quietly, but Derek ignored him. "They jumped me, Da! There wasn't anything I could do!"

"You could have walked away."

"They were beating me down!" Derek wished it didn't sound like whining, but it did, even to his ears.

"And now you're beating the family business down. How do you think I'm going to get this order done without you?"

"You could hire Peter and Augie. They said they would help," Derek suggested.

"When did you talk to them? I told you to go straight to our suppliers."

Derek dropped his eyes. "I only stopped for a bit."

"And now look at you. Lose your focus and you lose the mission."

Derek's shoulders collapsed, and his father continued. "How long are you in the stocks?"

"Two days," Derek mumbled.

"By the Forge," Da swore. "We can't lose two days. Now, I'll have to quit working on arrows to get the supplies I told you to pick up." He shook his head. Then, he took out the bag of silver. "Peter brought me the silver. You didn't mess that up, at least."

Seagulls cried to one another over the harbor. Down the pier, foreign captains barked orders to their sailors. Derek wanted to be with them, wanted to be boarding a ship to a foreign land, wanted to be anywhere besides broiling under his father's wrath. "I'm sorry, Da," he muttered.

Da glowered at Derek. Finally, he sighed. It sounded like he'd lost something and given up trying to find it. "I'll send your mother and sisters with food and water later." And then he left.

The remnants of the crowd split before him, no one willing to stand in the large man's path. They hid bits of rotten vegetables behind their backs. As soon as he was gone, the crowd closed again and turned their eyes on Derek. "A Fulstarter," they whispered. Derek hoped his father's name and station would protect him.

It did not.

A thin, pimply, rag-wearing boy of about fifteen with a black, oily ponytail stepped in front of the crowd and strutted as though he were royalty. Derek groaned. The ponytail and leather vest identified the boy as a member of a local street gang. Derek groaned as the boy marched back and forth. "Great," he muttered. "A Jotaro."

"Oh," the Jotaro member crowed, "Look at me! I'm the prince of Gillman's Way! Everyone step aside as I do daddy's bidding." The crowd hooted at the boy's antics. They called out taunts of their own.

"Swaggering ass!"

"Pompous princeling!"

The prancing, pockmarked boy paraded before the crowd. "You there, good sir," he cried with his nose lifted high, "mind your manners and shine my boots." He lifted a dirty, bare foot to a sailor, who immediately spit on it and began polishing the boy's toes with a tattered sleeve.

"There you are, my lord," the sailor said. "I pray it's polished to your satisfaction."

The boy turned his snout away. "We shall see," he said in a high-pitched voice, and his audience roared.

Derek turned from the crowd and saw Conrad watching him. "See?" the bully sneered. "Everyone knows. You think you're so much better than me just because I live on the streets, but the truth is you're too stuck up to see who you really are."

Derek's gut twisted at Conrad's words. His face burned, and his mouth twisted into a scowl. Who were these people to treat him like trash? What had he ever done to them?

The pockmarked boy hopped around Derek, making lewd gestures and spanking his own behind. A roar broke from the people around them. Someone threw a handful of coppers. The boy laughed and leaned his wiggling backside even closer to Derek's burning face, not realizing he was within Derek's reach.

But Derek did.

He shot out a long arm and snatched the raggedy boy by the seat of his pants. Caught off guard, the boy toppled back onto Derek, who slapped two arms in a tight hug around the struggling boy. The Jotaro squawked and kicked, but there was no escaping Derek. He was mad now. Mad at his sister for mocking him in front of a stranger. Mad at losing two weeks of freedom. Mad at his friends razzing him about his sister. Mad at being caught in a street fight. Mad at being insulted. Mad at letting Da down.

And now he had the perfect victim to unleash his fury on.

Scores of back-alley fights with Conrad and his goons had taught Derek one thing — fighting fair doesn't win fights. Derek pulled the prancing prince close and chomped down on his shoulder. The boy howled, and the crowd roared with laughter. Derek slipped a hand free and twisted a mittful of the boy's scalp. The kid yowled for help, which made the crowd laugh even more. Derek's anger blinded him to what he was doing. He let his fists and elbows and teeth run rampant. The Jotaro was tall and thin, with huge ears perfect for twisting. He never stood a chance against Derek.

Suddenly, someone yanked his prey away. Derek looked up, expecting to see an Iron Guardsman, but he was surprised to find the tall man from his father's shop instead. The man helped the pockmarked boy to his feet. "Are you alright, lad?"

The boy wiped a filthy wrist across his runny nose. "Yes, sir."

"Okay. Here are a few coppers for you." He held out a small cloth sack. "Run along and get something to eat."

The boy blinked and looked at the bag of coins. "Thank you, sir. Blessings of the Forge upon you, sir." The Jotaro drew his fingers in an arc across his forehead and then over his chest.

The tall man nodded and turned toward Derek. "Derek Fulstarter."

Derek dropped his eyes. "Yes, sir."

The man snorted. "Don't pull that humble facade with me, Derek Fulstarter. I know better than that."

"Sir?"

"You tried playing that role in your father's shop. I believed it at first, you acting like you want to be a cook and all."

"I like cooking."

The man snorted again. "Sure. Maybe. But I saw you."

Derek looked at the man. "Saw me?"

"After I left your shop, I circled back because there was something else I needed to talk to your father about. But guess what I saw?"

Derek shrugged. "What?"

"I saw these boys giving you a hard time." The tall man jerked a thumb at Conrad and his friends. Conrad opened his mouth to say something, but the stranger shot him a look, and the bully of Gillman's Way snapped his mouth shut. The tall man turned back to Derek. "I saw what you did with them."

"Then you saw it. They started it!"

The man waved a hand. "And you finished it. Here's what I know about you, Derek Fulstarter. You like fighting. You enjoy feeling like a victim because it justifies your fight."

"It was three on one!"

"All the better for you."

"I didn't want to fight them."

The man shook his head. "That's a lie and you know it. You wanted that fight, and you knew you could beat them. Where I come from, that isn't being strong. That's being a bully."

Derek's neck tingled. "I'm not a bully," he hissed between clenched teeth.

The man stepped closer, and the smell of leather armor and oil filled Derek's nose. He looked Derek dead in the eye. Fueled with a burning anger over the man's words, Derek did not look away. "My name is Niles Crowing," the man said. "I work for the rangers of Breechwood Forest. I am staying at the Ranger Outpost on the Black River on the east side of town. When you are done fighting against who you really are and need something to fight for, come find me."

Niles Crowing turned suddenly, and his chocolaty cloak whirled in the air. He flicked a quick hand toward Derek, and something clinked in the dust next to his hip. Derek shot out a hand and covered whatever it was. It felt cool and metallic. He rolled his hand over and opened it enough to take a peek. A large, silver key — a key just big enough to fit the padlock holding the stockade closed.

"Move aside, friends, and leave this boy alone. He's just a boy, after all. We all make mistakes." Niles strode through the crowd, who watched him as though he were royalty. Several onlookers from the crowd followed him as he left: a red-haired man, a priest of the Forge, and was that an ogress?

Why would Niles have dropped a key? Was it a key for the stockade locks? How did he get it? Derek kept his hand and the key close to his thigh so no one would see it. So many questions, and no answers in sight.

He was still watching Niles walk away when a girl's voice came from his other side. "Would you like some water?"

She was short, his age, maybe. Dirty, bare feet and her tattered dress spoke of a life on the streets. Her black hair was long, matted, and dusty. She wore it pulled into a loose bun on her head. A few pimples dotted her cheeks, but her eyes were bright and kind — a first since he had been thrown in the stockade. It may have been the heat, but somehow, beneath the dirt, the girl was good-looking, in a street beggar sort of way. She held a clay pitcher in one hand and a tin cup in the other.

She raised the tin cup toward him and smiled. "Water?"

"Don't talk to him," Conrad barked. "He doesn't deserve any."

The girl laughed. "Are you mad at everyone, Conrad?"

"Just stuck-up brats."

The girl turned back to Derek. "Don't listen to him. My brother's always mad about something or someone. It was just your day today."

Derek's mouth dropped open. "Your brother?"

She shrugged. "You can't choose your family."

The girl poured some water and handed it to Derek. He nodded his thanks and drank greedily. "What's your name?" she asked.

Derek drained the cup and handed it back. "Derek," he said.

"I know," she said with a sly smile.

"Then why'd you ask?"

Still smiling, the girl shrugged. "I just wanted to hear you say it."

Derek shook his head. "I have two sisters," he said, "but I'll never understand girls."

Conrad's sister laughed and took the pitcher and cup to Conrad, who grimaced. "By The Hammer, stop flirting. I'm going to throw up."

Derek felt his face burn, and this time it wasn't the sun. "I wasn't flirting!"

"Whatever."

The girl poured her brother a cup and raised it to his lips. He turned his head away as much as he could, which wasn't much because of the stocks. "Rinse that cup out first. I don't want to catch any asshole." He glared at Derek.

She laughed and held the cup to his mouth. "Shut up and drink," she said, still laughing. "You can't catch something you already have."

Conrad slurped at the water. It dribbled down his chin, leaving white streaks through the dust and blood. "Thank you," he wheezed. Then he asked, "What are you doing here? You know the docks aren't safe."

She chuckled. "Don't you worry about me. I'll be fine."

She poured another cup of water for Conrad, and then brought a second cup to Derek. She knelt next to him. "Ignore my brother," the girl whispered. "He's jealous of anyone who has something he doesn't, but he's a good guy inside."

She was close, so close Derek could smell that despite being covered with street dust, the girl smelled of sun and the sea. When she caught him staring at her, Derek cleared his throat. "Thanks for the water." He swallowed thickly, and then asked, "What's your name?"

"Dani."

"Isn't that a boy's name?"

Dani shrugged. "It's my name."

"Thanks for the water."

"Don't mention it." She looked out to sea, and then, without asking whether he wanted it or not, filled Derek another cup and handed it to him. He nodded his thanks, and while he drank, she asked, "How did you end up here?"

He wanted to say, *Fighting with your asshole brother*, but something about Dani made him feel settled, like a calm sea. And in that calmness, he found a truth. "I lost my temper."

She laughed. "Lost your temper? That's pretty stupid."

Since the calmness was still upon him, Derek said, "Yeah."

"Does that happen often?"

"Yeah."

A breeze came in off the waters. Behind the dark emerald stink of dead kelp under the pier came purer hints of the deep ocean, the sky, and freedom. Dani turned her face into the breeze and closed her eyes. "Next time you feel yourself getting angry, try breathing."

"Breathing?"

Dani shrugged. "Maybe it will help you control your temper, so you don't end up back here." She pointed at the stocks and smiled.

Derek looked at her and wanted to say something impressive, but all that came out was, "Okay."

Conrad made a noise like he was choking. "By the Forge, I'm going to throw up. Would you stop flirting?"

Dani laughed and gave Derek one last smile. "Who's flirting?" Then she stood and turned to leave. "I'll be back just before evening with blankets and something to eat."

Conrad strained against his stocks. "Dani, no! The docks aren't safe after dark."

Dani laughed. "I'll be fine, Conrad. Who's going to catch me? You?" She smiled at Conrad and gave a little wave to Derek. "See you later!"

Derek and Conrad watched her go. And because they were watching, they both saw the four boys — clad in the silver and gold vests favored by traveling Shadizarian oarsmen — grin at one another and follow her down the street. Conrad flailed and yanked at the stocks restraining him. "Dani! Look out!"

But she was too far away to hear him over the thrumming of the ocean and the chatter of thousands of people on the pier. Conrad strained and screamed against the stocks. The futility of his efforts made the passing crowd point and laugh. Some of them threw bits of food scraps at the crying boy. Exhausted and defeated, Conrad sagged against the standing stocks and wept.

Derek was straining to see Dani when the group of Shadizarian sun cultists re-appeared and danced in front of him again, beating tambourines and chanting. "Repent! Darkness is coming! The end of the world is nigh!"

Dockworkers walking nearby jeered the cultists. "Out of the way, fools. The sun sets. The sun rises. Nothing ever changes. Your god is a joke."

The cultists ignored the men and danced and chanted and beat their tambourines as they moved down the pier.

Derek bit the inside of his lip. He may have been an artisan's son. He may have lived a pampered life compared to Conrad, but he was born in Zuid Horn, one of the mightiest port cities in the realm. Derek knew what those Shadizarian boys were after, and he knew what was going to happen to Dani unless someone could get to her in time.

Derek rolled Niles' key in his hand. Soon it would be dark. The crowds would die down, and there would only be a few guards to watch over the hundred or so prisoners on the pier. Who would miss him if he slipped away to help Dani?

He looked over at Conrad. The boy's wrists were bleeding from where he had tried to yank his hands from the stockade. His face was crimson with rage. Here was the boy who, only a few short hours ago, Derek was brawling in the streets. Here was the boy who taunted him every chance he got, mocked his family, and

questioned Derek's worth. Why should Derek help him or his sister? Derek thought of his father. He thought of his family heritage. And, for some reason, he thought of Niles Crowing. And finally, he thought of his sisters, Liza and Sarah. What if the Shadizarian boys were coming after them?

Derek closed his eyes and sighed. He knew what he had to do

5

Derek Plays the Odds

Four yakariian warriors clambered over the edge of the roof to stand, glistening, under a burning night sky. Derek raised his club in defense, but he knew it was useless. Yakarii were trained fighters who feasted on the flesh of their victims. What chance did he stand against them?

The yakarii sniffed at the air through two mucous slits in their faces, just over their tooth-filled maws. One of them chuckled, its voice deep and raw. "You smell like fear, boy."

Another yakarii licked at the air with a long, black tongue. "Tastes like it too, I'll wager."

A third snickered. "I'll take that bet."

They spread out to either side, a wide net of hammerhead killers.

Derek's chest pounded. Behind him, two yakariian scouts were stealing his sisters away. He wanted to run to them, but if he did, and the other four chased him, what would he do against six yakariian warriors all at once? And what would they do to his sisters? No. There had to be another way. Derek looked to his right. Nothing but an empty roof with a few chimneys. He looked to his left, and his heart leapt. That was it! His escape!

Derek took off at a dead run to his left. He leapt from joist to joist and was at the edge of the roof in less than a dozen hops. The yakarii roared behind him. "Yes!" one of them barked. "A chase!"

Derek didn't waste any time looking back. He stood at the edge of a narrow, water-filled alley. Only a few paces distant, a three-story warehouse rose out of the flood waters. A dark window beckoned from the second floor. He didn't wait. Putting his feet on the lip of the roof, Derek swung his arms hard and jumped long, leading with his club. He smashed through the glass and rolled on the floor. The yakarii roared behind him. They bayed like hunting hounds, and Derek's bones shivered. He leapt to his feet and rushed to the wall next to the window. Then he raised his club over his head and waited.

He could hear the yakarii across the watery alley, on the other roof. "Let me take him," one of them said. "I'll be right back."

There was the slow crunch of footsteps, as though someone was backing up, the *pit-pit-pit* of someone running, and the solid *whump!* of someone leaping off the roof. That was when Derek swung his club into the open window.

His timing was impeccable. Derek's club met the leaping yakarii full in the face with a meaty *thwack!* The foul thing dropped hard against the window ledge, and before it could gather its senses, flopped backward into the flood waters below. Derek peeked out and saw it floundering. "Throw me a board!" the thing howled. "I can't swim!"

It might as well have been talking to a stone for all the help it received. The other yakarii pointed and laughed at its suffering, and when it went under for the last time, they almost fell over from cackling so hard.

Derek clutched his club, ready to take out the next yakarii to come across. But if his plan worked once, it wasn't going to go quite so easily the second time. "Spread out," one of the yakarii said. "He can't cover all the windows." The thing pointed to either side of where Derek stood. Sure enough, there were plenty of other windows for them to come through. He couldn't defend them all. What could he do?

Two of the yakarii strode eagerly down the roofline, while the other taunted Derek. "Why don't you just make this easy on yourself? No sense getting everyone worked up."

"No thanks," Derek said. "I like doing things the hard way."

"Suit yourself. You'll be dinner soon enough."

Derek checked on the other two yakarii. They were almost in position, ready to leap across. If they got in, there was no way he could defend himself against them both. He looked around the warehouse. Stacks of wooden crates ran from wall to wall. Overhead, a balcony spanned the entire room. There were two stairwells on either side of the balcony. In a flash, a plan formed in his head. He ducked away from the window he was guarding and sprinted down the room to the next window, where he knew one of the yakarii was about to make its leap.

Just in time, he heard the crunch of wood as the thing jumped. Its boney head crashed through the window, and glass exploded into the room. Derek swung with everything he had. His makeshift club cracked the thing's skull with a low *thunk*. The yakariian scout roared in irritation and reached for Derek with a clawed hand. He danced out of the way and stepped back in to deliver a sharp uppercut to the yakarii's jaw. The thing's head snapped back, and it flailed its arm for balance, but it was too far gone. The yakarii toppled backwards, and another scout dropped into the flood.

His victory was short lived. Just as the second yakarii flailed in the waters below, the other one smashed through the window at the far end of the room. Moments later, the chatty yakarii plowed through the same window Derek had blasted through. The thing hit the floor with a grunt and looked about. When its eyes fell on Derek, it growled. "Playtime is over, boy. I'm hungry."

Derek yelped and ran for the stairs. He grabbed smaller boxes as he went and pulled them down. The yakariian scouts rumbled

across the floor behind him. "That won't stop us, boy. You'll be in my belly before the sun comes up!"

He flew through the warehouse, dodging crates and sawhorses and piles of unspun wool. The yakariian scouts, natural runners, were closing the gap fast. Derek could hear them breathing, smooth and easy. His heart sank. Catching Derek wouldn't even be a challenge for these killers.

Derek scampered around a tower of boxes and found the staircase, only a few strides away. The yakarii were almost on him now. He ducked his head and made for the stairs as fast as he could, taking them two at a time. He was halfway up when the first yakarii reached the bottom. "All this running is only whetting my appetite, boy. There's no escape for you here, and that club ain't gonna help you."

"We'll see!" Derek shouted from the top of the stairs.

He was on the balcony around the upper warehouse now. The narrow walkway was dotted with tables stacked with ledgers and scrolls, ink pots and quills. Derek dipped through them, not even bothering to tip them over as he went. He checked over his shoulder every chance he got. The yakarii were close. The talker was already on the balcony, stalking Derek with long strides. The second was almost to the top of the stairs. "Head around the other way," the talker said, gesturing around the balcony. "Let's give him the old pinch."

The second yakarii roared its battle cry and sprang up the last of the stairs in two strides. It sprinted around the balcony on long, rangy legs. They would have him soon if Derek didn't act fast.

Light from the burning city streamed in through the windows, filling the warehouse with an eerie, orange flicker. The yakariis' tiny, close-set eyes glowed green in the dim light. Derek skidded to a stop in front of one of the windows. Unlike the lower windows of the warehouse, the upper windows were open, allowing a breeze to come through. The scent of burning pitch and foundry fuel lay heavy on the air. Derek's nose itched and burned. He put his back to the window and held up his club.

There was the quick scrape of boot over the wooden floor, and before Derek could look back into the warehouse, the first yakarii snatched Derek and yanked him out of the window. It tossed him to the floor as though he were a doll.

Derek groaned and pushed himself to his feet. He held his free hand before him and raised his club over his head. "I won't go down easily."

The talker chuckled. "I was hoping you'd say that."

Then they were on him.

The talker roared to distract Derek, while its partner leapt for his club. Derek hopped to the side and delivered a stinging whack to the thing's ribs. If the creature had been human, Derek would have shattered its chest cavity, but this was a yakariian scout. Heavily muscled and protected by dense bones, Derek's strike merely bounced off its side. The thing staggered to catch its balance and then wheeled on Derek again.

This time, they both came at him, their blades carving deadly arcs through the air. The creatures kept their cutting patterns tight, not allowing any openings for Derek to sneak in another attack. They circled him like gears turning in a mill, smooth and efficient. "You're quick, boy. I'll give you that."

Derek matched their movements, round and round. "I've got more than speed up my sleeve," he answered.

His back was to the window again. Rats or no, he knew this would be his only chance. He took a breath and leapt into the window frame again. "Rather go to the rats, would ya?" the talker asked.

Derek gave a quick glance below. Three stories above the flood, he hoped he would land between bodies. More than that, he hoped he could fight through the debris to find the surface. The floor creaked back in the warehouse, and he knew the yakarii were coming. Without another look, Derek leapt backwards, out the window. A jagged yakariian blade whistled through the open window where Derek had just been.

He held his breath and dropped.

"Derek!" came a shout from down the flooded street.

Derek looked, and then his feet punched through the water between the body of a drowned yakariian warrior and a floating wine cask. The dark water closed on him. His world was bubbles and oily water and limbs and too many rats. Derek clutched his club and swam for the surface. He pushed aside drifting blankets and bodies and somehow broke free. Derek gulped at the air and shook his head to clear the water from his eyes. Overhead, the yakariian scouts roared in frustration. "To the second floor! Don't let him get away!" the talker shouted.

Derek kicked and flailed at the water to keep his head up. The rats scattered over the debris at his impact, but they were already sniffing at him with their twitching noses. They would be back soon.

Then he remembered. Someone had shouted his name when he jumped. Derek looked up and down the flooded street. Sure enough, there was a boy paddling toward him in a canoe. With a few sure strokes, the boy brought the canoe alongside Derek. "What are you doing jumping out of a window?" the boy asked.

He knew that voice.

An explosion in the distance lit the sky for an instant and illuminated the boy's face. Derek was so surprised, he almost stopped treading water. "Conrad?"

Derek Makes a Choice

A moonless night fell on Zuid Horn, and the crowds heckling Derek and the other criminals broke away, filtering off to the pubs and taverns lining Ploughman's Wharf. Other than Conrad, his friends, and an old man brought in for public drunkenness, Derek was alone. The next prisoners in the stocks were almost twenty paces away: street children and dusty men and that sleeping ogre. He had tried getting Conrad to talk, but the street rat would only mutter about his sister. And the drunk? Too deep in his drink to do anything but snore. A lantern boy appeared, lighting oil lamps up and down the pier. Derek greeted the boy as he passed, but the dock worker wouldn't even glance in his direction.

Music and laughter whirled from the pubs. Here and there, street musicians and illusionists gathered little crowds, entertaining them with songs and sleight of hand. Scores of children ran about as well, bumping into sailors fresh off the ships, who shooed them away. That the children were pickpockets, Derek had no doubt. Occasionally, he even saw them pocketing their newfound goods. But he didn't say anything. Who would believe him? Anyway, could he really blame them? They needed to eat, too. He sighed and looked out to sea. It was almost time to act, but not just yet.

Great galleons rose and dipped gently with the tide beating against Zuid Horn's southern pier. A few forest giants worked slowly near the docks, loading and unloading mountains of crates. Ship to dock, dock to ship, like a living pendulum swinging back and forth. Derek watched the giants work, and his eyes drooped like heavy curtains. He blinked and shook his head to stay awake. No time for sleep now.

Derek munched on the remains of the smoked fish his mother and sisters had brought to the pier late in the afternoon. He had offered some to Conrad, a small platitude for Dani's cups of water, but the boy waved his offer away. Derek shrugged and ate what would have been Conrad's share. The fish quieted the rumbling in Derek's belly and helped pass the time as he studied his surroundings.

So many ships were coming and going from Zuid Horn, even at this hour, that the guide lanterns strung along their sides made the harbor and the black ocean beyond look like the star-filled sky. In fact, if Derek twisted far enough to see out over the bay, it was hard to tell where the ocean ended and the sky began.

A warm breeze came off the sea, bringing with it the scents of salts and oils from faraway lands. From his place in the stockades on the pier, Derek could make out the different smells coming from the larger boats. The flowery, light scents of sandalwood and vanilla? That had to be the merchant ships from Shadizar. That meaty, smoky smell that clung to the back of the throat like warm bacon fat? No doubt a schooner from Belveria bearing the finest smoked meats of the north. And when the breeze shifted, the source of that yellow stench reeking of urine and unwashed bodies? Minotaur slave carracks, with hulls stuffed floor to ceiling with prisoners to be sold in foreign slave markets.

Slavery had been outlawed in Zuid Horn for centuries, but as long as the minotaurs didn't unload their wares and paid their docking fees, the Iron Guard allowed the slavers to drop anchor at Ploughman's Wharf. Derek watched the nine-foot tall minotaurs swaggering down the dock, great battle axes strapped to their backs, and made sure to drop his eyes as they clopped past on iron-shod hooves.

Only a dozen guards watched the miserable line of souls locked in the stocks once night fell. There were a few more by the gibbet cages to keep street urchins from filching body parts to sell to necromancers, but Derek wasn't worried about them. He was too busy counting steps between the guards and reading their faces as they strolled past. They looked bored, as though they were the ones being punished by having to walk the docks during the night watch.

Derek wasn't sure what they didn't like about the docks. He enjoyed watching the great ships come and go. He also knew that some of these travelers came to Zuid Horn to buy wares from his father, which meant wealth and security. And who could complain about that? At least that's what Da always said.

The thought of his father sent a twinge of guilt through his gut. How could Derek have let his anger get ahold of him like it did? Derek was no stranger to losing his temper, but he needed to start controlling it if he was ever going to take over his father's business. Maybe Dani's advice to breathe would help.

A snuffling from Conrad brought Derek's attention back from the boats. The poor guy had been standing in the pillory all day under the blazing tropical sun. He had already staggered a few times, resulting in the boy practically choking himself. Throughout the afternoon, Conrad had cried out for Dani, but the passing crowd just laughed. Eventually, the street orphan simply sagged against his restraints.

In a gap between passing guards, Derek whispered, "Conrad!" When Conrad didn't reply, Derek said again, more urgently, "Hey! Let's get out of here!"

The drunk to Derek's left muttered and threw a dirty arm over his face. Derek rolled his eyes in disgust. "Conrad, are you

alright?" This time, Conrad nodded weakly. Derek checked over both shoulders to make sure there weren't any guards or tavern patrons strolling nearby. "Look, hang on. I'm going to get us out of here."

Conrad's head jerked up. When he spoke, his voice sounded like a gunny sack of chicken bones dragged over dry gravel. "Are you crazy? They'll catch us."

"Maybe, but we have to help your sister."

Conrad twisted in the pillory. He studied Derek with bleary eyes. "What?"

"I saw those Shadizarians following her."

Conrad flexed against the heavy beams of the pillory and then crumpled in defeat. "I need to get out of here, but the Iron Guard knows who we are! If we don't serve all our time, we'll have to go on the run."

Derek sighed. "Yeah, I know."

"Why would you help me?"

"I wouldn't. I'm helping Dani."

Conrad snorted. "Great. Just what I always wanted, a rich boy flirting with my sister."

"What? No, I..." but then he stopped because two Iron Guardsmen were coming.

They marched along the pier, the links on their armor jingling in time with their steps. "How long till the ball, now?" one of the guards asked the other.

"The Coming-of-Age Ball?"

"Yeah."

"I don't know, what, three weeks? A month? Who cares?"

"Gods, you know what it means, don't you?"

"We're pulling double duty."

The first guardsman laughed. "Not if you do it right. I'll get us up on the wall. That way, we won't be stuck in the thick of things."

"Do that," the other said, "and drinks are on me."

"You're on," the first guardsman said with a laugh. "I'll see what I can do."

Two guards clomped past. Derek watched them from the corner of his eye. After they'd gone, he checked for the next set of guards, who were still quite a way down the pier. This was the boys' chance. He leaned closer to Conrad.

"Look. I have sisters, too. If I saw slavers going after them, I... well, you know."

Conrad shook his head slowly. "Fine, but how are we getting out of here?"

"You'll see, but we have to go now. Can you make it?"

Conrad nodded.

Derek pulled out the key Niles Crowing had dropped. He slid on his rear until he was as close to the stocks as his restraints would allow. Then, he reached over and felt for the padlock. It was thick and cool, forged of low-grade iron. Derek flipped the lock so he could get at the keyhole. He bit his tongue, wiggled the key into place, and turned until it popped open. A quick moment later, he was free.

Derek looked up and down the pier. Except for the old drunk, who called for another round of wine, the stocks were empty for another twenty paces. After that, street children and the homeless dotted the stocks like buoys in the bay. They were too far away to pay any attention to him, so Derek was safe. He closed the ankle bindings to look like he had never been there and then checked on the patrolling guards. Closer now. He would have to move quickly. Conrad craned his neck to see around the pillory. "Hurry up!" he whispered.

"What are you waiting for?"

"Quiet," Derek hissed. "I have a plan."

Derek hopped to his aching feet and strolled down the dock, pausing to look at prisoners. When the Iron Guardsmen passed, they scowled. One of them, a weasel-faced man with yellow hair

and a tawny beard, pointed at Derek and grabbed the pommel of his long sword. "Out of the way, urchin." Derek gulped and scrambled to the side.

That was when the drunk sat up and glared at Derek with red-rimmed eyes. "Hey," the drunk said, "how'd you get out of your stocks?"

The Iron Guardsmen turned around. The yellow-haired, weasel-faced fellow eyed Derek and then turned to the drunk. "What did you just say?"

"He was here all afternoon, Cap'n Gorzoni," the drunk said, pointing at Derek. "Weren't ya?"

Derek tried to get his mouth to work. "Me? What? No, I wasn't. I came down here to look at the prisoners."

Captain Gorzoni frowned. "After dark?"

"Yeah," the other guardsman said. "Ain't no kids on the pier after dark, unless they're looking for trouble."

"Nothing but trouble, that one," the drunk said.

"What? I — no," Derek stammered. "I was just passing by."

"Where ya going?"

Derek thought quickly. "My mum sent me to pick up meat pies for dinner."

"Really?" the second guard asked. "Where from?"

"The Wayside Tavern," Derek said, naming the first wharf tavern that came to mind.

"They have meat pies?" Gorzoni asked.

Derek shrugged. "I guess so."

"No meat pies," the drunk mumbled, "but their brown ale is sweet as a siren's song."

Captain Gorzoni scowled at the drunk and waved the back of his hand at Derek. "Fine, get going then. Don't let us catch you down here again."

"Yes, sir," Derek said and ran off.

He stepped around a stack of wooden crates and then peeked back to check on the Iron Guardsmen. They were down the pier now, gesturing toward an old Shadizarian schooner. Derek pulled the key from his pocket and hurried over to Conrad. "I thought you left," Conrad said.

Derek tried the key in Conrad's lock. "I told you I had a plan."

Conrad grunted. "Can you blame me for not believing you?"

The lock popped open. Derek slipped the padlock out of the pillory and raised the gate. "Let's go," he said, waiting for Conrad to get out of the stocks. "We don't have much time before the next guards come."

Conrad tried to stand. He grabbed his back and groaned. "My back," he complained. "It's like someone's stabbing me."

Derek grabbed Conrad by the arm and helped him stand upright. He looked down the pier. The next pair of guards were just down the way. Amazingly, they had stopped to chat with some sailors and had their backs to the boys. "Come on," Derek said. "It's now or never."

They shuffled from the pier with Conrad's arm thrown around Derek's shoulders. Just then, the old drunk sat up again. "Hey! What are you boys doing?"

Derek and Conrad froze in their tracks. "My friend needs to pee," Derek said, thinking quickly. "We'll be right back."

"Don't got to leave for that," the drunk slurred. "I just go right here." He patted his sopping britches.

Derek coughed in disgust and helped Conrad away from the stocks. He hustled him toward the shadows.

"Hey!" the drunk called after them. "You're not supposed to leave!" And then, "Guards! Cap'n Gorzoni! Prisoners escaping!"

"By the Forge!" Derek swore. He pulled Conrad along as fast as he could.

"Told you," Conrad wheezed, struggling to keep up.

Clanking armor and heavy footsteps warned the boys that the Iron Guardsmen were hot on their tails. Derek searched frantically right and left for an escape. He dragged Conrad behind a pile of boxes stamped with the soaring eagle crest of Tyrsis and cut back on their trail. Finding a crevice between two crates, he pulled Conrad to the ground.

"Keep quiet!" he said. They ducked down just before two Iron Guardsmen appeared. The flash of yellow hair let the boys know Captain Gorzoni was on their trail.

"Did you see which way they went?" Gorzoni asked.

"Up there," the other answered. "Toward the pubs."

"Dirty street rats," Gorzoni. "Not worth a copper to chase them down."

"Count your coppers, and you'll be a rich man," the second said as they moved away.

Gorzoni laughed. "Too true! Too true!"

And then they were gone.

Derek peeked over the crate to watch them go. Checking about, he didn't see any more Iron Guardsmen. "Come on," he said, helping Conrad to his feet. "Let's go."

Conrad groaned. "What about Lars and Jenkins?"

"We can come back for them later. For now, let's get ourselves out of here first."

Keeping their heads low, the boys scurried from Ploughman's Wharf, doing their best to stick to the shadows.

Once they were off the wooden docks and back onto the cobblestone streets, the boys ducked toward a side street. Warm candlelight spilled from tiny pubs and food shacks. Smoke from grilling meats — ducks, chickens, pigeons, piglets, goats, and dogs — filled the air. The sweet scent of spilled wine and ale splashed up and down the alley. Bar patrons gathered in tight clutches, drinking, eating, and laughing.

The boys were almost past a wine shop, the Taste of Summer, when Conrad stumbled. Derek tried to catch him, but they both ended up on the cobblestones. A group of minotaurs gathered in front of the shop bellowed and pointed at the boys. Then they went back to their jugs of wine.

Conrad pushed himself onto his haunches. His wrists and neck were chafed and bleeding where the pillory had rubbed his flesh raw. His eyes were swollen and red. He ran a thick, white tongue over his cracked lips. "They're going to catch us. I can't go on any farther."

Derek helped Conrad lean against the wall. "Yes, you can. We are almost away."

Conrad raised his eyebrows in doubt. "It doesn't matter. They know who we are, especially you. Everyone knows you are Bryton Fulstarter's son. The Iron Guard will be at your house by morning."

Derek sighed and squatted against the wall next to Conrad. It was true. Derek imagined Da's face when the Iron Guard showed up at their shop. What would Da have to say then? He rubbed his eyes and pushed it aside. "I'll deal with that later. For now, let's focus on your sister."

"Great," scoffed Conrad. "Where do we start? We don't even know where she is. And what about the guards from Ploughman's Wharf? We have to get out of here."

"Don't worry. I've got a plan."

Conrad coughed. "Really?"

"Of course." Derek scanned the alley for anything that could help them.

The minotaurs across the way caught his attention. They were busy throwing back jugs of rhubarb wine, a Zuid Hornian favorite. Bulging sacks brimming with dry salted pork lay at their hooved feet. The minotaurs' huge woolen cloaks, dyed Minoan blue, lay draped over the wine shop's chairs. And on the tables with the waiting jugs of wine were several fat coin purses and a scattering of gold coins.

Derek smiled. The Iron Guard would be along soon. Everyone knew minotaurs fresh from the sea were rowdy, and these minotaurs were busy living up to their reputation, bellowing lewd songs about minotaur cows and downing pitchers of wine

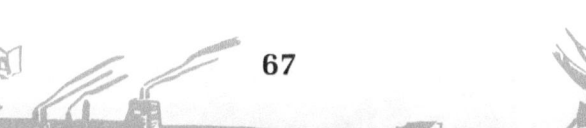

faster than the barkeep could bring them. The cloaks, the wine, and the coins. There was his plan, laid out before him. Derek got to his feet and crept toward the minotaurs, whose backs were to Derek and Conrad.

Conrad's swollen eyes flared. "What are you doing? You're going to get us killed!"

Derek held up his finger for Conrad to be quiet and then turned back to the minotaurs. He was almost to the cloak and the wine bottles when one of the minotaurs staggered backwards and bumped into Derek, knocking him to the ground. The minotaur wheeled and regarded Derek with bleary, red eyes. "Ho, what's this?" it growled.

"Excuse me," Derek stammered. "I didn't mean to get so close."

Another minotaur stepped in and extended a black taloned claw at Derek. "A liar! I saw him going for your cloak!"

The first minotaur turned and picked the cloak off the counter. It held the cloak in the air and sniffed long and deep. "Trying to filch my sweet cloak? This was a gift from my mother. I can still smell her on it."

For some reason, the minotaurs found this hilarious. They bellowed and roared. Derek took a quivering step back, but the minotaur with the cloak snatched him by the arm and hoisted him into the air. "Yes, my sweet mother and the Blue Crag Isles. A song, my lovely calves, to remind us of home!"

The other minotaurs raised their wine jugs and pounded tables in time to their singing. The thing holding Derek swung him back and forth with every line. His shoulder twisted in its socket, and Derek yelped. This brought even more laughter and calls for wine. Derek cast a pleading eye at Conrad, who could only raise his hands helplessly. The minotaurs' bellowing came to a triumphant crescendo. They raised their pitchers high and roared. Several waved their battle axes and stomped their hooves until the cobblestone pavement cracked.

Just then, a squad of Iron Guardsmen appeared at the mouth of the side street. Resplendent in full plate mail, heavy shields, and longswords, the guardsmen were the very image of battle-ready troops. Though the Iron Guardsmen outnumbered the minotaurs four to one, everyone in the alley knew the Guardsmen didn't stand a chance.

Despite the odds, the captain of the Iron Guardsmen moved to the front of his men and ordered them forward. "You there, minotaurs! We have received complaints of your disturbing the peace. You will cease and desist, or we will arrest you!"

The minotaurs fell silent and swung their great, horned heads toward the guardsmen. They dropped Derek, who scrambled over to Conrad as fast as he could. One of the minotaurs — a massive ten-footer with a pair of steel battle axes crossed over its broad back — hoisted its pitcher of bitter Zuid Hornian wine and drained it in one swallow. It tossed the ceramic jug against the wall, where it shattered over Derek and Conrad's heads, raining shards of broken pottery down over them.

The captain of the guard raised his hand. "This is your last warning," he started, but never finished. With a bellow that split the night like a ripped sheet, the minotaurs lowered their heads and charged. Massive hooves pounded the cobblestone, sending chips of flint flying with every step. Filled with drink and battle lust, the minotaurs didn't even bother to draw their axes.

At the other end of the alley, the Iron Guardsmen ripped longswords from their sheaths and raised their shields. "Steady!" their captain yelled. "Let's gut these cows and send them to the butchers!" His words were brave, but the lieutenant in the back row brought the warning horn to his lips and let loose three shrill blasts, alerting other guardsmen that a battle was underway.

They came together with a mighty crash. Shields buckled beneath the impact of several tons of minotaur flesh, talons, and horns. Longswords flashed, biting through the thick, black

minotaur hides. Hot blood sprayed the cobblestone alley into a slick mess.

The first row of Guardsmen vanished under the minotaurs' rush — trampled, gored, and dashed against the alley walls. If the second row of guardsmen felt any fear in the face of their comrades' demise, to their credit, they didn't show it. Swords held high, they charged in with blades hacking, reminding these pirates of the southern seas just why the Iron Guardsmen of Zuid Horn were so respected.

Derek and Conrad huddled against a wall near the door of a pub and watched in wide-eyed amazement. Conrad gripped Derek's arm. "We gotta get outta here. We lose either way!"

Derek couldn't agree more. "Can you make it to the end of the alley by yourself?"

"I think so. Aren't you coming?"

Derek nodded. "I'll be right there. I want to grab something." He started for the minotaurs' tables, now a jumbled mess of battered lumber.

Conrad grabbed his arm. "Are you mad? Let's get out of here!"

Derek shook his arm free. "Go!" Derek insisted. "I'll be right there." He turned and left before Conrad could argue more.

Derek ran back to the counter where the minotaurs had been drinking, grabbed one of the coin pouches, and then caught up with Conrad. He threw one of Conrad's arms around his neck and then helped him hurry out of the alley. "Where do you live?" Derek asked. "Maybe Dani is at home."

Conrad pointed into the heart of Zuid Horn. "Just head toward Gillman's Way." They shuffled along, and then Conrad muttered, "By the Forge, I hope she's there."

They hobbled away from Ploughman's Wharf, weaving between strolling families, sailors heading back to their ships, and dock workers ambling to the taverns. Soon, they were in the Warehouse District and crossing Mayfair Bridge over the Black River. From there, they could see the smokestacks of Zuid

Horn's great foundries, belching plumes of black smoke into the night sky. Orange sparks flickered with the stars. A high breeze parted the smoke and revealed the black Tower of High Sorcery. Even this far away, the sight of Gilgameth Tuft's tower made Derek shiver.

A unit of Iron Guardsmen marched past the boys just as they came to the Suppliers' District, where charcoal makers and blacksmiths had set up their shops for centuries. The boys hurried on and passed through a gate in one of the walls separating districts in Zuid Horn, and then they were back in the Artisan District, where Derek and his family had their shop. Derek readjusted Conrad's arm around his shoulder.

"You live in the Artisan District?"

Conrad snorted. "Why do you think we keep running into you?"

"Never really thought about it," Derek confessed.

"Obviously."

They came to Gillman's Way, and Conrad lifted his chin at a side alley. "Down there."

Derek stopped short. "Really? You live right next to me."

"Amazing," Conrad said, his voice flat. He took his arm off Derek's shoulder and swung it around to get the stiffness out. "Come on. It's just down here."

The alley was littered with broken crates, knots of molding cloth, and the bones of forgotten pets. A pair of black-haired rats squeaked and scurried away. Conrad came to a low box. "Here we are." He pushed the box aside to reveal a low door. He opened it and ducked inside. "Come on. Pull the box over the door once you're in."

Derek did as he was told and followed Conrad in the dark. There was a clacking with some sparks, and soon Conrad had an oil lamp lit to dispel the gloom. "Here we are."

The room had a low ceiling and was probably just a forgotten crawl space beneath some warehouse. Despite its location and the dirt floor, Derek could tell Conrad and Dani had done their best to make it their home. A dirty rug covered the center of the floor.

An open crate turned on its end made a low table, next to which lay two dusty cushions. A few boxes turned on their sides made makeshift shelves for their scant possessions — an extra shirt and pants, gunnysacks stuffed with overripe fruit, and a few posters advertising long-past stage performances.

Conrad noticed Derek studying the room. "Not like what you're used to," he said with a sneer but then caught himself. "Sorry. I didn't mean it like that."

Derek nodded and looked around the room some more. Two battered canoes hung from the walls, one stacked over the other, open side up. Folded blankets and grubby pillows showed that the canoes served as beds. A pair of oars hung over the canoes. "Where'd you get the canoes?"

"We found them on the beach a while back. Dani liked them and thought they would make good beds. Dani and me like boating the Black River now and then," Conrad said. "Don't cost nothing, and sometimes we find stuff."

Derek grunted and turned to Conrad. "Well, looks like she's not here."

"Yeah."

"Is there anywhere else she could be?"

Conrad's shoulders drooped. "I have no idea."

"Is there anyone who might have seen her? Anyone you guys know who might have seen her get... taken?"

Conrad thought for a moment. "Maybe, but most people who know anything will only talk if you have coin, and..." He gestured around the sparse crawlspace he called home.

"That's tough."

Conrad shrugged. "That's the street."

"We gotta find Dani and fast. If those Shadizarians got ahold of her, they'll want to get out of town as fast as they can. They were slavers, Conrad."

"I know who might know, but like I said, they won't talk without getting paid, and I don't have any money."

That's when Derek pulled the fat leather purse from behind his back. It jingled as he held it in the air. "Will this help?" he asked with a sly grin.

Conrad's eyes went wide. "Where did you get that?"

"The minotaurs left it on the counter at the wine shop when they were brawling with the Iron Guard. They should have been more careful."

Conrad laughed and shook his head. "Unbelievable." Then he looked Derek dead in the eye. "You know, I may have been wrong about you."

"How's that?"

"You know what I mean. I can't believe you're helping me after everything that's happened between us."

Derek shrugged. "Maybe I'm not helping you. Maybe I just like your sister."

Conrad frowned. "You make it hard to like you. You know that, right?"

Derek laughed. "Maybe."

"You know," Conrad said, "if we actually find Dani and save her, I don't know if I'll ever be able to repay you."

Derek took a deep breath. "We'll see. You never know when I'm going to need a hand."

"Well, when the time comes..." And Conrad left it at that.

Derek's World Goes Dark

Derek bobbed in the floodwater outside the warehouse. It had the gray reek of sewage drains and a metallic bite that made Derek's mouth run with spit. He treaded water to stay above the bodies and debris. Conrad eased the nose of his canoe over to Derek. Oddly, he was sitting in the front of the tiny craft. Derek grabbed the boat's edge and hung on.

"Conrad? What are you doing out here?"

"Following you."

Derek looked at the canoe in the light from the burning foundries almost half a mile away. "Wait. Isn't this Dani's bed?"

"By the Forge!" came a girl's voice from behind Conrad. "Get in! The yakarii are coming."

Derek craned his neck to look around Conrad. There was a small silhouette sitting at the back of the canoe. "Dani?"

Dani sighed in frustration. "Would you get in? We can talk later!"

"Sorry," Derek said. He tossed his club in the canoe and pulled himself over the edge. A wash of floodwater that reeked of sewage splashed into the bottom of the boat. "Hammer and Anvils," Conrad swore. "You stink."

"Conrad!" Dani hissed. "Get paddling."

And sure enough, the yakarii were on their way. Crates crashed inside the warehouse, and the heavy thump of yakariian boots pounded across the wooden floor. Conrad plunged his paddle into the water and pulled hard. Dani paddled too, but the floating boxes and bodies and rats made it almost impossible to move faster than the current. Footsteps in the warehouse drew closer and closer to the windows that opened like hungry mouths.

"Faster!" Derek yelled. "They're coming!" He twisted around to keep an eye out for the yakarii.

Their canoe edged past the warehouse just as the first yakarii stuck the bony crest of its head out the window. Its wicked tusks flashed in the light of the burning city. "There they are!" the thing shouted.

The second yakariian scout sprouted from a nearby window. This one was closer. "I'll get them," it growled and pulled a jagged dagger from its belt.

"Get down!" Derek yelled and yanked Dani to the bottom of the canoe.

A whirl of metal whistled over their heads and rattled off the side of a cooper's shop. "That was close," Conrad breathed. He peeked back at the yakarii and then ducked again, quick as a cat. A second dagger flew overhead. "Good thing the current is strong," Conrad said.

"Yeah," Derek agreed, "but we're going the wrong way. We have to get to the Merchant Gate."

"Why?" Conrad asked.

A third dagger rattled off the side of the canoe. Dani swore. "Can you two catch up later? We're being hunted here!"

"Right," Derek said. He kept low and looked around the canoe. "Do you have anything we can use as a shield?"

Dani pulled a backpack from under her seat and pushed it to Derek. "We've got some food and clothes in there. I don't know if it will stop a dagger, but it's better than nothing."

"Great," Derek muttered. He jostled past Dani and crouched on his knees. "I'll do my best. You two paddle." He held the backpack up as shield and peeked back at the warehouse.

Both yakarii leaned out of windows and over the flooded street. They held onto the sill with one hand and searched for throwing knives with the other. "Do you have any left?" one of them asked.

Its partner didn't respond but reared back its hand and hurled a dagger directly at Derek. His instinct was to duck, but he knew if he did that, the blade might hit one of his friends. Derek whipped Dani's thick, canvas pack at the flashing steel and whacked the blade aside. "Keep paddling!" Derek shouted. "We're almost out of range."

Another dagger came their way, but it fell short of the mark. The yakariian scouts swore and growled and then disappeared back into the warehouse. "I think we're safe," Derek said over his shoulder.

The current took them past a carpenter's shop and a weaver's studio. A movement in a window of the weaver's shop caught Derek's eye. Someone was peeking from behind a curtain. He tried to wave to them, but the shadow moved away from the window and fell back into darkness.

Dani looked to where he was waving. "People are still in their shops," she said in a low voice. "We should warn them about the yakarii."

Derek stopped waving. "I know. They've already got my sisters."

Conrad whipped around to face Derek. "What?"

"That's what I was trying to tell you," Derek said. "We've got to get to the Merchant Gate. Yakarii are swiping up people and taking them to the mines."

"Gods," Dani whispered, and traced her fingertips in an arc across her forehead and then over her chest.

Conrad put his oar across his lap and scratched at a scar on his forearm. "Hammer and Anvils, this itches like crazy." He looked back over his shoulder at Derek. "Where are your parents?"

"I don't know. They got swept away when the flood hit our shop."

Derek felt a hand on his back. "I'm sorry," Dani said.

"Me too," Derek said. "I haven't really had time to think about it. And guys, there's more. Peter's dead."

"Dead?" Dani asked.

Derek shook his head sadly. "And the yakarii kidnapped Augie and his parents when they nabbed my sisters." He looked at Dani and took a slow breath to clear his mind. "Can you help me rescue them?"

Conrad glanced over his shoulder. "You don't even need to ask." He pointed to a side alley coming up. "Dani, steer us down that alley. We need to cut across town."

Dani dug her paddle into the morass and pulled hard. The nose of the little craft swung over the floating debris toward the narrow gap between buildings. Rats scattered from their path but scurried back as soon as the boat passed. Rats. Derek shivered. The sight of their sleek hides and nude, wiggling tails made his skin crawl. He whispered a prayer to the Forge they wouldn't try to leap into the canoe.

The canoe rode low between buildings, so Derek couldn't see the smokestacks of the thirteen foundries at the city's heart, but what he could see was more than enough. Tall tongues of flame licked at the moonless sky, leaping high from the burning foundry fuel. Soot rained down, dusting everything with a powdery white coat and the taste of ash. Soaring behind the smoke and flames, the black Tower of High Sorcery surveyed the night of terror. Its image wavered in the heat of the fires. Derek ground his teeth. How much of tonight's destruction was the wizard's doing?

Conrad used his hands and paddle to guide the craft's nose into the alley. It was a tight fit, as the alley was more of a space between buildings than a proper passageway. "You ever been down here?" Conrad asked.

Derek shook his head. "Maybe when I was younger. I don't remember the way, really. You?"

"Nah," Conrad answered. "I'm just feeling my way."

The water ran almost level with the building to his right, so the roof was just barely above the flood. The building to their left rose three stories above them. Derek peeked in the windows as they floated by. Thin curtains waved in the windows. The room beyond the windows was darker than a grave. "Hello?" Derek whispered. "If anyone's in here, look out for yakarii. They're snatching people all over Zuid Horn."

Something moved in the dark. Before Derek could react, a taloned hand shot from the window and grabbed him by the throat. Claws like needles sank into the meat of his neck. He tried to breathe, but the thing was crushing his windpipe. He flailed with one hand and reached for his club in the bottom of the canoe with the other. His fingertips brushed against the hilt and sent it rattling over the floor of the canoe. His efforts to break free from the yakarii's grip pitched the canoe back and forth.

"Hey! Watch it!" Conrad yelled, but when he saw what was happening, he shouted, "Derek! Look out!"

Thanks for the warning, Derek wanted to say. He dug his nails in the sinewy forearm that held him. A low chuckle came from inside the warehouse.

"Got you now," a throaty voice growled. It pulled him closer, and the canoe banged against the wall of the building. "Just in time, too. I'm getting hungry." The yakarii's mandibles clicked and rattled in the dark. Its piggish eyes glowed a nasty green. "I think I'll carve you up where you stand and eat you right here," the thing said, "in front of your friends." There was the whisper of steel sliding over leather, and then a dagger in a yakariian fist leapt from the shadows.

Derek put his feet against the wall and pushed, but the yakariian scout was too strong. The dagger was almost at his throat when Dani screamed her battle cry. She brought the oar down hard on the thing's wrist. There was a crack and the scout howled. It dropped Derek and the knife at the same time. Without thinking, Derek snatched up the blade and slashed through the window and into the darkness. The base of the dagger met something meaty, an arm? A neck? He pulled hard and cut deep. The yakarii gurgled and stumbled back.

"Row!" Derek croaked, holding his neck. He tossed the bloody dagger into the bottom of the canoe.

Dani and Conrad paddled hard. There was less debris in the alley, and with a few strokes, the canoe shot down the narrow gap. When they came to the end of the alley, the water opened onto what was called "Feasting Lane" due to the many taverns and pubs that catered to traveling merchants. Like the alley, there was less debris here, and the canoe drew easily to the middle of the way.

Derek and his friends looked back at the alley and the building with the yakarii. From this side, they could see the building that rose three stories above the water had been a textile factory. Colorful sheets and blankets drifted from the building's drowned windows in the flood's current and waved like a carnival of kelp.

"Don't get your oar caught up in that," Conrad warned Dani.

"I know how to paddle," Dani grumbled. "It's my canoe, remember?"

Derek rubbed his neck and wheezed. His neck was slick with warm blood. The yakarii's nails had dug deep. "That was close," he said, his voice rough. "I don't want to do that again. Let's stick to the main streets."

"Agreed," Conrad said.

They glided down Feasting Lane. Conrad called out directions by pointing every now and then. He used his oar to push aside bodies and boxes, carts upended by the flood, and a fleet of the largest watermelons Derek had ever seen, bobbing with the current alongside them. Derek wanted to talk to his friends, wanted to know how they'd escaped the flood, how they'd managed to get one of their canoe beds out of their tiny room, but they needed silence now, especially with yakarii on the prowl. He thought of his sisters, somewhere on the northwest side of the city, slung over the beasts' backs like loot. He prayed to the

Forge they were still alive. And his parents? He bit his lip and muttered another prayer.

The canoe kicked hard to the side. "Hammer and Anvils!" Conrad swore.

Conrad maneuvered the canoe around a drowned ox that had gotten tangled up in some debris. Its head was anchored underwater, while the bulk of its bloated mass rose from the flood like a fat river stone. Water gushed and gurgled around the bobbing corpse. Derek leaned over to help push the canoe free. He reached out with a bare hand but pulled it away as fast as he could.

A pair of rats rode the dead ox as though it were an anchored barge. They had chewed away at the thing's side and were working hard at the dead ox's soft belly, exposing the glistening intestines. One of them sank its nose into the ox's innards and pulled out a rubbery mouthful. Derek tried not to breathe as they slipped past, but he could taste the bite of spilled bile in the back of his sinuses. His stomach turned and he looked away. That was when he saw something moving on a rooftop a few buildings down.

"Guys!" he whispered, "Something's moving on the roof!"

Conrad looked around. "Where?"

Derek pointed. "Up there. They're big, whatever they are, and there's at least two of them."

"Do they have your sisters?" Dani asked.

"There's only one way to be sure."

Conrad grunted and angled the canoe to the side of Feasting Lane to better hide from the yakariian scouts' view. They slid past a bakery and The Three Friars meat pie shop in silence. When they came to the end of The Three Friars building, Derek said, "Hold up here."

Dani dug her paddle into the water and held tight. The canoe eased over and bumped against the brick wall. Like many buildings in Zuid Horn, the walls were covered with thick grape vines. Derek grabbed onto the vines and pulled. They held.

"Perfect," he said. Derek grabbed his club from the bottom of the canoe. He stood up, a hand on the vines for balance. "I'm going after them. You guys stay close to the wall so they don't see you."

"You're what?" Dani almost shouted.

"Keep it down," Derek whispered. "I don't want them to know we're coming."

"Are you serious? There's two yakarii up there."

"Yeah, and they might have my sisters."

Conrad stood up. "I'm going with you." He pulled a short sword and scabbard from the front of the canoe and tied it to his belt.

Dani glared at the boys with an open mouth. "Would you listen to yourselves? A club and a short sword? You're a couple of boys against two — maybe more — yakariian scouts. You don't stand a chance."

Derek's jaw tightened. The side of his scalp tingled. "Dani, I don't have time to argue. If I don't get my sisters now, I'll never see them again." Derek hoisted himself up the vines. Conrad was right behind him.

"Are you crazy?" she hissed.

"No," Derek whispered, "I need to save my sisters." Then he was over the edge of the building and onto the roof. He heard Dani grumbling to herself below.

Conrad huffed over the edge. He squatted next to Derek and pointed a few buildings down. "There they are," he said. "Stay down."

The yakariian scouts were just ahead of them. In the dark, Liza and Sarah looked like a pair of dark lumps over the scouts' shoulders. "That's them," Derek whispered. "Let's go."

They scrambled over the rooftops on all-fours, keeping as low as they could. When they came to the end of the roof, a little leap helped them clear the alley to the next roof. Conrad hustled to the streetside of the roof and waved Dani forward, then he came back to Derek. "Dani's not happy," Conrad said.

"No kidding, but what does she want me to do? I've got to get my sisters before these yakarii catch up to the others."

"Others?"

"Yeah. These two were traveling with two more who took Augie and his family."

"By the Forge, everyone is getting nabbed tonight."

"Yeah."

The boys moved like shadows over the rooftops. Every now and then, Conrad crept to the side of the building to make sure his sister kept pace in the canoe. In short order, the boys were only a rooftop behind the yakarii. Kneeling behind a stack of new shingles, the boys were so close they could hear the creatures talking. "Another alley? I'm tired of jumping," one of them was saying.

"You're tired? I'm starving! Flood hit just as I was sitting down to a haunch of lamb."

"Lamb? Sounds good."

"Would have been. The skin was all crispy, too."

"I love it like that."

"Who doesn't?"

Conrad leaned over and whispered in Derek's ear. "What's the plan?"

Derek peeked around the shingles. The yakarii holding Sarah handed her to the other scout. She cried and kicked, but she was small — only ten years old, after all — and the yakarii had no trouble handling her. "Here, hold them both," the first one said. "I'll make the jump." It took a few steps back, got a running start, and leapt over the alley. It landed with a sliding crunch of pea gravel on the flat roof. "Alright, toss 'em," it said.

The boys watched the transfer of Derek's sisters. That's when Derek smiled. "I have an idea," Derek whispered. "Come on, let's get back to Dani."

Conrad followed Derek to the side of the building. Dani was waiting below in her canoe. "We're coming down," he said, pointing back to the yakarii. "Keep quiet. They're close."

Dani nodded and waited for the boys to climb into the canoe. Once they were settled, she asked, "What's the plan?"

Derek's chest tingled with excitement. He would have one chance to free his sisters. As nervous as he was, somehow, he had never felt more alive. He waved Conrad and Dani in close. "Aright. Here's what we are going to do..."

After Derek shared his plan, Dani's skill with the canoe and paddle won them a lead on the yakarii. Even though she was the lightest of the three, she sat in the bowman's seat and guided the craft through the litter-choked current as easily as though it were the middle of the Black River. More than once, Derek looked back at her in admiration. He wanted to say something, but silence was paramount.

Derek glanced at the sign for the shop next to them. David's Pottery. He had come there with his mother whenever she needed tableware, so he was familiar with the building. A trellis of grapevines ran around the edge of the roof, like so many others in Zuid Horn. "Slip into this alley," Derek whispered. "We'll go up here."

Dani held her oar firm in the current, and the nose of the canoe eased into the alley. Derek grabbed a windowsill and pulled them to stop. The faint current in the alleyway bubbled and licked at the sides of the small craft. "Alright," he said. "Let's go." He picked up his club and used a downspout to climb the side of the pottery shop. He was almost to the vine-covered railing around the roof when Dani called to him.

"Hey," Dani whispered.

Derek glanced over his shoulder. She was looking up at him. The distant fires highlighted the soft curve of her high cheekbones. Her short, dark hair glistened with floodwater. When she smiled, Derek's stomach twisted in a different kind of knot. "Be careful," she said. "I want to see you again."

"I will," he said, and then he was over the railing and onto the roof.

Conrad clambered up after him, and they darted across the flat rooftop. Conrad slid a short, steel sword from the sheath at his side. Its fine edge twinkled in the dim light. Two rooftops away, the yakarii ambled toward them. "They're coming," Derek whispered. "Hide over there." He pointed to the right of where he thought the yakarii would try to cross.

Conrad nodded, and the boys split up, one to each side of the oncoming yakarii's' path. The boys hunkered down behind the low railing, made sure the vines completely hid them from the yakarii, and then drew their weapons. Derek peeked through the vines and watched the yakarii carry his sisters closer and closer.

"We're almost there," the one with Liza over its shoulder said. It pointed past Derek. "See? There's the wall now."

Derek risked a look. Less than a quarter mile away, the great, iron walls of Zuid Horn rose into the inky night. At eighty feet, Zuid Horn's outermost walls dwarfed the defenses of every city-state in the realms. Thirty feet thick at the base and reinforced with steel rebar and an outer shell of iron plating, Zuid Horn's walls had repelled every assault since it was built. Da said the walls were a sign of the gods' favor, but wouldn't the gods have foreseen that the real threat to Zuid Horn would come from the sea?

"Not so bad," the other replied. "We might get out of the city before Ya'Gresh and Crika."

"We could be so lucky. I'm sick of his complaining. If we're late, that will be another thing for him to gripe about." The yakarii took Liza off its shoulder and handed her to its companion. "Here, take this. I'll go across first this time."

Liza kicked and squirmed. "Let me go!" she shouted. She brought a knee up hard and caught the yakarii under the chin.

It roared and clicked its mandibles. "Ku'Ra Gah curse you, girl!" it yelled and hurled her onto the flat roof.

She bounced so hard the wind wheezed between her teeth. She crawled and stumbled toward the far side of the roof. But the yakariian scout, with its rangy legs, was after her in a flash. "Think you can get away from me?"

The thing stalked with long strides after Liza. She scurried on her hands and knees, tried to pop to her feet, but tripped and went

down. Liza hit the roof hard and skidded. This time, there was no room to get up. She flipped over and scooted away on her backside as fast as she could. The yakariian scout was close. Too close. It towered over her and roared. Liza shrieked, and the thing picked her up and held her in the air.

"If it wasn't for Ya'Gresh, you would be dead, girl." The scout shook Liza back and forth, and then stormed back to its companion. It thrust Liza at the other scout, who snatched her with a taloned claw. "Now hold onto her," the first said, "or we'll have to break her legs so she doesn't run away."

Derek's heart pounded in his chest. How could he have been so arrogant? Dani was right. These were yakariian scouts. Trained killers. And they had his sisters. If his plan failed, not only could he die, but his sisters would, too. His entire family would be wiped out in one night!

A tremble started in his gut and worked through his limbs to his hands. Before he knew it, his whole body was shaking. He glanced at Conrad for support, but his friend had his eyes on the yakarii and Derek's sisters. "Pull it together," Derek growled to himself. "Pull it the hell together!"

The yakarii walked back a few steps and eyed the gap. "Alright," it said, and then it was off.

One, two, three steps and the thing launched itself upwards, its legs and lanky arms wheeling as though it could run through the air. It was at the apex of its arc when Derek saw the flaw in his plan. "Hammer and Anvils," he muttered. "I'm an idiot." But there was no time to change things now.

The scout flew through the air and crashed over the low railing. Derek and Conrad were on it before the thing had a chance to get its footing. *"Ya!"* Conrad cried, slashing at the yakarii with his short, steel sword. His blade bit into the thing's meaty shoulder and splashed a ribbon of black, yakariian blood across the pebble-strewn rooftop.

"What the?" the yakariian scout shouted and leapt away from Conrad.

This left the thing's back exposed to Derek, who came at it from behind with a devastating blow. The head of his makeshift club cracked hard off the yakarii's bony crest with a loud pop. It stumbled forward and threw its arms over its head. "Two of you?" it growled.

Derek and Conrad pressed their attacks, each working a side. But the yakariian scout was a trained fighter from a culture of warriors. The boys' surprise attack may have stunned the beast for a moment, but the heat of battle seemed to clear the thing's mind. It leapt to the side and pulled a jagged dagger from behind its back. "My turn," it said and dropped into a crouch.

The boys attacked from both sides. Derek swept at the thing's knees. His strike went low and bounced harmlessly off a tough shinbone. The yakarii laughed and hacked at Derek, catching him on his left arm. "No!" Derek cried and staggered back. He clutched the back of his arm, where hot blood ran thick. Derek gritted his teeth. His scalp tingled, and the sides of his vision blurred. The rage was near.

"How'd you like that?" the scout chuckled. "Plenty more where that came — argh!"

A splatter of black blood announced the arrival of Conrad's short sword, two feet of good, Zuid Hornian steel driven through the yakarii's other shoulder and out its upper chest. The creature grunted and reached for Conrad, but the orphan had too many years of eluding the Iron Guard under his belt. He slipped to a side, grabbed the hilt of his sword, and yanked it out of the scout's back with a wash of black ichor.

"Yes!" Derek raised his club and roared. His pulse ran hot with his temper. Dani's voice whispered at the edge of his mind, *Breathe, Derek, breathe*, but the anger was on him now, and he stuffed her advice away. He smacked the club in his hand and hunted for an opening.

The yakarii swayed, the mortal wound draining lifeblood down its chest and back. Derek could have let it bleed out, but the fury made him hungry for vengeance. He drove in and whacked at the thing's legs and then at its bloody chest. His club bounced off its arms and skull crest again and again. It swiped at Derek and roared in frustration as if the boy's attacks were a swarm of bees, stinging him over and over, not giving it a chance to staunch the bleeding that threatened its life. Striking high and low, driven by desperation, Derek pressed on. Images of his sisters and his parents flashed in his mind and fueled his white-hot anger. He knew the yakarii's blade was cutting him as often as his club found its mark, but he was too mad to care.

A shout from Conrad broke him from his battle trance. "Derek!"

Derek knocked aside a weak dagger strike and stepped away from the yakarii. The thing was covered in black blood. Its arms sagged, and it struggled to keep its dagger pointed at Derek. For his part, Derek was little better. The scout had carved him up good, and as his battle fury left him, Derek realized he was bleeding badly from half a dozen deep gashes.

Conrad peeked from behind the yakariian scout. His sword and forearms were slick with black blood. "Derek, your sisters."

"What?" Derek moved another step away from the fight and risked a look across the flooded alley.

The second yakarii held Derek's sisters in the air by the necks. Gods! How had he forgotten? When the yakarii saw it had Derek's attention, it said, "Throw down your weapons, or I kill the girls."

Derek's shoulders collapsed. The flaw in his plan. He saw it just as the first yakarii was jumping across the alley, and now it was too late. How could he have let his anger blind him? Now, his sisters would pay the price for his stupidity. "Drop your weapons," the thing said again.

The yakarii between Derek and Conrad wheezed for breath. It pressed a taloned hand against the hole in its chest, a bid to staunch the bleeding. With the other, it pointed a dagger at Derek's club. "Drop it."

Derek clenched his jaw. His mind raced. The foggy remnants of rage were still on him, and it was hard to think straight. If he gave up, the yakarii would have both him and his sisters, not to mention Conrad. If he fought, his sisters would die. The scout holding the dagger laughed. "Still have some fight left, do you? We'll see about that." Keeping its eye on Derek, it said to its companion, "Kill them."

"No!" Derek screamed.

Everything happened at once. The yakarii sprang at Derek and slashed at his throat. Derek stumbled backwards and flailed wildly with his club. He batted aside the scout's first strike but took a nasty cut to the neck when the thing turned the dagger around and swiped at him a second time. Derek howled and clutched the wound. The yakarii knocked him to the ground and drove its tremendous knees into his shoulders. It crushed Derek's neck with one hand and raised its dagger with the other. "Now you die," it hissed.

But its dagger never dropped.

Conrad's short sword popped through the thing's neck, severing its spine. Its beady eyes rolled back, and the yakariian scout toppled over.

Derek pressed a hand to the side of his throat. Blood streamed fast down his neck and chest. What was keeping him upright? The dagger must have just missed an artery. Conrad glanced at him. "You okay?" Derek waved him off with his club and turned to the yakariian scout holding his sisters across the flooded alley. "Let them go," Derek said, "or you die next."

The thing shook his head. "Impressive. I thought you cared about these girls. Guess I was wrong." It roared and flexed its mighty hands, sinking its talons into his sisters' necks.

"No!" Derek screamed. He tried to move, but everything felt thick and slow, like a dream. His hamstrings tingled like they were asleep. His throat tightened, and his breaths came hard.

Derek watched the yakariian scout strangle his sisters and felt his bladder let loose.

Liza and Sarah gurgled and kicked, their legs too short by far to reach the scout. Liza found Derek with her eyes. *Do something!* She seemed to plead. If he ever needed his battle rage, it was now. Why wouldn't his body answer?

His feet were lead. In fact, his entire body was tight, locked in place. Fear like copper filled his mouth. "Derek!" Conrad yelled, waving his sword. "Now!" His friend leapt over the vine-covered railing, found footing on the lip of the roof, and then dove across the flooded alley. Conrad fell short. He hit the water with a clumsy belly flop and whacked against the side of the far building. He clung to the roof with one hand and clutched his sword with the other. He tried to kick and swim out of the water, but the angle was all wrong. Unless he dropped his sword, he was stuck. "Derek!" he screamed over his shoulder. "Snap out of it!"

Derek's breathing came in quick bursts. He couldn't tear his eyes away from Liza. Veins bulged on her purpling face. She ripped and tore with her nails at the yakariian scout's hand and wrist, but its grip was iron. Sarah had stopped kicking, and the yakarii dropped her limp body to the roof. She lay like a bed of stones.

Liza's battering at the beast's hands faded to slapping. Finally, her hands flopped to her sides and hung like dead fish. Liza turned her wide, bloodshot eyes and found Derek. He wanted to go to her, to help her, to save her, but his world was drowning in bitter molasses. "Liza," he mouthed.

"You could have dropped your club," the yakarii growled. It flexed its tremendous hands, and there was a sharp crack. Liza's head jerked to the side. Her eyes rolled back, and then she was still.

The yakarii chuckled and dropped Liza's body. She hit the roof hard and didn't move. Then, the scout drew a pair of knives from its belt and walked over to Conrad, still clinging to the side of the roof. "Once I kill your friend," it said to Derek, "I'm coming for you."

Derek's mouth hung loose. Liza and Sarah. Dead? How could this be? A part of him screamed that he needed to help Conrad, needed to do something to save his friend, but he couldn't get over his new reality. First his parents and now his sisters. He was alone in the world.

"Derek!" Conrad yelled. "Help!"

Conrad's plea shot through Derek like an arrow and stirred the embers of his battle rage. The edges of his vision blurred until he could only see the yakariian scout. He flexed and screamed at the beast.

The creature looked up at Derek's challenge and smiled across the watery way. "Oh, so you're coming to me now? Saves me the trouble of hunting you down." He bowed mockingly. "You have my gratitude."

Derek snatched up his club, vaulted over the railing, and sprang for the far roof. Whereas Conrad was too short to make the leap, Derek's lanky, northern build easily cleared the gap. Pea gravel crunched under his feet as he skidded to a stop. His blood pounded in his ears. Derek raised his club and pointed it at the yakariian scout. "You killed my sisters."

"And now I'm going to kill you." The thing spread its arms wide and sank into a crouch. It stepped toward Derek and then jerked and dropped to all fours with a grunt, its close-set eyes wide with confusion.

"Not if I cut your hamstrings first," a girl's voice hissed. Dani rose slowly from behind the toppled beast, a bloody yakariian dagger in her hand.

The thing turned to slash at her, but Dani danced out of its reach. "Now!" she shouted.

Derek charged in and whacked the scout's wrist. Its dagger rattled across the roof. With his return strike, he smacked the other dagger away. A blur at his side told him Conrad had joined them, and now it was three on one.

"Hold on," Conrad said. "Let's find out why the yakarii are kidnapping people."

But Derek wasn't about to listen.

He roared and came in swinging. The yakarii was seven feet of hulking mass with black, taloned hands bigger than Derek's head. But with its hamstrings slashed, courtesy of Dani, its mobility was halved. Derek darted in and out, battering its arms, sides, and knobby head with his club.

The yakarii swiped at Derek and opened four jagged gashes on his chest. Derek ground his teeth and let loose a blow at the thing's elbow. There was a crack like a board breaking, and then the thing's arm dropped uselessly to its side.

"Derek, wait!" Conrad cried.

Derek ignored him. His vision blurred, and he hammered the yakarii again and again. The rhythm of his club beating the creature became the drumbeat of his rage. He swore, screamed, and cried but didn't understand a word of what he said. All he knew was that his family was dead, and this yakarii was to blame.

It was Dani who brought him back. Derek stood over the scout's body, beating the thing's corpse over and over. His lungs burned, and his club was slick with ichor. Her voice came to him like a breeze. "Derek," she said. "It's over."

And like leaves rustling in answer to the wind, his sanity returned. The battered scout's body lay at Derek's feet. When had the yakarii died? He dropped his club and backed away. The rage drained from him, and suddenly every part of him ached. Derek raised his palms and looked dumbly at his body. He was covered with blood — black yakariian blood and his own crimson — from head to toe. His eyes itched. Dirty as his hands were, he knew scratching them would only make the itching worse. His chest was so tight he couldn't get a decent breath. All he could do was gulp and pant. His throat and chin quivered, and then the tears came, and he was sobbing.

Dani put her hand on his shoulder. "It's over," she said again.

Derek dropped his head and let the tears come. "Derek," Conrad whispered. "Your sisters."

Conrad was kneeling next to Liza, holding her limp hand. Liza lay crumpled on the flat roof, her dark hair spread out like a pool of ink. The spray from the floodwaters had left her hair damp, as though she had just finished bath night, and the curves of her locks were smooth and rich. The last time he had seen her, when the yakarii was crushing her throat, her face had been purple and bloated and tight with fear. Now that death had released her, she looked like she was sleeping.

Derek came and knelt next to his sister, and he saw for the first time that she was beautiful. How could he have missed it? For all the teasing Peter had given him about Liza, how could he have missed that simple truth? Now he would never be able to tell her.

A pressure built in his belly and bubbled up his throat. Derek clenched his jaw to keep it in, but the grief boiled out as a moaning wail. He rocked back and forth next to Liza's corpse. First Peter, then his parents, and now his sisters.

The pain in his belly bent him in half. Derek pounded the roof with his fists and screamed, "No! No! No!"

"I'm sorry," Conrad kept saying. "I'm so sorry."

"My fault," he wailed. "All my fault."

"You did what you had to," Conrad said.

"No!" Derek screamed. "They'd be alive if I would have just left them alone."

"They'd be slaves."

"Better slaves than this." Derek flicked a hand at Liza's corpse.

He reached out and touched Liza's bare arm. It was still warm. "By The Hammer," he whispered, "I'm all alone."

"Derek." It was Dani.

He twisted on his haunches. Dani was kneeling next to Sarah's little body. She had her ear next to Sarah's mouth and a light hand on her thin chest. When Dani looked up, her eyes were wide. "Derek," she said. "Sarah's breathing. She's still alive."

Derek gets Crafty

The candle in Conrad and Dani's little room sputtered and spit. Derek knelt next to Conrad with a dish of water and a rag and wiped the blood from Conrad's wounds. "That should about do it," Derek said, checking things over one last time. "Got anything to eat?"

Conrad patted his chafed wrists and winced. "Yeah." He pointed to a sack next to a low box. "There's some apples in there."

Derek went to the sack and pulled out a pair of apples. They were bruised and riddled with worm holes. As hungry as he was, Derek almost put them back, but he didn't want to disrupt the new truce he had with the bully of Gillman's Way. He tossed one of the apples to Conrad. "Come on, let's go."

They left without saying a word. Once they were on Gillman's Way again, Conrad said, "We'll need help. We need to bust Lars and Jenkins out."

"Are you sure they'll help us?" Derek took a bite of the mealy apple. It was soft and too sweet and filled his mouth with the taste of rot. Derek forced himself to take another bite. "I mean, they hate me."

"True," Conrad said. He munched on his apple as they went and didn't seem to have any problem with the rotten taste. "But when they find out Dani's in trouble, they'll come along."

"Why's that?" Derek asked.

"Lars has a thing for Dani," Conrad explained and rolled his eyes. "He'd do anything for her."

"Great," Derek said. A nervous little voice from his belly wondered if Dani had a thing for Lars too. He pushed the voice aside. "Don't you think it would be better if we did this alone?"

Conrad shook his head. "We're going to need all the help we can get. Besides, worse comes to worst, Lars and Jenkins know everyone. If anyone saw Dani get kidnapped, they'll find out where she went."

"Fine, but this isn't going to be easy."

"Who said it would be?" Conrad asked.

The boys hurried back to Ploughman's Wharf. They walked near the taverns, where the smells of fish fried in bacon fat wafted on the sea breeze. To their right, toward the harbor, a line of prisoners in stocks and gibbets dotted the length of the pier. Most of the children in the stocks were asleep, but a few of them called out to Conrad as they passed. He gave one of them the apple core he had been gnawing on. "Hang in there," he whispered to the boy.

They wandered down the wharf, doing their best to act casual. A pair of guardsmen marched by. They didn't even give the boys a second glance. "Looks like things calmed down after the minotaur fight," Derek said.

"I'll say," Conrad said and pointed toward the gibbets.

Derek looked to the western end of the pier. The bloody bodies of half a dozen dead minotaurs stuffed into groaning gibbets twisted in the warm night air. "Yeah." Derek turned away. "A run in with the Iron Guard will do it."

"Nobody messes with Zuid Horn's finest," Conrad said, shaking his head. "They never lose."

Derek pointed up the row of prisoners. "Isn't that Lars and Jenkins up there?"

Conrad squinted into the dark. "I think so. Come on. Let's get closer."

The boys moved away from the lamplight of the taverns and toward the pier, where the merchants, sailors, and longshoremen used flickering torches to light the darkness. Stacks of crates and boxes and fishing nets made messy piles in front of each ship. These stacks grew and shrank, depending on whether the ships were just arriving or leaving Zuid Horn. Sailors, slaves, and merchants busied themselves by setting out goods for the morning market. Four forest giants waded in the harbor and carried goods between ship and shore. Thick waves grumbled in their wakes and splashed under the pier. Derek had never seen a forest giant smile, but as Da said, they must be making good coin, or they wouldn't keep coming back.

The boys ducked from crate to crate. When they were about twenty paces from Lars and Jenkins, Conrad pointed. "There they are. Do you have your key for the stocks?"

Derek pulled the key out of his pocket and held it up. "Right here." He scanned the docks and then yanked Conrad behind a crate. "Get down."

A pair of Iron Guardsmen clanked past. Derek and Conrad kept low and watched. As soon as the guards were far enough away, Derek nudged Conrad in the side. "Come on!"

The boys scrambled on light hands and feet across the pier until they got to Lars. The short boy looked up. His eyes were dark, and when he saw Derek, they grew even darker. "What are you doing here?" He was loud and angry.

Conrad quickly intervened. "Shut up, you idiot," Conrad hissed. "Derek is here to help."

Lars raised his brow. "With what?"

"Dani's in trouble," Conrad said.

The boy sat up straight. "What?"

Conrad looked over his shoulder and then squatted next to Lars. "A pack of Shadizarian sailors might have grabbed her. We saw them following her after she brought us water this afternoon." Conrad pointed to the alley where they had last seen Dani and the Shadizarians. "Derek busted us out of the stocks, and when we went to my place, Dani wasn't there. Where else could she be?"

Lars looked at them like they were crazy. "I don't know. A friend's house? Maybe she didn't feel safe staying alone."

Conrad's face went blank. "I didn't think of that."

Derek shook his head. "You didn't see them, Lars. They were following her. It was obvious."

Lars scowled. "So what? She's a good-looking girl. She gets followed all the time."

Derek's gut tightened. "I know the difference between someone looking for a girlfriend and someone looking for trouble."

"Oh," Lars mocked. "Now you're an expert on life on the street, are you?"

Derek clenched his jaw. "Come on, Conrad. We don't need this loser."

"Hammer and Anvils, enough!" Conrad barked and yanked Derek's arm. "Guards are coming." To Lars, he whispered, "Just shut up. We'll be right back."

The boys hustled behind a wet pile of fishing nets until the next pair of guards passed.

Conrad glared at Derek. "Can you knock it off?"

Derek threw up his hands. "What?"

"You know exactly what I mean. Get ahold of your temper, or he's not going to help us."

"I thought you said he would do it for Dani."

Conrad watched the guards marching past. "He will, but not if you keep insulting him. We may be street rats, but we have some pride."

Derek grunted. "Fine."

When the guards were far enough away, the boys crept back to Lars. "Look," Derek said, "you can stay here if you want. I told

Conrad you wouldn't help us, so it's no surprise to me. I'm going to check out that Shadizarian galley over there. If Dani's on it, I'm going to free her."

Derek turned to leave. "Come on," he heard Conrad say to Lars. "Dani needs us."

Derek looked over his shoulder to see what Lars would decide. The short boy with dark hair considered Derek with a frown. Finally, he sighed. "Fine, get me out of here. I'm coming too."

Conrad breathed a sigh of relief. "Thank you," he said.

Derek wasn't sure if Conrad was speaking to Lars or to Derek.

Derek went back and crouched next to the stocks. He pulled Niles' key from his belt and shot Conrad a quick look. "I'll stay here to get Lars out of his stocks. You go let Jenkins know what's going on."

Conrad nodded. "Got it," he said, and then he slipped into the darkness.

The key made quick work of the padlock. Derek lifted the heavy bar holding Lars and helped the street orphan stand. The boy wobbled on stiff legs. "Come on," Derek whispered, "before the next set of guards come."

Derek helped Lars hide behind a stack of crates on the wharf. Then they watched Conrad, who was whispering to Jenkins. Lars said, "Don't think this means we're going to be friends. I'm keeping my eye on you."

"Great."

"I know how people like you are."

"People like me?" Derek's scalp started to tingle.

"You know what I mean. People from soft homes who have everything handed to them. You've never had to work for anything your whole life."

Derek's jaw tightened. The edges of his vision started to close in. He forced his mouth to work. "I work in our shop every day."

Lars huffed in disgust. "See? That's exactly what I'm talking about. 'Our shop.' What a joke. Your daddy got that shop from his daddy. You Fulstarters have no idea what it's like to have nothing."

Derek's head throbbed. His jaw clamped shut. When he didn't have a comeback to the street rat's barrage, Lars continued. "People like you think you're doing us some big favor when you help us out, but it isn't real. You'll forget about Dani once your good deed is done, and then you'll go home to your soft bed and brag to all your rich friends about how you helped the poor. Wow. What a hero." Lars spit on the wharf. "This isn't about helping Dani. This is about putting yourself on some righteous pedestal."

Derek's entire body was on fire. He wanted to argue with Lars, to say that wasn't how it was at all, but the rage was on him now, and it made his throat tight and thick. Lars smirked. "What's the matter? Truth hurt?"

And then Derek let Lars have it. Right there on the dock, Derek grabbed the smaller boy by the shoulders and tossed him to the ground. Lars barely put up a fight as Derek drove his forearm across Lars' neck. "Take it back," Derek growled.

Lars struggled to breathe. "Can't take back the truth. Cat's out of the bag."

Derek reared back with a fist, ready to pummel Lars through the pier, but Conrad grabbed his arm. "By the Forge," Conrad swore. "I can't leave you two alone."

Seeing Conrad broke Derek's anger. He huffed and pushed himself off Lars, being sure to give the boy another shove before asking, "Is Jenkins with us?"

"Yes," Conrad said. "Use your key. There are no guards now. Hurry."

Derek got to his feet and ran as quietly as he could across the pier. He wished Conrad wouldn't have shown up when he did. Nothing would have felt better than letting Lars have it for what he said. But a kernel of doubt gnawed at Derek. Why was he really helping rescue Dani? His intentions were good, weren't they?

Derek slid to a stop next to Jenkins. The lanky boy had dark rings under his eyes, and his skin was a crispy pink. Other than that, he looked fine. Jenkins eyed Derek sheepishly. "You're really going to help us find Dani?"

Derek fiddled the key into the padlock and set Jenkins free. "Yes," he said. "Why wouldn't I?"

Jenkins rubbed the raw parts of his legs where the stocks had worn against them all day and then stood up next to Derek. "I don't know. I'm just surprised, that's all." They started back to Conrad and Lars. Before they got there, Jenkins rubbed the back of his head. "Sorry about that run-in on Gillman's Way today."

Derek stopped and searched Jenkins' face to see if he was being honest. When he saw the embarrassed cast of Jenkins' eyes, he said, "Don't mention it." They took a few more steps, and then Jenkins chuckled. "What?" Derek asked, thinking Jenkins was laughing at him.

Jenkins waved his hand. "Nothing. I was just thinking..." and he laughed quietly again. "It was kind of fun, wasn't it?"

Derek kept walking and laughed. "I guess. You guys weren't much of a challenge, though."

Jenkins grinned and slugged Derek in the shoulder. "We'll get you next time."

Derek smirked. "Sure."

Derek and Jenkins met up with the other two, and before long all four boys were standing in the shadows only twenty paces from the Shadizarian ship. It was massive as far as Shadizarian merchant vessels went. A gleaming coat of black tar ran in perfect lines from bow to stern. Tall masts of cedar, oiled with the sweat of a thousand slave hands, rose above the hull and disappeared into the moonless night. White canvas sails tied in neat folds hung tightly to the yards. Portholes for long, ash oars lined the lower decks, but these were now as silent as a dead man's eyes.

At least a dozen warriors in skirts of leather and steel, brandishing khopesh swords, stalked its decks. Pipe-smoking merchants from Zuid Horn ordered longshoremen up and down the planks. The sweating laborers carried barrels of wine, baskets of wheat, and chests of coal. Besides the guards, there were at least fifty men on deck.

Lars gave a low whistle. "So, how are we getting in?"

Derek grinned and jingled the purse of minotaur coins he had stolen earlier in the night. "I think I have an idea."

***

Two Shadizarian guardsmen stood watch in front of the Shadizarian ship, *The Delivery*. Just behind them, a stepped plank ran from the pier to the ship's deck. As Derek and the other boys approached, carrying stacks of steaming boxes and cream-colored jugs, the guards frowned and crossed their spears in front of the plank, barring entry.

"Where do you think you're going?" the guard on the right asked. His face was long, and its appearance was made longer still with the help of a thin, oily mustache.

Derek nodded at the boxes Conrad and Lars carried. "Dinner for the crew from the Crooked Hammer tavern. Hot beef stew, grilled shallots, warm bread and butter." He held up the jugs in his hands. "This here's last year's wine. It was a dry year, so they say it's good."

The guard on the left scoffed. "Bah. What would you boys know of good wine? You're too young, not to mention Zuid Hornian." Then, after a sniff, he added, "Let us have a taste of it, to see if it's fit for the crew." He reached out a hand, and Derek stepped out of reach.

"Sorry. Master Brighton says this is already paid for. Says it's for the crew."

The guard stepped toward Derek. "I'm part of the crew. How do you think I got to this swine hole, boy? Do you think I walked here?" He reached for the wine jug again.

"No, sir," Derek said, and ducked under the man's grasp. "But the master said it's for the crew, and you don't look like a sailor." Derek turned back toward the taverns lining the wharf. "Come on, boys," he said, walking away. "We can let the master deal with this lot." He winked at Conrad, who caught his cue.

"Come on!" Conrad whined. "I don't want to carry these boxes back to the Hammer to have old Brighton order us back here again. Let's just give these guys some rolls and wine and be done."

The guard with the thin mustache pounded the butt of his spear on the decking. "Now there's a boy with some sense. Just give us a taste, boy, and you can take the rest up to those other rats."

Derek stopped walking away but didn't come any closer to the ship. "I don't know," he said to Conrad. "It's supposed to be just for the crew. You know how the master gets."

"Just get on with it," Lars muttered, rolling his shoulders. "Either we deliver this, or we go back. I'm tired."

"There you go." The second guard pointed at Lars. "Listen to your friend."

Derek made a show of looking at each of the boys, and then finally he slumped his shoulders. "Fine, but don't take too much. If the master finds out, I'm the one who gets the lash."

The boys set the boxes and jugs down in front of the guards and took the tops off the boxes. Quick puffs of steam rolled off the hot beef stew. The guards sniffed in appreciation. "You weren't kidding. This smells good."

"Of course it is," Derek said, his nose in the air. "Everyone knows the Crooked Hammer serves up the best stew on the docks." Once the guards got a few mouthfuls, Derek signaled the boys to gather up the food and wine. "We've got to get this onboard. Can we pass?"

The Shadizarian guards didn't even bother to look up from the grilled shallots and bread. "Be quick about it and bring us any leftovers."

"We will," Derek said, and then he motioned for Conrad and his friends to follow him up the ramp and onto the deck of the Shadizarian ship.

The deck was littered with sailors repairing lines. Shadizarian guards strolled about with their curved swords and conical helms. Over by the central mast, a group of three men leaned over a map with a lantern to light their table. It was one of these men who called out to the boys. "You there! Boys! Who let you up here?" The man hustled over to them. He was wearing a sand-colored tunic fastened about the waist with a broad, yellow belt. A brace of wickedly curved daggers adorned his side.

Derek stepped forward. "Hello, sir. We're from the Crooked Hammer, just down Ploughman's Wharf, there." Derek leaned his head down the pier. "Our master sent us with dinner for your crew."

The man looked confused. "We didn't order dinner. We have our own cook." His accent was thick, rolling over the consonants and slurring the soft edges of syllables that Zuid Hornians preferred to cut short.

"I know, sir. Master Brighton is trying to win your business, sir. He figures if you like his cooking, your captain will call on him anytime you are in port."

"Did he, now? And why *The Delivery*? Or is your master doing this for every ship docking here tonight?"

Derek shrugged. "Not every ship, but most of them, sir. Most of the sailors from Tyrsis and Bearton already come to the Hammer, and we don't bother with the minotaurs. Who wants to do business with minotaurs, even if their coin is good?"

The man grunted. "Can't fault your logic there." He looked over the boxes. "What do you have?"

"Beef stew, sir. Grilled leeks, bread, and wine."

He seemed to consider it for a bit. "Fine. Let me see what the captain says. Stay here."

The man walked off to a small cabin at the front of the ship and disappeared through a well-polished door. The other men and sailors didn't seem interested in them, so Derek and the boys stepped closer to one another. "Well, I got us on the ship," Derek said.

"I have to admit, I'm impressed," Conrad said. "Good thing you had the coin to pay for all of this."

"Yeah," Lars sneered. "Must be nice."

The back of Derek's neck burned. "I told you. I filched that purse off some minotaurs."

Lars snorted. "Sure you did."

Derek's chest tightened, and Conrad stepped between them. "Knock it off, will you? Remember why we're here."

Derek and Lars scowled at one another one last time and then backed down. "Fine," Lars grumbled.

"Fine," Derek said.

They waited quietly with Derek and Lars sulking until the man came back. He walked over to them and shrugged. "The captain's not interested. Says we have our own provisions." He pointed to the gangplank. "Sorry, but you'll have to go."

"But sir," Derek said, "this food is paid for. It's a gift from Master Brighton."

"Who?"

"Master Brighton, sir. He owns the Crooked Hammer, makes the best beef stew on Ploughman's Wharf. You can ask anyone." The man eyed him suspiciously. "Is that so?"

"Yes, sir."

"It's paid for, you say?"

"Yes, sir."

"And why would he do that?"

"It's good business, sir. He's got more contracts with more shipmasters than any other tavern in Zuid Horn, and he wants yours."

The man narrowed his eyes. "Something tells me there's more going on here."

Derek's chest tightened with excitement. His mind raced, and in a flash, he had an idea. He chewed his bottom lip and sighed.

"I'm sorry if I seem too eager, sir. It's just that the master slips us each a piece of silver for every captain we get a contract with."

The man leaned back and smiled. "Well, that makes more sense."

"Apologies if we were too pushy, sir."

The man waved his hand. "It's fine. I was your age once too, scraping for every copper I could find." He looked them over. "You boys look like you've had it pretty rough."

Derek glanced at his friends. After an afternoon brawl and half a day and night in the stocks, they were bruised, bloodied, and sunburned. "Yes, sir," he said. "The master doesn't take failure well."

"So I see." He glanced at the table covered with maps and the two men waiting there for him. "I can get to that later," he said to himself. Then, to the boys, he said, "Come on. Let's go see the captain. Maybe we can get you a second chance to earn that coin." He gestured toward the small cabin at the front of *The Delivery*, and left without waiting for a response from the boys.

Derek grinned at Conrad. "Fortune is smiling on us," he whispered.

"Yeah," Conrad said. "But for how long?"

9

Derek Chooses a Path Forward

Another explosion rumbled over Zuid Horn. Light from the blast flashed against the smoke over the burning city, and for an instant, everything around Derek was bathed in an orange glow. He was with Conrad and Dani, kneeling over Sarah's body, his fingers on her purpled neck. "It's weak," he said to Dani, "but I can feel her pulse."

"Praise the Fires," Dani whispered, tracing her fingertips over her brow and upper chest.

Conrad shook Sarah's leg. "Can you wake her up?"

Derek rubbed the side of little Sarah's face. "Sarah, can you hear me?" She didn't respond. "Sarah?"

"We need a healer," Dani said.

"Do you think there are any left after tonight?" Conrad asked.

Dani shrugged. "We can only hope."

Derek rocked back on his haunches and ran his fingers through his hair. "By the Forge, what am I going to do?"

A breeze blew in from the harbor. In the distance, the cries and wails of the flood's victims echoed over Zuid Horn. Conrad looked toward the Warehouse District and Ploughman's Wharf. "We're not the only ones suffering tonight."

"'We?'" Derek barked, the spark of anger flickering under the coals of his misery. "What do you mean, *we?* You didn't lose anyone." He glared at his friend, and then the wet blanket of shame smothered his brewing rage.

Dani got up and walked around Sarah to squat next to Derek. She put her arm around his shoulders and held him close. Somehow, despite the stink of the flood and the ash falling from the sky all around them, he could still smell the sun on her skin. "You still have us," Dani said. "We're not going to leave you."

Derek's breaths came in jagged bursts. He wanted to tell her how much it meant that they were with him — how he was terrified to be an orphan, but if they would just promise to be with him forever, it wouldn't be so bad. There was so much he wanted to say, but it felt like there was a thick wad caught in his throat, and he couldn't get anything past it. He tried coughing, but the wad just got bigger.

Dani rubbed his back. "*Shhh.* We're here for you. We're here for you."

Derek closed his eyes and rested his head against Dani's shoulder. He heard Conrad crunch closer. "We can't stay here," Conrad said. "It's not safe."

As if to emphasize his point, a pair of yakarii roared their battle cries in the distance. Derek stood up and peered to the northwest. "That sounded like they're at the Merchant Gate. They're close."

Conrad scratched at the scar on his forearm and nodded. "We have to get out of here."

"I'm not leaving Liza." Derek got up and walked over to his sister. He squatted low and tried to slip his arms under her limp body, but she kept rolling out of his grasp. "Hammer and Anvils," he swore.

Conrad and Dani watched silently until Conrad finally whispered, "Liza's dead. She's not coming back."

"I know," Derek snapped. "You don't need to remind me."

"I know you know," Conrad said, "but we have to get out of here before more yakarii come."

"You're not helping." Derek felt his shoulders stiffen.

"I think what Conrad is trying to say..." Dani said, giving her brother a glance, "is that we can't bring Liza with us."

"What?" Derek shouted. "I can't just leave her here. What if they come back? You heard what they wanted to do to us. They'll eat her if we leave her here!"

"Yeah," Dani admitted. "We can't do that."

"Well, what am I going to do?"

Conrad took a deep breath. "Sailors bury their dead at sea."

A stone dropped in Derek's stomach. "No."

"Derek," Dani said, "we don't have a choice."

"How am I going to bury her at sea? It's not like I can summon an ocean."

"You don't need to," Conrad said quietly and jerked a thumb at the flood waters around them. "Someone already did that for you."

Derek turned to look at the Tower of High Sorcery. Smoke from the burning foundries broke against the tower's ebony ridges and trailed arms of ash into the distance like the shredded hems of a witch's robe. The wind shifted and touched the back of his neck, cooling the blood and sweat. Derek shivered.

He walked to the edge of the roof and looked at the flood below. Feasting Lane was choked with garbage, sewage, and the dead. Obscene sewer rats scurried over the flotsam and nibbled on the bodies of the drowned. A snarl of rats below Derek battled over a dog's corpse and filled the night with their hideous squeaking.

"You want me to dump Liza into that?"

Conrad came to stand beside him. "I don't think we have a choice."

The yakarii roared again, and the friends jumped. "Are they getting closer?" Dani asked. She hurried across the roof and stood with the boys.

"I think so," Conrad said. Then, to Derek, he added, "We have to go. Now."

Derek crossed his arms over his chest. "I'm not dumping my sister in there."

"Derek," Conrad insisted, "there's no room in the canoe."

"No."

"Derek," Conrad begged.

"No."

Dani stepped between the boys. "Look. We don't have time for this. Let's get Sarah loaded into the canoe first. Those yakarii are close."

Derek glared at Conrad, who sighed. "I'm not trying to hurt you, Derek."

Derek refused to budge. "What would you do if it was Dani?"

Conrad clenched his fists. "I get it, but you gotta think with your head. Your parents would want you to survive."

"My parents would want me to respect my sister."

"Are you sure? If it meant you and Sarah dying?"

"You guys," Dani said, stepping between them, "I think I see something."

She pointed at a rooftop near the Merchant Gate. At first, Derek didn't see anything, but then something moved over the crest of a peaked roof. "Yakarii," he whispered. Derek dropped to the flat roof. Dani and Conrad dropped next to him.

"I count three," Dani said.

"There's two more to the west," Conrad said. "On the side of that grain silo."

The creatures clambered over the rooftops on hands and feet. From this distance, they looked like giant spiders in the dim light. "They're coming this way," Dani said. She rolled on her side to face Derek. "We need to go. Now."

Derek gritted his teeth and punched the roof. "Fine. Help me get Sarah into the canoe." The friends crawled to Sarah's body. "We can't drag her," Derek said. "We'll have to pick her up. Conrad, you grab her feet. I'll take her shoulders." Derek crouched low and picked Sarah up, surprised by how light his youngest sister was. "Dani, you get the canoe ready."

"Right," Dani said. She bent as low as she could and ran to the alley side of the roof. Dani kicked her feet over the edge and dropped into the alley.

"Let's go," Derek whispered. "Stay low, so the yakarii don't see us."

"You know they can see in the dark, don't you?" Conrad asked, shuffling backward with Sarah's feet.

"I know," Derek said, "but let's not do anything to get them here faster."

The boys carried Sarah's little body to the edge of the building. Dani was waiting in the canoe below. "Okay," Derek said. "Conrad, you get in the canoe. I'll lower Sarah to you. Careful with her head."

Conrad put down Sarah's legs and crawled over the side of the building and hung by the tips of his fingers. He stretched as far as he could, but even then, he had to freefall a little. The little boat wobbled back and forth. "Watch it," Dani whispered. "You'll tip us over."

"I'm trying," Conrad said. He looked up at Derek. "Okay, let her down."

Derek eased Sarah's feet over the lip of the roof. He grabbed his sister under her armpits and lowered her down. Her head lolled in wild circles. "Hurry up," Derek said.

Conrad was on his toes in the canoe, his arms in the air. He swatted at Sarah's feet, and she swung back and forth. "Careful," Derek said. "I don't have a good grip here."

"I'm trying," Conrad said. "Wait. Let me get up on my seat. Maybe that will help. Dani, keep the boat steady."

"Oh, this isn't good," Dani muttered.

Conrad stepped carefully onto his seat. He climbed up and spread his arms wide to keep his balance. Once he was steady, he stood up and reached for Sarah.

"Got you," he said and wrapped his arms around Sarah's lower legs.

The yakarii roared again. Derek whirled around to find they were much closer now, only two buildings away, pointing and shouting at him. "Guys, they're almost here," Derek said.

"I'm trying," Conrad said. "Can you get her any lower? I'm on my toes."

"Stop rocking the boat!" Dani hissed.

"I'm doing my best here," Conrad growled.

Derek readjusted his grip. "I have an idea. Get ready."

Conrad looked up. "What? Wait!"

Derek didn't wait. He let go of Sarah's armpits and let his hands slide up her arms. She dropped like a stone until Derek caught her by the elbows. She slammed into Conrad and knocked him backwards. "Sorry!" Derek said.

Conrad flailed his arms for balance, but he was too far gone. The canoe shifted under his feet, and Conrad flipped into the flood.

"Conrad!" Dani yelled.

His head broke through the surface, sputtering and spitting. "I'm fine," he said and reached for the canoe.

"Hammer and Anvils," Derek swore. He looked over his shoulder. The yakarii were one roof away and closing fast. There were five of them that he could see — and probably more — sprinting toward him like lightning. "By the Bellows," he swore again. "There's no time. They're here. Conrad!" His friend looked up. "Catch!"

Conrad's eyes went wide. "What? You've got to be kidding. No!"

Derek didn't have a choice. He heaved Sarah as hard as he could and let go. She flew over the canoe, smacked off the wall across the flooded alley, and dropped into the debris-choked water next to Conrad. "Get her!" Derek yelled to Conrad. Then, without waiting for a response, Derek popped up and ran to Liza's body.

The yakarii were just across the opposite alley. They roared at one another. "There's a fresh piece of meat," said one.

"His liver goes to whoever catches him," said another.

Derek grabbed Liza by the armpits and picked her up. She was cooler now, and the thought of it made his stomach heavy.

He wanted to throw up, to run away, but there was no way he was going to let these yakarii make a meal of his sister.

He stumbled backwards and dragged Liza across the roof. It was coated in pea gravel and black tar, which rolled under his feet. He tripped, and Liza bounced on the roof. "Sorry," he muttered.

The first yakariian scouts leapt over the alleyway and hit the roof with heavy thuds. They eyed Derek and grinned. "Gotcha, little bird," one of them said. It slid a jagged longsword from its sheath and stalked toward him.

"What? Two manlings? It's our lucky day, boys! We've found a feast!"

Derek gasped and picked Liza up again. He kept his head down and tugged and yanked her across the roof. The yakarii were closing in fast. Three more thuds from the far alley, and now three more yakarii were after him. Derek's breath came in ragged bursts. His throat was on fire, and his legs and arms ached. He was close to the edge of the roof, he knew, but the yakarii were too close to risk a look. "Keep going," he muttered. "Keep going."

The yakarii spread out in a wide net, five wide. "You got yourself backed into a corner," one of them said. "No way out for you."

Derek gave Liza another tug and dragged her another three paces. The back of his heel hit a little rise, and suddenly he was tumbling backwards. His feet skittered over the loose pea gravel and then they were over the edge of the roof. He dug his fingers into Liza's armpits, hoping to use her weight to stop his fall, but she was so light that she just slid like a sled over the pea gravel. Derek toppled off the building and dragged Liza with him.

They fell together, brother and sister entwined in a knot of limbs, and punched through the greasy floodwater with a cold splash. He let go of Liza and thrashed to the surface. Trash was everywhere — jugs and pillows and broken pieces of wood, floating corpses of dogs and cats and people. "Liza!" Derek yelled and splashed. He flogged through the debris trying to find his sister, but every time he cleared a space, more flotsam rolled in to take its place.

Laughter like barking came from above. Derek looked up and saw the five yakarii watching him. "Does anyone have a spear?" one of them asked. "I can get him."

"Derek!" Conrad yelled.

The canoe came around the edge of the building. Conrad was at the front, reaching for Derek. "Give me your hand!" Conrad yelled.

"Liza! I've got to find Liza!"

The canoe pulled up next to him. "She's dead, Derek. Let her go."

"No! She was right here!" The corpse of an old woman wearing an apron rolled next to Derek. He shoved it away. "Liza!"

"Now, Derek! Get in the canoe."

The yakarii were back at the edge of the roof. "Gatta, let me use your spear."

Derek kept pushing through the debris. "Liza!"

"Derek!" Dani yelled. "She's dead. We have Sarah. We have to go!"

"By The Hammer," Conrad said. He turned around to face the yakarii on the roof. "Keep paddling, Dani! They have spears!" Conrad ripped his sword from its sheath and knelt low in the canoe.

The first spear ripped through the air with a high-pitched whine. Conrad grunted and twisted to the side. He brought his sword up in a hard arc and whacked the spear to his left. It punched deep into the belly of a dead cow with a thump and a gassy hiss. "By the gods, Derek," Conrad swore, "get in the damn canoe!"

Derek pushed a wine barrel to the side and looked for his sister. "But Liza," he started.

"Is dead, Derek," Dani said, her voice tight. "Just like we'll be if you don't get in here. Do you want us to die, too?"

Conrad grunted and deflected a second spear to the side. "I can't do this all night," he said.

Derek's limbs felt heavier than iron. All he wanted to do was let go and sink into the septic waste that had swallowed Liza, but he couldn't. Who would take care of Sarah? "Liza," he groaned, "I'm sorry." Derek turned and reached for the side of the canoe.

"Look out!" Conrad shouted.

The yakarii on the roof laughed and hurled another spear. Conrad grunted and swung to deflect it, but he was too early. The spear whistled over his shoulder and stopped with a meaty whack at the front of the canoe. Dani gasped, and Derek looked up. The Yakariian spear had skewered the lithe street girl straight through her lower back. Almost three feet of a black-tarred spear jutted from Dani's belly. Another three feet sprouted from her lower back.

"Dani!" Derek yelled.

"No!" Conrad screamed.

The yakarii on the roof cheered and hooted. "Nice shot," one of them said. The rest howled with laughter.

Derek's body coursed with strength. He pulled himself from the dark water in one fluid movement. A tremendous wash of floodwater and sewage flushed into the canoe with him. He cradled the girl in his arms. "Dani, Dani, no! No!"

Conrad howled, "Look what you did!"

Derek brushed the short hairs from Dani's forehead. "I'm sorry, Dani," he whispered.

Dani's eyes rolled in her head. Her mouth gulped like a fish on the shore. "You said you'd protect me."

A knot tightened in Derek's chest. "I wasn't thinking. It's just... Liza..."

Dani shook her head weakly. "Row," she sputtered. "Just row."

Derek picked Dani up and set her next to Sarah. She groaned and sputtered when the spear's shaft bumped against the canoe. "Sorry," Derek said.

Once Dani was squatting next to Sarah, Derek picked up Dani's paddle. "Keep those spears off us. We're getting out of here."

"A little late," Conrad growled.

Derek dug the paddle deep into the water. He pulled the tipsy craft across the wide expanse of Feasting Lane and toward an alley

across the way. "Hey," he heard one of the yakarii say. "They're getting away. Do you have another spear?"

"Nah," another answered. "But they got two bleeders with them. Let's find a way across this street. We can track 'em by scent."

The others hooted, and they vanished from the edge of the roof.

Derek used his paddle to push debris from their path. In short order, he turned the nose of the canoe between the second floors of a tavern and a butcher's shop. It was quieter here and darker. Dani's breaths came in quick pants. Conrad sheathed his sword and picked up his paddle, his sure strokes shooting the canoe between buildings. Derek could feel his friend burning a hole in his back. He had to say something.

"I'm sorry," he muttered. "I wasn't thinking straight."

Conrad snorted. "Way to get our sisters killed, idiot."

Derek felt the rush of blood burn his face. "Dani's still alive," he said. "We can save her."

"Really? How are we going to do that? The city's destroyed, you fool. Your parents are dead. The temples are ruined. There's no one left."

Derek glanced at Dani and took a breath to calm himself. He had to control his temper. It had gotten him into enough trouble for this night. "Wrong. I know someplace that could survive this flood, and I'll bet the person who can save her is there right now."

Conrad breathed hard. Between the buildings, his breath huffed like a bull snorting. "Really? Where are we going, genius?"

"To the Ranger Outpost. If we are going to save Dani and Sarah, we need to find Niles Crowing and the Magnificent Seven."

10

A Friend in Need

Aboard the Shadizarian slaver, *The Delivery*, Derek and the others followed the first mate and carried their boxes of steaming stew, grilled shallots, and jugs of wine into the captain's quarters. The room was a smallish affair, maybe four strides across, but it was big enough to be outfitted with a cot covered in Shadizarian silks, a thick rug woven in majestic copper and golden hues, and a small table covered with maps. Several padlocked chests sat against the walls, tucked under bookshelves that overflowed with ledgers, quills, and ink pots.

The captain was seated at the table when the first mate ushered the boys into the room. He wore his long, dark hair down so that it brushed the shoulders of his silk, crimson vest. His thin hands bloomed from the long sleeves of a finely tailored shirt, and he rubbed the bridge of his nose with manicured fingers. Two sheathed daggers lay on the table before him.

The first mate walked over to the captain's table. "These are the boys I told you about."

The captain looked up from his map and glared at the first mate. "I already told you. I didn't order dinner."

"Yes, sir. The boys say their master is sending this sample to win your business for future trips."

The captain's eyes narrowed until they were dark slits. "Is that so?"

Derek and the others nodded but held their tongues. The captain leaned back in his chair and twirled one of the daggers on the table with his finger. It spun round and round on a map of the southern coast. "You there," he said, lifting his chin at Derek. "Where did you say this food came from?"

"The Crooked Hammer," Derek said. "It's just down the pier."

"I sent Khali to check it out. It's a tavern," the first mate said.

"Did he talk to the owner?" the captain asked.

"No, sir. I can send him again if you would like."

The captain waved his hand. "No need." He turned his attention to the boys. "Do you know who I am?" The boys all shook their heads. "I am Amir Safina, sub-commander of the Shadizarian royal fleet. There are many in this city who would see me dead." He leaned forward and peered at the boys. "Would you see me dead?"

Derek's mouth went dry, and his heart pounded. From the corner of his eye, he saw the first mate's hand drift to the pommel of the dagger at his belt. Derek swallowed hard. "N-no, sir," he stuttered. "We are just following Master Brighton's orders."

"I've seen assassins cloaked in black, wrapped in sheer silk, and garbed in beggar's rags. Are you assassins dressed as boys?" When the boys shook their heads, Amir Safina said, "Well, how do I know the food you bring me isn't poisoned?" He leaned back in his chair, and his face hardened. "Open your boxes."

"Sir?"

"You heard me. Open your boxes. Uncork your wine." The boys did as they were bid. Amir Safina eyed them intently. "Now eat."

"But, sir," Derek said, "Master Brighton ordered us to deliver this to you."

"And I'm ordering you to eat and drink."

The boys looked at one another. "You'll explain to him, sir, if he asks about us eating the food. Won't you, sir?"

"Eat."

The boys sat with crossed legs on the floor, each with an open box before him. They broke off bits of bread and sopped it in the beef stew. Using their pocketknives, they jabbed bits of grilled leeks and hungrily stuffed them into their mouths. Other than the rotten apples from Conrad's stash, none of the boys had eaten since the day before, when they were arrested, and they were famished. They quickly finished their first boxes of stew and moved onto a second. Conrad was pouring the boys cups of the common, thin wine served with all meals in Zuid Horn when the captain put up a hand.

"Alright, enough. I just needed to see you taste the food. You don't need to eat all of it."

The boys stopped eating and closed their second boxes. Lars snuck one last piece of bread into his mouth. Amir Safina eyed the boys again, but this time his gaze was softer. "Who did you say your master was again?"

Derek stood up but kept his eyes down. "Brighton, sir. Master Brighton."

"He doesn't feed you much, does he?"

"Not his job, sir. We just make and serve the food. We don't eat it."

Amir Safina grunted. "You boys are cooks?"

"Yes, sir. Sometimes. Well, I am, anyway." Derek jerked a thumb at Conrad, Lars, and Jenkins, who were still eyeing up the boxes of stew. "This lot just cuts and stirs."

"And yet you go hungry?" The captain shook his head. "I worked in a kitchen when I was a lad. You know what they say about cooks who go hungry?"

"That we're fools?" Derek offered.

Amir Safina laughed, and Derek sighed in relief. The captain pointed a playful finger at him. "You've been around a kitchen." He waved Derek forward. "Bring me a box of your stew, boy, and see that my men get theirs as well."

Derek set a fresh box before the captain and poured him a cup of dinner wine. Amir Safina sniffed at the stew. "Not bad," he said. Then he took a sip of the wine and frowned. "But you Zuid Hornians know nothing about wine." He drained the cup in one swallow, then pointed to the first mate. "Fetch me two bottles of dry from the galley. Bring a cup for yourself and join me for dinner." Then he pointed at Derek. "And give the other bottle to this boy's master."

The first mate bowed sharply. "Yes, sir," he said and left in a hurry.

Amir Safina watched him go, and then he turned back to Derek. "Your master, what was his name again?"

"Master Brighton, sir."

"Brighton, yes. See that he gets the wine from me. Tell him that he's got my business." The boys bowed and turned to go, but the captain called them back. "Boy."

"Yes, sir?"

"A ship's always got room for a good cook if you're interested. I pay well, and you'll see the world."

Derek's chest swelled with pride. "An honor, sir, but I don't know what Master Brighton would say about that."

Amir Safina scoffed. "How old are you, boy?"

"Sixteen, sir,"

"Sixteen? Pretty tall for sixteen, aren't you?"

"Yes, sir."

"Well, you're old enough to make up your own mind. Why apprentice under a tavern slop chef when you could run the galley of a Shadizarian merchant ship?" When Derek hesitated, the captain added, "Tell you what. Send the wine back with your friends. You take a look around the ship. See what you think. We aren't leaving until noon tomorrow. You come back and give me your decision then."

"Yes, sir. Thank you, sir."

The first mate returned. On his way to the captain's table, he handed Derek a bottle of dry, Shadizarian wine. "Careful with that, boy. It's better than the best Zuid Horn has to offer."

Derek accepted the bottle with a weak smile. "Yes, sir." He handed the bottle to Conrad, explaining to the first mate. "My friend, here, will take the wine to Master Brighton. The captain said I could look around a little."

The first mate raised his brow. "Did he, now?"

"Yes, yes," Amir Safina said, dismissing the first mate's comment with a backhanded wave. He took another bite of the stew and sighed. "I offered the boy a chance to travel with us. Here, sit down with me and eat for a bit. The stew is good. You can catch up with the boy later. We need to discuss something."

Seeing their chance to leave, the boys bowed again and backed out of the room. "Thank you, sir. It's been an honor, sir." Then they were out of the captain's quarters.

Once they were a bit away from the door, Conrad whispered, "I can't believe that worked! You'll get to scout the ship!"

"Gotta know how business works," Derek said, looking at Lars. "It's one of the advantages of being a rich snob."

Lars glared at Derek, but Jenkins ignored the simmering fight. "I don't care where you came up with the idea. That was amazing!"

"We aren't done yet," Derek insisted. "Help me get the crew fed. I'll stay behind and check things out. Meet me next to the Crooked Hammer, and we'll plan our next step once we know a little more."

The boys distributed the boxes of stew and leeks amongst the crew, most of whom didn't even give the boys more than a second glance before flipping open their stew boxes and getting down to the business of eating. They universally complained about the thin wine, but the boys insisted they couldn't help that. "It's what goes with meals in Zuid Horn," Derek explained.

When all their boxes of stew and jugs of wine were distributed, the boys gathered at the top of the gangway leading to the pier.

They reviewed their plan to meet next to the Crooked Hammer once Derek was finished and shook hands. Derek made sure Conrad had the bottle of Shadizarian wine.

"Save that for when we're done," he said.

Conrad waved, and then he was off.

Derek moved about the upper deck, chatting with guards and sailors, asking questions as any boy would do, given free reign of a ship. The first mate reappeared and introduced himself as Awwal Bahhar. "So, what do you think so far?"

"I've never been on a ship before," Derek admitted. "I don't know if I could be much help."

"Don't worry about that," Awwal said with a laugh. "You're a cook. You don't need to know how to sail."

"That's true." Derek looked around. "I've seen the upper deck. Where's the kitchen?"

"You mean the galley? That's what you call a kitchen on a ship. It's below deck. Come with me."

Awwal led Derek to a narrow stairwell and started down. He grabbed one of two lanterns hanging on the wall to light their way. Two closed doors flanked the bottom of the stairwell. A few paces later, the passage widened a bit, creating alcoves wide enough for three hammocks to hang, one above the other, on both sides of the hallway. Under each set of hammocks, three small chests were bolted to the wall and the floor. Other than that, there was no evidence of personal artifacts lying about. The passageway reeked of dust and sweat.

Awwal moved at a quick clip, pointing things out as he went. "There are three decks on *The Delivery*. The upper deck is where men spend most of their time during the day. Now that we're in port, only a skeleton crew is kept here overnight. Most of the sailors are in the city, wasting their wages."

Derek followed along behind Awwal as he went. "What's this deck for?"

"This is where you'll spend most of your time. The men bunk here, keep their goods in lockers," he pointed to the bolted chests under the hammocks, "and take their meals." The rows of hammocks ended, and the passageway opened to a neat clutch of narrow tables and benches. "Most of the men prefer to eat up top, but if the weather is bad, they'll eat down here." Awwal gestured for Derek to follow him. "Come on. The galley's just ahead."

At the end of the hallway, they came to another stairwell leading both to the upper deck and to a lower level. There was a doorway to the left. Awwal opened the door and stepped aside so Derek could see. "This is the galley."

The room was two paces deep and only one pace wide. On one side, there was a box brimming with charcoal. On the other, there was a series of low ovens with chimneys that led out through the side of the ship. Large cast-iron pots and pans hung from the ceiling. A wooden bucket nailed to one wall housed spatulas, long forks, stirring spoons, and ladles. Next to the bucket was a block of knives and a whet stone. Derek drew a knife from the block and ran his thumb across the edge.

"Not very sharp," he commented. "Where's the cook now?"

Awwal looked back out the door. "On shore, I suspect. He's a moody fellow, gets moodier the longer we're at sea. He's better for a while after he's had shore leave, but no one likes being around him. I suppose that's why the captain's looking for a new cook. An ornery cook is bad for morale."

The voices of sailors came from the passageway. Derek peeked out and saw that some of them were returning. Like the boys he had seen following Dani, the Shadizarian sailors wore britches and vests shimmering with gold and copper threads. He turned back to Awwal. "The kitchen is pretty small. Where do you keep your food?"

Awwal pointed to the stairwell. "Down in the hold. Come on, I'll show you."

They went down the stairs and were about to skip a floor when the stench of ammonia and unwashed bodies assaulted Derek. He covered his mouth and nose with a hand. "What's on this floor?"

Awwal shrugged. "Slaves for rowing, mostly. Take a look."

Derek took the lantern from Awwal and held it up. The room was packed with benches full of sleeping, almost naked slaves. Their heads were shaved, and their backs and arms bore the marks of regular beatings. A few of them looked up blearily, but most of them kept on sleeping. Derek had never seen slaves before, let alone so many of them.

His face must have shown his surprise because Awwal asked, "What's the matter?"

"I've never seen slaves before."

Awwal grunted. "Really?"

Derek shook his head. "Zuid Horn is a free city. Has been for a long time."

"Does it bother you?" Awwal asked, studying Derek closely.

"A little, to be honest. I've always known slavers were allowed to keep their wares on their boats. I just never thought it would look or smell like this."

Awwal shrugged. "You get used to it. Zuid Horn isn't like most of the world. There are slaves everywhere. I wouldn't be surprised if slavery comes to Zuid Horn someday."

"Maybe," Derek said with a frown. He looked at the slaves again. Was Dani here? He needed to keep Awwal talking. "Would I have to cook for the slaves, too?"

"Of course," Awwal said. "But they are just slaves. A simple gruel will do for them. Come, let me show you the hold."

Derek was about to follow Awwal down the stairs when the light from his lantern fell on a pair of wide eyes that were watching him. Although her head was shaved, Derek recognized Dani immediately. His breath caught in his throat. How was he going to get her out of here? Dani sat up straight on her bench. The chains holding her wrists, ankles, and neck jingled in the dim light. Derek waved a hand, motioning for her to sit back down.

"It's going to be alright," he whispered.

He held the lantern up higher, and more heads popped up. Of the dozen or so people squinting into the light, at least half were children. Something about them looked familiar, and then one of the boys looked at Derek and gave a little wave. Suddenly, it clicked in Derek's mind. That was the boy Conrad had given his apple core to when they went to free Lars and Jenkins from the stocks. A nauseous wave turned Derek's gut.

These were the people chained to the stocks on the pier earlier tonight.

Derek gasped, realizing how close he had come to being taken as a slave. The others must have been taken right after Derek and Conrad had freed Jenkins and Lars. The whole thing was incredibly close, yet here was Derek, in the hold as a free man, where fate had meant for him to be chained up as a slave.

"We're going to save you," Derek whispered.

"Who?" Dani asked.

"Me and Conrad," Derek said, "and some others."

"Are you coming?" Awwal called from the stairwell.

Derek practically jumped out of his skin. "Yes, sorry!" he yelled back up the stairs. Then, to Dani, he quickly whispered, "Don't worry. I'll protect you!" Dani's eyes were wide with fear, but Derek could see a glimmer of hope sparkling where it hadn't been when he first saw her. "I'll be back," he said, and hurried to catch up to Awwal. "Sorry," he said when he met the first mate on the stairs. "Like I said, I'm just not used to seeing slaves."

Awwal nodded and continued down the stairs. "They are common in Shadizar. We need them to do the jobs no Shadizarian will do."

"Where are they from?"

"Markets, mostly. The captain sends buyers into slave markets when we dock. Sometimes we buy them from other ships we pass. Anywhere, I guess. I don't really think about it. They are just slaves."

The stairway twisted about itself until they were in the belly of the boat. It was dark and dank. Rows of barrels, casks, and wooden crates filled the base of the ship from top to bottom. "We keep our trading wares in the back, but the foodstuffs are right here so the cook can get at them easily."

Derek opened a crate and peeked inside. There was a burlap sack filled with dried rice. He picked up a handful and let the grains run through his fingers. "Wow. This is nice rice."

"Shadizarian," Awwal said with a sniff. "The best in the realms."

A sleek shadow darted between the crate and the wall. Derek yelped and jumped back. "What was that?"

Awwal laughed. "A rat. You won't find a ship on the seas that isn't plagued with them. We need to get a good ratter down here to clean them up. No one can get them all, but a good ratter can keep them under control."

"A ratter?"

"Someone to kill the rats."

"That's a job?"

"For a slave. Like I said, slaves do the jobs Shadizarians don't want to do."

Derek nodded and backed out of the storage room. "Not a job I'd want."

Awwal nodded. "See? Now you understand why we have slaves."

"I guess," Derek said and looked around the dark passageway.

Now that he studied it, he realized that every available space was stuffed with cargo. Racks of scroll tubes lined the walls along the ceiling. Under that were boxes stamped with the insignia of city-states throughout the realms. By his feet was a row of boxes from the western yakariian warlords. Stacked on top of these were a few crates from the northern city-states of Bearton and Tyrsis. And just down the passage a bit, a blanket had been thrown over several boxes. The blanket wasn't big enough to cover them completely, so Derek could see the bottom of a brand that had been burned into the side peeking out.

The crossed battle axes of the southern islands.

So, the Shadizarians were trading with the minotaurs. Derek put that information in the back of his mind for later. To Awwal, he said, "It will take me a while before I learn where everything is. There's so much down here."

"There is," Awwal agreed. "My guess is that the captain will keep the current cook on until you know your way around. Then, the next time we're in some port, he'll cut that bitter man free." The first mate slapped his palms on his thighs. "Well, seen enough?"

"Yes, sir," Derek replied.

"Do you have any questions?"

Derek thought for a bit. "If I sign on, what about the other cook? Won't he be angry if he finds out I'm going to replace him?"

Awwal waved his hand dismissively. "Don't worry about that. We'll just tell him we got him some help. That will keep him from bellyaching too much."

"If you think that will work," Derek said with a shrug.

"It will be fine," Awwal said. "I think you'd be a good fit here."

"Thank you. I've got a lot to think about."

Awwal started climbing back up the stairs. "That's for sure. Either way, you made a good sale for your master at the...what did you say the tavern's name was?"

"The Crooked Hammer."

"Yes, the Crooked Hammer. You're a good boy. The captain can see that. I suspect that's why he wants you onboard."

They were quiet as they climbed the stairs until they came out on the upper deck. Awwal patted Derek on the back and guided him toward the gangway. "Take your time thinking about things tonight. That's a big decision you have to make."

Derek stopped at the top of the plank leading off the ship. "I will, sir."

"And you'll come back in the morning, before we disembark?"

"Yes, sir."

"Alright, then. See you in the morning."

"Yes, sir."

Derek hurried down the plank, thankful to have the solid pier under his feet. He turned back to wave and found Awwal watching him. The first mate waved. Derek waved back and then hurried off in the direction of the Crooked Hammer. Just before he rounded a corner, he turned back to look at the ship again and saw that Awwal was still watching him. The first mate of *The Delivery* waved again. Derek ducked behind the corner and sprinted for the Crooked Hammer as fast as he could.

***

Derek, Conrad, Lars, and Jenkins crouched in an alley just down from the Crooked Hammer. Four boxes of beef stew lay open before them. They squatted on the ground as Derek told them what had happened on *The Delivery*. By the time Derek finished his tale, Conrad's face was flushed a dark crimson. "Are you sure it was her?"

"Absolutely," Derek said. "And the others, I'm sure they were in fetters with us on the pier this afternoon. I'm telling you, the hull was full of them."

Conrad ran his fingers through his hair. "Dani," he muttered. "What are we going to do?"

Lars pounded a fist into the hard packed street. "I knew it! Every time a ship from Shadizar shows up in Zuid Horn, people go missing."

"What?" Derek asked. "This has happened before?"

Lars snorted. "Maybe not to you rich kids, but us rats on the streets, we always have to watch our backs."

"Why doesn't the Iron Guard do anything about it?"

Lars sneered. "The Iron Guard? They don't care about people disappearing. They only care about keeping things quiet."

Jenkins wiped up the last of his stew with the heel of his bread. "It's true. Do you really think the Iron Guard would look into missing street kids? Who do you think pays them?"

Derek thought for a bit. "The Merchants' Guild."

"Exactly," Jenkins said, swiping Derek's unfinished bread and scarfing it down. "The Merchants' Guild is probably glad we're gone — cuts down on pickpockets."

Derek sighed. "It just doesn't make any sense. The Iron Guard has always protected Zuid Horn."

"Protected the city, sure," Lars spat, "but not its people."

Derek pressed his lips together. He wanted to argue that the Iron Guard were the good guys, that they were there to help everyone, but was there another side to the story? "I'm not sure what to think right now. There's got to be someone who can help us."

Suddenly, Conrad sat up. "Wait, how much money do you have left from the minotaurs? Maybe we can buy Dani back."

"How are we going to do that?" Derek asked. "The Shadizarians don't want anyone to know they are kidnapping people in Zuid Horn. If we got someone to try buying Dani back, the Shadizarians would know we have something to do with it. Or, at least, they'll think they're getting set up." Derek shook his head. "It would never work."

Conrad wouldn't give up. "But what about your dad? Could you get him to try to buy her back?"

Derek snorted. "My dad? By the Forge, I can't even think about him right now. He's going to kill me the way it is. First, I get arrested, and then I get tied up with Shadizarian slavers, all because..." and he stopped.

Jenkins looked at him quizzically. "All because what?"

Derek didn't answer but kept talking to himself out loud. "No, it's crazy. But it might be Dani's only chance."

Conrad glared at Derek. "What are you talking about?"

Derek dug in his pocket. "I can't believe I didn't think about this sooner."

"Think about what?" Lars asked.

Derek produced a cast iron key tied to a thin, leather thong. He held it up in the dim light streaming from the Crooked Hammer across the alley. "When Conrad and I were in the stocks, a man stopped by to see me. His name is Niles Crowing. Niles stopped by our shop earlier in the morning and made a huge purchase for the Ranger Outpost just outside the Foundry District."

Lars and Jenkins stared at one another and then back at Derek. "And?" Lars asked.

"And," Derek continued, "he seemed really interested in me and what I wanted to do with my life, like he actually cared."

"Touching," Lars muttered.

Derek ignored him. "No, don't you get it? He went out of his way to seek me out and then even dropped this." Derek held up the key. "A key to the Iron Guard's stocks, right next to my hand. Guys, what if he knows about the Shadizarians stealing people from the stocks? What if he was trying to save me?"

Conrad nodded. "I see where you're going with this. If he knows, maybe he can help us."

"Exactly," Derek said.

Lars snorted. "Sounds far-fetched to me. And even if it was true, why would this Niles want to help Dani?"

The boys all looked at one another, the question Lars asked hanging between them. Finally, Derek said, "There's only one way to find out. We have to ask him."

"Okay, fine," Lars said. "But how do we find him?"

"Well, we know his name," Derek started, "and that he's a ranger."

"Great," Conrad said, rocking back on his heels. "He's probably halfway across Breechwood Forest by now. We're never going to find him in time."

"Not necessarily," Jenkins said.

"What do you mean?" Derek asked.

"You said he put in a big order for the Ranger Outpost. Just because he's a ranger doesn't mean he's out in the forest. I see rangers hanging out at the outpost all the time. Maybe he's staying there."

"Good point," Conrad said. "I saw rangers there when Dani and I canoed the Black River."

"Then that's where we need to go," Derek said. "It's our only chance of finding someone who can help us."

"You know what they say..." Conrad said, getting up and brushing the dust off his pants. "A friend in need is a friend indeed."

"Let's hope so," Derek said, and started jogging deeper into Zuid Horn. "Come on, guys. Time is short."

The others got up and tossed their empty stew boxes into a nearby trash midden. They caught up with Derek, and the four of them disappeared into the night.

As soon as they were gone, a dark figure broke from the shadows and squatted where the boys had been sitting. The figure poked around in the dirt, walked over, examined the stew boxes they had thrown away, and then broke into a sprint up the alley, heading after the boys.

11

Derek Returns to the Source

Derek and Conrad guided their little canoe through Zuid Horn's flooded streets along the edge of the Artisan District. Gray ash rained down, and with it came the sharp stink of foundry fuel. Screams filled the air between the thunderous explosions from the burning factories. Too often, yakariian battle cries followed those screams. Derek tried not to imagine what was happening to people all over Zuid Horn, but it was hard not to, with Sarah unconscious and Dani groaning in the canoe right behind him, six feet of a yakariian spear running through her belly.

Her breaths came in quick gasps. Every time their canoe bumped against a table or a body or a barrel riding out the flood, Dani yelped and pleaded, "Get it out!"

"We can't, Dani," Derek said, his chest tighter than a fist. "Not yet. Not here."

"It hurts."

"I know. I'm sorry, Dani. I'm so sorry."

Derek used his paddle to push a drowned dog from their path. It bobbed beneath the surface and rolled to the side. He turned around to check on Dani. She was straddling Sarah, who was passed out in the bottom of the canoe. His eyes kept going to the spear. Derek didn't know much about vitals, but he had helped butcher a pig once. From what he remembered, most of the stuff that would kill you quick, a shot to the heart, lungs, liver, spleen, was tucked under the ribs. Dani's spear probably ran straight through her intestines — a gut shot, which meant a slow, painful death.

Unless they could find Niles Crowing in time.

"Hold on," Derek whispered to Dani. "We're getting closer."

Dani winced. "I'm so thirsty," she wheezed. "My tongue is burning."

Derek twisted a bit more to see Conrad. "Do you have any water with you?"

His friend's face was bent in a dark scowl, but behind the frown, his eyes were wide with fright. "Yeah," he nodded, "but we shouldn't give her any." Conrad paddled hard, and the canoe shot forward into the gap Derek had just cleared.

"Why not?" Derek asked.

"Do you remember Mark Talisman?"

"That kid who got killed a couple of years ago?" Derek turned around and paddled. The canoe lurched forward, and Dani groaned. "Sorry," he muttered.

"It's okay," Dani whispered. "Just keep paddling. Keep talking. Keeps my mind off the pain."

"I was there when it happened," Conrad continued. "He got jumped by a couple of Jotaro."

"Jotaro? I thought that gang only worked Ploughman's Wharf."

"Yeah, well, Mark was down there, mouthing off, and they followed him up to Gillman's Way. Caught him behind Killjoy's Leatherwares and knifed him up good."

"What happened?" Derek pushed aside a tangled mess of sheets, and the canoe wobbled. Dani groaned. "Sorry," Derek said again.

"Be careful!" Conrad barked. "You're ripping her up."

"I'm trying!" Derek insisted. His neck tingled, and his jaw clenched. The anger was rising in him. He had to fight it, needed to fight it, if he was going to save Dani. Derek took a deep breath to calm his nerves and paddled. "So, what happened?"

Conrad cleared his throat. "Anyway, Mr. Killjoy hears Mark yelling and the Jotaro laughing, and he comes out of his shop with a club. The Jotaro run off, and all I hear Mark saying is, 'I'm so thirsty. I need water.' Mr. Killjoy goes inside and gets a jug of water. Mark drinks it all down and asks for more. Mr. Killjoy goes inside to get another jug, and by the time he comes back, Mark is dead. Then, the Iron Guard shows up. One of them tells Mr. Killjoy you shouldn't give water to someone who's been stuck in the gut. Kills them faster."

"Why?" Derek asked.

"Who knows?" Conrad said. "It's just what he said, and I'm not taking chances with Dani."

A yakariian battle cry ripped through the night. Derek looked over his shoulder at the rooftops behind them. "They're close."

"Too close," Conrad agreed. "We have to find a faster way to the Ranger Outpost."

"Yeah," Derek said, "but we can't go along the Black."

"Why not?"

"Are you deaf? That's where all the explosions are coming from."

"Those yakariian scouts are getting closer. We don't have time to play it safe."

Neither does Dani, Derek thought, but he kept his mouth shut.

Debris and the dead choked the streets. Derek sat in the front of the canoe and used his paddle to clear corpses from their path. Massive rats, larger than the tom cats that prowled Zuid Horn's back alleys, slank about the dark windows of the buildings they passed. Several rode the larger bodies of the drowned, nibbling at the fresh feast.

One of these rats, larger than its brethren, sniffed at the canoe as it drifted past. It clambered over a drowned goat to get a bit closer. It sniffed first at Derek and bared its teeth. Derek swung at it with his paddle, but it was too far away. The thing backed away a bit and then froze, its beady eyes locked on Conrad.

"Get out of here!" Conrad yelled.

The rat squeaked and scurried away over the floating debris and disappeared into the darkness. Derek kept paddling and watched it go. "Strange," he muttered.

Conrad grunted. "I guess."

Derek looked back at Conrad. The boy's face was pale and glistening with sweat. "You okay?" Derek asked. "You look sick."

Conrad shook his head. "All these rats. Something smells funny about them. Makes my stomach turn." He rubbed his forehead in his elbow. "I'll be fine."

"Huh," Derek said, "I can't smell them over the sewage."

The yakariian scouts behind them roared again. "By The Hammer," Derek swore. "They're catching up quick."

"Are those the same ones we ran into before?" Conrad asked.

"I hope not," Derek answered. "Let's head for the Black River and cut through the Foundry District."

"You clear the way," Conrad said. "I'll steer."

It was past midnight, and the thundering rush of the initial flood had quieted considerably. The water still rolled toward the center of Zuid Horn, but its pace was more like a lazy river than a raging torrent. When Derek mentioned it, all he got out of Conrad was a grunt and, "Magic, no doubt." Derek shivered and kept paddling.

Conrad maneuvered the laden canoe from the back of the boat with a practiced hand. With the threat of the yakariian scouts on their tail, the boys stuck to the middle of the street, where the current was fastest.

Soon the canoe was past the artisan neighborhood and into Zuid Horn's industrial heart, centered along the Black River, which twisted through the middle of the city. First came the coal houses, where wealthy merchants dried lumber from Breechwood Forest, kept the best boards for sale, and turned the scrap into some of the

135

finest hardwood lump coal available. They paddled past the tops of warehouses, now mostly underwater, with their ruined crates and lofts full of lump coal. It would take weeks to dry out the coal in Zuid Horn's tropical humidity. Derek wondered if any of the foundries would be left after the fire and flood to take advantage of the cheap coal.

Next came the blacksmiths' shops, conveniently clutched together between the coal yards and foundries. Most of these were completely underwater except for their chimneys, which reached out of the water like fingers grasping for the moonless sky. These businesses and homes were a complete loss. Several buildings had been torn apart, like Derek's house earlier in the night, leaving attics and lofts exposed. Here and there, survivors called to the group in the canoe, but with four people already in the small boat, there was no room for anyone else.

"We can't," Derek said to a drenched woman holding an infant in her thin arms. "We've got two wounded already."

"Please!" the woman begged. "Have mercy!"

Derek gritted his teeth and turned away. He hated refusing the woman help. There were more survivors on rooftops ahead, waving and calling to the boys. What was he to do, with Sarah unconscious in the canoe's belly and Dani with a spear through her gut?

"We can't," Conrad said in answer to Derek's thoughts. "We've got to stay focused on our own."

"It's not easy," Derek muttered.

"We got yakariian scouts on our tail. We can't stop."

"But the yakarii will get them."

"The yakarii are probably taking hundreds of prisoners tonight. We can't rescue them if we get caught too."

"Water," Dani whispered. Her voice was barely a breath.

Derek turned back to check on her. Dani slumped against the side of the canoe, with the spear running diagonally across the gunwale. She kept a hand on either side of the wound to keep her body from sliding back and forth and leaned against the thwart to steady herself. Her head lolled with the rhythm of the current, and her mouth sagged like a loose bag. A yakariian scout roared. It sounded like it was just down the block.

"Hang on, Dani," Derek said. Dani groaned. Letting out a sigh, Derek went back to paddling. The woman and her baby would have to find help elsewhere.

They shot down the boulevards, the current quickening as they drew closer and closer to the heart of the Foundry District. A wild crackling filled the air. Derek looked over the rooftops ahead. Sparks from the burning foundries leapt into the clear night sky. There was the crackling and something else that made the hairs on the back of Derek's neck stand up. It was a sound like growling or roaring, bigger than a forest giant.

His gut told him something dangerous waited just ahead, and his heart told him to flee, but Dani and his sister needed help fast. With the yakarii on their tail, they had no choice but to go forward. Derek poled the canoe around a final corner, and they came face-to-face with the first of the burning foundries. They all stared in stunned silence.

The Farran Foundry stood five stories tall. One of the proud monuments of Zuid Horn's elite, it had provided iron and steel for many of the realm's greatest armies. Zuid Horn famously kept itself neutral in most conflicts so it could profit by supplying both sides of the battlefield with swords, spears, armor, and shields. The Farran Foundry had been among Zuid Horn's first foundries, and now it was falling into ruin on the night of the city's destruction.

The building's uppermost floors were on fire, and it was obvious that these were not normal flames. Even the children in the canoe, who had no schooling in the magical arts, could see that. Coils of fire twisted themselves into a gigantic, humanoid shape at least three stories tall, with arms that easily spanned the street. It punched fist after fist into the foundry, setting the wood and brick structure further ablaze with every blow. The flaming creature reached deep into the foundry and ripped out more and more of the building's guts with its massive, fiery hands and tossed the burning remains into the watery streets.

Derek and the others shielded their faces from the fire's heat and watched in horror as the creature climbed to the top of the foundry, where the flames were highest. It bent low and drove its hands into the heart of the inferno, squatting so low its shoulders were almost flush with the top of the building. It seemed to latch onto something and then strained and heaved and pulled another creature just like itself from the flames. Once the second fire monster was free, they both pounded and tore at the building until it collapsed in a crackling crash. Just before the foundry plunged into the floodwaters, the flame creatures leapt to the next burning building and started ripping that one apart as well. Bricks and beams flew into the air and splashed into the flooded streets below.

Waves from the monsters' battle with the buildings rocked the tiny canoe back and forth. "We can't stay here!" Derek shouted to Conrad. "These waves will capsize us!"

Dani's spear rattled against the canoe's gunwale. She wailed in pain. "The waves are ripping me up!"

"Keep us steady!" Derek yelled.

Conrad tried to steady the canoe, but the wild waves and the current's steady draw toward the destruction kept them moving closer and closer to the battle between fire and water. "I can't do it!" Conrad yelled. "Something is pulling us in!"

Derek paddled against the current, but his efforts produced little effect. "Blazing Forges! What is going on?"

Dani gripped the edges of the little boat and screamed, "Get this spear out of me!"

"Dani, it might kill you," Derek argued over his shoulder.

"It is killing me now!"

He searched the streets. Not far away, he spotted just what he needed. "Conrad, make for that alcove." He pointed to the top of the archway of a flooded shop. "We can put the canoe in there."

The boys dug in with their paddles and knifed across the surge. They made their way to the alcove in short order. Conrad grabbed the brick overhang with both hands to keep them in place. Derek spun around in his seat. "Hold it steady."

Conrad watched with nervous eyes. "Can you help her?"

"This is a bad idea."

"Just get it out," Dani hissed between clenched teeth.

"By The Hammer," Derek swore to himself. He glanced at Sarah, unconscious next to Dani. How could he lose someone else he cared about tonight? He took a breath. "Okay, hold on."

He knelt next to Dani, careful not to crush Sarah, who was crumpled in the canoe's belly. Derek put one hand around the wound, where the spear jutted from Dani's torso. He carefully wrapped his fingers around the haft of the spear, just below the head. Derek leaned forward and looked Dani in the eyes. "Are you ready?"

Dani nodded.

"If it's too much, just tell me, and I'll stop."

"Just get it out," she breathed.

Derek took a slow breath to steady himself. He pulled the spear toward him, and Dani howled. Derek's hands flew off the spear. "Be careful!" Conrad yelled.

"I'm trying! I've never done this before." Derek's neck burned.

"You better not kill her."

Derek's scalp tingled. *Why would Conrad even say that?* "Do you want to do it?"

Conrad's face fell. "No."

"Alright then. Shut up and let Dani decide if I should stop."

Derek's breaths came short and fast. He tried to calm himself down, but the anger, fueled by fear for Dani, was on him now. He found Dani's eyes again. "Dani?"

She nodded. "Do it."

Derek swallowed the lump in his throat and pressed against her torso. She winced but didn't scream. The spear slid through

the hole in her body, bit by bit. Dani sucked air in short gasps, her eyes clenched. The spear emerged, shiny and slick, at Derek's beckoning. He gaped at the weapon, his mind unable to comprehend what he was doing. It was as though he were dreaming or watching someone else, and the part of his mind that was incredibly clear, incredibly present, was telling that person what to do. *Wait for the breath. Slow. Pause. Wait for the breath. Okay, now. Go.*

The spear appeared one finger-width at a time. He was more than halfway now. Dani's head lolled in sickening circles. Every now and then, the silvery gray of intestine would peek through the hole in Dani's gut, and he would have to stuff it back inside her torso. *Careful now. Make sure it isn't caught on a splinter. Tuck it back in. That's it. Not much blood. Is that bad?*

He was almost at the end of the spear when something heavy — several somethings heavy — thumped on the roof above their alcove. "They're close," a deep voice growled from above. "I can smell the girl's belly. She ain't got long now."

Derek snapped a quick look at Conrad. The boy's eyes were wide and white in the light of the burning foundries. "What are we going to do?" Conrad mouthed.

Derek checked the spear. Less than a hand's length to go. He leaned close to Dani and whispered in her ear. "We're almost done. Can you make it?"

Dani dropped her head against Derek's shoulder and nodded weakly. Her head was drenched in sweat. Her short hair clung to her head in tiny, damp curls. Derek took a breath to steady himself and was amazed to find that even against the stink of the flooded sewers and the burning foundries, Dani still smelled like the sun. Derek pressed the side of his head against hers. "Okay. It will be over soon."

Then he pressed her belly as gently as he could and, with one smooth motion, pulled the rest of the spear free. Breathing in sharp bursts, she collapsed against Derek's shoulder. He handed the spear to Conrad and held Dani as tightly as he dared. "Dani, I'm so sorry," he whispered. "This is all my fault."

Dani shook her head. Her face was drawn and pale. She gestured to the flaming buildings. "Go."

"But the yakarii? They'll see us."

The creak of wood overhead made Derek look up. A yakariian scout was hanging over the edge of the roof, looking directly at him. "What do we have here? Found 'em, boys!"

Derek helped Dani lie down in the canoe. He hopped to the bow seat and grabbed his paddle. "Conrad! Go!"

The boys pushed out of their alcove with a white spray. More yakariian arms sprouted from overhead and dangled like thick vines. Derek ducked just out of reach as he passed beneath them. "Look out!" he warned Conrad.

But Derek saw that Conrad had other ideas. He grabbed the spear Derek had just taken out of Dani and slashed at the outstretched arms like they were pork roasts. The yakarii pulled back their arms and howled. "Don't let them get away!" one of them roared.

"Spear them!" called another.

"We're out!" bellowed a third.

"Over the rooftops! After them!"

The canoe blasted from the shop's alcove. "Not too close to the foundries," Derek said. "Those giant fire creatures could knock a chimney on us."

Conrad leaned back in the stern and drove his paddle deep into the water to turn the canoe. "I'm trying, but the current is sucking us in!"

Derek looked ahead, desperate to discover what could be pulling their boat toward the flaming buildings. He found his answer in an instant.

The foundries blazed overhead like volcanoes, spitting sparks and ash into the air. Several fiery giants straddled the burning

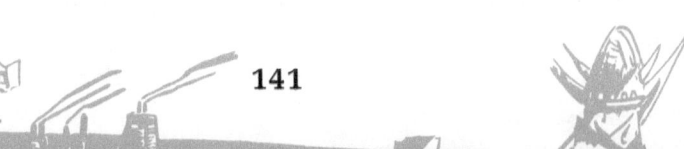

buildings, dealing destruction with their blazing fists. Below, where the flood rushed past the foundries' second-floor windows, the waters foamed from the churning of three tremendous water elementals. Shaped like the serpents of old, these creatures slithered through the waters like eighty-foot anacondas, wrapped thick coils around support beams, and squeezed until wall after wall came down. Water from the flood rushed into the creatures as they grew bigger and bigger.

That's what made the current flow toward the buildings, Derek thought. One of the massive creatures sank watery teeth into a wall of bricks and hurled it into the air. "Look out!" Conrad shouted, pointing to the sky.

Bricks, mortar, and broken timber splashed into the inky flood next to the canoe. A sheet of water exploded and dropped on them like a heavy blanket. The boys spit and sputtered, but they somehow managed to keep their tiny craft afloat.

Derek wiped his eyes with the back of his wrist and checked on Dani and Sarah. The bottom of the canoe was filling up with water. "We've gotta get out of here!"

Dani struggled to sit. She tugged at Sarah to keep her head above the water. "Cut between the foundries," she wheezed. "Get to the Black River."

Derek shook his sopping head. "Those water elementals are sucking up too much water. We'll get pulled in."

"Then get to those warehouses," Dani instructed, holding her belly with one hand and supporting Sarah's head with the other.

"Which ones?" Derek asked.

"There," Dani said, pointing at the warehouses across the boulevard from the foundries with her chin. Then her eyes went wide. "Wizards!"

Derek scanned the buildings on the other side of the wide street. Movement atop a flat-roofed coal warehouse caught his eye. Three people dressed in the black garb of the wizarding class — two men and a woman — stood on the roof, moving their arms

in delicate patterns and muttering incantations. Their eyes were trained on the fire and water elementals.

Derek waved at them and shouted, "Hey, hello! Can you help us?"

One of the men glanced at Derek, but he immediately turned his attention back to the destruction. "No help there," Dani muttered.

Derek stopped waving and paddled. "I'll say. I thought the wizards were supposed to protect Zuid Horn, not destroy it."

"It doesn't make sense," Dani said, her voice little more than a whisper.

"Da was right," Derek growled. "Never trust a wizard."

"Will you focus on paddling?" Conrad barked. "We have yakarii on our tail!"

Derek's neck burned. "Like I didn't know that."

"Knock it off, you two," Dani hissed, her face knotted with pain. "Derek, put your anger into paddling. Get us out of here."

Derek lowered his head and paddled as hard as he could. Water flew with each furious stroke. The draw on the canoe from the growing water elementals was strong, but Derek's fury and pain from the night's events burned hotter than the foundries. Bit by bit, the loaded canoe made its way across the flooded street.

They were just out of range of the largest falling pieces when Conrad said, "We're almost there. I didn't think we were going to make it."

That was when the foundry collapsed.

There was a tremendous crack, and the building came down in a rush. The load-bearing beams of the lower floors burst through the outer walls. Bricks and iron bars hurtled through the air and skittered across the water. One by one, the floors collapsed with dusty, explosive coughs, spitting out nails and glass and flame. When the bulk of the ruined foundry finally hit the water, a massive wave pulsed outward, rocketed across the street, and flipped the canoe.

"Dani!" Derek shouted, and then he was under.

He came to the surface, wiped oily water from his eyes, and looked around. The water stung the dozen or so gashes covering his body from the night's adventure, but in his panic, he ignored the pain. Dani was an arm's length away. Conrad already had an arm around her, and they were making for the warehouse, where a ladder to an upper-level storage loft sprouted out of the water.

"I've got Dani," Conrad said, though he struggled to stay above water. "Get your sister!"

Derek's gut clenched. How could he forget? "Sarah!"

She floated next to him, face down, her legs trapped under the capsized canoe. Derek grabbed her and flipped her over. He kicked hard to keep her head above water and then squeezed her torso. "Come on, Sarah. Don't leave me. Cough it out. Cough it out."

On the third hard squeeze, Sarah coughed up a lungful of water. Her eyes flared open. "What?" she sputtered. "Derek?" Her voice was raw and broken.

Derek held her tight. "I've got you. You've been out for a while."

She looked around. "Liza? Mum and Da?"

Derek felt like he was going to throw up. He knew he had to tell her the truth, but now was not the time. "Not now. We need to help Dani."

"Dani?" Sarah pushed away from Derek. "Where?"

"Over here!" Conrad shouted.

He and Dani were across the street from the collapsed foundry, at the base of a ladder to a storage loft. He had one hand on a ladder rung and another wrapped around Dani's waist. Her head lolled loosely against her chest. Conrad strained to heave her out of the water, but he slipped, and she dropped back down with a thin splash. Conrad snatched her by the arm and looked at Derek with pleading eyes.

"Help me get her up this ladder."

"Are you strong enough to swim?" Derek asked Sarah.

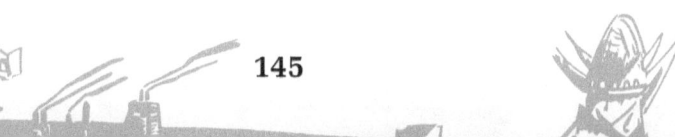

"I think so." She struck out for the loft and made slow progress. "What's wrong with Dani?"

Derek grit his teeth. "Not now. Get to the ladder." He had just started after her when a cruel chorus of laughter sounded from a few rooftops away. "Look at the little fishies," a yakariian scout cackled, "flopping in the stream."

"Someone get a net. Let's catch us some dinner!"

The yakarii howled and barked as they scrambled over the rooftops. They would be on Derek and his friends in no time. "By The Hammer!" Derek swore. "We're swimming into a trap." He put his head into the flood's muck and swam for the ladder with desperate strokes.

He caught up to Sarah in short order. Despite her strong start, her progress was quickly slowing. "I can't make it," she gasped. "The current."

Derek grabbed her by the back of her shirt and tugged her forward. "Come on!"

At the base of the ladder, Conrad and Dani struggled to climb even the first rung. Conrad was behind his sister, trying to push her up the ladder. "Come on, Dani. You can do it."

Dani shook her head weakly. "Can't. Too tired."

Derek searched for the incoming yakarii. They were one rooftop away now, cresting an accountant's office. Their dimly lit forms rose and fell like ocean swells against the night sky. "They're almost on us," Derek said. "We're not going to make it."

Conrad whirled on him. "Shut up!" Then, to Dani, he begged, "Come on, just climb."

"Conrad!" Derek shouted. "There's no time. And we won't be safe in that loft." He looked for the canoe. The current was dragging it toward the snarling water elementals at the base of the burning foundry. "I've got to get the canoe! Sarah, hold on!"

Derek didn't wait for his sister to respond. He made for the escaping canoe as fast as he could. If the canoe got much farther, it would be destroyed by either the raging water elementals or the collapsing foundries. He hadn't gone more than three strokes when he stopped and tread water in amazement.

Less than a stone's throw away, a tall, lanky man was poling a punt — a flat-bottomed boat with a square-cut bow — right for him. The man's face was hidden by a deep hood. "Derek Fulstarter," said the stranger. "What are you doing down here?"

He knew that voice. "Niles Crowing?"

The figure stopped poling long enough to throw back his hood, revealing a lean face, framed with long, black hair. A brilliant mustache and dark eyes that sparkled in the firelight added a mischievous glint to his smile. "None other."

Niles brought the low boat alongside Derek and helped the boy get aboard. "The Seven? Are the rest..."

As if in answer to his question, the yakarii who had been chasing Derek and his friends cried out. Derek turned in time to see them clutch their necks and drop, one by one, into the dank flood. Standing in their places on the roof were four man-sized shadows. One of them waved to Niles, who lifted his chin in response.

Niles smiled. "Would I go anywhere on a night like this without them?"

"Lenny?" Derek asked.

There was a sharp clap, and a tiny man, less than a foot tall, appeared on Niles' shoulder. The little man was dressed in a smart brown coat with black patches on the elbows, a matching bowler cap, and brown trousers hemmed neatly at the knees, which revealed that one of his legs was actually a wooden stump.

"At your service," Lenny the Unlucky Leprechaun said with a crisp bow.

"Lenny!" Derek shouted at the Leprechaun. "Sarah's drowning! Can you get her?"

Lenny bowed in response. "Good as done!" Then he clapped his hands and vanished into thin air.

Derek looked around for the little man and found him helping Sarah clamber aboard a floating wine cask.

He barely had time for a sigh of relief when a loud, woody bang made Derek whirl. The double doors leading to the loft Conrad and Dani were trying to climb had been thrown open. Something large moved in the darkness. Derek squinted into the shadowy loft and then gasped.

A massive bulk, topped by the most hideous face Derek had ever seen, filled the open, double doors. The head was huge, almost as large as a horse's, with wire-stiff bristles springing from the scalp and running in jagged lines down the neck and back. Two beady pig eyes glowered beneath massive brows that crowned a triumphant mountain of a nose. Beneath that, a great, sweltering maw ringed with razor-sharp fangs and two blackened tusks opened to reveal a glistening, red tongue. The creature's body filled the doorway with thick arms, a broad, flabby belly that hung loosely from beneath a well-polished coat of plate mail armor, an iron skirt, and wide, leather boots. This was an ogress, and a tremendous specimen at that.

Derek sighed in relief. He waved at the creature, and she waved back. "Wendy!" he shouted. "Dani's hurt! Can you get her into the loft?"

Wendy the Ogress scanned the flooded street. She glanced at Niles and Derek in the punt and the four members of the Magnificent Seven on the adjacent rooftop before settling on Conrad and the girls below. The ogress's eyes went wide.

"Goodness!" she cried, and faster than Derek would have thought possible given her bulk, she swung onto the ladder, scampered down with a surprising nimbleness, and snatched Dani out of the water. "What's happened to you, girl?" Wendy the Ogress asked, cradling Dani in an arm that rivaled a tree trunk.

Dani said nothing but let her head collapse against Wendy's shoulder. Wendy shot up the ladder and disappeared into the loft. Conrad and Sarah followed the ogress up the ladder and into the darkness. "Father Ferrum!" Wendy bellowed from the shadows. "Get in here! We have two children who need you."

Derek turned to Niles. "Father Ferrum is here?"

Niles nodded. "We're all here." He waved to the four figures on the rooftop and pointed to the loft. They waved back and hurried toward the warehouse holding Wendy and the children. "What happened to Dani?" Niles asked.

"She took a spear through the side." Derek paused. "It was my fault."

"Your fault?"

Derek swallowed the knot in his throat. His chin quivered, and then it all came out in a rush of tears and gasping sobs. He told Niles about losing his parents, their home, their run-in with the yakarii, Liza, and finally, the spear that was meant for him but ended up skewering Dani instead. "After everything she's done for me," Derek moaned, "and that's how I repay her."

They were at the ladder to the loft now. Niles grabbed the iron rungs and tied up the punt with a length of hemp rope. "Is that how she sees it?"

"How else could she see it?"

Niles shrugged. "Did you ask her?"

"We haven't exactly had time to chat," Derek said, a little more sarcastically than he'd liked.

"Well, Father Ferrum is here. He'll get Dani patched up. Maybe you'll get a chance to talk then."

Father Ferrum. The old priest was a master healer, skilled in both practical and magical healing. If anyone in Zuid Horn could save Dani, it would be him. "I doubt she'll ever want to talk to me again."

"You won't know until you try," Niles said. He jerked a thumb toward the loft and studied the wounds crisscrossing Derek's body. "Let's get you in the loft. Looks like Father Ferrum will have to do a little work on you, too."

Derek started up the ladder. His body ached from the long night's adventures, but a glimmer of hope lit the darkness in his heart. Now that they had finally found Niles Crowing and the Magnificent Seven, maybe they would be safe at last.

12

Derek Develops the Best Laid Plans

By the time Derek, Conrad, Jenkins, and Lars stood across the street from Zuid Horn's Ranger Outpost, it was well past midnight. The two-story building was built of ironwood hewn from deep within Breechwood Forest, the tropical jungle surrounding Zuid Horn. The wood was a deep brown, almost black, and so strong that many warriors preferred an ironwood club from Breechwood over steel longswords from Bearton. Forge masters used the same trees to make the charcoal that fueled Zuid Horn's steel and iron industry. Scores of warehouses along the Black River stored the valuable, and flammable, resource.

Oil lanterns hung from support beams and posts all around the outpost. Lamplight reflected off the polished ironwood and bathed the building in a golden aura. Rows of barrels stood in strict formation along the first-floor wall, so they could be easily loaded onto merchant wagons. Charred brands identified the barrels' contents. Wines, ales, pickled vegetables, and even meats stored in salty brines were among the riches brought in by the wide-roving rangers. Zuid Hornians were always hungry for the taste of exotic goods, and the rangers were more than happy to profit from the city dwellers' insatiable appetite. Shelves in the alleys on either side of the building supplied extra storage space for salted hides waiting to be tanned, boxes of forest roots and barks in need of preparation by alchemists, and baskets of choice, edible mushrooms.

None of this was new to Derek. He had been to the outpost many times with his father, as the rangers were frequent customers. But the rangers' large order this morning made him look at the ranger station differently. Usually, Da made arrows for solitary rangers. He never filled bulk orders. Was Niles Crowing telling the truth? Were the rangers about to make the Fulstarters their primary supplier? It would be a windfall and security like never before. Derek felt terrible that his temper had put the Ranger Outpost contract in jeopardy. He had let his father down, but knowing that Dani was enslaved on a Shadizarian ship steeled his resolve. The girl's unprompted kindness while Derek was a prisoner in the stocks would not be forgotten.

Several men wearing dark cloaks gathered before the Ranger Outpost. They had long ash bows slung over their backs and longswords and daggers made of Zuid Hornian steel at their hips. Derek and his group were far enough away to only catch an odd phrase or a bit of laughter now and then. The lanky men in dark cloaks studied the boys as they approached.

One of them crossed his arms over his chest and grumbled, "A little late for young ones to be out, isn't it?"

"We're here on business," Derek said.

"Ho! Is that so?" The man turned to grin at his fellows. "And what are you selling?"

"Nothing for sale," Derek continued. "We are here to see Niles Crowing."

This brought the men up short. "Niles Crowing? That scoundrel? You boys would do well to steer clear of that old trickster."

Conrad's face scrunched up in confusion. "Trickster? He's not a ranger?"

The men burst into laughter. One of them even had to wipe tears from his eyes. When they had control of themselves, he said, "Ranger? Boys, I don't know what he's been telling you, but Niles Crowing is no ranger."

Conrad's face fell. "He's not?"

"By the gods, no."

Derek scratched the back of his neck. "But he came to my da's shop. Bryton Fulstarter? He ordered several score of arrows for the outpost."

The man looked at Derek, a soft pity in his eyes. "Bryton's boy, eh?"

"Yes, sir."

"Might have guessed with your height."

Derek needed to win the rangers' trust to get to Niles Crowing, and this turn in the conversation had just handed him a way forward. "How do you know my father?"

"Son," the ranger continued, "that's a long story. But because I've known your father for a long time, let me set you straight about this 'friend' Niles of yours. Niles may have put in an order for the outpost, but he's no ranger. Our captain hires him to do odd jobs all the time."

Derek felt his hopes drain down his back. If Niles wasn't an adventurer, how was he going to help them rescue Dani? "So, he's not an adventurer?"

"Oh, I didn't say that. Niles Crowing and the Magnificent Seven are adventurers alright. They just have a strange way of getting things done." He paused. "You know, they bend the law a bit."

Derek considered that and then looked at Conrad, who urged Derek on with his eyes. "Well, do you know where he is now?" Derek asked.

"Sure," the ranger said, jerking a thumb over his shoulder. "He's inside. He's got a room on the first floor, next to the mess hall. The captain likes to keep an eye on him, gives him jobs to keep him out of trouble." The man leaned toward the boys in a conspiratorial kind of way. "If we didn't keep him busy, he'd be out trying to save the world. You know, going on quests and whatnot with the Magnificent Seven."

"The Magnificent Seven?" Jenkins blurted.

Another of the rangers snorted. "You boys really don't get around much, do you?"

"You'd be surprised," Derek said. "So, who are they?"

"That's Niles' adventuring group. You'd be hard-pressed to find a rowdier bunch of brawlers — a street magician, a dirty thief, an unlucky leprechaun, an ogress, a Shadizarian lancer, a drunken priest of the Forge, and a retired gladiator. Nothing but bad news there, boys."

Jenkins stood on his toes and tried to see around the rangers. "Are they in there now?"

"No. They stay on the other side of town. The captain lets Niles have his own room here, like I said, so he can keep an eye on their leader." The man looked closely at the boys. "I'd stay away from him if I were you."

Derek considered that for a bit. "That sounds like good advice, but I promised my da I would speak to him about that contract today. I can't go home until I do."

"And you waited until after midnight to come see him?"

Derek shrugged. "I kind of got distracted."

"Distracted?"

"Chasing girls."

The man snorted and looked at the other rangers. "What do you think?"

"I don't care," one of them replied, "if they leave when they're done. I don't think the captain wants a bunch of kids hanging around."

"Alright," the first ranger said. "Follow me." He turned and took the boys into the outpost.

They followed the ranger inside the two-story building. The first floor was open, with piled furs, salted meats, stacks of fine lumber,

traps, and trading supplies neatly arranged in rows. Every stack had a tag attached to it, indicating where it was going and to whom it belonged. There were several rangers milling about the room.

To the boys' right and left, long counters ran the length of the walls. Stark men in tattered cloaks leaned against the counters, throwing back thin, clay cups of rye whiskey and reminiscing over tales from the woods. By their feet sat bundles of furs strapped together with thick bands of leather. Backpacks, fat with riches from the forest, hung heavily over their shoulders. A low fire simmered in a stone fireplace, drying out the tropical humidity without overheating the room.

"Over here," the man said, pointing to a doorway under a stairwell. "Looks like he's in." He rapped on the door sharply. "Crowing, you have visitors."

There was a shuffling of papers from the room, and then a voice. "Well, send them in."

The ranger pushed the door open and bowed to the boys. "There you go. Don't be long." And he walked away to join a few men drinking at a counter.

"Let's go," Derek said, moving the group forward. "We've come this far." He knocked on the door and walked into Niles' room.

Niles was sitting sideways at a small desk. He barely looked up from his writing when the boys entered. "I was expecting Derek," he said, returning to his ledger, "but not the rest of you." He pointed to a neatly made cot with a crisp, wool blanket tucked over the top. "Well, take a seat."

The bed was long enough for all four boys. Niles continued writing, pausing only to dip his quill in an ink stand. A light scent of cloves and wet ink hung in the air. Derek listened to the turkey feather scratching across the parchment. There was something soothing about it. His father had taught him his numbers and letters early on so Derek could help with record keeping around the shop. But ink was expensive and paper even more so. That's why the Fulstarters used slate and chalk to keep orders straight, rather than paper. It was temporary but better than nothing. Maybe if Da landed this contract with the rangers, they could have proper records in their shop.

A mountain of ledgers was open before Niles with charts full of names, numbers, and check marks. A pile of maps, mostly rolled into neat cylinders, rested next to the ledgers. A few of the maps were unrolled on a side table and held down with various weights, daggers, and an empty, brass mug. Derek leaned forward to see a little more of the map. He could make out the bulging, southern coast of the realms with a great, green spread representing Breechwood Forest, and an iron gray circle marking Zuid Horn's location on the southwest coast.

Conrad and the others fidgeted on the edge of the bed. Derek made a motion for them to calm down, but Conrad leaned in close. "Ask him," he whispered.

"Not yet," Derek said.

"Ask me what?" Niles said, scratching away on his records.

Derek looked at the others. Conrad encouraged him with a nod, so Derek said, "We need your help."

Niles put his quill in the inkwell. "Do you now?"

Derek opened his mouth to speak, but Conrad cut him off. "Yes, sir. Some Shadizarian slavers nabbed my sister off the pier. They've got her chained to a rowing bench on *The Delivery*."

Niles eased back in his chair. "How do you know she's chained to a rowing bench?"

"Derek saw her, sir," Conrad said. "We snuck onto *The Delivery*, and Derek got to scout the whole ship out. That's how he found Dani."

"Dani is your sister?"

"Yes, sir."

"And you were on *The Delivery*?"

"Yes, sir," Conrad said.

"Impressive. How did you pull that off?"

"It was all Derek's plan," Jenkins cut in. "He had some gold he stole from a bunch of minotaurs, and we used that to, um..." but that was all he could say because Conrad elbowed him hard in the ribs. Jenkins gave a little, *"Oof!"* and dropped his eyes to the floor. "Sorry," he mumbled, and then was quiet.

Niles rubbed his chin and studied the boys. "Sounds like you've had quite the night."

Derek let out a slow breath. "I'll say."

"Tell you what," Niles said, grabbing the empty pewter mug off his table. "I'm going to grab a Woodsman's Ale, and when I get back, you're going to tell me your story."

Once Niles was back in his seat with his brown ale, Derek's recounting of the last day went quickly. When Derek was finished, he said, "And so that's why we came here. You obviously dropped that key by me for a reason, and I kind of hoped it was because you wanted to help us."

"First of all," Niles said, stretching in his chair, "I didn't drop a key."

"But you did," Derek insisted.

Niles leveled a look at Derek and raised his brow. "I said, 'I didn't drop a key.'"

"Oh," Derek said. "Right."

"Speaking of which, can I have it back?" Niles extended a hand.

"What? Oh, of course." Derek dug the key out of his pocket and handed it to Niles.

"Wonderful," the swashbuckler said, tucking the key into his belt. "And now that you've broken out of the stocks, you are fugitives from the Iron Guard."

"Yeah," Conrad muttered, swinging his legs on the side of the bed, "about that. Can you help us? We are just trying to save my sister."

"I understand," Niles said, "but the Iron Guard and the rangers don't have formal connections. They are the executors of the law in Zuid Horn."

Derek sat up suddenly. "But what if we could free the people the Shadizarians kidnapped? The Iron Guard would have to let us go if we did that."

Niles laughed. "That's not exactly how the law works, but okay." He crossed his lean arms over his chest. "Where did you say you'd seen the people in the hull before?"

"They were in the stocks with us," Derek said.

"And how do you think they got onto *The Delivery*?"

The boys looked at one another. Derek muttered, "Oh no."

"What?" Jenkins asked.

Conrad sighed. "Think about it. Who was watching over the prisoners on Ploughman's Wharf?"

Jenkins shrugged. "The Iron Guard."

"And who could have let the prisoners out of the stocks and sold them to the Shadizarians without anyone knowing?"

Jenkins screwed up his face. "The Iron Guard? You think they are selling Zuid Hornians into slavery?"

"It makes sense," Lars said. "Think about it. People go missing all the time." Lars looked at Derek and frowned. "And who would care about a few missing street rats?"

Derek was still skeptical. "I don't know. Maybe. It just seems odd that the Iron Guard would be caught up in something so dirty. Someone would say something. There would be rumors, right?"

Niles got up and closed the door. He sat back down and motioned the boys closer. "Look, I've had a suspicion that something like this was going on for a while. I just couldn't prove it. And to be honest, I don't think most of the Iron Guard is involved in a slavery ring. It is probably just a few men working on Ploughman's Wharf." Niles took a deep breath and rubbed his hands together. "I've got a plan that might free your sister and get the evidence we need to prove there is a dirty underbelly in the Iron Guard. If we can do that, we might be able to keep some Zuid Hornians from being sold into slavery and convince the legitimate members of the Iron Guard to overlook your little jailbreak." He studied the boys closely. "What do you think?"

"I think it's our only choice," Derek said.

"I'll do anything to save Dani," Conrad agreed.

Niles smiled and leaned back in his chair. Pointing at Conrad and Derek, he said, "Are you boys willing to infiltrate *The Delivery*?"

"We already did," Derek said.

"True enough," Niles conceded. "But this time I need you to do it for real."

"What do you mean?" Conrad asked.

"I need you to get onto that ship, work it, and gain their trust. Get access to the captain's quarters. Find proof of the Iron Guard's involvement. Shadizarians are meticulous record keepers. With a little searching, you should be able to find what you need." Niles stopped suddenly. "Wait. Can any of you read?" Conrad's shoulders slumped. "No."

"Us either," Jenkins said, jerking a thumb at Lars.

Derek nudged Conrad lightly with his elbow. "I can," Derek said. "Da taught me so I could keep track of accounts in our shop."

"Excellent," Niles said, closing several of the ledgers on his desk.

Conrad fidgeted on the edge of the bed. "Okay, so what should Derek look for, and how do we get that information to you? How do we rescue Dani?"

Niles held up his hands. "Whoa, slow down. One thing at a time. You'll be looking for accounting books listing slaves bought in Zuid Horn, any names of merchants or Iron Guardsmen involved. Maybe there will be scrolls or maps. You'll know when you see it."

Conrad looked at Derek, his eyes heavy with doubt. "Can you do that?"

Derek shrugged. "Shouldn't be a problem if I can find where they keep their records. Probably in the captain's quarters."

"Exactly," Niles said. He got up and walked to a chest, opened it, and dug through neatly folded shirts, britches, and extra blankets. "Next, what you'll need is a way to let us know when you found proof that the Iron Guard is selling Zuid Hornians into slavery." Niles stopped digging and pulled a vial from the bottom of the chest. He held it in the air like a trophy. Passing the silver vial to Derek, he said, "Take this."

Derek turned the vial over in his hands. "What is it?" Niles grinned. "That is a little something from a magical wellspring in the yakariian lands, far to the east."

"Okay. What do we do with it?"

"Once you have the proof we need, go to the back of the boat, pull the cork, and toss the whole thing into the ocean. It's gotta mix with seawater, otherwise it won't work."

"And then what?" Conrad asked.

"And then we will know that it's time to rescue you and the others. But remember, don't give us the signal until you have proof that the Iron Guard and the Shadizarians are working together. Shadizarians are notorious record keepers and will destroy records as fast as they can if they think they are in trouble."

Derek and Conrad glanced at one another. Derek felt the confidence they once had in Niles sinking like a stone. "Wait. You're going to take over a ship?"

"Yes."

Derek took a deep breath. "I saw at least a dozen guards on the ship tonight. The rest were probably at a tavern."

"Yeah," Conrad said. "I'll bet they have twenty guards on that ship when they are at sea."

Niles tugged at his black and silver beard. "Twenty? Is that all?"

"That's all?" Conrad asked. "How can you say that? Twenty guards, plus another twenty sailors. That ship is a floating fortress! You'd need an army to pirate it from the Shadizarians."

Niles smiled. "Leave that to me. I know where to find just the kind of help we need for a mission like this."

"Where's that?" Derek asked.

Niles' smile twisted into a smirk. "Have you ever heard of The Magnificent Seven?"

13

Derek finds a Temporary Refuge

After Niles helped Derek into the second floor of the warehouse, they found Wendy the Ogress cradling Dani at the far side of the wide attic, squatting on her massive haunches against a pallet of charcoal. Conrad was kneeling next to the ogress and rubbing Dani's arm.

"Hold on, Dani. Father Ferrum is almost here." He looked up when Derek and Niles came close. Conrad frowned at Derek and then turned his attention to Niles. "The healer is with you, isn't he?"

"He's on his way," the swashbuckler said. There was a thump above them and the quiet tread of light feet moving over the roof. "Ah, here they come now."

A series of large shadows swung through an open set of double doors at the back of the building and landed lightly in the dark loft. The first shadow — tall, slim, and dressed in robes that swished over the rough planks of the attic's floor like wind through autumn leaves — broke from the others and hurried toward Dani.

"We need a little light in here," said a voice that clipped consonants the way a gardener thins seedlings. There was a rustle of cloth, and a low, red light flared into the dusty room. Derek threw up an arm to shield his eyes. "Pavaraci Moonfist?"

"Master Fulstarter," came the reply. "Imagine finding you in the thick of things."

Derek lowered his arm and blinked against the brightness to find the elven wizard bending over Dani, inspecting her wounds. Pavaraci had his hood thrown back, revealing the high cheekbones and fine features of his kind. The tips of his pointed ears poked through a crown of rich, black hair woven into a single braid that lay like a good rope down his back. His brown robes looked almost black in the low, red light. A worn, white band of cloth etched with black runes dangled about his shoulders. Pavaraci probed the edges of Dani's wound with delicate fingers.

"Hmm, yes, this doesn't look good at all. Not at all. Father Ferrum, you need to take a look at this."

A shadow emerged from the dark. Thick and heavy, the figure moved with purposeful strides to the wizard's side. "Move aside, elf. This is a priest's work. Wizards will only do more harm here."

Derek did his best to stifle a grunt. He remembered what Da had said about never trusting a wizard. Pavaraci, who appeared to not hear Derek's grunt, sniffed. "We all have our talents. You'll need me before the night is over, I'll wager." The elf moved aside but peered over Father Ferrum's shoulder. "It's infected."

The priest of the Forge snorted in irritation. "Of course, it is, elf. She's got a hole through her big enough to sail a barge through. Drop her in that rolling sewage out there, and it's a miracle she's still alive." He knelt on the floor and dug through a satchel slung over his shoulder until he produced a tube of rolled leather. Ferrum unbuttoned a latch and unrolled the tube on the floor. The edges curled closed like dying fingers. "Derek," the priest called without looking up. "Come hold my tool kit open."

Derek rushed over and held the edges of the tool kit down. Knives, scalpels, and screws glinted in the red light from the elven wizard's magic. Father Ferrum drew a lean set of scissors from the kit and snipped the lower half of Dani's tunic open, revealing the spear wound. It looked like a toothless mouth, trying to say, "Oh." The skin around the wound was dark, red, and inflamed. Derek reached out to touch it, and Father Ferrum slapped his hand away.

"What are you doing?" the priest asked.

"Sorry. I just wanted to see if it was infected."

Father Ferrum shook his head. "Can't you feel the heat pouring off it? This girl will be dead by sunrise if I don't heal her." He looked at Derek. "You don't look so good yourself. I'll see to you in a bit."

The priest inspected Dani's wound again, sized up the hole with his fingers, and then drew something from the tool kit that looked like scissors but with the blades sharpened on the outer edges. He held the tool up in the red light to inspect it and grunted to himself. "What happened to her?"

Derek cleared his throat. "A yakariian scout got her with a spear."

"Where is it now?"

"I pulled it out."

"You *what*?"

"She asked me to get the spear out of her, so I pulled it out."

The priest shook his head. "You're lucky you didn't kill her."

"I'll say."

Dani moaned, and her head lolled from side to side. Wendy the Ogress took Dani's head with a massive paw and gently held the frail girl against her chest. "Enough with the questions, Ferrum. Heal this child before it's too late."

The priest waved his hand. "Yes, yes. Lay the girl down. This won't take long."

The ogress grumbled and laid Dani on the floor. Derek shifted back to make room. "What are you going to do?"

"You'll see," Father Ferrum said. He unbuckled his chest armor and stripped off the tattered tunic he wore underneath.

Derek gasped at the man's body, covered as it was with a thick webbing of white scars. "What happened to you?" Derek asked.

Father Ferrum traced a light finger around the wound in Dani's gut and then touched the same spot on his own belly. "You don't know? I'm a healer, boy. I use the magic of the Forge to heal people's sickness and injuries."

"Okay," Derek said and pointed to the scars covering the priest's hide. "But what about all of that?"

"Magic has a price, boy. You don't get something for nothing. If we want to heal this girl, someone's got to pay the price." He flipped the scissors around in his free hand, so the razor point touched the priest's belly in the same spot where Dani had her spear wound. Father Ferrum closed his eyes and chanted. "Master of the Forge, receive my pain. Master of the Forge, receive my pain."

Derek's gut tightened. He wanted to shut his eyes, wanted to turn away, but some sick fascination kept his gaze glued on the horror before him. Father Ferrum took a slow breath and then pressed the scissors until the tip popped through his scarred hide. The priest winced and pulled the handles open, widening the wound.

"By the Forge, stop!" Derek begged, but Pavaraci Moonfist pulled him away from the healing ceremony. Derek shrugged off the elf's hand. "Make him stop! He's going to kill himself!"

"The worst is over, Master Fulstarter," the wizard said. "I'm surprised you are so upset. Father Ferrum has healed you before."

"I know," Derek said, "but I didn't have to see what he was doing. Now that I know... Just make him stop!"

Pavaraci Moonfist shook his head. "To stop now would be to throw away the magic that Father Ferrum has captured."

"What?"

"Father Ferrum has paid the price, and the Lord of the Forge is answering his prayers. Look!"

Derek turned back to the priest. A warm, orange glow, rather than blood, drained from Father Ferrum's fresh wound. The priest of the Forge caught the magic in his hands and poured it like water over the hole in Dani's belly. The girl's eyes flared open

as the magic trickled through her. Dani's breaths came in quick gasps, and even in the wizard's low, red light, Derek could see life returning to her face.

Conrad's eyes widened. "You're doing it! She's getting better!"

And indeed, she was. The gaping hole shrank before their eyes, until all that remained was a pink knot of scar tissue. Dani blinked and sat up, her eyes round with wonder. She ran her dirty fingers over the new, pink skin closing what had just been a death sentence.

"I'm better," she whispered. "I don't believe it."

Father Ferrum sank back onto his haunches and pressed a tight hand over the wound in his belly. "Believe it, girl. The Lord of the Forge still has plans for you, or he wouldn't have answered my prayers. Be sure you are listening for his call."

Dani shook her head from side to side. "I've never touched real magic before." She ran the tips of her fingers over the round, red bump on her belly. "It's amazing." Then her face lit up. "Can anyone become a healer?"

The priest produced a long needle and thick thread from his healing kit. Without so much as a wince, he began stitching himself up. "Anyone can become a healer, but few are willing to pay the price."

"But if someone was willing, could they do it?"

Ferrum's fingers worked methodically with the needle and thread. Pinch, stitch. Pinch, stitch. "The initiation and apprenticeship take years. Most acolytes abandon the faith long before their training is complete. Others don't survive. But, yes, the path of the healer is open to anyone willing to endure the walk."

"And you can heal anything?"

"To a point, yes."

Derek listened, fascinated. "My sister, Sarah, hurt her neck. Could you heal her?"

Father Ferrum looked up from his work. "What happened?"

The image of Liza dying flashed through Derek's mind. His

chest tightened. "A yakarii choked her until she blacked out, but she came to when the canoe flipped."

"Let me see."

Derek motioned for Sarah to step closer, but his sister shook her head and backed away. Niles grunted. "Poor girl's not interested, Ferrum. After seeing Dani getting healed, who can blame her?"

Father Ferrum looked for Sarah, now edging into the shadows. "Are you going to be alright, girl?"

Sarah shook her head vigorously and stepped behind Niles. "I'm fine." Her voice was scratched and raw.

Derek shrugged and watched Dani probe the pink flesh of her belly. Suddenly, a thought came to him and was out of his mouth before he could stop it. "Father Ferrum, could you bring the dead back to life?"

Ferrum's round face fell into a frown. "We don't talk about that, boy. Magic can do almost anything for those willing to pay the price, but to use the Lord of the Forge's gifts in such a way would be an abomination. Let the dead be dead. They have earned their rest. Do not wake them from their slumber."

Derek bit his lip. "But it's possible?"

The priest finished stitching the hole in his belly and cut the thread with scissors from his kit. "Aren't you listening? Don't even think about going down that path. There are all kinds of magic users in the realms, boy, and they all pay a price for what they do. Priests trade pain for healing. Mystics devote their lives to meditation and training. Druids make deals with nature. The Forge only knows what wizards do..."

"You don't want to know," Pavaraci Moonfist said with a wry smile. "But the priest is right. Forget about raising the dead, Master Fulstarter. That path is too dark."

"But —"

"But nothing, boy!" the priest roared. "Think about what you've already seen tonight. What do you think it would cost to bring back the dead?"

Derek's scalp tingled. "I don't care what the price is. Do you know what I've lost tonight?" His voice rose and threatened to crack. "My sister was murdered in front of me. I watched my parents drown. I talked to my best friend just before the flood got him." Derek clenched his fists. "What about the price I've paid? Isn't that worth anything?"

"Derek," Dani called. "Breathe." She was kneeling on the floor, one hand over her freshly healed belly. Wendy the Ogress loomed behind her like a protective mother ox. "Please, Derek," Dani said. "We need you to keep calm."

He took several slow breaths. New, pink flesh peeked between Dani's fingers where the spear had gutted her. Derek swore silently. He wouldn't fail Dani, not again. He turned to face Father Ferrum.

"I'm fine. I'm fine," he muttered.

"Boy," Father Ferrum said, standing slowly, "You've suffered tonight, no one will argue with you there, but do you think you're the only one who has lost family and friends in this flood?"

Derek's chest tightened. "We've all paid our price. Now how about some magic to get revenge on whoever killed my parents?"

Father Ferrum opened his mouth to reply, but Niles cut him off with a grunt. "Funny you should say that. You saw the wizards out there?"

"Of course."

"And their elementals tearing down the foundries?"

"Who could miss them?"

"Well, the Seven and I were on our way to have a little talk with our black-robed friends."

"You were?"

Niles nodded. "Why do you think we were down here? We could see the wizards' magic all the way from the Ranger Outpost. Do you really think we would sit by and watch them destroy Zuid Horn?"

Derek looked around. "Speaking of the Seven, where are Manny and Almun?"

"Oh, they're around. They'll find us later. Don't worry about that."

Dani worked herself to her knees. Conrad moved to help her stand, but Dani waved him off. "I've got it," she said to her brother. Then, to Niles, she said, "But it doesn't make any sense. I thought the wizards were supposed to protect Zuid Horn. Why would Gilgameth Tuft betray us now?"

Niles shook his head. "That, my friends, is exactly what we are going to find out."

"Do you have any ideas about why this happened?" Dani asked.

Niles shook his head. "None at all."

A booming explosion came from outside as another foundry collapsed. A rush of water slammed against the building. The fire elementals roared, and the serpentine water elementals hissed.

When the booming and the roaring and the hissing quieted down, Derek muttered, "Why are the wizards even here in the first place?"

Pavaraci Moonfist cleared his throat. "Wizards throughout the realm are assigned cities to overlook. They control the use of magic in the realms, keep rogue wizards under control, and generally help keep the peace — even the Black Robes, like our friend here in Zuid Horn, Gilgameth Tuft. In return, each city collects a small tax to pay the wizards."

"Sounds like extortion," Conrad muttered.

"Maybe," Pavaraci conceded, "but it is a system that has been in place for centuries. And except for a few, very rare cases, wizards have never turned on the cities they were assigned to defend. And so, regarding tonight, an important question remains unanswered."

Derek let out a slow breath. "Why would Zuid Horn's wizards destroy something that was bringing them profit?"

"Exactly," Pavaraci said.

A disgusted snort came from the back of the room. "Why does anyone break a vow? For the promise of even more profit."

Light footfalls announced the arrival of a hooded man. He pulled his hood back to reveal a lean face crowned with thick black

hair, dark eyes, and an unshaven chin. His arms were bare beneath sleeveless, leather armor. Spidery, white scars crisscrossed his skin. A brace of throwing daggers accompanied several pouches hanging from a belt about his waist.

Pavaraci sighed, "I doubt it is as simple as that, Kassar. Master Tuft isn't motivated by money."

"Power, then? Of the thirteen major foundries in Zuid Horn, only four still stand."

Niles Crowing rubbed his mustache. "You're suggesting that Tuft is angling for influence with the surviving foundry families?"

"What else could it be?" Kassar the Swift crossed his arms over his chest. "Profit and power. What other factors drive the world?"

Derek shook his head in disgust. All this destruction, all this death, just so someone could turn a profit? Da was right. Wizards were scoundrels, no matter how powerful they were.

Father Ferrum interrupted Derek's thoughts with a grunt. "A wonderful view of humanity from a thief."

"I speak what I see."

"Maybe," Niles replied. He walked over to a desk against the wall of the attic. Stacks of books, an ink pot, and a goose-feather quill adorned the desk, along with a wine bottle and a bowl. Niles picked up the bowl and sniffed. "Grilled eel and rice," he said. "Still warm." He held up the bowl. "You kids want some?"

Derek's stomach grumbled, but he wasn't going to have any unless Dani wanted some. "Dani?" Derek asked.

She shook her head. "It's all yours, Niles."

Derek sighed and watched the tall man walk around the desk. Niles lifted his chin at the weathered street thief. "Kassar, check the rest of the attic to see if we are alone up here." He sat down at the desk and helped himself to the bowl of eel. Kassar disappeared back into the shadows.

Wendy looked around. "Speaking of being alone, where are Lars and Jenkins?"

Conrad shook his head. "We haven't seen them yet. I was with them earlier tonight, before the flooding. They were heading over to the Warehouse District."

Wendy grunted. "I'm sure they'll show up."

Conrad nodded. "I hope so."

"Don't worry," Wendy said. "We'll find them, one way or another."

Derek growled, his frustration growing again. "I don't care about Lars and Jenkins. They can't help us right now. The wizards who killed my family are out there. Why can't we go get them?"

Niles drummed his fingers on the desk. "Let's not give up on your parents yet. There is a chance they survived."

Derek felt like a thick, wet blanket had been draped over his shoulders. A fever was growing in him, and it broke out in a cold sweat on his forehead. "Maybe."

Niles got up and grabbed Derek by the shoulder. "Hey, look at me."

Derek glanced at Niles from under heavy brows. "What?"

"You're tired, you're wounded, and you're probably infected from swimming in that water. Here, eat this." Niles handed Derek the rest of the grilled eel and rice, and then motioned for the healer. "Father Ferrum, come over here and heal this boy. He's just about to fall over."

The priest came over and inspected Derek. He took out some ointment, smeared it over Derek's wounds, stitched up the worst of them, and gave him a tonic to drink. When Father Ferrum was done, Niles pulled Derek aside and said, "Look, we don't know where your parents are. We don't know they are dead, just that they are missing. Right now, there is nothing we can do for them, right?"

Derek nodded numbly. "Right."

"Once the water goes down," Niles continued, "we can organize a search, okay? But right now, you've got to make a choice. Do you need to rest here with Wendy and your sister, or do you want to come with me to discover why the wizards would betray Zuid Horn?"

Derek looked at his sister, who was nestled under Wendy's thick arm. "Sarah can stay here?"

"Of course," Niles said.

"Will she be safe?"

Wendy grunted and flexed her ham-sized fists. "What do you think?"

Derek managed a tired smile. "No, I mean, is the building safe? It seems like every other house is coming down with the water."

"The worst of the flood is over, boy," Kassar the Swift said, reappearing from the shadows next to a support beam. "If this warehouse was going to come down, it would have come down already."

Derek sighed and looked at Conrad. "How are you doing? Do you need to sleep?"

"Yeah," Conrad said and scratched at the scar on his forearm. "I'm tired and feel like I'm going to throw up, but there's no way I can sleep yet."

"Me, too," Derek agreed. He turned to Dani.

"How about you? You just got healed up."

"I'm exhausted," she admitted, "but I can't sleep either. I'm coming with you."

Derek rolled out his neck and turned to Niles.

"Alright, so what do you have in mind?" Niles smiled. He got up from the desk and started across the attic. He waved Derek, Conrad, and Dani along. "Come on. I want to show you something."

The children followed the lanky swordsman over the dusty floor, with Kassar and Pavaraci falling in behind them. Derek studied the patterns of the flickering light and scowled at the dusty cobwebs lining the ceiling between the rafters. Niles walked to the end of the attic, to the door they had originally come through, and pointed at the burning foundries. "Look."

Derek and his friends looked out the double doors. From the second story of the warehouse, they had a good view of Zuid Horn. Tall, black iron walls encircled the city, with ornate spires reaching into the dark night. Here and there, the bulky estates of foundry owners rose above the one- and two-story hovels of the city's working and artisan classes. And in the middle, at the heart of the city, the flaming ruins of Zuid Horn's famous foundries still blazed under billowing clouds of inky smoke. The scent of ash and burning charcoal filled the air.

Giant fire elementals of flame and pitch straddled a nearby foundry. They raised balled-up fists and pounded the burning building, spreading fire and destruction with every blow. The resulting explosions felt like thunder bursts in Derek's chest.

He pointed at the magical creatures. "They're still here."

Niles nodded. "It means the wizards are still at it. Elementals have no life on this plane without the wizards' help."

"Plane? What does that mean?" Dani asked. Fire from the burning buildings flashed in her wide eyes.

Pavaraci Moonfist moved closer and pulled the sleeves of his wizard's robes back a bit. "Allow me to explain. Students of magic learn that rivers of power move through many layers of existence. The world we live in, this world," Pavaraci gestured to the city outside the window, "is just one of countless planes. Another one of those planes is the Plane of Fire. Another is the Plane of Water. Those wizards controlling the fire and water monsters have created a gateway for them to enter this world and do the wizards' bidding."

"And they use their magic to control the monsters," Dani finished without taking her eyes from them.

Pavaraci nodded. "Exactly." The wizard looked at the girl who was so fascinated by the fire elementals. "You have an interest in magic?"

Dani blinked and faced the Elven wizard. "I've never thought about it before tonight. What chance would a street urchin have of becoming a wizard?"

The elf opened his mouth to respond, but Derek cut him off. "I still don't get it. Why would wizards destroy Zuid Horn?"

"I don't know," Niles said. "But we are going to find out."

"How?" Derek asked.

Niles pointed to the elementals. "The wizards have been busy all night. They are powerful, but their strength won't hold out forever. We are going to wait for them to use up the last of their magic."

"And then what?" Conrad asked.

Kassar the Swift drummed his fingers on the hilt of his dagger. "Then, children, we are going to have a little talk with our black-robed friends."

14

Derek Discovers Life at Sea

It was almost noon, and it was time for Derek to make a decision. Derek and the boys were on Ploughman's Wharf, just across the dock from *The Delivery*. They huddled behind a stack of wooden crates stamped with the black flag sigil of Belvera, a city-state hundreds of miles northwest of Zuid Horn.

Dozens of Shadizarians were all over *The Delivery*, prepping it for the voyage ahead. Human guards outfitted in sleeveless leather armor and steel-plated kilts strolled casually back and forth along the pier and across the wide deck. Four guards with khopesh swords checked the wares and papers of porters hauling goods up the gangplank and into the ship's hull. From their spot behind the crates heading to Belvera, the boys could see Awwal Bahhar, the Shadizarian first mate, chatting with merchants and ordering freight to be moved here and there. A pair of forest giants loaded goods directly from the pier onto *The Delivery*. The captain was nowhere to be seen.

The boys ducked behind the boxes. Derek leaned his forehead against the stack and took a deep breath. Despite the short rest at Conrad's place, he was exhausted. Looking at the other boys,

Derek could see they were tired as well. But even if they were tired, none of them said anything. Their resilience — even that of the ever-whining Lars — impressed Derek, suggesting that his initial impression of Dani must have been correct. There must be something special about Dani because these boys were willing to risk everything to save her.

Each of the boys had a sack to carry his personal belongings: a change of clothes, a blanket, some extra food. None of them had ever been to sea before, and after discussing things at Conrad's place, they decided traveling light would be best. Derek also had the rest of the minotaur's gold in his bag. He had never carried so much gold in his life, and although he felt nervous about bringing it on a ship, he didn't know what else to do with it. It wasn't like he could take it to his parents' house. They thought he was still in the stocks. A twinge of guilt wrenched his gut again. Being in the stocks for two days when Da needed him was bad enough. How long would he be gone now that he was going out to sea?

Conrad thumped him on the arm. "Hey, are you alright?"

Derek jerked up. "Me? Yeah."

"You looked like you're falling asleep."

"No," Derek said. "Well, maybe. I was just wishing I could let my parents know what's going on."

"Look!" Jenkins said, pointing at *The Delivery*.

Several sailors were at the moorings, getting ready to cast the Shadizarian slaver free. Awwal Bahhar was on the deck, near the top of the gangplank, barking orders to his sailors on the pier. A few sailors with ledgers stood near him, going over a stack of crates piled alongside the ship, waiting to be taken below.

"This is it," Derek said. "If we are going to save Dani, we have to leave now." He looked at each of them in turn and saw the determined set of their eyes. He nodded, again impressed at how much this girl meant to these boys who he had thought were just simple bullies. "Alright then," he said, picking up his bag and slinging it over his shoulder. "Let's go."

They ran across Ploughman's Wharf together, dodging slow-moving carts stuffed with casks of fermented cabbage and barrels of cider. Just as they circled around a ponderous hill giant with a wagonload of fresh fish over its shoulder, a hand shot out of the crowd and pulled Derek to the side.

"Hey!" Derek yelled. He whirled away from the hand but calmed down when he saw it was Niles Crowing. "Oh, it's you."

"Do you have the vial I gave you?"

Derek patted the burlap sack he was carrying. "I've got it right here."

Niles shook his head. "No, not in a bag. Keep it on you, so you know where it is."

Derek dug the vial out of the bag and tucked it into a pocket sewn inside his shirt. "Are you sure this is going to work? How will the Shadizarians not see you following us?"

"I told you," Niles said with a grin. "The Magnificent Seven and I will take care of that. You just get what we need to prove the Iron Guard is selling Zuid Hornians into slavery. Get that, dump the vial, and we will take care of the rest. And remember, don't dump the vial into sea water until you have the evidence we need. If the Shadizarians even suspect we are onto them, they will destroy everything."

The thought of boarding a Shadizarian slaver made Derek shake a little, although he would never admit it to Conrad. "Okay," he said to Niles.

"Hey," Niles said. "Look at me."

Derek lifted his gaze. Despite Niles' gruff appearance and the reputation he seemed to have among the rangers, his eyes were kind and understanding.

"I know you're scared," the swashbuckler said. "I would be too, but what you're doing is going to help a lot of people. Doing what's right, especially when you're scared, is what being brave is all about."

Derek nodded, but his throat was too tight to speak.

"Oh, and don't let the Shadizarians know you've met me," Niles said. "Don't even mention the Magnificent Seven. They've run into us before."

"They have?" Derek asked, immediately feeling his spirits lift, though he wasn't sure why. "What happened?"

"Not now," Niles said, turning Derek around and pushing him toward *The Delivery*, where the gangplank was being drawn up from the dock. "I'll tell you that story after all of this is wrapped up. Now go! Don't keep them waiting. Good luck!"

"Thank you, Niles!" Derek took a step away, but then he stopped. "Niles, could you say something to my parents, please? They're going to be worried."

Niles nodded. "I will. Now, go!"

Derek turned to go and then stopped again. "Wait," he said, digging out the minotaur's gold. "Could you give this to Da? He can use it to hire some help with that order for the Ranger Outpost."

Niles took the bag of gold and tucked it into his belt. "Where'd you get this?"

"I stole it from some minotaurs."

Niles raised his eyebrows. "Minotaurs, eh? That's what your friend was mumbling about last night. You are your father's son, aren't you?"

Derek did his best to smile, though he had no idea why so many people seemed to have the wrong idea about who his father was. He turned and hurried toward the Shadizarian slave ship. Conrad and the others scrambled to keep up with Derek's long strides. Derek waved his free arm overhead as he yelled at *The Delivery*.

"Wait! Wait for me!"

Awwal Bahhar looked up from a ledger. He squinted down from the deck of *The Delivery* and held up a hand against the noonday sun. When he saw it was Derek and the boys, he ordered the gangplank back down to the pier. Once it was set, Awwal called Derek and the others aboard.

"So," he said as the boys huffed for breath with their bags over their shoulders, "you decided to join us."

"Yes, sir. We did," Derek said. "We're ready for an adventure."

The Shadizarian nodded his approval and then turned to the sailors checking inventory next to him. "See? I told you the boy would return. Maybe now we will have a decent cook."

The other sailors laughed and went on inspecting their merchandise. The first mate looked at Conrad and the others. "And you've brought your friends."

Derek's gut flipped. Hadn't the first mate offered them all jobs? He was too tired to remember. If Conrad and the others couldn't get aboard, he would have to rescue Dani by himself. Derek had to think quickly. "Yes, sir. They were wondering if you had room for them, too."

Awwal Bahhar smirked at a nearby sailor. "We'll find room for them. Come," he said, waving the boys onto the ship. "Bring your things. We'll get you settled in and to your stations before we leave the harbor."

Derek breathed a sigh of relief. The boys were turning to follow the first mate when a shadow drew Derek's attention back to the gangplank, where a short man in a worn, blue cloak draped over a long-sleeved, tan shirt and thin, canvas pants scurried onto the ship. He was a Shadizarian, Derek saw, for his eyes were painted with the black eyeliner Shadizarians favored. His straight, black hair was long on top but shaved almost to the skull on the sides and back, revealing a scalp infested with well-picked, red sores that oozed a clear pus. The man glanced briefly at Derek and then went directly to the first mate, who shook his hand.

"Ah, Ahriman," Awwal Bahhar said. "You're back."

Ahriman said nothing but gestured for Awwal to come close, which he did. Ahriman whispered into the first mate's ear, and every now and then he gave Derek a quick look. Derek tried not to squirm. Why did Ahriman keep glancing at him?

When Ahriman was finished with his whispering, Awwal said, "I see. Well, we can talk more later. For now, why don't you get yourself something to eat? I need to get these boys settled in." Ahriman bowed to the first mate and then rushed away.

Awwal Bahhar took Derek and the others not to the stairs that Derek had previously gone down, but to another set on the opposite side of the ship. "It turns out," he said over his shoulder, "that we need some strong, young hands like you boys. I will talk to the captain, but I don't see why we wouldn't hire the rest of you on. You're friends of Derek's, after all." He started down the stairs, moving to the side to allow some sailors lugging a cask of water onto the upper deck. The first mate came to the bottom of the stairs and kept going down a musty hallway at a quick clip. "Since you boys all know one another," he said over his shoulder, "would you mind bunking together? We've got a few open hammocks back here."

He brought them to a place where the hallway widened a bit. Several hammocks were slung along the hallway, with chests built into the walls behind the hammocks. Awwal showed the boys how to use the tiny chests to store their scant personal belongings. "I'll need to check with the captain just to make sure we can hire you, but I'm going to take you to your jobs so we can get going." Awwal was away without another word.

The first mate led the boys down the hallway, grabbed a lantern, and then led them down another stairwell which opened into a dark passage leading to the back of the ship. Awwal adjusted the wick of his lantern and then hurried off. His lantern rocked back and forth, splashing drunken shadows on the walls. Derek bustled to catch up to the first mate before he could hurry away again. "Sir? Excuse me."

Awwal Bahhar half-glanced over his shoulder but did not break his stride. "Yes?"

"I know I will be working in the galley, but what will my friends be doing?"

"*The Delivery* needs nimble hands all over the ship once we are at sea. We need boys who can climb the rigging to set sails, repair ties, swab decks, move cargo, and kill rats. In fact," Awwal said, looking at Conrad, "I'll put you to work in the hold. We've had more rats than a man can count since the last time we were in Bearton. Nasty, black things. They killed off our cats, and the captain won't let us have rat terriers onboard. What do you say? You up for a little rat hunting?"

Conrad nodded enthusiastically. "Yes, sir!"

"Good. Ah, here you are." Awwal came to stop before a stout wooden door. He took out a key and opened a door that led to a dark stairwell. "What did you say your name was?"

"Conrad, sir."

"Alright, Conrad. You'll find a cudgel hanging on a hook at the bottom of the stairs. Use that to kill the rats when you see them. I think there's a lantern at the bottom of the stairs as well."

"Yes, sir. Thank you for taking us on, sir."

Awwal smiled as he watched Conrad hurry down the stairs. "No need to thank me. You're doing us a favor."

Derek watched the first mate close the door. For an instant, Derek could have sworn the inside of the door was shredded with scratch marks, but Awwal closed the door so quickly it was hard to say what Derek saw. Awwal locked the door and then turned to face Derek.

Awwal must have noticed the shocked look on Derek's face because he said, "I must lock the door. Otherwise, the crew will sneak into the hold and take what they like. Have you ever tried to control a crew after they've had their fill of Tyrsis mead?" Awwal shook his head. "Impossible."

"Yes, sir," Derek said. He could understand the logic of locking the hold, but what about those scratches? And how was Conrad going to find a lantern in the dark?

"Now for you two," Awwal Bahhar said, looking at Jenkins and Lars. "I don't have much for you right now, and I really must get to the captain. Do you boys mind doing a bit of rowing to help get us out of port?"

"No, sir," Jenkins said. "But I've never done any rowing before."

"Me either," said Lars. "Don't worry about it," the first mate said, waving his hand. "You'll pick it up in no time."

Awwal led them back onto the main deck. Sailors were bustling about, shouting to one another as *The Delivery* pulled away from Ploughman's Wharf. The oars were out now, bristling above the railings like twin ridges of spines. Several men were in the masts, barking orders from on high. Two forest giants hauled *The Delivery* into open water. Their pace was slow but steady.

Derek hurried along behind Awwal but veered a bit so he would be closer to the railing. By going up on his toes, he could see Niles next to a mound of fishing nets back on the pier. Derek wanted to wave, to let Niles know he saw him, but just in time he remembered Niles' warning. Niles seemed to understand, as he touched two fingers to his temple in a loose salute.

"Are you coming?" Awwal called.

"Yes, sir!" Derek shouted and hurried over to the steep stairwell where the others were waiting. He looked back for Niles one last time, but the lanky swashbuckler was gone.

Awwal eyed Derek suspiciously. "You're not having second thoughts, are you?"

"No, sir," Derek said. "I just wanted to see Zuid Horn from the harbor. I've never been off the pier before."

"Oh, you'll get to see plenty of cities from afar with us," Awwal said. "I promise you that."

He led the three boys down the stairs to the rowing deck. Again, the stink of ammonia and unwashed bodies assaulted Derek's nose. His stomach lurched into his throat, and he put his hand over his mouth.

Awwal laughed. "You'll get used to the smell of hard work. Soon, you won't even notice it." He looked over the benches filled with slaves chained to their seats. Pulling Lars and Jenkins before him, Awwal said, "Alright, boys, this is going to sound strange, but I'm hoping you understand when I explain it to you."

Lars and Jenkins nodded, their eyes on the rowing deck. The boys were behind the chained slaves, most of whom were shirtless. White and red scars like thick, wriggling worms crisscrossed the slaves' backs.

"The slaves are a rough bunch," Awwal said. "I feel bad putting young boys like you next to them, but I don't have any other jobs for you right now, and if we want the captain to take you on, he needs to know you are willing to work. Do you understand?"

Lars and Jenkins nodded again, but their faces were starting to show the seeds of doubt.

"Good," Awwal went on. "Now, to make things a little easier on you, we're going to have to trick the slaves a little bit. Can you do that for me?" Again, the boys nodded. Awwal continued, "Okay, if there is one thing slaves hate, it's a free man. If this lot thinks you boys are getting paid for doing the same work they are forced to do, things could get rough for you down here. We need to make them think you are slaves. Understand?"

"Yes, sir," said Lars.

"What we are going to do is I'm going to haul you in there and treat you like slaves in front of all of them. I'm going to chain you up, so they will really believe it. Okay?"

"Chain us up, sir?" Jenkins asked.

"You want them to think you're slaves, don't you?"

"Well..." Jenkins started. The boy looked at Derek, the color of his face draining away as Derek watched. Then he looked over the slaves, and Derek looked with him. Just then, Dani turned in her bench and stared with wide eyes at the boys. Jenkins stood stock still, his gaze locked with Dani's. "I'll do it," he said without looking away from Dani. "Lock me up."

"Me too," said Lars, who was also looking at Dani.

Awwal smiled. "Good boys. This will work better for you in the end. I'll come for you first chance I get, right after I talk to the captain. Alright?"

The boys said nothing. Fear gnawed at Derek's innards. He looked at Dani, who was still twisted in her seat toward the front of the rowing deck. The short bristles of her shaven head glistened with sweat. Even from across the room, he could see that one of her eyes was swollen shut. The other one, dark and haunted, found him. She opened her mouth to speak, but Derek made a slight movement with his eyebrows telling her to stay quiet. Her shoulders slumped, and she turned around. Derek glanced quickly at Jenkins and Lars. They were watching Dani.

Jenkins steeled his jaw. "Yes, sir," he said to Awwal. "We can do this."

"Good," the Shadizarian said, patting the boys on the back. "Let's go."

He led them through the rows of slaves, shoving them aside where he needed to, stepping over benches and cursing the whole way. "Row master!" he called out, and a huge Shadizarian in a tight, red vest emerged from the shadows.

Cords of muscles rippled under the man's bronze hide. His bald head glistened with beads of sweat. He pushed his way through the slaves, delivering stinging whacks with the handle of his whip as he went. When he made it to Awwal and the boys, he crossed his arms over his broad chest and studied the boys. "What's this?"

Awwal pushed Lars and Jenkins forward. "I got a couple more rowers for you. Just got them off the docks. Where do you want them?"

The row master looked at the boys and scowled. "I need strong arms down here, not more of these worthless scarecrows you keep sending me. How do you expect me to get *The Delivery* back to Shadizar? On the backs of miserable louts like this? I'll be dead before they get us home."

Awwal laughed. "Don't you worry. These boys are stronger than they look."

"They'd better be," the row master said with a grunt, "or I'll bleed them." He wheeled around and in one movement uncoiled his whip and lashed it across a slave's back.

The thin man's shirt split open with a crack that sent a bolt of lightning down Derek's spine. He watched in horror as a wide, red smear trickled down the man's back. The other slaves gasped and quickly ducked their heads.

Awwal nodded. "Not bad. So, where do you want these two?"

The row master growled and pushed his way through the slaves, toward the front of the rowing deck. "What do I care? Put them there," he said, pointing to a pair of open seats a few rows behind Dani. "If they don't work, they'll bleed."

"You've made that perfectly clear." Awwal pushed Lars and Jenkins toward the open seats. When they arrived, he grabbed Lars by the arm. "Get over here, whelp." He shoved Lars onto a bench and shackled his wrists and ankles. He pointed at Jenkins and then to the other open spot. "You sit there."

Jenkins sat down and allowed Awwal to lock the manacles around his wrists and ankles. "Once we are at sea, I expect you boys to do the work of two men," Awwal said loudly. "No resting, or it's the whipping post for you." He pointed to Derek. "Come on, you. To the galley."

Derek followed Awwal over the benches to the bow side of the ship. He looked over his shoulder to see Dani, Jenkins, and Lars all watching him. Doubt wriggled in his gut. How was his plan to free Dani ever going to work if they were all shackled? "Hurry up!" Awwal barked. "You have work to do."

Derek hopped over the last few benches to keep up. "Yes, sir," he said. Then, with a last look over his shoulder, he left his friends chained to their oars and followed Awwal Bahhar up the stairs and toward the galley.

Derek could smell and hear the galley long before they got there. A stinking cloud of grilled fish and vinegar steam spilled into the stairwell. A fat, shirtless man with thick, black hairs covering his chest and back filled the kitchen, wielding a chopping knife in one hand and a dirty towel in the other. Rivulets of sweat dribbled over the rolls of fat on his body and dripped into the bubbling soup.

"By the gods," he swore when he saw Awwal holding his nose by the doorway, "I told you I need help feeding this measly lot. When are you going to get me a slave?"

Awwal laughed. "Watch your tongue, or I'll cut it out and feed it to the captain. I've kept my word." He reached behind his back and pulled Derek before him. "Here is your help, Saehrimnir, you greasy goat."

Saehrimnir stood with fists on his wide hips. His thin, stained breeches were stretched taut against the meaty bulk of his thighs. When he laughed, it was like a donkey braying. "Where did you pick this wretch up?"

Awwal shrugged. "He came to us last night. He's done work in a kitchen before and said he wanted to see the world."

Saehrimnir laughed again. "Won't see much of the world chained in a galley, that's for sure." The fat man tossed his knife onto the cluttered counter. Squatting with a grunt, he pushed aside a bucket near the stove and pulled out a thick chain and manacles. He snatched Derek with a sweaty paw and slapped the manacles about Derek's ankle. "There's your ticket to seeing the world," he said with a grunt as he got up, "for all the good it will do you."

Derek looked down at the manacles and then at Awwal, who shrugged. "I'll talk to the captain," the first mate said in a low voice, and then he left.

Derek watched him go. He was about to call out, to ask what was going on, but Saehrimnir thrust a turning knife into Derek's hands. "Here. Take this." Then he handed him a bucket of potatoes. "These need to be peeled and quartered before we are out of the harbor. Get to work. I'm running down to the hold to grab some more. There's a lot of rats on this ship that need feeding."

Saehrimnir squeezed past Derek, a jiggling wall of sweat and fat. Derek screwed up his face in disgust and looked at the potatoes as the portly cook thumped down the stairwell like a blob of thick gravy. A wave of despair washed over Derek. How was he ever going to get out of these chains? And how was he ever going to find evidence connecting the Iron Guard with these Shadizarian slavers? Derek sighed and started in on the potatoes. He would have to keep his eyes peeled. That's all there was to it.

15

Derek Becomes a Pawn in Bigger Game

Derek, Conrad, and Dani scurried over the slippery rooftops, doing their best to keep up with Niles Crowing and Kassar the Swift. Kassar led the way, leaping from building to building over flooded alleys. Niles Crowing wasn't far behind, his nimble footwork a testament to his reputation as an adventurer. The street wizard, Pavaraci Moonfist, hung close to Derek and the others.

"Just to keep an eye on you," he maintained, but Derek could tell the bookwormish wizard struggled to keep pace with the masters of stealth leading the way. Derek helped the thin magician when he could, but sometimes, Derek noticed, Pavaraci used a little magic to keep up.

The sky was gray in the east. Wispy fingers of light spread through the stars, pinching them out one by one. Rising above the coal black walls surrounding Zuid Horn, the towering canopy of Breechwood Forest shivered in the breeze off the ocean. This same breeze rushed over the city, taking with it great columns of black smoke pouring from the burning foundries.

Derek took stock of the city as he scrambled over the rooftops. Of the thirteen largest foundries in Zuid Horn, only four remained. And of these four, two would be little more than burned out husks before the sun rose. No matter the reason for Gilgameth Tuft and his apprentices destroying the city, Derek couldn't argue with their effectiveness. Four fire elementals straddled two of the remaining foundries, punching and tearing at the walls. Steel beams within the walls screeched in protest and drowned out the fire creatures' howling.

In order to better sneak up on the wizards, the little group of adventurers took a path that led them away from the Foundry District and then back again on the wizards' north side. They were almost in position, and Derek's heart raced with excitement. As excited as he was, Derek struggled to keep pace with Niles and Kassar. After the night's events, his limbs felt like they were weighed down with leaden chains. Conrad and Dani stumbled every now and then but bit their tongues whenever Derek asked if they needed to stop for a rest.

They had just leapt from the flat, tarred roof of a tannery to the peaked, clay-tiled roof of a charcoal distributor when Niles waved his arm at them. "Try to keep it down," he whispered. "We're as close as we can get for now."

Derek and the others crept carefully up the roof. Niles and Kassar lay prone against the tiles, their eyes just over the peak, and pointed to a rooftop ahead. "There they are," Kassar whispered.

It was hard not to see them. Three black-robed wizards—two men and a woman — were on a flat roof, their concentration upon the fire and water monsters absolute. Every now and then, Derek thought he could see the magic moving through the air, his vision wavering like a mirage on a hot road. "What do we do now?" he asked.

Pavaraci finally crawled up the last bit of roof and collapsed between Niles and Derek. "The next time we decide to do a little roof hopping," the wizard huffed, "I'm taking our flying carpet."

Niles laughed. "You do that." Then, he turned his attention back toward the three wizards controlling the elementals. "What do you think, Moonfist? Is it time?"

The wizard gave a tired sigh, wiped the sweat from his forehead, and studied the scene four rooftops away. "They are powerful," he admitted. "Stronger than me. In any other city, they would be masters of their own towers. But they are tired. See their faces?"

Derek looked at the wizards. Their leader, a lithe woman with a shaven head, barked orders to her companions, who carried out her wishes without comment. She used a language Derek didn't recognize, her voice scratchy and hoarse. Heavy rings darkened her eyes, and the skin of her face sagged from her bones.

The male wizards wore their hair straight, long, braided, and black. That much would have let them pass for any other Zuid Hornian. But their pale complexion, so thin Derek could see spider-like veins running under the surface of the skin, spoke to the years they spent confined in the Gilgameth Tuft's Tower of Sorcery.

"Gross," Derek whispered. "They're paler than spider bellies."

Pavaraci grunted. "That's the way with all who study dark magic. They pour themselves into their studies, to the detriment of their humanity. Eventually, they lose themselves and are little more than hollow shells for funneling magic between planes."

Dani and Derek exchanged glances. Derek frowned. "Remind me not to take up magic."

Pavaraci twisted so he was on his side, facing Derek and Dani. "Not all who study magic become twisted." He held up his arm so his brown sleeve dangled in the air between them. "Look at me. I've been studying magic for almost three decades. My robes are brown."

"Poor logic," Kassar the Swift whispered. "Your fashion sense borders on tragic."

"Enough," Niles hissed. "We are here to talk to wizards, not discuss clothing." He shook his head. "How long do we have, Moonfist?"

Pavaraci flipped onto his belly again and studied the scene. "Soon," he said. "Summon the others."

Niles slid down the roof away from the wizards. The swordsman pulled a long strip of canvas from his belt and what looked like a silver pebble from his pouch. Niles slipped the pebble into the makeshift sling and twirled it rapidly around his head. A high-pitched whistling filled the air until Niles released one end of the strip and sent the pebble sailing over the city. The pellet soared into the sky. Suddenly, a white flash pulsed bright and hot. Then, it vanished.

Niles scampered up the roof and lay next to the group again. "Any time now," he said.

They lay low on the roof and watched in silence. Dawn was coming. The stars were gone, and the sky glowed like a warm fire. Derek stretched his neck and listened to the floodwater gurgling past. On the buildings across the way, the dark, high watermark from the night's flood was several hands above the water's current level. The floodwater was receding.

What would be left after the waters were gone? Liza was dead. Derek's parents were gone. His best friend, Peter, was dead. The yakariian slavers had Augie and his parents. What could possibly be left after the waters dried up?

Derek dropped his head onto his arms and closed his eyes. He felt a tiny hand, Dani's hand, on his back. "You okay?" she asked.

"Me? I'm fine," Derek said, a little too bitterly. "Why wouldn't I be? Almost everyone I love is dead." The back of Derek's scalp tingled. "I'm just fine."

Dani rubbed his back lightly. "None of that was your fault, Derek."

"I didn't say it was," he said, his voice rising. Pavaraci shushed him, and Derek lowered his voice. "But I had chances to save them all, and I failed every time. Some hero I turned out to be."

"You did your best."

"Yeah, and how did that work out for you? My 'best' got you a spear through the gut. If we wouldn't have found Father Ferrum, you would have died."

Dani nudged closer to Derek and ran her fingers through his hair, right where his scalp was tingling. "Yeah, well, you found Ferrum, and I'm not dead. You saved me. Again."

Something relaxed in Derek's chest. It was warm and tickly should have been wrong in light of everything that had happened on this night, but somehow, it felt right. And, just as amazing, the tingling in his scalp was gone. Derek rubbed his eyes in the crook of his elbow and then turned to look at Dani lying on the banked rooftop next to him.

They were close, so close that it almost looked like there were two Danis next to him — one in the sky and one on the ground. They were both beautiful, he realized in the morning light, with their short, dark curls and eyes that saw through his fumbling, angry shell. But the one in the sky, the image of Dani that floated just out of his reach, was lighter, freer, and Derek realized, happier. He blinked and moved back a bit so the two images merged, and both Danis came together again next to Derek on the roof.

And then a thought burst out of him so quickly that it had to be the truth, "You're the best thing that's ever happened to me."

Dani smiled. "You've got a lot of life left to live."

"I'm trying to be serious."

"I know."

"By The Hammer," Conrad complained from Dani's other side. "I'm going to throw up."

"And you all need to keep it down," Pavaraci hissed. "We're hunting wizards here, not finding dates for the Coming of Age Ball."

"Sorry," Dani whispered to the elven wizard. Then, to Derek, she said, "We'll get through this. You'll see." She scratched little circles on his back. "Rest."

Derek sighed. It seemed like he had just closed his eyes when Dani shook him. "Derek, someone is coming."

Derek propped himself up and rubbed his face. The sun was over the eastern horizon. Had he nodded off? The fire and water elementals were gone, and the wizards a few roofs over were speaking quietly amongst themselves and pointing to the ruined foundries. Derek couldn't hear what they were saying. Pavaraci Moonfist lay to his left, Dani to his right, with Conrad on his sister's other side. A sloshing came from the waterway next to their building. Derek pulled himself away from the crest of the roof and crept over to the street side to peer down.

Below him, Father Ferrum poled a long, narrow boat toward the three black-robed wizards. A pile of chain mail armor lay folded neatly on a seat in front of him. Next to it sat a sturdy mace with an ironwood shaft and a round shield of ironwood, thick leather, and steel. The priest's robes were emblazoned on front and back with an embroidered anvil and hammer, encircled with rays of white and gold. Ferrum was a priest of the Forge, the holy deity that blessed Zuid Horn with the realm's strongest steelworks — outside of the Mountain King's forges, of course. He was singing a hymn, and when he was close enough, the three wizards stopped talking and watched him approach.

"Father Ferrum!" Derek whispered to Pavaraci Moonfist.

"Late, as always," Pavaraci said, keeping his eyes on the wizards.

"Where are the others?"

Pavaraci rolled his eyes. "Quiet now. You'll see soon enough. Now watch!"

The priest waved at the three wizards in black. "Hello! I am Father Ferrum, priest of the Forge. I am looking for survivors in need of aid. Are you alright, friends?" Ferrum poled his boat to rest against a building across the wide, flooded street from the wizards. He placed the long pole in his boat and held onto the building with one hand to keep the current from taking him away. "Is there anything I can do for you?"

The wizards in black moved to the edge of the flat roof like smoke drifting over a burning field. They stood with their hands folded in their sleeves and looked down on the solitary priest. "We don't need your help, priest," the woman said. "Move along."

Father Ferrum studied the smoldering buildings. He didn't move. "A lot of destruction here. It's a pity, all these foundries gone. Well, all except the Bering and Stoates foundries." He pointed to the two surviving foundries. "I wonder if the other foundries will be able to rebuild after the flood..." He looked directly at the wizards. "And the fire."

"There are many in need of your assistance," said the man on the left. "I hear the people living by the wharf were hit particularly hard. Perhaps you should go where you are needed."

"I could," the priest agreed, running his fingers over the rim of his shield, "but then I might miss discovering how the heart of Zuid Horn's steel production was destroyed in a single night. Everything gone, save two foundries. Think about it," Ferrum said, leaning forward a bit to play with the handle of his mace. "Six months ago, Zuid Horn won contracts to outfit Shadizar's King Folio and his son-in-law, Lord Valis, in their war against one another. The contracts were divided between the thirteen major foundries in Zuid Horn." The priest paused and let his heavy gaze fall upon the wizards. "Until tonight."

The wizards scowled. "Watch your tongue, priest," the woman said, "before it gets you in trouble."

Ferrum shrugged. "I am but the voice of a people crying out in need. As a servant of the Lord of the Forge, I feel a need to understand why the city's foundries, which provide a living for thousands of people, were destroyed tonight. All the foundries, that is, except two — two which stand to profit greatly from the suffering of their competitors. From my limited understanding of the greater working of things, it certainly seems suspicious."

"You are correct on one point, priest," the wizard on the left said. "Your understanding is limited in many areas."

Derek sucked his breath between his teeth. Was what Father Ferrum implying true? Both Dani and Conrad leaned closer to hear better.

Ferrum held his mace at arm's length and studied its craftsmanship. "Of that, I have no doubt. But as a priest of the Forge, I do understand the role the foundries play in Zuid Horn's livelihood. The foundries were gifts of old from His Holy Hammer.

Who would be willing to destroy them, especially for something so base as war profiteering?"

The woman's scowl darkened under her pale visage. "What are you trying to say, priest?"

Ferrum stood in his boat and pointed his mace at the three wizards. The friendly countenance of his face was gone, replaced with a steely gaze. "I'm looking for an answer, witch, so be straight with me, or I'll be the death of you. Why did the wizards destroy Zuid Horn and its foundries? Are you in league with the Bering and Stoates clans?" He gestured with his mace to the destruction all around him. "Is this your sad plan to line your pockets with a few coins? Tell me, witch, since when have wizards stooped so low?" The woman screeched and tore the sleeves off her robes, revealing lank arms covered with spidery tattoos. "Witch? You pompous fool! Your words betray your ignorance and your arrogance — fatal flaws that today spell your doom!" She raised her hands in the air, her fingers outstretched until the tendons flexed like tree roots. An emerald light danced between her palms and formed a shimmering orb. She screamed a curse at Ferrum and hurled the flaming, green sphere across the water at him.

Watching from four rooftops away, Derek gasped. "We have to help him!"

Pavaraci waved him off. "Hold on, Derek. Not just yet."

But Derek noticed that the brown-robed wizard had produced a gnarled stick from the folds of his robe. Derek turned his attention back to the battling priest and wizards.

Ferrum stood firm in his boat, his iron-shod boots wide against the sides. He lifted his mace over his head, and as soon as the flaming sphere reached him, the priest of the Forge swatted it away like spiderwebs. The boat rocked gently under Father Ferrum. He laughed derisively. "Is that all you have, witch? You're tired and weak from your night's devilry. Now, let me show you what the Lord of the Forge provides for his servants!" Ferrum spread his arms wide and chanted in the deep,

song-like manner all Zuid Hornian blacksmiths used to keep time at the bellows. A rich blue glow pulsed from the hammer-shaped amulet around his neck, and the priest of the Forge rose into the air. As he passed the rooftops, he lifted his free hand, and a great, glowing hammer appeared in the air next to him. Ferrum swung in a powerful arc, and the magical hammer flew at the wizards. They threw up their hands, hastily erecting magical barriers, but the hammer smashed through their defensive spells like stone through glass and exploded in a white flash in front of the wizards. All three wizards crumpled to the ground.

Derek lifted an arm to shield his eyes from the light. He felt Pavaraci moving quickly beside him. Roof tiles broke under the wizard's feet and clattered down to plink loudly into the flooded street behind them. Once the light died and Derek could look again, he saw Pavaraci was already bounding to the next rooftop with impossibly powerful leaps. Derek couldn't believe what he was seeing, but it looked like Pavaraci was clearing the length of an entire rooftop with each jump.

"Magic?" Conrad whispered.

"Of course," Derek replied. "Come on. Let's get closer."

Dani's eyes were wide. "Let's!"

Without another word, Derek, Conrad, and Dani crept closer to the battle. Derek paused and searched the sky for Father Ferrum. The priest had floated down and was about to land on the wizards' roof. The wizards scrambled to their feet in a tangle of robes.

Just ahead of Derek, Pavaraci Moonfist took one last leap and landed lightly behind the black-robed wizards. They whirled at the sound of gravel crunching under Pavaraci's boots. When they saw who it was, the woman sneered.

"Moonfist. I thought I recognized the priest." She cast a glance over her shoulder at Father Ferrum, who had touched down on the roof and stood with his mace held high, battle ready. "But now I see this for what it is." She and her two compatriots crouched and spread their hands. Magic crackled and sparked between their fingers. "Where are the rest of the Magnificent Seven? Is that hack, Niles Crowing, with you, or are you just out doing his bidding?"

At her word, several figures pulled themselves onto the rooftop. Leading the way was a powerfully built northerner with flaming red hair braided in a coil down his back. His fiery beard was thick and full, spilling over a battered leather chest-plate. He wore blue steel greaves on his legs and similarly fashioned bracers on his forearms.

"Father Ferrum," the northerner called. "How rude of you to host a party and forget to invite your friends." He drew two razor-sharp hatchets from his belt and twirled them with expert precision. "I would have brought something for the gathering, had I known. Maybe one of those little cheese plates you favor from Ploughman's Wharf?"

The priest laughed. "Manny Haccian, you old gladiator. Just in time to help me question these rats." Ferrum held out his left arm. "*Tornare!*" There was a thrumming pulse and a flash of light as Ferrum's shield flew from his canoe, through the air, and onto his arm. He clanged his mace and shield together, the steel glowing light blue in the morning sun.

"Wow," Dani muttered and sat up to see better.

Derek grabbed her arm and pulled her down next to him. "Stay down," he hissed. "This is over our heads."

Dani dropped to the rooftop next to Derek. "Isn't it amazing?"

Derek shrugged and refocused on the nearby rooftop. The northerner, Manny Haccian, rubbed his thumbs over the shafts of his hatchets. The blades sizzled with red flames. "Let's find out what these miserable rats know," he growled. "This will be fun. I've never cared much for wizards. No offense, Pavaraci."

"None taken," the brown-robed wizard replied, moving in a slow circle around the woman and the two men. "I'm also curious to learn what my magical brethren have been up to tonight."

The black-robed wizards crouched in a tight circle, facing outwards. Magical barriers rose and shimmered around them, but just as soon as the spells of protection went up, Pavaraci Moonfist and Father Ferrum brought them down.

"You're tired," Pavaraci observed. "Not much magic left in you after tonight, is there?"

"I'm warning you, Moonfist," the woman hissed, "you'll pay for this when my master learns what you've done." She twisted a ring on her finger, and an iridescent shell sprang up around the black-robed woman and her companions.

Pavaraci Moonfist muttered quietly and rippled his fingers. The magical shell fell. "I don't doubt you there, but I suspect the Council of Nine will want to know why wizards are involving themselves with the destruction of a city they were sworn to protect."

"We don't have to answer to the likes of you," one of the men barked.

"We'll see about that," Haccian growled, moving several steps closer.

Two more light thumps on the rooftop announced the arrival of Niles Crowing and a lean Shadizarian. The Shadizarian kept his head neatly shaved but allowed himself the indulgence of a neatly trimmed, perfect black beard. His face was deeply tanned and lined from years under the sun, and he carried a long, slim lance loosely over one shoulder.

"Well, Niles," the man said, his Shadizarian accent thick on his tongue. "It looks like we are the last to arrive."

"Not quite, Almun Aqadh," Niles said, his hand upon the pommel of his keenly polished rapier. "There's one more." Then, to the red-haired northerner, whose eyes blazed with battle lust, he said, "Hold up, Haccian. There's another way."

Manny Haccian spit and growled. He flipped his hungry hatchets around in his meaty fists. "Not nearly as fun, I'll bet."

Suddenly, the black-robed woman flailed her arms in the air, hopped about, and clawed at her neck and back. "Get it off me!" she screamed. She ran in tight circles and swatted at her back like she was trying to pull something out of her robes. Her male

companions rushed to help her, but they were clearly as confused as she was.

Haccian watched the woman hop about and lowered his hatchets. "Actually," he smirked, "this might be better."

Niles drew his rapier and stepped forward. "Enough! Lenny, show yourself!"

There was a small popping sound, and the tiny man with a peg leg appeared on the woman's back. He held a gleaming knife to the wizard's bare neck. "Calm yourself there, lass," the leprechaun said, "or I'll have to open your throat."

Her companions chanted an incantation, but the woman called them off. "Stop, fools! He's a leprechaun. You've got nothing left that will affect him." When her companions abandoned their spells, the black-robed woman held up her hands. "What do you want?" she snarled.

Niles smiled. "I thought you might come to see things our way."

"Our master will hear of this."

Niles Crowing looked over his shoulder at the Tower of Sorcery, "That will be interesting. Does Gilgameth Tuft know what his apprentices were up to tonight?"

The woman growled deep in her throat but kept her silence.

"Well," Niles said, "I commend your loyalty to your master, but we have two more subjects to question, so we really don't need you. Thousands of people died in tonight's destruction." He came to stand directly before the wizard. "I will know who was behind it." His voice was flat and businesslike.

"You'll get nothing from me."

Niles sighed. "As you wish." He glanced at Lenny the Leprechaun, perched on the black-robed woman's back. "You know what to do."

Lenny's tiny mouth dropped. "Niles, this isn't our way."

"A city was destroyed, Lenny. More than half of its people were killed. These people know why." His face was set. "Do it."

"But Niles!"

Niles' face was stone, his gaze cold on the woman. "Do it."

Lenny took a deep breath. "I'm sorry," he said to the woman, and he pressed his knife sharply to her neck.

The air split with a deafening crack. Everyone stumbled on the roof, staggering to keep their balance. In an instant, the morning light and the warmth of the tropics were gone, replaced with a deep darkness and a chill that made bones shiver. Standing between Niles and the woman was a bent man dressed in fine, black robes. He was short, only coming up to Niles' chest. Both of his hands were wrapped around a twisted staff, and he leaned on it heavily.

One rooftop away, Derek and the others huddled in the suddenly dark and cold morning. "Who is that?" Dani whispered.

"I don't want to know," Conrad managed to stutter.

Derek had a suspicion. A chilling fear gripped his chest, and he was unable to speak. The stooped man had gnarled hands and a bald head. His nose was almost comically large. It would have been laughable, except for the smeared ruin of his face, most of which looked as though it had melted off. His dark eyes were locked on Niles.

"Master Tuft," Niles said with a smile. "I thought you might show up." Niles kept his gaze on Gilgameth Tuft and said, "It's alright, Lenny. We got what we wanted. Let her go."

There was another tiny pop, and Lenny appeared on Niles' shoulder. "I thought you were serious," Lenny said.

Niles ignored him. "Master Tuft, my apologies for threatening your apprentice, but dire circumstances warrant dire actions."

"Under normal circumstances, you and your friends — including the children — would be dead right now." Gilgameth Tuft's apprentices looked around, confused.

"Leave the children out of this," Niles said.

"You were a fool to bring them into such trouble," the master wizard answered. Then, turning slightly, he said, "Naomi."

The woman bowed her head. "Master?"

"Take the others and return to the Tower of Sorcery."

"We are drained after last night, master. We cannot leave."

Gilgameth Tuft dipped his hand into his robes and produced three rings. There was a flash of light, and they appeared on his apprentices' fingers. "Go."

The apprentices bowed, twisted the rings about their fingers, and then vanished one after the other. Tuft took a slow breath and regarded Niles. "I understand you are a mercenary."

Niles Crowing stiffened a little. "Yes."

"I would like to hire you."

"Hire me?"

"Yes."

Niles raised his brow. "To what purpose?"

"I should like you to discover who brought this destruction to Zuid Horn."

"Excuse me?"

"You don't really think I was responsible for this, do you?"

Niles studied the wizard to see if he was joking.

"This wasn't your doing?"

Gilgameth Tuft snorted. "Of course not."

"We saw your apprentices destroying the foundries with water and fire elementals."

"My apprentices were acting under my command. Ten of the thirteen foundries went up in flames simultaneously with the explosions. The foundries were ruined beyond repair and the fire was spreading. I ordered them to use the fire elementals to do a controlled burn. We had to act quickly to keep the flames from spreading more than they did. Most of the coal and lumber yards had already caught fire. A good part of the artisan neighborhood was ablaze, and the wharf burned like a bonfire. There wasn't enough water in the Black River to put it all out. I had no choice but to summon the sea."

Niles went stiff. "You brought the flood?"

"What choice did I have? The city would have been ashes by morning if I did nothing."

"But you killed thousands of people!"

Tuft shrugged. "And probably saved thousands more. What of it?"

"You're a wizard on the Council of Nine! You are charged with protecting the city you live in, but you destroyed it!"

Gilgameth Tuft's eyes flashed in the magical twilight. "Do not presume to instruct me on what I am charged to do! Zuid Horn was attacked. I saved what was left of this city so that it can be rebuilt." He paused and regained control of himself. "It does not matter if you do not understand why I did what I did. What matters is discovering who was behind this attack and ensuring it never happens again."

Niles nodded slowly. "Agreed."

"Are you for hire, then?"

"You have apprentices. Why depend on mercenaries?"

"They are powerful, yes, but magic has its limits, as you just saw."

Niles lifted his chin slightly. "Why us?"

Gilgameth Tuft's tongue flicked at his thin lips. "The reputation of Niles Crowing and the Magnificent Seven has reached even the highest chambers of the Tower of Sorcery. Most impressive for a band of your composition." He studied the adventurers gathered on the rooftop. "Are you for hire? I will not ask again."

Niles looked around at the Magnificent Seven. "For Zuid Horn?" One by one, the Magnificent Seven minus Wendy the Ogress nodded their consent. Niles turned back to Gilgameth Tuft. "You know our usual rate?"

"A bit steep, but yes."

"Triple it," Niles said without missing a beat.

"Done," the wizard said. "Report to the Tower of Sorcery as you gather information."

Niles let out a low breath. "Do you have any idea who might have done this?"

Gilgameth Tuft considered the question briefly. "The waters will be gone by midday. I would check each of the foundries for signs of foul play. They will be coated in silt and mud, of course, but you might find some clues to help you."

On the nearby rooftop, Derek shook his head. "Working for Gilgameth Tuft. What would Da say?"

"Quiet," Conrad whispered. "He'll hear you."

Derek waved off Conrad's worry. "He needs us to solve this mystery. We don't need to be scared of him now." He turned back to watch the confrontation between Niles Crowing and Gilgameth Tuft.

The wizard walked across the rooftop toward the Tower of Sorcery, on the far side of Zuid Horn. Niles and Manny Haccian hurried to get out of his way. When he reached the edge of the roof, he turned suddenly, causing Niles and Manny to jump back and raise their weapons.

Gilgameth Tuft smiled. "Oh, I almost forgot. I should like to have some assurance that your work for me remains your primary focus."

He rolled the fingers of one hand. Electric green snakes appeared in the air. Faster than either Niles or Manny could react, Gilgameth Tuft flicked his fingers and sent the snakes over the roofs to the children, where they wrapped themselves around Derek and his friends and lifted them into the air. Derek fought and kicked, but he found no give.

"Niles!" he screamed.

Niles ran forward. "Derek! No!" Niles waved at Father Ferrum. "Stop them!"

The priest grasped the medallion around his neck and began chanting, but Gilgameth Tuft waved his fingers, and suddenly Ferrum was red-faced, struggling for breath. The master wizard rose into the air, taking Derek, Conrad, and Dani with him.

"The children will stay with me in the Tower of Sorcery," the wizard said, "until you discover who did this to Zuid Horn."

Derek screamed and struggled to free himself, but the green, crackling snakes held him fast and lifted him and the others into the sky. Soon, he was several stories above the rooftops and could see the flooded and charred ruins of Zuid Horn. Niles Crowing waved at him from below, his face a portrait of pain.

"I will free you!" he cried. "Hold on!"

Derek was too scared to respond. Ahead of him, Dani and Conrad were already hurtling toward the upper chambers of the Tower of Sorcery. Its obsidian walls rose bleakly from the ruin around it. There were neither doors nor windows, save a series of open portals near the top, where a sleek deck looked out over the city. As they drew closer, Derek saw several figures moving about. Some of them looked human, but many more did not. Derek swallowed hard and fought back the tears, not knowing what terrors awaited them in Gilgameth Tuft's dreaded fortress.

16

Derek Discovers He Hates Cooking

The Delivery had been at sea for almost a week before Derek had a chance to escape the galley. His life had fallen into the dull monotony of a slave's routine. Every morning, Saehrimnir kicked Derek awake and tossed him a bucket of carrots to be peeled or fish to be scaled or oats to be ground, threatening to put his eyes out if it wasn't done quick enough.

"And don't think I won't," Saehrimnir growled through greasy lips. "I know how lazy boys can be."

Derek had only seen Awwal Bahhar twice in that week. The first time was when Awwal passed the galley on his way to the upper deck. Saehrimnir was with Derek in the galley, swearing and sweating over a boiling pot of turnips, so Derek couldn't say anything. He would have to be careful with how he approached the first mate, Derek knew. That Derek and his friends were slaves was obvious now, but perhaps by playing naive, he might win a chance to explore *The Delivery*.

The second time Derek saw Awwal, Saehrimnir was in the belly of the ship fetching fermented cabbage from the hold. Derek saw his chance and called to the first mate. "Sir, what's going on?"

Awwal leaned against the doorway, his body swaying in rhythm to the rocking of the ocean. "We are heading around the western cape, north of Zuid Horn. In a few days, we'll be running alongside the Coastland."

"No," Derek said. "I mean, what has the captain said about the others and me? Will he hire us?"

"Oh, that," Awwal said, clearing his throat. "Yes, he said he would hire you on."

Derek held up the chain around his ankle that had kept him in the kitchen for almost a week. "Do we have to go on pretending to be slaves?"

Awwal chewed the inside of his lip. "About that, you may have to pretend you are slaves a bit longer."

"Why?"

"Well, it turns out there wasn't as much work as I thought on *The Delivery*. The only work the captain had for you was in the kitchen, rowing for the two others, and rat hunting for your friend."

"But why do we have to keep acting like slaves if we're not?"

Thumping feet and a barrage of swearing sounded up the stairwell behind Awwal. He leaned toward Derek and whispered, "Do you know how many slaves are on this ship?" Derek shook his head. "A lot," the first mate said. "Including Saehrimnir. What do you think that swine would do if he found out a free boy was working next to him, getting paid for what he is forced to do?"

Derek nodded and played along. "When am I getting paid?"

Awwal looked over his shoulder. He dug quickly in his pocket for a few coins and handed them to Derek. "Here. Now keep quiet and do what Saehrimnir says. If he finds out you aren't a slave, you might get hurt."

Derek tucked the coins into his belt just as the fat cook appeared behind Awwal at the top of the stairs. "Out of my way, you lazy Shadizarian, before I drop this cask of cabbage."

"Watch your tongue, slave," Awwal said, despite stepping nimbly out of the way, "or you'll get ten lashes to help you remember your place."

Saehrimnir brayed with laughter, spraying spittle everywhere, including into the bucket of cabbage he was carrying. "And then who would feed this lot?" He kicked at Derek, who sidestepped Saehrimnir's boot with a jingle of his chains. "This boy? He can barely boil water."

"You never know," Awwal said, giving Derek one last look before heading for the stairs and fresh air. "That boy might be your replacement."

The cook didn't even bother to look at Derek. "I doubt that," he growled.

Derek leaned into the stairwell to watch Awwal go. Saehrimnir kicked at his chain. "Boy, get those turnips cut up. We've got a crew to feed."

Derek sighed and started on the turnips.

Three days passed, and there was no further word from Awwal. Derek was sitting in the kitchen, boning out a bucket of fish and wracking his mind over what to do. How was he going to get out of these chains? He needed to explore *The Delivery* to find evidence connecting members of the Iron Guard with the Shadizarian slavers. Derek knew that if he could just get free, even for a short while, he stood a good chance of getting what he needed. He had a pretty good idea of the ship's layout, thanks to the tour Awwal gave him when they came aboard the first time. All he needed to do was get out of these chains.

He ran his finger over the vial Niles Crowing had given him. Once he got the papers to prove that the Iron Guard was involved in a slave ring with Shadizarians, he could summon Niles Crowing and the Magnificent Seven, then free himself, his friends, and the other slaves on the ship. To top it off, by exposing the corrupt Iron Guardsmen, Derek was hoping the law would overlook the inconvenient fact that he and his friends had broken out of the stocks.

Or so he hoped.

Now that he was in the belly of a slave ship, doubts gnawed on him like a dozen rats. What if he couldn't get out of the kitchen? What if he couldn't get into the captain's quarters? What if he couldn't find the ledgers to prove the Iron Guard was corrupt? And the big one — what if Niles Crowing couldn't really save them? What if the signal didn't work and the swashbuckler was unable to take the heavily armed slave ship? Derek and his friends would be slaves forever. Despair draped its gray arms over Derek.

His head sank to his chest. "What have I done?" he muttered.

Derek pulled another fish from the bucket and pressed it to the cutting board. He slid his fileting knife down one side of the spine, freeing the flesh with a practiced hand. Derek thought of his mother and the times he had watched her preparing fish for dinner. How could Derek have left her like this? He could see Mum worrying her fingers into knots over his disappearance. Her eyes and voice would be raw from weeping. The thought of his mother crying made his chin tremble.

Derek tossed the filet into a pail of cold water and dropped the bones and carcasses into a sack. He grabbed another fish and kept cleaning.

And Da? What was he thinking? Would he be angry that Derek vanished right when he needed him most, or would he be upset, like Mum, that his boy was gone? It was hard to say. Derek never knew what he needed to do to make Da happy. His father never said much about how he felt. Even his resting face looked angry. Derek stabbed at the fish. Why couldn't Da just be happy letting Derek do what he wanted?

Derek's jaw tightened and sweat broke out on his forehead. It was the anger coming on, he realized, but what good was it going to do him while he was chained in a ship's galley? He remembered Dani's words on the pier and closed his eyes. Derek breathed slowly. In and out. In and out. Bit by bit, the anger faded, and he opened his eyes again.

Saehrimnir pulled a fistful of filets from Derek's bucket. The flabby chef slopped the dripping fish onto a cutting board and hacked them into bite size bits before scraping them onto a hot grill. The pieces sizzled and spit, filling the tiny kitchen with the smell of burning bones and Saehrimnir's unwashed body. Derek watched the slave work, and a realization dawned on him.

Why was he complaining about Da not supporting his dreams? Even Derek didn't know what he wanted to do. A few weeks ago, Derek's dream was to work the grill of his own tavern, but his experience working as a cook on *The Delivery* was simply miserable. Derek didn't think he would ever want to cook again! How could he have blamed Da for not supporting him? He should have been grateful he had parents at all. Derek shook his head. How could he have been so blind?

Derek lifted his head and set his chin. No. He was going to find his way out of this mess, return to his parents, and be the son he knew he could be.

"First things first," Derek said to himself.

"Eh?" Saehrimnir grunted from the stove. He didn't even bother looking up.

"Nothing, sir. Just clearing my throat."

Saehrimnir shook his head and continued turning fish on the wide grill. "Hurry up boning those fish," he said. "I'm ready for the next round."

"Yes, sir," Derek said.

He picked the next fish out of the bucket. It was a huge salmon, with silver scales that flashed in the swinging lamp light. This one was too big for the cutting board, so Derek pinned it on the floor with his knees and used his tiny knife to open it along its spine from head to tail. Then, he slid the blade along the backbones and methodically fileted the fish.

Derek was running the knife along the salmon's ribs when he stopped and touched the bones with his finger. An idea was forming. It was crazy, but it just might work. He looked at the lock around his ankle, gauging the size of the keyhole. Then, he looked back at the salmon rib bones. Derek smiled. Yes, they were just thick enough, he thought, looking at the lock around his ankle. But he would have to dry them first. Making sure Saehrimnir was busy with the grill, Derek grabbed a fistful of salmon bones and tucked them behind a box of salt on the shelf, just behind him. Now, all he had to do was wait.

Two days later, the salmon bones were dry enough for Derek to test on his lock. Saehrimnir had taken a bucket of gruel down to the slaves, and Derek knew he wouldn't be back for a long time. He checked the stairwell and, seeing no one, hurried to the shelf where he had hidden the dried salmon bones. Sitting next to the door so he could listen to the stairwell, Derek went to work on the lock about his ankle with his rudimentary lock picks.

The first two bones snapped because Derek twisted too hard. He had to shake the lock to get the bits of bone free. On the third try, he felt several of the tumblers slip free before the bone broke again. It was on the fourth try, though, that he found success. Using two bones, he worked the tumblers of the lock back one by one until he felt he could go no further. Then, bit by bit, he turned the bones until he heard a quick, metallic click, and he was free.

Derek slid the lock off his leg and rubbed the raw skin beneath. He was free. Even though he hadn't moved, somehow the stale air of the galley smelled fresher. Derek was contemplating his next move when he heard Saehrimnir huffing and puffing his way up the stairs, banging the feed bucket behind him the whole way. Derek fit the manacles loosely, but not completely, around his ankle again.

The portly cook waddled into the galley. Derek squished himself against the shelves to avoid touching Saehrimnir's glistening rolls of fat as he passed. The cook tossed the bucket into the corner, where it bounced with a woody rattle. "Get this kitchen cleaned up," he grumbled. "I'm done for the night." Then he left.

Derek watched him go. As soon as the cook was down the stairs to the slaves' quarters, Derek scrambled to clean the kitchen, careful not to let the fetters about his ankle snap shut. Time dragged, but eventually Derek had the kitchen clean. Derek paused to wipe his face and catch his breath. Then he knelt and took the chains off his ankle.

He stood up a free man.

Leaning into the stairwell, Derek checked to see if anyone was coming. There wasn't, so he scurried back into the kitchen and arranged some baskets to look like a sleeping boy. To finish the effect, he threw the thin blanket Saehrimnir had given him to sleep on over the top. He inspected his work, deemed it passable, and then snatched foodstuffs off the shelves — a box of dried pheasant back mushrooms, fermented soy, oil, salt.

Derek tossed the dried mushrooms into a bowl of water to rehydrate them. Then, he knelt close to the stove and blew on the last glowing coals. He brought the heat up again, put an iron skillet on the stovetop, and warmed some oil. When the edges smoked a bit, Derek carefully arranged the mushrooms in the pan, dribbled more oil and fermented soy over them, and waited for the undersides to turn brown. He hurried to the stairwell to see if anyone was coming. Seeing the coast was clear, Derek rushed back to the stove, flipped the mushrooms, and took the skillet off the heat. Letting the residual heat finish the job, Derek readied a plate, grabbed a fork, and laid the cleanest serving napkin he could find over his arm.

By this time, the sauteed mushrooms were ready. Derek took them off, one by one, and arranged them carefully on the plate. Then, taking a deep breath, he carried the plate of mushrooms out of the kitchen and up the stairs to the upper deck.

The first thing Derek noticed was the blast of fresh air. After almost two weeks chained in the galley, he had forgotten what ocean air smelled like. It was past sunset, but a bit of the lingering day still had a hold on the western sky. Overhead, a half-moon chased after the sunken sun, shedding enough light for Derek to easily see his way along the deck.

Sailors had finished eating. Now they were moving about battening hatches, braiding lines, and repairing sails. Some of the sailors chatted with the guardsmen, who strolled along the railing wearing padded cloth armor with hide shields slung over their backs. They wore tunics bearing the sun sigil of Shadizar's King Folio. The same symbol adorned the warriors' shields.

Derek walked past them, directly to the captain's quarters. The window in the door was dark. If he ever was going to explore for evidence linking the Shadizarians to the Iron Guard, he would never find a more perfect time.

Derek was almost to the door when a passing guard stopped him. "You there. Where are you going?"

Derek held up the plate of mushrooms. "A treat, sir, for the captain."

The guard leaned close and sniffed at the steam. "That smells good. What is it?"

"Mushrooms, sir. The way we make them at the Crooked Hammer."

"Is that so?" The guard reached for the plate. "I should probably test them to make certain they are good enough for the captain."

Derek twisted out of the way. "Sorry, sir. I can't let you do that. There wouldn't be enough for the captain."

The man scowled but stopped going after the mushrooms. "Fine. Deliver your goods, but be quick about it, slave. There's a storm coming, and all the slaves need to be below deck."

"Yes, sir!" Derek said, and he hustled to the captain's quarters without another interruption. Finding the door unlocked, he slipped inside.

Moonlight streaming through the cramped cabin windows provided enough light for Derek to find his way into the room. He had been there before and could now make out the shadows of shelves lining the walls, the captain's bed against the far wall, and the table stacked with maps in the center of the room. Derek crept to the table and put the plate of mushrooms in the dead center. He spread the napkin out wide while waiting for his eyes to adjust to the dark. Try as he might, it was simply too dark to see anything of value. He eyed the moonlight coming through the windows. Maybe there was enough light.

Derek grabbed a ledger and was a step away from the window when he heard someone talking near the door. Derek whirled and put the book back down on the table where he found it. His eyes darted about in the dark. Where could he go? The room was so small and sparse. Derek cursed his foul luck, but it was too late to not stick with his original plan.

Taking two quick steps, Derek slipped around to the front of the desk just as the captain, Awwal, and Ahriman — the suspicious man who had boarded *The Delivery* just after Derek and the boys — came through the only door in or out of the cabin. The captain had a lantern with him, and when he stepped into the room and saw Derek standing there, he stopped so suddenly that Awwal walked right into him.

"Hello, there. What's this?"

Awwal stepped around the captain and came up short. "Derek? What are you doing here?"

Ahriman scowled at Derek. His hand drifted near the curved dagger at his waist. Derek swallowed thickly. "I brought something special for the captain, sir." He lowered his eyes in proper fashion and extended a hand toward the plate of steaming mushrooms.

"Is that so?" the captain said. The captain crossed the room and sat down at his desk. He sniffed at the mushrooms. "Smells good. Did you make this?"

"Yes, sir."

Awwal walked into the room and crossed his arms in front of Derek. "How did you get out of your chains?"

Derek put on a confused look. "They were unlocked the whole time."

"They were?" Awwal sounded doubtful.

"Yes, sir. I didn't say anything because you told me I had to convince the others I was a slave. It was all part of the disguise, sir, wasn't it?"

The captain coughed. "Disguise?"

"Yes, sir," Derek went on. "Awwal said I needed to convince the others I was a slave, or they would get angry that a free boy was willing to do their work, just to see the world." He turned to Awwal. "Isn't that right, Awwal?"

The first mate shrugged. "That's what I said."

"I see." The captain took out his dagger and moved the mushrooms around a bit. "So, you made me these mushrooms?"

"Yes, sir."

"Does Saehrimnir know about this?"

"Oh, no, sir."

The captain sliced off a bit of mushroom and stabbed it with the tip of his dagger. The mushroom was almost in his mouth when the thin-lipped Ahriman rushed forward. "My captain! Don't eat that! He could be trying to poison you."

The captain froze with the dagger just before his lips. "Why would this boy try to poison me?"

Ahriman stepped around Awwal to stand before the captain's desk. Something about the way he moved reminded Derek of a cobra slipping through the shadows. Ahriman leaned close to the captain and whispered in his ear.

"I see," the captain said, eyebrows raised in surprise. He turned his attention to Derek. "How do I know you're not trying to poison me?"

Derek froze. He looked at the captain. "Sir?"

"How do I know you're not trying to poison me? Ahriman here tells me you and your friends aren't who you say you are." Derek felt a knot tightening in his throat. "We just wanted to see the world," he whispered.

"Maybe," the captain said, "but Ahriman went to the Crooked Hammer. The owner had never heard of you boys, says he never sent boxes of stew and jugs of wine to *The Delivery*." The captain leaned forward and pushed the plate across the table. "Care to explain that?"

Derek looked quickly to Awwal, who moved to stand between Derek and the door. Derek looked at Ahriman and saw that the snaky man had one hand behind his back. His eyes were no more than black slits. Derek's heart thumped in his chest. He tried to swallow, but his throat was suddenly as dry as grit.

The captain leaned forward. "You're not making a good showing for yourself, boy." He pushed the plate forward a little more. "Eat these."

"Sir?"

"Eat the mushrooms. If you are trying to poison me, as Ahriman says, you're going to die first."

Derek reached for the plate with trembling fingers and pinched a bit of mushroom. "Take a bigger piece," the captain insisted. "I want to make sure."

Derek did as he was ordered. He finished one piece, and the captain urged him on with a wave of his hand. "And the rest?" One by one, Derek ate all of the mushrooms. Something about the taste of home gave him strength, and suddenly he had a possible solution to his dilemma.

Wiping his wrist across his mouth, he said, "They aren't poisoned, sir. I just wanted to impress you so I could get out of the kitchen."

The captain leaned back in his chair. "Is that all you wanted?"

Derek looked up at the captain. If he was going to sell his story, it was now or never. He took a deep breath. "I'm sorry about lying to you about the Crooked Hammer, sir. But it's true, my friends and I just wanted to see the world."

"On a Shadizarian ship? Why not sign on with a Zuid Hornian merchant?"

Derek hesitated, and Awwal's scowl darkened. "The captain asked you a question, Derek."

"Yes, sir. It's just embarrassing, now that I think about it, sir."

"Answer the captain, Derek."

"Well," Derek started, "about a month ago, a Shadizarian merchant ship docked in Zuid Horn. My friends and I happened to be there as the passengers were disembarking."

"Go on," Awwal said.

"We were people-watching, and all of a sudden this girl comes down the gangplank."

"A Shadizarian girl?"

"Yes, sir. And we just couldn't stop looking at her. She was the most beautiful thing we ever saw. Right then and there, we all agreed that if we could come up with a plan to get to Shadizar, we would take it, the first chance we got."

"To meet Shadizarian girls."

Derek waited just a bit. "Yes, sir."

Awwal and the captain looked at one another. The captain shrugged. "Can you blame him?"

Awwal chuckled. "I suppose not."

The captain leaned back in his chair and turned his attention to Derek. "So, that was all you wanted?"

"Yes, sir."

The captain took a breath and looked at Awwal. "What do you think?"

Awwal shrugged. "What harm could he do? Let him cook meals for the officers. It will burn Saehrimnir, but that fat goat needs a good prodding every now and then."

"And you?" the captain asked Ahriman, who had been silent during Derek's story.

The small man circled around behind the boy, looking at him from many angles. Derek did his best not to twitch. "I don't trust him," Ahriman said. "The boy lies about working for the Crooked Hammer, escapes from his chains —"

"They were unlocked!" Derek hoped he sounded believable, but the knot in his stomach was tightening.

Ahriman scoffed. "Unlikely. And he shows up, uninvited, in your quarters while you are gone." Ahriman turned a slow scowl on the captain. "And there is something else I didn't tell you that may sway your opinion of the boy." Derek felt the blood drain from his face. What else could this Shadizarian snake know about him? Ahriman circled Derek, keeping his hands behind his back. "Tell us, boy, who did you visit the night before you joined our crew? Who were you talking to on Ploughman's Wharf before you boarded *The Delivery*?" Derek opened his mouth, but nothing came out.

Ahriman whirled back to the captain. "Nothing to say? Then I will say it for you." He pulled his hands from behind his back, producing two slim, black daggers. "This boy and his friends were visiting Niles Crowing!"

"Niles Crowing?" the captain asked, sitting up. "*The* Niles Crowing?"

Derek stumbled back. "Niles Crowing? What? No!"

"Don't deny it, you Zuid Hornian weasel," Ahriman sneered. "I saw it with my own eyes." He sheathed one of the daggers and then grabbed Derek's collar, pulling him so close that Derek could smell garlic from yesterday's turnip stew on his breath. "Your pathetic story about chasing girls just shows you to be the liar I know you are." Derek struggled to get away, but Ahriman pulled him close and pressed the black blade against Derek's neck. "Don't move," Ahriman hissed, and he began patting Derek down. He stopped when he felt Niles' vial tucked into the secret pocket in Derek's shirt. "Ho, ho! What do we have here?" He removed the dagger from Derek's neck and used it to slice Derek's shirt open. The vial tumbled out and rolled on the floor. Ahriman pushed Derek away and scooped it up. "Just as I thought," he said.

The captain squinted at the vial. "What is it?"

Ahriman carefully unscrewed the vial's cap. A faint, golden glow shone from within. "This, my captain, is liquid magic, taken from one of only a handful of sites in the realms. Niles Crowing uses this to spring the surprise attacks for which he is so famous."

The captain leaned forward. "Does he, now?"

"Indeed, my captain," Ahriman said, smirking at Derek.

Turning to Derek, the captain smiled. "Thank you, my boy."

"'Thank you?'" Derek managed to stutter.

"Yes. Niles Crowing has been a thorn in my sovereign king's side for many years. You've just given us a tool to lure him into a trap." The captain settled into his chair and stretched his arms behind his head. "Imagine it, Awwal. We arrive in Shadizar with a hull full of new slaves and the heads of Niles Crowing and the Magnificent Seven to boot." He laughed, and to Derek's ears, it was the cruelest laughter he had ever heard.

Awwal grabbed Derek by the arm. "What should we do with this one?"

The captain dragged a finger through the mushroom juice on the plate and tasted it. "Hmm... This is good. Give him ten lashes for lying to us. Then, take him back to Saehrimnir in the galley."

"Yes, sir." Awwal turned and dragged Derek to the door. "Come on, you."

"Oh, and Awwal," the captain called.

"Yes, sir?"

"This time, make certain the boy's chains are locked."

17

Derek Finds a Way to Help

A week had passed since Gilgameth Tuft brought Derek and his friends to the uppermost reaches of the Tower of High Sorcery. Each of the children had a small room connected to a common living area, a private spot for toiletries, and an invisible servant to take care of their every physical need. Even though the children said nothing, it was as if the wizard could read their minds.

"Why am I providing you such luxuries?" he had asked just before he left them. "I have my reasons. For now, let's just say I need you healthy and alive to ensure Niles Crowing upholds his end of the bargain."

The friends had spent the first few days huddled together in terror. The door to their apartment complex was locked, but they could hear things slithering and moaning in the corridors on the other side. Nights were the worst, when the air about the tower rippled with magical creatures, almost invisible to the naked eye, coming and going on missions for Gilgameth Tuft.

By the third day, though, when the children concluded that nothing was going to harm them, they began to let down their guard and enjoy the relative safety and comfort that the realm's most powerful wizard afforded them. Meals appeared three times a day, once more than Derek was used to and three times more than Conrad and Dani could afford on their own. They spent their time on the balcony overlooking Zuid Horn, trying to recognize streets and buildings that had been destroyed in the flood. But with everything buried under a blanket of sea salt, mud, and ash, even the most commonplace of landmarks were difficult to discern.

If Derek had to describe Zuid Horn after the flood in one word, it would have been "gray." Silt from the ocean covered everything. Silt was on the ground. It was in the rubble. It was in the air every time the breeze kicked up. The gray dust smelled of salt and seaweed, and as the week went on and survivors of the flood tried to dig themselves free of the ruins, another smell grew in intensity — the reek of the rotting dead.

Intertwined with the bits of broken boards, charred shingles, and shredded sheets were the bodies of those who were not fast or strong or lucky enough to have escaped the flood. The sweltering, tropical sun intensified the effect and brought bubbles of sweet stench to the children on the tower's balcony with every warm breeze. Clouds of black and green swamp flies, fat and hungry, buzzed over the city. Great flights of carrion birds wheeled overhead, landing in squawking flocks to fight over the bloated trophies. As horrendous as the smells and sights of the ruined city were, Derek and the others found that they could not stop staring at the scene unfolding below them.

Yakariian warriors and scouts, who had been tolerated within the city for centuries, ranged through Zuid Horn in wild packs, rounding up humans and dragging them away in slave trains. Derek watched the trains disappear on the Coast Road, the trail leading from Zuid Horn to the Hagedorn salt mines, far to the northeast. He wondered if Augie and his parents were already there, and if he would ever see his friends again.

"Where is the Iron Guard?" Dani asked as they watched from the balcony.

"Drowned, most likely," Conrad said. "Trapped in the best armor money can buy."

It was just past noon, a week after Gilgameth Tuft had brought the children to the Tower of Sorcery. Derek, Dani, and Conrad stood on the upper balcony overlooking Zuid Horn. They leaned against the obsidian railing and breathed through their shirts to cut the reek of the dead. To the east, a waxing gibbous moon rose over Breechwood Forest.

"I feel so helpless," Dani said. "If we could just go down there, clear some rubble, feed someone, help children find their mothers."

Conrad elbowed his sister. "Dani," he said, dipping his head toward Derek. "Derek's parents?"

Dani pursed her lips. "Oh, right. Sorry."

Derek waved them off. "It's alright."

They turned their attention back to people moving in the city below. The people looked like mice scurrying over the tangled destruction. Some cleaned the streets and created narrow walkways to get from ruin to ruin. Others focused on what was left of their houses, now either torn in half or filled with ocean silt. The cries of people discovering the bodies of their loved ones rose and fell across the city. Derek wondered if anyone had discovered his parents' bodies yet, and if anyone would cry if they did.

"Do you think Sarah will go looking for your parents?" Conrad asked.

Derek shrugged. "Not on her own. There's no way Wendy will let her out of her sight."

"Good point," Conrad said. "Maybe she took them to your house."

"What's left of it," Derek muttered. He turned away from the balcony and slumped into their shared living space. A few plush cushions lay spread over a thick rug. Derek threw himself down on them, covering his face with the crook of his arm. All he wanted was to be left alone.

Conrad eased himself onto a cushion and scratched absent-mindedly at the scab on his forearm. "Sorry about Dani bringing up your parents."

Derek shifted. "Don't worry about it."

"I know how hard it must be, you being trapped in here and all, not knowing what's going on with your sisters or where your parents are."

"I said, don't worry about it."

Conrad stretched out on the rug next to Derek and propped himself up on his elbows. "Okay. I was just trying to help."

Dani came in from the balcony and crouched at the low table outfitted with glistening fruit and a jug of clear water. She poured a small cup of water and brought it to Derek. "Thirsty?" The back of Derek's scalp tingled. "No."

She held the cup out, closer to him. "Are you sure? Sometimes I get crabby if I'm thirsty."

The edges of his vision shimmered. His chest tightened, and he clenched his fists. "I said no."

She backed away, her eyes hurt. "I was just trying to help." Derek glared at Dani and Conrad. He saw the pity in their eyes, and before he knew it, he was screaming at them. "Just stop it! Every time we go out on the balcony, you have to say something about my parents! You think I don't know that my parents are probably dead? You smell that?" He pointed to the balcony, where the thick curtains billowed in a warm, sickly-sweet breeze. "Smell that? That's my parents rotting out there. That's Liza. Who's going to find them? Me? You? I'll never see them again, never get to bury them." Derek's chest was tight with rage. He wanted to hit something, but there was nothing to lash out against.

Conrad and Dani exchanged glances. "We just feel bad for you," Conrad said.

"Feel bad for me? You?" Derek exploded. "What do you know about losing parents or a house? You've never had any!"

And as soon as the words were out of his mouth, Derek knew he had crossed a line, and the anger left him like a candle doused in a well, only to be replaced by a burning shame. "I'm sorry. I didn't mean it like that."

Conrad's face tightened and his eyes narrowed.

"I'm sorry," Derek whispered again. "I don't know where that came from." He swallowed, and then, "It's not how I really feel."

"Maybe it is," Dani said.

Her footsteps shuffled out to the balcony. He wanted to go to her, but he couldn't move. Derek sighed and sank into the cushions. He buried his face in a pillow. "I'm such an idiot," he muttered.

"Yep," Conrad said.

"You know I didn't mean that."

"You must have been thinking it, or you wouldn't have said it."

Derek rubbed his face. "By the gods, what is wrong with me? Why would I say that?"

There was a soft rustling, like two sheets moving over one another, and then a voice came from a chair near the balcony. "Because you are in pain."

Derek and Conrad leapt to their feet. Derek held a pillow in front of himself. Conrad's fists were up as though he were boxing. Sitting in the chair, next to the curtain billowing in the breeze, was Gilgameth Tuft.

They hadn't seen him in a week, and he looked exactly like he had on the night he whisked them away from Niles Crowing and into the Tower of Sorcery. Only, something was different. There was no chill in the air, and Derek's chest didn't feel as though icy fingers were sinking through his flesh. Tuft just looked like an old, bald man, hunched in a chair, leaning on a crooked tree limb that served as a staff. In the light of day, the scars of a horrific burning still marred his face, but other than that, he looked like he could have been anyone's grandfather.

"Excuse me?" Derek asked.

"You were short with your friends because you are in pain."

Derek's breath caught in his throat. "No, I'm not."

"Aren't you?" Gilgameth Tuft asked. "I've been watching you for a long time, Derek Fulstarter."

"You have?" Derek managed to squeak.

"Yes."

"Why?" he asked, although a large part of him didn't really want to know.

"It doesn't matter," the wizard said, waving his hand. "What matters is that all of us carry pain of one variety or another. What matters is what we do with it."

Derek kept the pillow he was holding between himself and Gilgameth Tuft. "I'm not in pain. I'm fine."

"Are you? How deeply have you looked in here?" The wizard patted his chest, the sleeves of his robes waving like kelp. "We all carry ghosts, and until we confront them, we are haunted by their groaning."

Derek and Conrad looked at one another and shrugged. "I don't understand," Derek said.

Gilgameth Tuft smiled. "I'm sure you don't. Not yet, anyway. But you will, in time. Look to those you have known the longest. That might be a good place to find help."

Derek and Conrad glanced at one another, unsure what to do next. A shadow moved across the balcony, and Dani burst back into the room. "Look, Derek, I know..." Then she saw Gilgameth Tuft and stopped dead in her tracks, eyes wide.

The master wizard waved a bony hand at her. "Come in. Join your brother and your friend." When Dani hesitated, he sighed. "I'm not going to hurt you, child. If I wanted to hurt you, I would have done it a long time ago."

Dani hurried across the room and stood between Derek and Conrad. Gilgameth Tuft studied them. "You wish to leave the tower."

Derek dropped his eyes. Had the wizard been listening? "Yes," he whispered.

"You know why I need you here, don't you?"

"We are collateral to make sure Niles Crowing discovers who destroyed Zuid Horn."

Gilgameth Tuft nodded and rubbed his bony hands together. The thin skin, spotted with age, slid back and forth. "You have served your purpose well."

Derek stood up straight. "Niles found the scoundrels?"

"Not yet," Gilgameth said. His forehead was deeply wrinkled where it wasn't scarred, and his ears drooped broad and low. "But he has been working without sleep for a week. You are an effective incentive for him."

"What has he learned?" Derek asked.

"Niles has spent the past week scouring the destroyed foundries for clues." Gilgameth Tuft leaned forward and ran palsied fingers over his thin thighs. "He has found something they all have in common."

Derek stepped closer to the wizard. "What's that?"

"All of the foundries have blast marks in their lower levels."

"Blast marks? They burned to the ground. How can he tell they are blast marks?"

Gilgameth made a tight ball with his hands. "When a powerful explosion takes place, fire and energy rush out from a central location." The wizard opened his hands like a blooming flower. "Its path leaves telltale signs. In this case, dark grooves in the foundries' basement walls."

Derek imagined Niles in the cellars of the drowned foundries. He could almost smell the gray silt Niles had to plow through, mucking step by step through the gray slop. The stink of rot and sea and molding wood wafted at the back of his nose. Derek imagined the blast marks, streaked as though a bear had clawed at the stone masonry with thick nails.

"Sabotage," Derek whispered.

"Yes," the wizard answered.

"What about the two surviving foundries?"

"Niles found minor blast marks in both, as well. It was just dumb luck that their furnace fuel never caught on fire."

"So, it wasn't about destroying their competitors."

Gilgameth Tuft tucked his hands into the loose sleeves of his robe. "Apparently not."

Derek blinked, and his mind was back in the room. "But who would do something like that?"

Gilgameth Tuft cocked his head to the side and peered at Derek. An uneasy itch tickled Derek's chest. He felt like a mouse being studied by an owl. The wizard's mouth slid into a smirk. "That's what we are going to find out."

Derek looked at Dani and Conrad. "You're sending us to help Niles?"

The wizard laughed. "Oh no. We need to let Niles Crowing and the Magnificent Seven do what they do best. You would just get in their way."

"But," Derek protested.

Tuft held up a hand. "But when he is done, he is going to want what I promised him, and I plan to deliver on my word."

"He wanted triple his normal fee."

"Yes, that. And he wanted you and your friends back, free of harm."

"Oh, that," Derek said.

"And I can't do that if you get so worked up while you are here that you kill one another, now can I?"

Derek dropped his face in shame, remembering what he had just said to Dani and Conrad. "You heard that?"

"It was hard not to." Gilgameth Tuft rolled his bent shoulders and studied Derek, then Dani, and finally Conrad, one after the other. "And so, I have a proposition for you."

The children looked at one another, suddenly suspicious.

"You do?" Conrad asked.

"I do. You were fighting about your parents."

Derek felt his face blaze. "Yes," he mumbled.

"And you are frustrated because you don't know what happened to them."

Derek chewed the inside of his lip. "Yes."

"That's what I thought. Here is my proposition. Niles will keep on working as long as he thinks you are under my control, correct?" Derek and the others nodded. "Well," Gilgameth Tuft continued, "that doesn't mean you need to be in the tower, does it?"

"I suppose not," Derek said, not sure where the wizard was going with this.

"What if I let you out to look for your parents?"

The children looked at one another, almost speechless. "Really?" Conrad asked. "You would trust us to do that?"

The wizard straightened his bent spine and peered under hairless eyebrows at Conrad. "Trust? What do you think you will do? Run away? I am Gilgameth Tuft, charged with overseeing Zuid Horn and a member of the realm's Council of Nine. Do you really think I couldn't find you if you broke our agreement?"

Derek turned to Conrad and Dani. He couldn't believe the gamut his emotions and his fortune had run in such a short time. Something in his gut told him this was all wrong. This was Gilgameth Tuft, after all, the most renowned broker of evil in the realms. And here he was with Derek and his friends, just sitting in an apartment and chatting.

The wizard looked so normal, so old, that Derek found it hard to believe this was the man legends described, the wizard who had sold his soul for immortality and power, who ruled Zuid Horn with an iron fist, whose enemies disappeared at the slightest provocation. Still, if the possibility to search for his parents — if they were still alive — existed, he knew he had to take it.

Dani and Conrad slowly shook their heads, but Derek ignored their silent warnings. "We'll do it."

Gilgameth lowered his head and smiled, his thin lips pulling back to reveal yellowed but strong teeth. "Excellent."

Derek looked at Dani and Conrad. They were still shaking their heads and mouthing, *"No,"* but Derek was too excited to get out of the tower to worry about what his friends had to say. "When can we go?" he asked.

"Right now," the wizard said. "But first, I have something for the three of you that may help you on your journey, if you are willing to pay the price." He dipped his thin fingers into a pocket in his robe and produced three rings. He held them in the cup of his hand. They shimmered in the balmy air. "These rings have been dipped in the Wellspring beneath Bengazii."

"Bengazii?" Derek said. "It doesn't exist."

"Never heard of it," Conrad said.

"Some of the traders at Augie's inn used to talk about it. They said it was a city on the eastern edge of the Desert Sea."

Conrad scoffed. "There is no eastern side to the Desert Sea. Everyone knows the sands go on forever."

Derek shrugged. "Well, the merchants say Bengazii traded with Shadizar a thousand years ago. But that's just a legend."

"Bengazii is real enough," Gilgameth Tuft said. "I've been there. And these rings," he waved his fingers over the rings, and they appeared on each of the children's hands, "are called the Rings of Many Skins. With them, you may assume the form of any creature you like, from as small as an ant to as large as an elephant."

Derek looked at the ring on his hand as though he had grown a new appendage. "We can change shapes whenever we want?"

The wizard held up three fingers. "You may change shape three times. After that, I need to take the rings to Bengazii and dip them in the Wellspring again."

"Thank you," Derek said, running his thumb over the edge of the ring. "I don't know what to say. I wasn't expecting you to be, well... like this."

The black-robed wizard wrapped his arms around his small frame. "Yes, well, you would do well to mind what you have heard of me. Most of it is true."

Derek froze, wondering if he had crossed a line again. "I'm sorry, sir. I didn't mean to offend."

"No offense taken. My path to power has taken many dark turns, as the color of my robes would indicate." He held out his arms again, letting the long sleeves dangle in the warm breeze. "But the truth is, I remember what it was like to be an orphan, and I will always carry a soft spot in my heart for those without parents." His eyes took on a faraway look. "And those who never knew them."

Derek nodded. "Thank you."

Dani cleared her throat. "You said something about 'paying a price' if we use the rings?"

Gilgameth Tuft nodded. "I did. The use of magic does not come without a price. The magic in these rings, for example, requires much effort to acquire, and even then, it is limited."

"If the magic is already in the rings," Derek asked, "why do we have to pay a price?"

The master wizard smiled. "Because it is my magic. I paid the price for it, and I will not dole it out without repayment."

Derek nodded. "Fair enough. What's your price?"

"I am looking for a new apprentice."

A chill rippled through Derek. Was it fear, or was it excitement? "An apprentice?"

"My current apprentices are close to completing their training. Soon, they will be assigned towers and territories to oversee," the wizard said. "When they are gone, I will need a new apprentice."

Derek looked at Conrad and Dani. They were both shaking their heads. "Don't," was all Conrad said.

Derek ran his thumb over the ring on his finger. He had grown up hearing tales of Gilgameth Tuft and his evil deeds. His parents, Da especially, didn't trust wizards. Yet, here was not only the opportunity to get out of the Tower of Sorcery, but the power to find and save his parents — not to mention Augie and his parents, as well. If it meant sacrificing himself to become Gilgameth Tuft's next apprentice, wasn't that worth it? After all, isn't that what heroes did?

Derek took a slow breath. "I'll do it."

Conrad stepped closer and whispered. "Derek, what are you doing?"

Derek frowned. "Imagine what we could do with these rings! If my parents are still alive, we can find them. This is our chance to help Augie, too."

"But is it worth it?"

Derek waved him off. "I'm willing to pay if it means getting my parents back." Dani looked like she was about to say something, but Derek cut her off and turned to the wizard. "It's a deal."

Gilgameth Tuft looked at them. "Well, you seem quite certain. What about your friends? They will be using the rings as well. Do they accept that one will pay the price for the others?"

Derek glanced at them. Conrad was shaking his head.

Dani looked sad. "You're going to regret this," she said.

"Come on, guys. Think of the people we could help."

"Yeah," Conrad said, "but at what cost?"

"Let me worry about that." Derek took a deep breath. "Please? For my parents? For me?"

Conrad sighed. "Fine."

Dani nodded. "Alright."

Tuft eyed the children. "To be clear, one of you will pay the price for using the rings?"

Derek and the others nodded their consent.

"Very well." Gilgameth Tuft murmured an enchantment, and the ring on Derek's finger buzzed. "The magic is yours to use as you will."

Derek closed his eyes and breathed a sigh of relief. "Thank you."

Gilgameth Tuft bowed slightly from his chair. "It is my pleasure." He used his staff to stand up and then hobbled to the balcony. His gait was stiff, and he favored his left hip. "Now, I suppose you want to get started as soon as possible."

Derek looked at Dani and Conrad, who simply shrugged and nodded. "Yes," Derek said, "if we could."

"You needn't say another word." Gilgameth Tuft gestured to the balcony. "Come out here, and I'll let you out at the base of the tower."

Derek and the others followed the ancient wizard to the railing. "When you have found what you need," Tuft said, "come back to the base of the tower. I will let you in. Do you understand?"

"Yes, sir," Derek said with a nod.

"And remember, not a word to Niles. He needs to think you are in the Tower of Sorcery."

Derek nodded. "Not a word."

The wizard fanned his fingers in front of the children. "Alright then, off you go. I'll put you down at the base of the tower."

The children shimmered, and then they were gone.

18

Derek Faces Another Storm

erek's back was on fire. At the tenth lash from the row master's whip, Derek's shirt hung from his bloody shoulders in long, jagged strips. The deck below his feet was slick with crimson. Awwal, standing near the whipping post, held up his hand.

"Enough. Take him down."

A pair of hands grabbed Derek by the shoulders and yanked him up. Awwal unlocked the shackles around his wrists, and Derek's knees buckled beneath him.

"Take him to the galley. Be sure his chains are secure." The first mate gave Derek a suspicious glare and then looked into the wind. "And be quick. Those clouds are coming in fast. It's going to be a bad one. I'll need all hands on deck."

Derek struggled to lift his head. Pain like white lightning seized his back from the effort. He gasped and let his head fall again, but Derek had seen what he needed to see. Massive, black clouds rolling in fat formations from the west were piled high and barreling down on *The Delivery*. The sea was dark and rising. White caps rode the waves like cats' claws, slashing against *The Delivery's* side and growing in strength.

The deckhands dragged Derek down the stairwell and tossed him in the galley. He bounced against the open shelves and landed on the rough planks of the galley floor. An avalanche of jars, satchels of herbs, sacks of salt, and ladles collapsed on top of him. He let out a yelp when a glass jar of pickled cucumbers broke and poured vinegar and salt over the open wounds on his back.

"Enough, slave," one of the deckhands growled as he clapped a pair of manacles around Derek's ankles, "or we'll take you to the whipping post again." Over his shoulder, the deckhand said to his partner, who was standing in the open doorway, "Better wake up Saehrimnir, that lazy cow. If he doesn't get these shelves battened down, we'll lose half our kitchen in this storm."

His partner gave a grunt and headed down the stairs into the ship's belly.

The deckhand stood up and gave Derek a good kick. "Clean this mess up. If Saehrimnir sees his galley like this, he's likely to give you a beating of his own." Then, he turned and left.

Derek whimpered and rolled to his knees. A tin cup and several jars of Shadizarian pepper fell off his chest and rattled to the floor. The ship rolled under him, the waves growing in intensity as the storm drew closer and closer. Derek gripped the rickety shelf for balance and restocked the shelves with his free hand. Saehrimnir thumped and swore his way up the stairwell. He emerged from *The Delivery's* dark underbelly and filled the galley's doorway with his bulk. Saehrimnir was in his sleeping clothes, which consisted of little more than a greasy loincloth.

"By the Pit, what in Ra's name happened to you?"

Derek looked down at the strips of flayed flesh missing from his shoulders. "Ten lashes," he whispered.

The bloated chef scratched his jiggling belly and grunted. "Deserved it, no doubt."

Just then, *The Delivery* pitched hard to stern. Saehrimnir toppled into the small kitchen and onto Derek, smothering him under a load of sweaty blubber and thick, black hairs. "By Ra!"

Saehrimnir swore again. He rolled off Derek, who tried to spit the taste of the cook's armpit out of his mouth. "The boys were right," Saehrimnir said. "A storm is on us. Get the coal bucket, boy, and clear out the oven. If we don't get those coals out of here, we'll have a fire that will burn the ship down. Hurry!"

Derek shuffled to the end of the cramped kitchen where the coal bucket and its tiny shovel were kept. The chains about his ankles jingled with every step. He snatched the bucket and shovel, and just as he was in front of the stove, the ship pitched again. Derek slammed into the hot stove top, searing his palms and wrists. He dropped the coal bucket with a yelp. Saehrimnir flailed his arms to keep balance.

"Watch yourself, or you'll knock me over!" The cook stumbled toward the doorway. "Hurry up with those coals. I'll get a bucket of sand from the ballast to douse what's left."

Derek threw open the oven's door and shoveled a scoopful of hot ash into his bucket. "What should I do with this?" he asked, holding up the bucket.

Saehrimnir latched onto the railing as he tried to maneuver his bulk down the stairwell. "Throw it overboard! Don't be an idiot." And he started down the stairs again.

"But I'm chained up!" Derek yelled.

The cook considered for a moment and then came grumbling back to Derek, digging a black skeleton key out of his loincloth. "Awwal will have my hide for freeing you, but if the oven busts open and we don't have this fire out, we are done for." He took off Derek's chain and started for the stairs again. "I'm getting sand. Now hurry up!"

Derek threw himself into his task. It wasn't easy, what with *The Delivery* pitching sharply in all directions, but he had the belly of the stove cleaned out before Saehrimnir found his way back from the ship's hold.

Derek slapped a cover over the coals, picked up the bucket, and grabbed a shelf to help himself stand. The floor dipped and sagged under his feet, rising and plummeting with the waves. Derek swung back and forth, knowing he needed to get to the upper deck, but not knowing how to get there with only one hand free. He slid his hand along the shelving, and that helped him get out of the kitchen, but once he got to the stairwell, a sudden pitch to the side sent him sprawling into the walls. He threw out his free hand, snatched a railing, and drew himself toward the deck one handhold at a time.

A chilled wind roared and filled the stairwell with a white, swirling mist that tasted of salt. Water from the sea and rain splattered down the hatch, making each step a treacherous trap. He fought against the ship as it rose and fell. Twice, he slipped and banged his shins, but he held the bucket of hot coals with a death grip.

Finally, Derek made it to the top step and gaped at what he saw. Sailors clung to masts and railings all over *The Delivery*. Some had ropes around their waists, binding them to the ship. Others, rope-less, held on for dear life. Between waves, the sailors struggled to draw down sails and batten hatches. Awwal barked orders from the middle of the deck, his legs braced wide as a wave broke over the railing. Several men lost their grips and slid past Derek. Two of the men were saved by the tethers holding them to a set of bolted, iron chests, but a third disappeared when the wave sloshed over the far railing and the tether holding him snapped. He disappeared without a sound, the frayed end of the rope that had been around his waist the only sign he had ever existed.

"Man overboard!" Awwal yelled, and several men nearby rushed to the railing to search for him.

The first man to the railing pointed into the frothy sea. "There he is! Get a barrel to him!"

Derek watched for a moment as they found a barrel tied to a rope. One of the sailors hurtled it into the sea in the man's general direction and then clung desperately to the railing. Derek shook his head. The man was gone, he knew. Who could survive the growing waves?

Derek turned his attention to the task of emptying the coal bucket. Now that he was out of the ship's belly, Derek found he could predict the pitch and roll of the ship better than when he was in the galley because he could see the waves coming. He hurried across the slippery deck, sliding to a stop by the railing. Looping one arm around a rail, Derek wriggled the lid off his coal bucket and emptied the bucket into the sea.

"That was easy," Derek said to himself.

"Rogue wave!" Awwal yelled.

Sailors scrambled for cover, screaming to Ra for mercy. Derek looked around, confused, until he saw the source of their terror. Bearing down on *The Delivery's* bow was a wave as tall as the Tower of Sorcery in Zuid Horn. Derek dropped the coal bucket, wrapped his arms and legs through the railing, and squeezed for all he was worth. *The Delivery* rose and rose, its bow pointing higher and higher into the sky. Anything that wasn't tied down on deck slid to the back of the ship, slowly at first, but then faster and faster until some of the lighter chests skidded across the deck and flipped into the air to disappear into the sea. Derek closed his eyes and prayed to the Forge.

In the middle of his prayer, the bow of the ship leveled off, and Derek opened his eyes. They were at the top of the world, the sea far below them. The sky was dark and low. They were so high upon the crest of this wave, Derek felt that if he reached up, he would be able to touch the black clouds. Row upon row of waves, as mighty as the wave they were riding, stretched out before them. Derek's stomach tightened at the sight of them, and his arms felt impossibly heavy. He was already exhausted from the ten lashes. His back screamed from the salt water in his wounds. How was he going to survive this? The ship slipped from the crest and dropped as though it had fallen into a canyon, its bow dipping almost straight down. Derek let go of his bucket so he could cling to the railing with both hands. The bucket tumbled through the air and smashed against the wall of the captain's quarters far below him. He watched as anything that wasn't properly tied down slid past and down the deck to batter the captain's small room. There was a sharp wrenching sound, and then the cracking of bolts snapping. Derek looked up to see a huge, iron chest, half as tall as he was and again as wide, sliding straight toward him.

Derek hugged the rails as the chest shot past. It hurtled toward the captain's quarters and blasted through the wall with an explosion of splinters just as *The Delivery* reached the bottom of its plummet. The bow of the ship plunged beneath the sea, but the ship's buoyancy popped it to the surface again. Another thick brush of seawater washed over the prow, clearing the deck of loose debris. Derek held on as the wave washed over him, and the ship began to climb the far side of the next wave.

For a moment, the deck was almost flat. Sailors rushed about, securing lines, tethering sails that had come loose, and closing hatches that had popped open. Awwal stood in the middle of it all, barking orders right and left. Derek let the railing go. For the briefest of moments, he looked to the stairwell leading to the galley and safety. But then he looked to the captain's quarters, with the new hole in the wall from the iron chest, and he knew he would never have a better chance to search the captain's room again. Derek bit his lip and made a break across the deck, dancing out of sailors' ways as he went.

To his surprise, the door was unlocked. Derek slipped inside and closed the door behind him. The room was in complete shambles. Papers were everywhere. Shelves were overturned. The captain's small table and chair were flipped against the far wall. The remains of the captain's dinner were splattered over the floor. Derek saw all of this and suddenly froze.

There, in the dim light, the captain was looking straight at him. Terror flooded Derek's limbs, giving him strength. He searched frantically for a weapon, then rushed to the overturned table, tore off a table leg, and held it over his head.

But the captain didn't move.

Derek crept closer. Why wasn't the captain moving? Derek peered at the Shadizarian, and then realized why the man was so still. There, buried in the captain's ribcage, was the iron chest that had punched through the wall. Broken bits of ribs, like skeletal fingers, reached around the edges of the iron chest and poked through the captain's finery. His eyes were frozen wide, as though he had been looking at the wall when the chest exploded through it. The captain's mouth sagged open, but his ruined lungs offered no wind to give voice to his pain.

Derek lowered his makeshift club. The floor rose and fell under his feet. He crawled across the room on his hands and knees and searched through the papers littering the floor. He held them up in the dim light, green from the storm, and looked for anything that would tie *The Delivery* to the rotten underbelly of the Iron Guard. Derek flipped through ledgers and scrolls and reams of papers as the ship pitched and heaved.

Just as he was about to give up, he felt his chest surge with excitement as he found a scroll dated from only a week earlier. Derek scanned the scroll, running his finger under his reading to help him keep his place as the ship rocked from front to back. "By the Forge, this is it," he whispered.

Rolling the scroll into a tube, Derek hurried to the captain's shelf and wedged the scroll tube behind it. He breathed a sigh of relief just as the ship's bow began rising up the side of another huge wave. Derek grabbed an iron hand loop in the wall, probably designed just for that purpose, and held on as *The Delivery* rose and rose. Papers and cups and inkwells and quills tumbled to the far side of the room. The bow continued to rise, and the table and chair slid across the room until they slammed into the far wall. Derek watched the captain's body, with the iron chest still embedded in his chest, slide across the room to be buried under the debris raining down.

Derek's feet slipped out from under him. He dangled in the air, his gut churning as he realized that at the pitch *The Delivery* was rising, it could very well flip over, its hull belly-up in the sea. There would be nothing he could do to save his friends who were trapped below deck, chained to their seats.

Then, as if his thoughts had summoned them, Derek heard the screams of the dozens of slaves below the captain's quarters, begging for help, praying to their gods for mercy. Derek panicked, knowing he had to get to his friends. But with the front of the ship still rising, he would have to wait until they crested this wave and began their next descent. He hung on for dear life and watched as bits of paper and silver perfume jars and jingling copper coins from Shadizar slid over the floor and tumbled through the hole in the wall created by the iron chest that killed the captain.

Thinking of the captain, Derek found the Shadizarian's broken body buried in a pile of rubble against the far wall. The dead man's limbs jutted from the midden heap like a broken scarecrow. *The Delivery* pitched, and the entire pile slid toward the door, which burst open and now flapped wildly in the storm. Bit by bit, the trash dropped out the door, taking the captain's body with it. The captain flipped through the opening, his arms windmilling as his mangled corpse fell through the air past several wide-eyed sailors, careened off the central mast, and landed with a muted splash in the black sea behind the ship.

Derek felt a vomitous bubble rising in his throat. There was no way the ship would survive this storm. He had led his friends on a death mission, and it was all his fault. Knowing it was his fault was worse than knowing this storm was going to kill them. Despair weighed him down, making the grip he had on the iron ring more tenuous than ever. A part of him wanted to let go of his hold and join the captain in the churning seas, but another part of him told him to hang on. He was still alive, and, as far as he knew, so were his friends. There had to be a way out.

The ship's timbers groaned when *The Delivery* reached the peak of another crest and hung there, precariously, before starting down the long slope to the other side. His feet found the floor again, and he collapsed. Sailors shouted to one another on the deck, and Awwal barked orders. "Close the oar ports! Three came open on the starboard side! You there! Check your lashing! It's coming loose!"

Derek hurried across the room before the ship began its descent down the next wave. He had to get below deck before Awwal caught him in the captain's quarters. Derek opened the door to only to find his way blocked by a shadow squatting in the slashing rain. "There you are, you little rat!"

Ahriman! The Shadizarian assassin gripped the doorframe with one hand. With the other, he slid a slim, curved dagger from behind his back. "I don't know how you got out of your chains this time, but there's no one to save you now." He grabbed the side of a bookshelf and pulled himself into the room one hand at a time as the ship dropped into the canyon between waves.

Derek scrambled away, tripping over his feet. The floor was dropping fast, and with nothing to hold onto, Derek went skidding across the room. He heard the scraping of clutter rushing toward him from the opposite side of the captain's quarters. Ahriman eased himself down the far wall like a spider, moving from a bolted shelf to a fixed, iron chest, creeping closer to Derek all the while. "I should have knifed you when I saw you yapping with Niles Crowing back in Zuid Horn. That wretch has caused nothing but problems for Shadizar."

Derek searched frantically for a weapon. Amazingly, he found the table leg he was going to use against the captain and held it over his head.

Ahriman laughed. "You think a boy with a table leg is going to stop a Shadizarian assassin? Think again."

Ahriman held onto the shelf as the ship's bow dipped lower and lower. Outside, the roar of wind and waves almost drowned out the sailors' screams. But inside, Derek's attention was fixed on the dark man in the wet, canvas cloak working his way toward him. Derek tried to move back, but clutter from the pitched room blocked his way. He risked a glance over his shoulder. He only had two steps before he would be at the far wall. When he turned his attention back to Ahriman, he found the assassin was almost on him.

Derek gasped and stumbled backwards, holding his makeshift club between himself and Ahriman. Ahriman crouched and crept over the clutter. A necklace slipped from under his tunic, and Derek saw it was the silver vial from Niles Crowing. Ahriman noticed Derek looking at it. The assassin fingered the vial with his free hand and sneered. "Tell me, dead boy, did you really think Niles Crowing was coming to save you?"

Derek's throat tightened. Ahriman studied Derek with glittering eyes. "Nothing to say? Let me tell you what's going to happen. I'm going to knife you and toss you overboard. Then, when we get to Shadizar, my masters will use this vial to trap Niles Crowing once and for all." Ahriman slashed with his curved dagger, and Derek leapt to the side.

Derek knew he needed to stall if he wanted to find a chance to survive. "What's the point?" Derek asked, circling the best he could as *The Delivery* pitched and rolled. "The ship is going to capsize unless we all work together!"

"*The Delivery* will weather this storm," Ahriman continued, stalking closer and closer. "We will arrive in Shadizar, and your friends will be sold into slavery. Awwal and I will make a pretty profit, and in a few months, we'll turn around and head back to Zuid Horn." He slashed at Derek, tearing a thin gash across Derek's arm. Ahriman licked his lips and edged closer. "And this time, Derek Fulstarter, I'll hunt down your sisters."

"What?" Derek's back seized up.

Somehow, even the ship's dangerous pitch ceased to be of importance. The assassin's lips peeled back to reveal a row of wet, yellow teeth. "That's right, Derek Fulstarter. I know who you are. It wasn't hard to find out. How long did you think the son of an artisan could get away with playing an unsung hero?"

He leapt at Derek and drew two quick slashes across Derek's belly. Derek clutched his bleeding gut, expecting to feel the slippery snakes of his intestines wriggling out, but the cuts had only broken the surface. Derek looked at his bloody fingers, and the assassin laughed. "That's right," Ahriman said. "I'm playing with you just like I'm going to play with Liza."

At the mention of his sister's name, the back of Derek's neck tingled. The vision around the edge of his awareness flashed white, and a surge of energy coursed through him. "No!" Derek screamed, and he leapt at the Shadizarian, swinging the table leg in great arcs.

Ahriman laughed and danced out of the way. "Ho, ho! This one's got a bit of life left in him!"

Derek swept the club back and forth, putting everything he had into each swing. His stomach burned where the assassin's blade had carved him up, but his anger from hearing the Shadizarian's threat to his sister drove him to near madness. He worked Ahriman across the heaving room until he had the assassin backed into a corner.

Ahriman grinned wolfishly. "All that rage," he said, "blinds you in a fight."

Derek screamed and swung furiously. Ahriman's eyes gleamed as he ducked under the blow. Laying the edge of his dagger against Derek's ribs, the Shadizarian slipped past him and ripped a slick gash alongside Derek's chest. Derek howled and stumbled into the corner, clutching his bleeding ribs. Ahriman snickered and whirled on Derek again.

"Too easy," he said.

Clutching his belly with one hand, Derek held his table leg before him. "Leave my sisters alone."

"I don't think so," Ahriman said, circling Derek as the ship's floor rose and fell under their feet. "In fact, I think I'll grab Sarah as well. They'll fetch a hefty price in Shadizar."

"Leave them alone!" Derek screamed.

Ahriman bent his face into a mockery of a frown. "Just think of how desperate your parents will be. One day, your sisters will be there, and the next," he kissed the air, "poof. Gone."

"You snake!"

The assassin's mouth twisted into a sneer. "I want you to die knowing you made your parents miserable."

Derek tightened his grip on the table leg and attacked Ahriman with a howl. The Shadizarian moved like a cobra, darting in and out, stinging Derek again and again with the tip and edge of his dagger. Derek was bleeding from a dozen wounds, but none of them were deep enough to be a killing blow. Derek felt his head growing light, and he staggered as the bow of the ship dipped into another deep valley. Ahriman moved lightly to track Derek and smiled at the boy's failing strength.

"I've enjoyed playing with you, boy, but now it ends." The assassin drew a second dagger from behind his back and stalked toward Derek.

There was a loud crack from outside the captain's quarters. Sailors shouted, and Derek heard Awwal scream over the storm, "Look out!"

Suddenly, the ceiling exploded into a thousand splinters as the main mast crashed through the roof. Wet lines, wrapped sails, and the polished cedar of the cross-post dropped into the room with a wash of rain and seawater. Derek fell back against the wall, and then a surge from the waves threw him forward against the mast, now lying on the floor of the captain's quarters in a tangle of lines, bound sails, and clay roof tiles from the smashed quarters. Derek squinted through the rain and mist, knowing an assassin was still in the room with him.

Ahriman was on the floor, holding his head with one hand, a dagger in the other. The Shadizarian was on his knees, and the back of his head was bleeding. The man's threat to Liza and Sarah echoed in Derek's head. A wave of strength pulsed through him, and he tightened his grip on his table leg. Derek launched himself over the ruined mast and landed lightly on his feet in front of Ahriman. The assassin looked up, his eyes dazed. Derek didn't wait for pity to stay his hand. He took his makeshift club in both hands.

"For my sisters," he growled, and he caught Ahriman under the chin with a mighty blow.

Ahriman's mouth exploded in a spray of red and white. His broken teeth clattered over the wet floor, and he collapsed on his back. He fought back to his elbows, but Derek dealt him another blow, and the Shadizarian assassin collapsed for the final time.

Derek's lungs burned. Rain and salty mist filled his eyes. He dropped to his knees and felt the ship roll and pitch under him. His body was battered. Lashed at the post, sliced by a trained assassin, and exhausted from fighting for his life, Derek wanted nothing more than to drop into a sleep, but he knew his friends were counting on him.

"You!" a voice shouted from where the door to the captain's quarters used to be. "What are you doing up here?"

It was Awwal. The first mate stood in the doorway, gripping what was left of the frame with white knuckles. Walls of seawater broke over the walls and doused the room. Wind howled through the two remaining masts and screamed through the railings. Awwal glared at Derek, then noticed the assassin's body and the wash of blood spreading over the floor. Awwal's eyes narrowed.

"What did you do?" he asked and stepped carefully into the room.

Derek tried to stand but fell on his backside. He scooted away as fast as his broken body would let him. "He tried to kill me!"

Awwal crossed the room one careful step at a time, his well-earned sea legs keeping him steady. "I should have listened to Ahriman," Awwal said, sliding a rapier free from the scabbard at his side, "and killed you when I had the chance."

Derek scrambled to Ahriman's broken body and tore open the assassin's tunic. The silver vial lay against his chest at the end of a leather necklace. Derek grabbed the vial and yanked hard, but the leather held. "What are you doing?" Awwal shouted but then

seemed to understand what was happening. He growled, "Oh, no you don't."

Derek looked up in time to see the first mate lunging across the floor, his rapier aimed at Derek's heart. With nothing else to do, Derek rolled to the side, over the assassin's body. The tip of the rapier missed his heart but plunged into the meat under Derek's collarbone.

The boy screamed, and the first mate grinned as he twisted the steel in the boy's chest. "You deserve worse than this for all the trouble you've caused me." He drew the rapier back and readied himself for a killing blow.

Derek felt the blood draining in thick pulses from the hole in his chest. One arm hung limply at his side, but in his good hand, he still clutched the silver vial. He remembered Niles' words in the Ranger Outpost. *"Once you have the proof we need, go to the back of the boat, pull the cork, and toss the whole thing into the ocean. It's gotta mix with seawater, otherwise it won't work."* There was no way Derek was getting to the back of the boat now, but he hoped there was enough seawater in the ruined captain's quarters for the magic to function. He wedged his thumb under the lid, he flipped it open, and dumped the glowing contents into the seawater sloshing back and forth all around him.

Awwal looked at the thick, amber liquid glowing brightly in the dark of the storm. "No!" he screamed, and he whirled to watch the magic at work.

A thin, vertical line, taller than a man and glowing more brightly than the sun, flashed from where the amber liquid mixed with the seawater. Derek collapsed on his back and held up his good hand against the magic's light. He watched as two massive, taloned hands burst from inside the line and pulled it into more of an oval shape. There was a roar, and a massive head pushed through the magical gateway, which was quickly taking the shape of a doorway.

Derek recognized the beast as an ogress, with yellowed tusks and angry, black eyes. The creature squeezed its bulk through the passage and rose to its full height. It was armored from head to toe in plate mail. Its fists were housed in gauntlets of iron, which it pounded together as it roared at Awwal. The gauntlets buzzed and gave off a golden glow. The Shadizarian shrank back, his weapon held high.

"No!" he screamed and leapt at the ogress.

Awwal slashed with his rapier, years of raiding and pirating giving his blade a quickness that would cut most adversaries to shreds. But the ogress, surprisingly nimble, knocked aside the Shadizarian's slashes and grabbed Awwal by the sword arm. Derek watched in horror as the creature jerked the first mate hard to the left and then back to the right. There was a sickening, wet crack as the first mate's sword arm snapped. Awwal screamed and writhed to escape. His face was ghastly white, and his arm bent wildly above the elbow where no joint should have existed. The ogress raised Awwal to its face and roared, the sea and the wind lashing them both.

"You'll pay for this!" Awwal screamed, and reached for the dagger he kept in a scabbard at the back of his belt.

Derek threw himself to his feet. Snatching the table leg in his good hand, he staggered to the battling pair. Awwal yanked the dagger from its scabbard and reared back to plunge it into the unsuspecting ogress's neck.

"No!" Derek shouted and swung with everything he had left, catching Awwal in the arm.

The first mate howled and dropped the dagger, which hit the floor at the same time as Derek.

The ogress yanked Awwal to the side. It glared at the dagger on the ground and then at Derek, who had crumpled into a miserable heap. The creature roared and reared a fist back, ready to finish the Shadizarian off, when a voice came from behind it. "Wendy, enough. A lady shouldn't play with her food before she eats. Take some of that rope and tie him up. We'll need him for questioning."

Derek blinked through the rain, rubbing his eyes with his good hand. A man in a flapping cloak was standing there, and he wasn't alone. A priest of the Forge, a pair of warriors, a man in a tattered cloak with a face like a weasel, a wizard with a cloak that flapped in the wild wind, and — Were his eyes deceiving him? — a leprechaun.

The man came close and knelt beside Derek. Derek smiled because even though his eyes were blurry with exhaustion, he recognized the man with the closely clipped beard and kind, brown eyes. "Don't worry," the man said. "It will be alright now. You did fine."

Derek nodded and let exhaustion overtake him. He fell asleep smiling because he knew everything would be fine. Niles Crowing and the Magnificent Seven had arrived.

19

Derek gets Salty

Derek and Dani and Conrad sloshed through the silt and rubbish left by the flood a week earlier. Every dozen paces or so, one of them would lose a boot to the sucking mire. Conrad suggested going barefoot to save time, but after Derek almost impaled his foot on a nail just below the surface, they all donned their footwear in a hurry.

It was hard going in the streets. There was the muck to tromp through, of course. But just as bad was the constant losing of their way. Without the landmarks they were used to seeing, Derek and his friends had to rely on the gaunt survivors they passed for directions. Most of these sad scraps of humanity just stared at the friends with deep-set eyes. While Derek and the others had been eating three meals a day in the Tower of High Sorcery for the last week, the people of Zuid Horn had been scrambling for even the tiniest morsels to fill their crying bellies.

The friends had almost rounded the corner to Gillman's Way when they realized what was so odd about the city, besides its destruction. Other than the occasional wail that rose over the squawking vultures and ravens, Zuid Horn was silent. They hadn't seen an alley cat or even heard a dog bark all the way to Derek's house. When a city starves, anything that moves is fair game for the cooking pot.

That wasn't to say the streets lacked for meat. The problem was that after a week in the sun, none of it was edible. Worse, while the rubble was littered with the decaying corpses of pack animals and pets, most of the corpses they saw were the former citizens of Zuid Horn. On every street, human limbs and torsos jutted from the mud. Once, Derek stepped into what he thought was a debris-free patch of muck, only to find he was stepping on a bloated corpse. When his weight bent the foul thing in half at the waist, its head broke the surface with a wet, sucking slurp and exhaled the remnants of its last breath into Derek's face.

Disgusted, he led the others to the rooftops, where they had run ridgelines and leapt from building to building during the flood. Occasionally, survivors shouted at them to stay off their homes, but starving and weakened as they were, none of them had the strength to stop the friends.

From the rooftops, the children could see the city's destruction more clearly. Along the thoroughfares, where the water had rushed most fiercely, the bulk of the buildings were destroyed. Down on Ploughman's Wharf, the destruction was complete. Any of the buildings along the great walls around Zuid Horn were also a complete loss, as that was where the ocean met its match and doubled back on the city proper. A great, black scorch mark marred the center of town where the foundries once lay. The charred remnants of the buildings reached for the clear blue overhead, like the outstretched hands of dying men pleading to gods who neither listened nor cared for the worries of men.

When they made it to Gillman's Way, they took a short breather on the roof of a carpenter's shop, Peter's home. Grief's cold whisper echoed in Derek's heart. How many times had he played here with his best friend? He remembered climbing onto this very roof with Peter and the scolding Peter's father had given them. Now, his best friend was gone, and his family probably was, too. What kind of world was this going to be, when almost everyone he had loved was dead or gone?

Derek took a sad breath and moved as close to the edge of the roof as he dared. "This was Gillman's Way."

The water had rushed ferociously here. Derek remembered the night of the flood and the way the growling tempest had torn the face of his family's home apart. That had been night, when the dark obscured the full extent of the sea's destruction. Now in the daylight, Derek could see that most of the buildings on Gillman's Way had been torn in half like his family's shop, and there were precious few survivors to reclaim what was left.

Derek stared numbly at the devastation and didn't realize Dani and Conrad were standing next to him at the edge of the roof until Dani spoke. "This is terrible," she whispered.

Dani's hand on his back made him flinch, but then he let himself relax with a heavy sigh. "Yeah. It's so much worse in the daylight."

Something moved in the ruins of the shop below them. A voice called out, "Hey, you kids shouldn't be up there! That roof ain't safe."

The children peered over the edge. A large man, with broad shoulders and a thick chest like Derek's father, plowed through the muck to glare into the sunlight at them. Derek recognized him immediately. It was Peter's father. "Master Lignarius!" Derek shouted.

Atrifex Lignarius snorted. "Master, eh?" He made a sweeping gesture to take in his shop. "Not much of a master, I'll say, when I can't build a home to withstand a flood." He shook his head. "You haven't seen my wife or son, have you?"

Derek shook his head and swallowed the lump in his throat. He knew he needed to tell the truth about Peter, but how do you tell a man his son is dead? "I don't know about Mrs. Lignarius, sir."

"But Peter? Have you seen my son?"

Derek closed his eyes. In a flash, he was back at the night of the flood, standing on the roof of his ruined house, watching the waters rush past. There was Peter, his corpse rolling in the current, his pale eyes staring. There was Liza, screaming to the boy she loved.

"Derek!" Peter's dad demanded. "Have you seen my son?"

Derek nodded once.

A shudder rippled through the big man. He held his temples with both hands and staggered in the muck. "I knew it," he muttered. "I just knew it."

The large man wept then, and Derek felt the tears coming to his own eyes.

Master Lignarius rubbed his face and looked up. "Felt it in my gut, I did. Something told me Peter was gone. Does Liza know?"

A knife twisted in Derek's chest. "She's gone too."

Master Lignarius shook his head. "Too much death. Too much death. How will we get past this?"

"I don't know."

Peter's father took a long, slow breath. "Why don't you kids come down here? There's something I have to tell you." Artifex Lignarius pointed to the alley. "Go to the alley side of the roof. I put a ladder up there after the flood. That will be easier for you to get down. Hurry now. I'll see what I can do about getting you kids something to eat."

Derek and the others hurried to the roof's edge and found the ladder as Master Lignarius had promised. They climbed down and then slogged through the mud to the front of his shop. The carpenter was gone, but they could hear him bustling about upstairs in his loft. "I'm up here," he called. "Come on up."

They climbed the stairs to the second floor. Dark splotches of — What, blood? — colored the stairwell. Derek held his breath and continued upstairs. They found Artifex squatting in front of a heavy, wooden chest, reinforced with iron bracings.

"Got my reserves here," he said over his shoulder. "My wife always liked to keep the dried foods up here. Didn't like the rats nibbling at it, she said."

While Artifex dug through his food chest, Derek took in the loft. Despite his sixteen-year friendship with Peter, he'd never been upstairs. Unlike Derek's home, which had a second-floor loft open to the main floor below, the Lignarius loft was only accessible by a stairwell, which could be closed off by a sturdy, wooden trapdoor. Derek saw fresh cuts on the lumber where Master Lignarius had reinforced the trapdoor, as well as new bracings over the windows.

"Looks like you've been busy," Derek said.

Artifex turned from the chest. He had a wineskin of the light wine Zuid Hornians favored, as well as a reed basket filled with dried figs, apples, and raisins. When Derek pointed out the trapdoor and boarded windows, Artifex nodded. "Haven't had a choice, what with the yakariians running rampant at night."

"Still?" Conrad asked and glanced at Derek.

"Packs of them." Artifex passed Dani the basket of dried fruits.

Dani looked at the fruits and then at Derek. She didn't have to say anything for Derek to know what she was thinking. After three meals a day for the last week in the Tower of Sorcery, it seemed almost immoral to eat any of this poor man's food. But what part of any deal with Gilgameth Tuft was moral? Dani let the food basket sink into her lap.

Master Lignarius continued, "Nobody's seen hide nor hair of the Iron Guard, and without them, the world's gone crazy."

"Iron Guard gone?" Conrad said. "Any idea where they went?"

"Dead, most of them," Artifex said, closing the food chest and then using it as a seat. "The flood got them."

"You haven't seen any Iron Guard at all?" Dani asked.

"Well, maybe I exaggerated. There's been a few around, but from what I hear, most of them headed up the coast, to the salt mines."

"Salt mines?" Derek asked.

Master Lignarius nodded and cracked his knuckles. "Yes. That's what I was going to tell you about." He turned to face Derek. "It's about your parents."

Derek shot up like a bolt of lightning. "They're alive?"

"Yes," Artifex nodded, but his face held no joy. "I think so, anyway."

"What's the matter? Where are they?"

The master carpenter looked toward the boarded-over window. "The yakariians got them the day after the flood. A pack of those animals came down Gillman's Way, rounding up anyone they could find. I had almost a dozen people holed up in here when a pair of yakariian scouts came snooping around the shop. They banged on the trap door there, demanding we give ourselves up. We refused, of course, and they came back with a handful of others. I had my father's spear and tickled one in the gut through my murder hole there." He pointed near the trapdoor, and Derek noticed a series of holes along the floor he hadn't seen before. "I got another one right in the neck. They left us alone after that. Boarded up my windows that night, and I've been safe here ever since."

"But what about my folks?"

"They weren't with me, Derek. I never saw them, to be honest. I'm just telling you what I heard from Old Judith."

Old Judith was an herbalist who ran a tiny shack down the way from Derek's house. "Old Judith is alive?"

Master Lignarius shrugged. "Who's to say who would survive and who would die? Anyway, she said the yakariians dragged your da from his shop. They roughed him up a bit, demanding that your mum come out of her hiding place, or they'd kill him. You can guess what she did, even when your da told her not to."

Derek looked at his hands. "How long ago was this?"

Artifex scratched his head. "What is it now... five, six days ago? Not long after that is when the Iron Guard left. The lot of them marched off to the mines, knowing the yakarii would sell off what they couldn't use as slaves first chance they got."

"How many Iron Guardsmen are left?" Dani asked.

Artifex shrugged. "Who knows? Not many. Not enough, anyway. Those few of us that survived do what we can to get on with the rebuilding, but you see how the streets are. Ain't no food. Ain't no clean water. Just thin wine and whatever people had squirreled away in their lofts."

A fierce fire was smoldering in Derek's gut. He wanted to move, had to move. Derek slapped his thighs and stood up. "We need to go. I have to rescue my parents."

"Derek," Dani said, "be patient."

Master Lignarius waved for Derek to sit back down. "Hold on, now. Calm yourself. If you go marching off to the salt mines, you'll end up a yakariian slave or worse." The grizzled carpenter shook his head. "No, you stay here, and let the Iron Guard do their job. It's what your parents would want."

Derek considered for a moment. "But you just said there aren't many Iron Guardsmen left."

The carpenter looked at Derek and sighed. "What could you do that the Iron Guard couldn't?"

"Maybe we could sneak them out?"

"We?" Artifex asked.

Derek looked first at Conrad, and then at Dani. "We're a team."

Artifex looked at the brother and sister. "You're okay with this?"

Conrad stepped forward and stood next to Derek. "We're in it together."

Dani came up to stand beside her brother. "Me, too."

The carpenter sighed heavily and rubbed his face. "I was hoping you weren't going to say that. There's been too much death in Zuid Horn this week, too much slaving. Now to have you three running off, not long after your adventures with the Shadizarians, it's like you're throwing away your second chance at life."

"What kind of life would I have if I wasn't looking out for the people I love?" Derek asked.

"There's that," Master Lignarius admitted, "but I'm just thinking about what your parents would want." Artifex gave another heavy sigh, and then he turned around to open the iron chest he had been sitting on. He pulled out some more dried fruits and meats, put them in a cloth sack, and handed it to Derek. "Here. If you're going to go running off getting yourself caught by the yakariians, you might as well do it on a full belly."

Derek accepted the gift with a low bow. "Thank you, Master Lignarius."

The carpenter waved his hand. "No master here. Just Artifex, if you please. I'll be a master if I can rebuild everything I've lost, but how do you rebuild a broken family?"

"I don't know if any of us can," Derek said. They turned and headed down the stairwell.

The silence was heavy and awkward. Conrad coughed. "There will be plenty of rebuilding to be done, that's for sure."

"True enough," Artifex said, tromping down the stairwell behind Conrad. "And it will be harder still until my wife gets back." His voice broke at the last of it, and he stopped on the stairs just before he reached the bottom. Derek and the others turned to face him. The carpenter's eyes were shiny and wet. "I understand why you kids are doing what you're doing, but I gotta stay here for my wife, in case she comes back. Maybe she survived the flood. Maybe she's still out there. I don't know. If you see her, if you find her at the mines and the Iron Guard haven't freed them, could you..." but he couldn't finish.

"We'll do what we can, if we see her," Derek said. "I promise."

The friends said their goodbyes and hurried the best they could down the mucky street. The mud sucked at their boots as they made their way to Derek's house. "That was hard."

"You did good," Dani said.

"I guess." Derek plodded through the muck. They walked in silence for a while, and then Derek said, "I can't believe they're alive. We have to get to the salt mines."

"Have you ever been there?" Conrad asked.

"No," Derek admitted, "but I've heard merchants talking about them at Augie's inn."

"Everything I've heard about them is pretty bad. Most slaves don't make it for more than a couple of months before, well, you know." Conrad poked his toe at the mud.

"That's why we have to get there as fast as we can," Derek said. "That is, if you two are still willing to go." He turned to his friends. "Sorry for speaking for you in the tower. I shouldn't have been so pushy."

"No," Dani said, "you shouldn't have. But we understand, don't we, Conrad?"

Conrad nodded. "You know we're here for you."

"Thank you," Derek managed through a tight throat.

"How far away are the mines?" Dani asked.

Derek thought for a bit. "About a week's travel, but that's by foot."

"By foot?" Conrad asked. "Riding would be faster, but where are we going to get horses? I doubt there are many horses left in Zuid Horn after the flood, and we don't have any money anyway."

Derek smirked and held up the ring from Gilgameth Tuft. "Who said anything about horses? I say we fly."

Dani and Conrad grinned. "Yes!" Dani said. "Do you know how to get there?"

"It's easy," Derek said. "Just follow the Coast Road. And if we lose that, we just follow the coast. From what the merchants say, the mines are right off the beach."

The friends looked at one another, amazed that they were about to start their search for Derek's parents and the kidnapped Zuid Hornians, and glad for the distraction it might provide. Derek fiddled with the wizard's ring on his finger.

"Let's go to the loft in my house," he said. "If we are going to try these rings out, we shouldn't do it in the middle of the street."

Derek led Dani and Conrad through the muck. They slogged down Gillman's Way, greeting the occasional survivor. The story they heard was the same again and again. Derek's parents had been taken by yakariian warriors, along with dozens of other survivors. The last anyone had seen, the entire lot had been marched off to the mines. No one had seen Peter's mother.

"Here we are," Derek said when they made it to his house. "Let's go upstairs."

The face of the house was missing, revealing the sleeping loft his family had used for generations. Even from the ground, Derek could see his mother's closet had been torn open. Its door dangled from the hinges like a loose tooth. The bed mats were torn to shreds, and holes dotted the wall, as though the looters had been searching for secret compartments.

"Looks like someone tried to loot the place," Conrad said.

Derek nodded with a grunt. "Not much to find. Da's money box was on the first floor, and he brought most of each day's earnings to the Bank of the Forge, anyway. Ever since that break-in when I was a kid, he never had more than a handful of silver in the shop." Derek pointed to the ladder leading to the loft. "Come on."

They climbed up and settled down on a tattered pile of blankets that used to serve as a bed. Each of the children took off their rings and studied them. "How do you think we use them?" Dani asked.

Derek shrugged. "I don't know. Maybe we just say what we want to be."

"Maybe," Conrad said. "Or what if all we have to do is think about what we want to be?"

"Do we have to wear the rings or not?" Dani asked.

Derek sighed and rubbed the back of his neck. "I can't believe we didn't ask how to use them."

"I was just excited to have a magic ring," Conrad admitted.

Dani held up her ring in the sunlight. "I've never had a magic *anything* before." She dropped her hand and leaned back on her elbows. "I wish Niles was here. He would know what to do."

"So do I, but we don't have time to look for him. Besides, we promised Gilgameth Tuft we wouldn't have contact with Niles."

They were quiet for a while, and then Dani suddenly stood up and put on her ring. "I'm just going to do it," she said. "I've been wanting to do magic." Conrad and Derek watched as she closed her eyes and said, "Ring, I want to be an eagle."

A yellowish haze formed around Dani. It made Derek's eyes hurt, so he turned his head away for a moment. When he looked back, she was gone. A beautiful golden eagle squatted where she had been standing. Dani the eagle looked around.

Derek and Conrad stared at Dani with open mouths. The eagle flapped its wings and hopped up and down, squawking and shrieking. "Dani?" Conrad asked. "Is that you?"

Dani the eagle flapped her wings in reply.

"Wow," Derek whispered. He stood up and slipped his ring on his finger. Closing his eyes, he said, "Ring, I want to be an eagle."

A warm pulse flooded through Derek's veins. He felt dizzy, as though the room were growing around him, and pieces of his body were flailing out in a million different directions. He closed his eyes against a wave of nausea, and when he opened them again, he shivered in surprise. His vision was exceptionally crisp. He watched as a spider on the ceiling sipped at a droplet of water. Each feather on Dani's head stood out to him as though she were a twelve-foot-tall forest giantess. When he looked at himself, he found that he was covered with a glossy coat of golden feathers.

Dani the golden eagle was studying Derek. "Amazing," she said.

Derek flapped his wings. "Hey! I can understand you!"

Dani laughed and hopped around. "We're birds!" she sang.

Conrad gawked at the bird versions of Derek and his sister. "Are you guys alright?"

"We're fine!" Derek squawked. "Hurry up!" But Conrad gave no sign that he understood.

Finally, Conrad stood up and put on his ring. "Ring," he said, "I want to be an eagle."

And in a few moments, there were three eagles squatting in the loft where just a brief moment before, the three friends had been. The eagle versions of the children laughed and hopped about, wondering at their new incarnations.

"This is amazing!" Derek said. "But we should go. Come on, follow me!" And without another word, he ran toward the edge of the loft, spread his wings, and lifted himself into the air.

He dipped low into Gillman's Way and dropped toward the muck-laden street. His mind froze. Should he glide? Should he flap? Derek the eagle threw his wings wide and flapped for all he was worth. He wobbled and careened across Gillman's Way, right toward the ruin of Beru's old shop.

"Stop flapping so hard!" Dani laughed. "Just listen to your body!"

Derek tried to stop flapping his wings, but that only made him drop faster. A soft, golden whirl flashed by him as Dani shot past.

"Watch, silly!" Dani flapped once to gain altitude and then spread her wings wide. She sailed over Gillman's Way, and with another flap, rose above the gray streets. "Come on!" she sang. "This is great!"

A hot flash of anger boiled in Derek's throat. "Wait!" he screeched, but Dani only laughed and flew higher and higher. Derek growled the best he could with his bird throat and copied Dani's method. One flap, spread the wings wide. To his irritation, it worked perfectly.

"Not bad," Conrad the eagle said from next to him. "It's like you've been flying your whole life."

Derek flapped to gain more altitude. "Whatever," he grumbled.

Conrad pointed his beak at Dani, soaring overhead. They could hear her laughing and singing. "She's really got it," Conrad said.

"I guess."

Conrad looked at Derek. "What's gotten into you? One minute, you're happy to be an eagle, and the next minute, you're all angry."

Derek turned away from his friend. How could he explain something he didn't even understand himself? Of course, he was embarrassed that he wasn't good at flying, but who would really expect him to be? No, the truth of it dawned on Derek as he watched Dani enjoying herself as an eagle, flying high above Zuid Horn. Something about seeing Dani so comfortable with the magic when he was the one who had agreed to pay the price for the magic rings made his scalp tingle with irritation. It was embarrassing to even think of it.

"It's nothing. I'm just being stupid."

Conrad laughed. "Well, that's nothing new."

They caught a rising bubble of warm air and rode it over the city. Derek felt the air, thick beneath his wing feathers. The way it supported him reminded Derek of being in the ocean with his father, with his strong, artisan hands bracing him against the waves, holding him up, keeping him from dropping under. Derek felt a tickle in his chest, and he wondered if he would ever see his mother or father again.

He let loose that pain in a mighty screech, pushed hard against the current and rose higher and higher over Zuid Horn. Conrad called for him to come back, but that was not what he needed now. He looked up and saw Dani far above him. There was no way he could catch her, and when he realized that, the smoldering flame of anger flared to life again. Despite his irritation with her, he heard Dani in his memory telling him to *breathe...breathe... breathe*, so he closed his eyes for a moment and breathed the anger away.

The city shrank below him until it was little more than a gray smear dotted with soot black flecks. Breechwood Forest stretched out like a green quilt, a puffed field of emerald butting against the aquamarine blue of the sea. There were ships in the harbor, miniscule specks with colored sails spanning the rainbow. Zuid Horn might have taken a disastrous blow, but it would rebuild itself and prosper once more.

But what was a boy of sixteen to do about any of that? All he could worry about was getting what was left of his family back together. After everything he had been through, this one simple thing was all that mattered. Derek looked below and saw Conrad struggling to keep up. Despite Derek's bad temper and all the bad choices he had made, Conrad was still with him. He was the most loyal friend Derek had ever known. Derek's chest surged with the replenishing breath of friendship, and he wheeled in a great arc until his friend could catch up. Dani was off on her own, high overhead. She would come back to them when she was ready.

When Conrad finally caught up to Derek, they let loose a mighty pair of screeches and turned northwest, toward the coast, toward the salt mines, and towards the parents that, this time, Derek would not let down.

20

Derek Keeps His Word

Derek's sweet slumber in the captain's quarter of *The Delivery* only lasted for a brief moment before a blast of energy coursed through his body and jolted him awake. He sat bolt upright. The wind was still howling, the rain was still pouring, and *The Delivery* was still rising and falling with the sickening waves.

A large man holding a dagger emblazoned with the Holy Anvil of the Temple of the Forge knelt next to him. Blood ran from half a dozen wounds all over his chest and belly. Sparks of dwindling magic crackled over his outstretched hands.

He spoke, "There you are, boy. Welcome back."

Derek rubbed the seawater out of his face. "You're a priest of the Forge."

The man smiled. "That I am, boy. Was an orphan before the temple took me in years ago."

Nile Crowing appeared from behind the man and knelt beside Derek. "Derek, this is Father Ferrum. He is a friend of mine. Are you feeling better?"

Derek looked at his arms and pulled the tattered remains of his shirt up to inspect himself. His blood was everywhere, but there were no open wounds. In fact, he felt no pain at all. White scars told the tale of Ahriman and Awwal's attacks, but that was it. Even his back felt better. He touched a scar gingerly. "I'm healed. How?"

Father Ferrum smiled. "By the grace of the Forge, boy." The priest drew a needle and thread from a pack at his side and began stitching up the wounds covering his body.

"What happened to you?" Derek asked.

The priest of the Forge shrugged. "Someone had to pay the price for your healing."

Derek wanted to ask more, but a heavy thumping interrupted him. A towering, red-haired man stalked up behind Niles and Father Ferrum. The man had a pair of ironwood-hafted hatchets in his hands. He eyed Derek and nodded. "The boy is better? Good. We'll need all the hands we can get to take this ship. The storm's dying down. We should go soon."

Niles looked over his shoulder at the hatchet-wielding man. "There will be time enough for that, Manny." Niles turned back to Derek. "Derek, this is another friend of mine, Manny Haccian. Manny, this is Derek."

Manny grunted and lumbered toward the ruined door. "I'll keep an eye on things. This could get ugly quick!" he shouted over the wind.

Derek sighed in exasperation. How much uglier could things get?

Niles leaned close to Derek. "Manny used to fight in Shadizar's gladiatorial pits. I broke him and Alum Aqadh free years ago, and they've been with me ever since."

Niles pointed to a lanky Shadizarian following Manny to the splintered door. Alum Aqadh wore slim slabs of leather armor over his thighs, shins, and forearms. He wore a coat of chain mail that glimmered in the dim light of the storm. On his head was the conical helmet of the Shadizarian army.

Derek lifted a chin at Alum Aqadh. "Was he in Shadizar's army?"

"Yes," Niles said, offering Derek a hand and then pulling him to his feet. "One of King Folio's best lancers."

"How did he end up in the fighting pits?"

Niles shrugged. "Hard to say. His story changes every time I ask him. Sometimes, he was betrayed by an old lover. Other times, his brother sold him into slavery. I think the real reason is too embarrassing for him to admit. All I know is that since he's been with me, he's been nothing short of honorable."

The deck pitched, and the table leg Derek had used as a club in his fight against Awwal and Ahriman rolled across the floor and bumped into his leg. Derek bent to pick it up. "I didn't think I was going to use this again, but it did the job with these two." Derek pointed at Awwal and Ahriman.

Niles laughed. "A table leg?"

"Yes."

"Amazing." Niles pulled a short rapier from his side and handed it to Derek. "Here. Do you think you can handle this?"

Derek held up the thin blade in the rain and frowned. "I've never used a sword before. I think I had better stick with this." He patted his table leg and handed the rapier back to Niles.

"Probably better that way," came a voice right next to Derek's ear.

Derek leapt and turned in the air, but there was no one behind him. Niles laughed until he doubled over. "Show yourself, Lenny, before our young friend dies of fright."

A sharp, popping noise introduced the figure of a tiny man, no bigger than a street cat, dressed in brown trousers and a traveling coat. He wore a trim hat with a sparrow's feather tucked into the brim. Stranger still, the little man had a fine wooden stump where his left leg should have been.

Niles, still laughing, knelt on the ground. "Derek, allow me to introduce you to one of my longtime companions, Lenny the Unlucky Leprechaun."

"Pl-pleased to meet you," Derek stammered, barely able to remember his manners.

"The pleasure is mine." Lenny bowed. "So," he asked Niles, "what's the plan?"

Michael Weber

"We need to take this ship and take it fast. The sailors are busy with the storm, so let's take advantage of that." Niles leaned a bit to peer out the cabin door. "Derek, how many soldiers are on *The Delivery*?"

"Between twenty and thirty, I think. To be honest, I spent most of my time chained up in the kitchen."

"And what about sailors?" Lenny asked.

"The same again, from what I could tell," Derek said. "But with this storm, I don't know how many of them washed overboard."

Niles suddenly clapped his hands. "How could I forget! Pavaraci!" he yelled over his shoulder. "Do you have that potion for Derek?"

The brown-robed wizard stepped cautiously through the rubbish until he was next to Niles. His feet were braced as wide as they could go to keep his balance on the wildly bobbing ship. Pavaraci patted down his pockets produced a slim bottle and handed it to Niles. "Be careful with that. I only have a few left."

Niles nodded his gratitude and gave the glass bottle to Derek. "Here. Drink this."

Derek took the vial and studied it. "What is it?"

"It's a little something I mixed up," Pavaraci Moonfist explained. "It will allow you to breathe either air or water."

Derek looked at it dubiously. "It's not going to hurt me?" Pavaraci laughed. "We are here to save you, Derek. If you go overboard in this storm, you're going to thank me."

Derek uncorked the vial and sniffed at the contents, which stank of seaweed and sea salt. "I've never used magic before," he admitted.

"There's always a first time," Lenny the Unlucky Leprechaun said.

Pavaraci shooed Lenny away. The leprechaun disappeared with a pop and reappeared on Niles' shoulder. Pavaraci frowned at the one-legged leprechaun. "Don't scare the boy." The wizard turned to Derek and put a hand on his shoulder. "Derek, if you don't want to use it, you don't have to. Just keep the vial close. If

265

you need it, use it. If you don't use it, you can give it back when this is all over."

Derek breathed a sigh of relief and tucked the vial into his tattered belt. "Well, thank you. I'm just kind of nervous about magic, that's all." He glanced at Father Ferrum, who was putting on his armor. "No offense."

"None taken," said the priest.

Niles waved Derek and the Magnificent Seven closer to him. "My friends, we have a ship to commandeer. Derek, you signaled us. Did you find evidence that the Iron Guard was selling Zuid Hornians to the Shadizarian slavers?"

Derek rubbed his face with his hands. "I almost forgot!"

He hurried to the remains of the captain's bookshelf. Derek had to step over shattered clay tiles and cedar planking where the main mast had crashed into the captain's quarters. The rain was dying down, but enough came through the hole in the roof to give Derek a good soaking. He reached behind the bookshelf and pulled out the scroll tube he had hidden there. Derek opened the tube and peeked inside. Despite all the water, the pages confirming the Iron Guard's corruption were safely dry inside.

"Here," he said, handing the scroll to Niles. "It's all here."

Niles took the tube and knelt on the floor. He held his cloak up with one hand to shield himself from the rain. He pulled the scroll tube's cork out with his teeth and then tapped out the papers. Derek watched Niles scan the documents. The swashbuckler's eyes grew larger as he read. He kept nodding and muttering, "This is it. This is it."

Derek felt a gentle touch on his back. He turned to find Wendy the Ogress frowning at his back. "What happened to your shirt? Why is it ripped?"

Derek felt his face getting hot, despite the cold rain. He readjusted his tattered shirt, hoping it would better cover the marks from the row master's lash. "It's nothing," he said, amazed that the lashings no longer pained him. "Father Ferrum's magic must have completely healed me."

Wendy the Ogress leaned around Derek to better study his back. "Nothing? I don't think so," she said. "Show me."

"Do I have to?" Derek asked, and when Wendy's scowl deepened, Derek had a strange feeling, like he was disobeying his mother. He sighed, pulled off his shirt, and turned around.

Wendy gasped. "Niles! Did you see this?" The ogress grabbed Derek and spun him around so Derek's back was facing Niles.

Niles Crowing looked up and gave a sigh. "Yes."

"Yes? And you let this happen?"

"Wendy, you know how the magic works. We can only open the gate once. I had to wait until Derek could prove the Iron Guard was working with these slavers."

The ogress glared at Niles. "You risked this child's life to complete your quest?"

Derek looked between Wendy and Niles. He hadn't thought of Niles as willing to sacrifice him and his friends. Hadn't they been the ones to ask Niles for help? But Wendy the Ogress shed a new light on things, and the relief Derek had felt when Niles and the Magnificent Seven arrived eroded like a sandcastle under the waves.

Niles carefully rolled the documents back up and tucked them into the scroll tube. "Wendy, how many children and innocents have been dragged into slavery thanks to the Iron Guard's little scam?"

"But look at his back!"

Niles glanced over his shoulder. Derek followed his gaze to see sailors scurrying about on deck, trying to help *The Delivery* weather the storm. Niles gestured for Wendy to lower her voice. "Wendy, keep it down. You're going to get the fight you are looking for, but remember, I'm not one of the slavers. I'm trying to stop them. Do you remember what the Shadizarians did to my sister?"

Wendy the Ogress opened her mouth to argue, but at the mention of Niles' sister, the great toothed maw clamped shut.

"We'll talk about this later," she grumbled to Niles. Then she turned to Derek. "Who did this to you?"

Derek jerked a thumb toward the whipping post. "The row master."

The ogress growled and took Derek by the wrist. She led him to the ruined door, and together they peered out. "Which one is he?"

Derek scanned the deck and found the row master working with a group of sailors to batten down a sail that had come loose. "That one, over there. The man with the red vest."

"That's all I needed to know. Thank you," Wendy said, turning Derek back to Niles. "Come on. Let's see what Crowing has planned."

Wendy and Derek returned to find Niles tapping a cork into the scroll tube. "Derek, I'm sorry this has been so tough on you and your friends, but the four of you have done a great thing for Zuid Horn."

Derek was glad the storm was so dark, or Niles Crowing and the Magnificent Seven would have seen him blushing crimson. "Thanks."

"Alright," Niles said to the group, "we are dealing with slavers. These worms have come into our city and stolen our people. It's going to be messy, but let's keep the captain alive so we can bring him to trial. Maybe we can find out who else is involved in all of this."

"Yeah, about that..." Derek cut in, "The captain is dead. His body flipped out to sea just before you all showed up. And that," Derek said, pointing to Awwal, who was expertly hogtied with one of Wendy's nasty ogre clan knots, "is the first mate."

"Well," Manny said, clacking his hatchets together, "that makes things easy then."

A shadow from the corner rippled and moved toward them. Derek rubbed his eyes, and when he looked again, a pale man wearing a black leather vest, black bracers, a navy cloak, and a belt of curved daggers stood next to Niles.

"Maybe not so easy," the man said with a voice that reminded Derek of an arrow in flight. "How many soldiers and slavers are on this ship? Almost sixty?"

"More or less," Derek said.

"If that's the case and we go plowing through them, the ones in back will have time to react to our first strike. Bashing skulls isn't the best route here. No offense, Wendy," the man said.

"None taken, Kassar," the ogress said, flexing her meaty fists until her iron gauntlets creaked. "But bashing skulls is what I'm best at."

"That it is," Kassar admitted. "But we can't get to all of them at once. If a pack of sailors see things are going badly, what's to stop them from slipping below and using the slaves as hostages? They all know what's going to happen if we take this ship back to Zuid Horn. They will be swinging in gibbets on Ploughman's Wharf soon after we arrive."

Niles nodded. "Derek, this is Kassar the Swift, the last member of the Magnificent Seven and a man I've owed my life to more than once." He turned to Kassar. "You make a good point, my friend, and that's why our attack won't only come from the main deck."

"It won't?" Wendy asked, sounding disappointed.

"Of course not," Niles said, smirking at Derek. "I have a plan."

"Bah," Manny growled. "I was hoping to crack some bones."

"You're not the only one," Wendy the Ogress said.

"Quiet," Niles said, drawing them closer. "There will be plenty of bone cracking for the both of you." Manny and Wendy grinned at one another. The combination of Manny's broken teeth and Wendy the Ogress's fetid breath made Derek's stomach churn. Niles ignored them and continued. "Now, listen up, and I'll tell you what we are going to do."

***

A short time later, Derek was standing next to the elven wizard and biting his nails. "I've never used magic before."

Pavaraci Moonfist sighed. "So, you said earlier. Stay back a little while I am casting the spell, and you will be fine."

Derek, Niles Crowing, and the Magnificent Seven crowded together in a tight circle at the back of the captain's quarters. Pavaraci knelt in the middle of the pack. He traced a spiraling circle on the wooden planks of the floor with a slim dagger. Then, he sprinkled silver dust into the groove. The wizard muttered in a low voice, rolling and hypnotic like the sea, and suddenly the silver dust burst into a bright flame. Derek turned his face from the light, and when he looked back, there was a wide hole in the floor where the spiral had been. Staring up from the hole were several pairs of confused eyes.

"The rowing deck!" Derek exclaimed in a whisper. Derek strained his eyes into the dark and was surprised to see a face he barely recognized looking back at him. "Lars!"

The orphan from Zuid Horn sagged in his seat. The fight that had always been in Lars' eyes was gone, replaced with a dull stare. In the dim light of the rowing deck, Derek could see the boy was close to death. His face was gaunt and pale. Great welts across his back told of the row master's fury during the past week. One eye was swollen shut, and one cheek was bruised, bloody, and draining a thick, yellow pus.

"Lars!" Derek whispered. "Niles is here."

A hand pulled Derek gently away from the hole. "Remember your mission, Derek," Niles said. "There are a lot of people we need to save on this ship."

"But Lars looks terrible."

Niles frowned and took Derek by the shoulders. "I know, and Father Ferrum will help him. But first, we need to secure this ship. Can you do what I told you to do?"

Derek nodded. "Get the key to free the slaves, and then rally them to attack from below."

"Can you do that?"

"I think so."

Lenny the Unlucky Leprechaun stepped next to Derek. "I'll keep an eye on the boy." He clapped his hands, and suddenly the leprechaun was sitting on Derek's shoulder.

"Good," Niles said, and then looked at the table leg in Derek's hand. "You sure you don't want a rapier? It's a lot faster."

Derek shook his head. "This club saved me from a Shadizarian assassin and a sword master." He bounced the table leg in his hands. "We're becoming fast friends."

Niles chuckled and turned to Pavaraci. "Alright. It's time."

The brown-robed wizard stepped in front of Derek and opened a small leather pouch. He took out a pinch of white, crystal-like dust and sprinkled it over Derek. Pavaraci began chanting, and Derek took a step back as the dust fell on him. "What's that?" he asked.

Lenny the Leprechaun, sitting on Derek's shoulder, tugged on Derek's ear. "Don't move. Pavaraci is casting the spell. You don't want him to mess up when he is casting a spell on you. I've seen that before, and it isn't pretty." He lowered and raised his peg leg.

Derek gulped and stood as still as he could. Sparks of light flickered over the wizard's fingers, trailing behind Pavaraci's nimble gestures. The sparks grew in number as he chanted, until the dots of light fused into a shimmering blanket that hovered in the air. Pavaraci grasped the sparkling blanket with delicate fingers and flicked it once, so the blanket rose and then settled over Derek and Lenny.

The world darkened slightly, as though a cloud had passed over the sun. "Well done, Pavaraci," Niles said, looking at Derek and Lenny. "Other than a faint wiggle in the air, I can't see them at all."

Pavaraci frowned. "I'm working on that. Maybe I'll have it ironed out for next time. They should be fine in the dark, below deck."

"Yes," Niles agreed. "They will be fine. Okay, Derek, where are you?'

"Right here." Derek waved his hand. Niles gave no indication he could see him.

"Good," Niles said. "Pavaraci's magic won't last forever. You need to get the key and rally the slaves. Can you do that?"

Derek nodded, but Niles didn't respond. "You have to answer him," Lenny whispered from Derek's shoulder. "He can't see you, remember?"

"Right," Derek whispered to Lenny. Then, to Niles, he said, "Yes, I can do that."

"Good," Niles said. "I'll give you a few moments to rally the slaves. Then, the Magnificent Seven and I will get started up here." Niles looked around the group. "Ready?"

Low grunts answered from all around. Derek moved to the hole Pavaraci had made in the floor. He grasped the edge and swung down.

"Good luck!" the elf whispered, and then stitched his magical portal closed.

Several slaves jerked back when they heard something they couldn't see moving near them. The frightened slaves chattered amongst themselves.

"What's going on?"

"Who was that?"

"There's something down here!"

"Quiet, or they'll bring the whip!"

The slaves rustled and fidgeted on their benches. Their chains rattled in the dim light. Derek wanted to go to them, to let them know he was there to help. Just as he was about to speak to the nearest slave, a bent man with a scraggly beard, Lenny the Unlucky Leprechaun whispered in Derek's ear. "Don't say anything. Most people don't trust magic. Stay focused on your task!"

Derek kept his mouth shut and eased up the narrow lane between the fettered slaves. Lars was on his right. Now that he was closer and his eyes had adjusted to the dim light of the rowing deck, Derek could see the full extent of the punishment Lars had taken. Long, dark welts and gashes crisscrossed his back. His head was shaven, none too carefully, as there were blood-crusted scabs marking where the barber's razor had sliced too deeply. His eyes were swollen almost shut, and his mouth hung open, a thin line of saliva rolling off his bottom lip. Lars' wrists were purple and raw around his manacles, and the boy slumped on his bench, swaying with the rocking of the boat. Other than that, he showed no interest in the world around him.

All the anger and irritation Derek had ever felt for Lars vanished in a flash. He reached out for the battered orphan, but again, Lenny encouraged him. "I know you want to help him, but the best way to do that is to free everyone. There will be time enough for healing later. And remember, Pavaraci's magic won't last forever. Come on."

They kept pushing forward. A few benches later, they came to Jenkins, who looked a little better than Lars, but not by much. Jenkins had a bloody back, courtesy of the master's whip, and his face was only slightly bruised. The boy was looking over his shoulder, trying to see what people in the back of the rowing deck were whispering about. Derek wanted to stop, to let Jenkins know that help was finally here, but Lenny brought his attention back to their mission. "Careful, now. A pair of guards just came down the stairs."

Derek looked up the aisle between the benches and saw two shirtless guardsmen step into the rowing deck. Rain and seawater ran in rivulets off their bodies. Their hair hung in limp coils against their faces, and dark streaks from their Shadizarian eyeliner ran over their cheeks. Their bare chests and arms glistened in the dim light of the slaves' quarters. One of the men stepped forward and scowled at the slaves.

He held up a thin reed and whistled loudly for attention. "Listen up! The storm's dying down. We'll be rowing soon to break out of the back end of this thing. We lost our main mast, so your lousy backs will be what gets us home. Any of you not pulling your weight gets the reed. If I see any of you slacking, the lot of you will get a visit from Waga'a Alam here."

The speaker jerked his thumb at the brute standing just behind him. A stout man brandishing a wide board with square-headed nails driven through it stepped forward. His eyes were deep-set and hidden in shadows, save for a cruel glitter that flickered when he smirked at the slaves. An older man seated in the front row leaned away from Waga'a Alam, and the Shadizarian wheeled on him.

"Did I say you could move?" Waga'a drew back the spiked board and lashed at the chained man, knocking him from the rower's bench in one blow. "Get back to your bench," Waga'a growled and struck the man again. Strands of blood so dark it was almost black flew in arcs from Waga'a's spiked club with each blow.

Derek was several benches from Waga'a, so he couldn't see the blows landing, but he heard the chained man's cries. The back of Derek's scalp tingled, and his vision shivered at the edges of his periphery. "I can't watch this," he said. A nervous knot twisted his innards and grappled with his limbs. He needed to act. Derek rushed Waga'a and his spiked club, waving his table leg over his head.

"Not yet!" Lenny hissed.

Derek ignored the leprechaun's warning and hopped another bench, closer now to the Shadizarian bully.

Waga'a towered over the crumpled slave, his face aglow with a wicked glee. Blood from the beaten man spattered his face and bare chest. His arm was ready for a finishing blow when Derek, still completely invisible thanks to the wizard's spell, came to the slave's defense.

Derek swung hard at Waga'a's unprotected gut. There was the thick *whump* of Derek's club whacking meat, as well as the crisp, white snapping of Waga'a's ribs. The Shadizarian crumpled to the floor, wheezing for breath. Waga'a's partner gave a shout of surprise, but Derek didn't care.

The rage was on him. Derek's mouth twisted into a grimace, and his eyes were set. After serving as a slave on *The Delivery*, Derek was ready to explode. Without giving the second guardsman a chance to figure out what was happening, he swung with all his might at the man's unprotected jaw. Teeth and lip and cheek exploded against the wall with a wet splat, and the second slave driver went down in a heap. A shout went up from the slaves.

"What's happening?"

"Who's there?"

Waga'a Alam groaned from the floor. He clutched his shattered ribs with a trembling hand and crawled toward his spiked club, which had gone clattering over the floor of the rowing deck. Derek breathed hard and stalked toward the downed man. Derek took in a deep breath and raised his club over his head. "No!" Lenny shouted and yanked on Derek's ear. "He's down! You're not a murderer!"

Derek froze, and it was as if a mask, dripping with gore, had been torn from his face. He looked about and saw slaves staring wide-eyed in confusion. The broken bodies of two men lay at his feet.

His breath came in sharp, quick bursts as the rush of anger drained from his limbs. Derek dropped the arm bearing the makeshift club, and he felt himself shaking. He heard Lenny let out a breath of relief. "Thank the Forge," the leprechaun whispered. "You're not a killer, Derek. You don't want to take that path yet, even if they deserve it."

Derek nodded and kept his silence. Waga'a fought to get to his knees. That's when the slaves in the front row saw their chance.

"They're down!"

"Get them!"

One of the men nearest to the Shadizarian raised the length of chain confining him to the bench and whacked the slaver over the head. Waga'a Alam hit the floor and lay there, the back of his scalp split wide. A dark bubble rose like a warm spring from the wound and spread in a coppery puddle over the rough, wooden deck.

"We need to move," Lenny whispered. "Pavaraci's magic won't last forever. Where are the keys?"

Derek stepped to the slavers' bodies. A large, brass ring with a clutch of iron keys hung from Waga'a's belt. He kicked it so the keys jingled, and the man who had felled the slaver looked down. His eyes lit up when he saw the keys.

Just then, there was the crackle of magic and a tremendous explosion from the upper deck. A rousing shout sounded from the sailors and guardsmen up top. The ceiling thrummed with the thunder of more than fifty boots charging into battle. The sharp, blue ring of steel on steel rang from above, and the cries of dying men filled the air.

The slaves chained in the rowing deck looked about with wide eyes.

"What's happening?"

"We're being attacked!"

"Pirates?"

Derek hustled to the stairwell, where a second, third, and fourth set of key rings hung from a rusty nail in the wall. He snatched the key rings and turned back to the frightened slaves.

"People of Zuid Horn!" he shouted above the chaotic chattering. "Niles Crowing and the Magnificent Seven are here, but you must help them! Take the keys from Waga'a's belt. Free yourselves! When you are ready, rush the deck! Use your chains and anything you can find to fight for your freedom!" He tossed the key rings at the Zuid Hornian slaves in the front row. The key rings bounced off their chests and clattered at their feet. They looked at the keys in shock. "Now!" Derek insisted. "Before it's too late!"

Slowly, the slaves awoke from their stupor. One by one, the Zuid Hornians in the front row snatched the keys from the floor and freed themselves and passed the keys to the slaves behind them. Derek watched the shackles come off and rattle on the floor. Several of the slaves who had freed themselves moved in a clutch toward the stairs. "Wait!" Derek shouted. "Wait until you are all freed, and then rush the deck together!"

Dani, her face bruised and beaten from the slavers' whippings, stood and peered into the stairwell. "Derek? Is that you?"

"Yes!" he called. "Wait until everyone is freed, and then rush the upper deck all together. It's the only way this will work."

"Where are you?"

"I'm in the stairwell, on my way to save Conrad."

"By the gods, how is he?"

"I don't know, that's why I have to go. Please, just get everyone free and rush the deck together. It's the only way to help Niles Crowing and the Magnificent Seven."

"Who?"

Derek was about to explain, but Lenny sighed and stopped him. "Don't bother," he said.

"Never mind," Derek called to Dani. "I'll see you up top." And before she could say another word, he turned toward the stairs.

Rather than heading to the upper deck, Derek took the stairs leading to the belly of the ship. "Hey!" Lenny shouted. "Where are you going?"

Derek skipped down the steps two at a time, using the walls for balance as *The Delivery* pitched to-and-fro in the last waves of the storm. "My friend has been locked up as a ratter in the ballast hold since we left Zuid Horn. I don't know if he's alive."

Light from the stairwell barely made it to the lower decks. All lanterns had been extinguished in the storm, so Derek had to feel his way along the dark, narrow corridor. He felt his way past stacks of crates that had been battened down, over piles of lines and nets that had come loose, and through puddles of wine that splashed about after cases of the fine, Shadizarian vintages had broken loose and fallen from shelves during the storm. Finally, he felt the padlocked doorway that led to the ratter's hold.

"Here it is," he whispered. "But it's locked."

"Smash it with your club," Lenny said.

"I would, but I can't see."

"Hold on," Lenny said. "I've got a little something I filched from Pavaraci."

Derek felt Lenny rustling about, and then a bright light filled the hallway. Derek blinked against the light. "Well, so much for that," Lenny said.

When Derek's vision returned, he saw Lenny was holding a small, glowing stone. He also realized that he could see himself, and the leprechaun sitting on his shoulder, once again. Derek sighed. "I was hoping the invisibility spell would last longer."

Lenny shrugged and handed Derek the glowing stone. "It did what it was supposed to do. I've known some wizards who use magic to fool you into thinking you are invisible. That makes for a stink, I'll tell you."

Something moved in the darkness behind them. "Boy, is that you?"

Derek whirled and raised his club. He heard Lenny slide a tiny knife from its sheath. There was a popping sound, and Lenny was gone from Derek's shoulder. Derek wasn't worried about the leprechaun. He knew that voice and peered down the packed hallway. "Saehrimnir?"

The fat chef waddled out of the darkness. He held a massive meat cleaver in one hand and guarded his eyes against the light with the other. "What are you doing down here, boy?"

Derek took a step away from the northerner. "I'm looking for my friend."

Saehrimnir glanced at the padlock. "The ratter? Don't worry about him. He's the safest one on this ship — if any of us can be safe, what with the storm and now these pirates."

"Pirates?"

"Are you deaf, boy?" Saehrimnir growled. "Haven't heard it up top?" He shrugged his round shoulders, and the fat of his chest bounced like a Shadizarian belly dancer. "What does it matter?" the plump chef asked. "Shadizarians? Pirates? We are slaves either way."

Derek lowered his table leg. "Those aren't pirates. They are with me."

Saehrimnir scowled. "This ain't a time for stories, boy."

"It's the truth," Derek insisted. "It's Niles Crowing and the Magnificent Seven."

"Who?"

"Niles Crowing. He's famous."

Saehrimnir scoffed. "Not where I'm from."

Derek sighed. "Look, all I want is to get my friend out of this hold and then get up top so I can help my friends take over the ship."

"Oh, *friends* now, is it?" Saehrimnir used one hand to pull up the avalanche of his belly fat and dug a ring of keys out of an impossibly small loincloth. "Well, then, who am I to stop you?"

He found the key he was looking for and stuck it in the padlock. The lock clanked open, and Saehrimnir swung the door wide. It screeched in the musty hallway. A breeze reeking of stale urine and rotting carrion wafted up the stairs. Derek covered his mouth and gave Saehrimnir a questioning look.

"Come on," the cook said, stepping into the ratter's hold. "And bring your light." He waddled into the shadows. "I'm not going to ask where you got your magic stone from, but I've seen them before. Used to be an adventurer myself."

Derek stepped over the threshold and into the ratter's hold. "You did?" he asked, looking for Conrad over Saehrimnir's shoulder. "That was years ago, before I was caught thieving in Shadizar. Could have taken my hands as a punishment, but they sold me to the captain of *The Delivery* instead. First time in my life where I had two square meals a day." Saehrimnir slid soft fingers over the blanket of blubber covering his hips. "Two squares taste pretty good if you grew up on the streets."

Stacks of belted and bolted crates lined the walls. A pile of dead rats, easily fifty high, lay mounded by the door, evidence of Conrad's work. Saehrimnir picked up a rat by the tail and inspected it. "Looks like your friend got some good ones." The dead rat twirled by the tail. "Good meat on these. We should skin 'em up."

Derek coughed. "No thanks. I just want to find my friend."

Something scurried in the boxes by Derek's head. He leapt against the far wall just as the nude tail of a monster rat disappeared behind a tower of rice bags. Derek caught his breath and hurried after Saehrimnir.

A dull explosion sounded up top, followed by muffled cries. "We'd better move fast if you want to help your friends," Saehrimnir said. "What's the ratter's name?"

"Conrad."

"Call him. I don't like being down here anymore than you do." A shadow flashed to their right, and Saehrimnir's cleaver flashed in a blur. There was a wet *thunk*, a squeak, and then a wriggling sound. "Geh," Saehrimnir grunted. "That's a big one."

Derek stepped close and peered around the cook. A gigantic rat, almost the size of a small dog, twitched in two halves on top of a crate of pickled herring from Bearton. A bit of the brine oozed out of the crate through the gap Saehrimnir's cleaver made.

"Shame about them rat innards leaking in there," Saehrimnir said, scraping the juicy bits away from the three-finger wide hole he had made. "That's good herring." He dipped his finger in the herring brine and rat gut mix and popped it in his mouth. The fat chef sucked at his finger with greasy lips. "Not bad," he said, gesturing to the mix. "Try some."

Derek's stomach rolled. He was about to throw up when a scuffling sound behind him made him whirl. A lanky shadow of a boy, no more than a skeleton, lurked at the rim of the glowing stone's light. "Conrad?"

The boy from Zuid Horn staggered closer. His eyes were rimmed with black, heavy bags. A nasty gash that looked suspiciously like a bite drained cloudy pus down the boy's forearm. "Did you free Dani?" His voice was just a whisper.

"Yes," Derek said, easing toward his friend. "I freed them all."

Conrad's shoulders slumped in relief. "Thank the Forge."

"Mother of Anubis," Saehrimnir whispered from behind Derek. "Is that your friend?"

Derek nodded. "Yes."

"He doesn't look good. Let's get him out of here. This is no place for anyone, even a clutch of dirty slaves like us. Damn Shadizarians. No telling what a fellow could catch down here." Saehrimnir frowned at the bite mark on Conrad's forearm. He squeezed past Derek, leaving a shiny patch of sweat and kitchen grease on Derek's shoulder and face. "If your pirate friend... What was his name? Miles Crawling?"

"Niles Crowing."

"Whatever. If he is going to take *The Delivery*, he is going to need our help. Come on. Let's get up top and cleave us some Shadizarians." Saehrimnir smirked and hefted his butcher's cleaver. Then, he turned and left the boys to follow him.

"Can you walk?" Derek asked Conrad.

The boy shook his head weakly. "I'll be fine once I get out of here. Let's make sure Dani is safe." Conrad drew two ratter's knives from the frayed rope that served as his belt and hurried after Saehrimnir.

The boys and the waddling cook climbed through the belly of the ship and wound up the stairwell to the rowing deck. Save for a few people too battered to walk, all the benches were empty. Conrad ran up and down the aisle. "Where's Dani?"

Derek shrugged. "I don't know. She was here before. She must be up top."

The clash of arms and screams of the dying were closer now than in the ratter's hold. Conrad stared with wide eyes at the ceiling. "We have to help her!" He pushed past Derek and Saehrimnir and charged up the stairs.

Derek and the cook were right on his tail. Saehrimnir struggled up every step and panted heavily behind Derek. "You go on," the blubbery cook said, stopping for breath. "I'm building my strength for battle." Saehrimnir held a railing with one hand and braced himself on a knee with the other.

The boys left the cook behind and vaulted the steps to the main deck. They stopped just short of clearing the last few steps, amazed at the battle before them.

A wave of slaves from the rowing deck, their bruised backs gleaming wetly from the spray of sea foam, wielded lengths of chain as though they had practiced from birth. The Shadizarian guardsmen and sailors tried to get themselves close enough to work their rapiers on the slaves' hides, but the freed Zuid Hornian slaves took turns lashing out with the heavy links. As Derek and Conrad watched, a guardsman stepped in too close and caught a healthy arc of iron links across the mouth. The man collapsed and didn't move.

Niles Crowing and the Magnificent Seven harassed the pack of slavers from the other side of the ship. From where he stood on the stairs, Derek could see Wendy the Ogress. She towered over the masses and showered blows upon the Shadizarians with fists the size of salted hams. Bodies flew with every swing. Shadizarian sailors smashed against masts with bone-crunching cracks. Guardsmen flew over railings and tumbled into the stormy sea. Wendy's eyes were wide with battle lust, and then they focused on a large man in a red vest. The row master! The ogress roared and charged the man who had inflicted so much suffering on the Zuid Hornians.

Derek cheered her on just as the battle surged and blocked his view. "Hammer and Anvils!" he swore.

Just ahead of Wendy, Manny and Alum Aqadh worked side by side, Manny with his whirling double hatchets and Alum Aqadh with his lance and shield. Manny charged in, his attacks a blur of steel and black ironwood. The Shadizarians fell back under his pressing fury, raising their small bucklers in a vain attempt to protect themselves from the raining blades. Alum Aqadh wove like a viper through the conflict, slashing and thrusting at the Shadizarians' exposed underbellies. When they raised their bucklers to ward off Manny and his hatchets, they opened themselves to Alum's deadly lance. The dead and dying lay in groaning piles about the pair, leaking crimson gore across *The Delivery's* deck.

Not far away, Kassar the Swift and a dashing Niles Crowing fenced a knot of *The Delivery's* surviving officers with expert precision. Kassar's knives and Niles' rapier flashed in the light of the passing storm. Half a dozen of Shadizar's finest scimitars couldn't find a gap in the Zuid Hornian mercenaries' defenses. Niles and Kassar kept their backs to one another as the officers circled, darting out with stinging steel to make the Shadizarian pirates pay with blood if their defenses slipped even for the briefest of moments. One by one, the circle of enemies thinned, until just a handful were left to wheel about Niles and Kassar like a pack of hungry wolves.

A crack, a flash of light, and the sizzle of charred flesh drew Derek's attention to the starboard side of the ship, where Pavaraci Moonfist and Father Ferrum worked in tandem, weaving a deadly blanket of magic through their foes. Pavaraci's fingers sparkled as webs of silver and lightning leapt through the air and ensnared the charging Shadizarians before they could get too close. The sailors jerked to a stop, unable to move while caught in the wizard's magic. They struggled against the magical bonds, but the wizard's spell held fast.

Father Ferrum clutched his holy anvil necklace in one hand and summoned a host of ghostly warriors to wade into the battle. Their glowing hammers crashed through the mystically held sailors and guardsmen. The Shadizarians fell in droves beneath the summoned spirits' assault, but their sheer numbers gave them courage. A group of sailors who had escaped Pavaraci's magic crept around the battle toward the wizard and the priest of the Forge.

"Look out!" Derek yelled from the stairs.

Somehow, impossibly, Father Ferrum heard Derek. His quick eye caught the advance, and he smiled grimly. Ferrum raised his mighty mace and chanted to his god. Derek felt the stirrings of battle lust in his chest. He raised his table leg and let out a whoop. "Come on, Conrad," he said. "We have to help them!"

There was a pop and a shuffle on Derek's shoulder, and Lenny the Unlucky Leprechaun was back with him again. "There, portside! We can fill the gap before the sailors break through!"

Derek looked, and sure enough, the Shadizarians were pressing to smash a hole in the slaves' line of defense. The Zuid Hornians, exhausted from their beatings and long days of rowing — along with their inexperience in battle — were being pushed back, despite their initial enthusiasm. Derek spun his table leg in a tight circle. "For Zuid Horn!" He rushed to the line and smashed into the gap, flailing about wildly with his makeshift club.

"Watch yourself!" Lenny warned. "You're going to smack the wrong person!"

A shout cleared Derek's vision long enough for him to see he was battling next to Lars. The boy was bleeding from half a dozen wounds. Lars looked up. His eyes were wild with excitement. "Derek!" the boy shouted. Lars whipped his chain and caught a sailor across the chin. The Shadizarian reeled back into his mates, his mouth a toothless, bloody gash.

"Lars!" Derek stepped shoulder to shoulder with the street orphan.

He could see Jenkins just beyond Lars, slugging it out with a dagger-wielding sailor. Another slave came to Jenkins' aid and leapt on the sailor. The pair spun like dancers, and Derek realized it was none other than Dani on the sailor's back, the length of her chain wrapped tightly about his neck. The Shadizarian tried to slash her with his dagger, but Dani jerked and twisted to avoid the blade's keen edge. Every effort the sailor made to cut Dani only helped the Zuid Hornian girl tighten the iron noose.

Just as Derek was about to rush to his friend's aid, Jenkins delivered a mighty blow to the sailor's knee and dropped him to the deck. The Shadizarian's face burned purple from lack of breath, and when Dani finally let loose her chain, he collapsed at her feet, never to move again.

Derek wanted to go to his friends, but another guardsman leapt into the gap. The guardsman slashed at Derek with a curved scimitar and caught the boy with its tip. Derek screamed and clutched at the cut across his shoulder. The Shadizarian grinned wickedly and crouched, hunting for a chance to bleed the boy again. Derek roared and charged, his table leg a brown blur under the stormy sky. His vision closed from all sides until all he could see was the slaver before him.

He drove the man back so fast the Shadizarian tripped over his heels and skittered across the deck on his backside. Derek saw his chance to finish the slaver off and pressed on with long, grim strides. "No!" Lenny yelled, but the rage had Derek now, and he ignored the leprechaun.

The man snarled at Derek and pulled a thin throwing knife from his belt. Derek saw what the guard was up to and rushed across the deck, his flight fueled by fury and Father Ferrum's magical chanting. Derek closed the gap before the man could let the blade fly. A solid shot from Derek's table leg ended the matter.

Derek's vision cleared for a moment, and he realized that although he had defeated one opponent, Derek had made a brilliant, tactical blunder. In his battle fury, he had pulled away from the line of Zuid Hornians. Now, Shadizarians surrounded him from all sides.

"This isn't good," Lenny the Unlucky Leprechaun muttered from Derek's shoulder. There was a pop, and Derek knew Lenny was gone.

"Nice timing," Derek muttered.

The battle raged around them, and Derek's world closed until only the five men surrounding him remained. They circled him like hyenas, crouched and snarling, waiting for someone to make a first move.

They didn't have to wait long.

Another pop announced Lenny's return, this time upon one of the sailor's shoulders. "Surprise!" the leprechaun shouted. He sank a thin dagger into the man's sword arm.

The sailor howled and fell back from the circle, swatting at the tiny man on his shoulder. Lenny rode the flailing fool like a wild bull until they disappeared into the crowd.

Derek knew he would get no better chance. He sprang on the nearest sailor while the man was still staring in open-mouthed wonder at the leprechaun. A well-placed blow from Derek's table leg dropped the man on the spot. He knocked down a second man the same way, and then the fight was down to two-on-one. He spun his table leg over once and felt the easy weight of it in his palm.

"Let's get this over with," he growled.

Cries of pain and rage blended into a roar on the deck of *The Delivery*, yet some part of Derek's mind told him the end of the fight was near. Most of the sailors and guardsmen had fallen, but many of the former slaves had as well. Yes, the battle was almost won. All he had to do was survive this final encounter, and he and his friends would live to see another day.

The combatants circled one another, none of them willing to make the first move so late in the battle. Derek turned with the sailors, careful with his feet so he wouldn't slip on the slick blood covering the deck. When he faced *The Delivery's* stern, he saw something that froze the breath in his throat.

Lars was sprawled on the deck, his neck opened from ear to ear. The boy's gray face was raised to the sky, his eyes dull. Derek felt a scream build in his chest, and it burst in a bubble when he saw Dani kneeling over another body — Jenkins. She cradled his head to her chest. His lanky arms dangled at his side.

Derek's vision whirled. How could Lars and Jenkins be dead? He was just fighting next to them. He was only gone for a moment. He hadn't heard them scream or cry for help. But now they were mortally wounded, their lives bleeding out on *The Delivery's* deck. These were his friends — recently met to be sure, but friends nonetheless — who had followed him on a crazy mission to free Dani from slavery. They all knew what the risks were, but Derek never really believed any of them would die.

And yet there they were.

A quick movement from his side sparked some life back into Derek's fighting spirit. One of the Shadizarian sailors swiped at

Derek with a chipped dagger. It caught him in the thigh and burned like fire, but it brought the sailor close enough for Derek to take a whack at him with his table leg. The blow buffeted the man into his comrade, and they stumbled for balance. Derek leapt at the sailors and twirled his makeshift club over again and again. They fell back beneath his fury, and in the space that opened, Derek became aware of someone fighting beside him. He dared a quick glance and then whooped.

"Conrad!"

Battered and worn, his enemy-turned-friend had rushed to his side after so many dark days in the ratter's hold. Conrad clutched a scimitar he must have snatched from a fallen guardsman. Derek slapped him on the back with his free hand, and together they faced the Shadizarians who were back on their feet like crouched desert lions, their daggers at the ready.

The four came together with a crash. Derek and Conrad came in swinging wildly. Though untrained, they had youth and speed and the rage every slave feels toward their master fueling their assault. The Shadizarian sailors had years at sea under their feet, and the reach and strength of older men behind their daggers.

Back and forth, the combatants rolled across the slick deck. Derek and Conrad fell back before the sailors and their lightning-fast swipes. The Shadizarians were careful with their daggers, setting up openings in the boys' defenses with a series of feints and thrusts. Derek and Conrad bled from half a dozen knicks and cuts. Derek's arms felt like lead. His table leg, once light and balanced, felt more like a log. The sailor across from Derek snickered and lunged at him, opening a nasty gash across his thigh. Derek stumbled and tried to bash the man, but he was off balance, and the sailor merely laughed and batted the table leg aside with his open hand. Then, before Derek could act, the sailor closed the gap between them like a cobra and sliced up Derek's ribs with a pair of deep rips.

Derek's face sagged, and when he saw a knowing gleam in the Shadizarian's eye, he understood a simple, sad truth. The sailor was toying with him. Derek was about to die.

A quick glance to his side showed Derek that Conrad was faring no better. Normally a tough, gritty boy, Conrad was weakened from his time in the hold. He bled from cuts crisscrossing his torso. He limped from a nasty gouge in his thigh. Conrad fell back, and the Shadizarian he fought pressed forward until the sailor was side by side with Derek.

That was when Derek saw his chance to help Conrad.

The Shadizarian, so caught up in fighting Conrad, had forgotten about Derek right at his side. As soon as the sailor stepped past him, Derek put everything he had left into a vicious backhanded swing with his table leg that caught Conrad's Shadizarian full in the back of the head. The man dropped like a stone.

Conrad watched the man fall, and then looked at Derek with grateful eyes, which suddenly flew wide. He pointed behind Derek. "Look out!"

Derek twisted at Conrad's warning, but the Shadizarian Derek had been fighting was on him now. The man wrapped a tight arm around Derek's neck and plunged his dagger between Derek's ribs again and again. Derek's chest opened like fire, and suddenly, he couldn't draw a breath. He gulped like a fish, but no cooling air rewarded his efforts. The Shadizarian spun Derek around and pulled him close. Derek could see the smeared eyeliner under the man's eyes, and the black stubble riding his cheeks and neck.

"Have a taste of Shadizarian steel, dog," the man hissed, and he stuck Derek in the gut.

Derek's knees went weak. He clung to the man and tried to stand, but the man shoved him away, and Derek collapsed to the deck. A blur flashed beside him as Conrad rushed to his aid. "Derek!"

The Shadizarian laughed and tried to spring over Derek, who reached for the man's ankle as he leapt. The sailor stumbled, and

Derek dragged him to the deck. "By the Pit," the man cursed. He kicked at Derek, but Derek clung to his leg like a dying vine. "Why won't you just die?" The sailor flipped over and scuttled on his hands and knees back toward Derek. He pinned Derek to the deck with one hand and drew back his dagger for a killing blow.

Derek's face and throat burned from lack of breath. He held up his arms to fend the man off, when Conrad of Gillman's Way leapt at the Shadizarian. Conrad caught the man beneath the ribs with his scimitar and drove deep. The sailor collapsed with a groan.

Conrad kicked him away from Derek and rushed to his friend. "Derek!"

Derek tried to speak, but he couldn't draw enough breath to voice a single word. He pressed his fingers against the wounds in his chest, and that seemed to plug the holes long enough to allow Derek to take tiny sips of air. Conrad held his friend in his arms. "Niles!" he cried.

Derek's world spun. *The Delivery's* remaining masts rocked to the ocean's deep swell. Dark clouds whirled overhead and dropped glittering spears of rain upon the survivors. Sprays of white mist burst in plumes every time *The Delivery's* bow dropped into the valley between waves. The edges of Derek's vision grew fuzzy, and the sounds of battle around him dimmed. *So, this is what it's like to die,* he thought. *It's not what I expected.*

Two figures pushed themselves into Derek's sightline — Niles Crowing and Father Ferrum. Niles' mouth moved, but Derek couldn't hear a word of it. His ears were filled with the warm rush of his impending death. Strangely, Derek wasn't afraid. He thought of his father and felt bad for letting him down. He felt regret over Lars and Jenkins falling to the Shadizarians' blades. And Dani? He prayed to the Forge she would be alright.

Derek's vision had collapsed to a thin, white line when a bright glow from Father Ferrum's hands made Derek squint. His chest warmed with a deep tingling, and then a rush of refreshing air poured down his gullet. Derek gulped and sat up with a start.

His ribs and gut were sore, but somehow, he was alive. "What?" he asked.

Father Ferrum gently pushed him back down. A widening crimson stain spilled down the priest's chest. "Rest, boy. The battle is over. We have won. You are going to be fine, by the grace of the Forge."

"You're bleeding."

"Never you mind, boy."

"You paid the price again?"

"I said, 'Never you mind.'"

Conrad's eyes were wide, going from Derek to Father Ferrum's bloody chest. "Can you help our friends Lars and Jenkins? They are just over there." He pointed down the deck.

The priest nodded. "Wendy," he said over his shoulder, "watch over Derek, will you?"

Wendy's massive face appeared over Father Ferrum's shoulder. "Help the others," she said. "I have this one."

The priest limped off, and Wendy squatted next to Derek with a loud thump. Driblets of gore ran from her thick thews in the rain. She picked Derek up as though he were made of straw and cradled him in her warm lap. The ogress reeked of unwashed body parts and sweat and rotten meat. Somehow, Derek had never felt safer.

Wendy was humming an ogre battle chant when Niles Crowing came back to them. He smiled at Derek. "You look like someone dragged you through Sheol."

"I feel like it," Derek said. "My friends?"

Niles held up his hands. "They will be fine. You kids are a tough bunch. I thought Lars was a goner, but somehow, he held on there until Father Ferrum could patch him up with his magic."

"Dani?"

The girl, hearing her name, rushed over. "I'm fine." She smiled and called out to her brother, "Conrad! Derek is awake!"

There was a patter of feet on the deck, and Conrad appeared next to his sister. He opened his mouth to say something, but then he seemed to think better of it and nodded at his friend instead.

Derek shifted in Wendy's lap and looked at Niles. "Thank you for saving us," he said. "We wouldn't have made it without you."

Niles looked surprised. "Saving you? You kids did all the work. Look around. All these people would have been slaves without you. Zuid Horn owes you a great debt."

Derek looked around the deck at the survivors of the battle. People were crying over the dead, hugging one another with relief, and talking to the rest of the Magnificent Seven. Like the battle, the storm was over, and the ocean was quieting down. Derek breathed a sigh of relief. "Do you think the Iron Guard will forgive us for breaking out of the stocks?" Niles laughed. "Oh, I would say so. But first, we have the little matter of exposing the corrupt underbelly of the Iron Guardsmen working on Ploughman's Wharf."

"How are we going to do that?" Dani asked.

Niles grinned and glanced at Pavaraci Moonfist, who was chatting with a pair of freed slaves. "Oh, don't worry about that. I've got a plan."

21

Derek's Temper Finds a Home

Soaring on the warm updrafts rising along the coast in their magical bird bodies, Derek, Conrad, and Dani followed the Coastland Trail that paralleled the black pebble beach for the better part of the next week. They traveled faster than any horse could ride and easily outpaced the slave train heading north along the trail.

When Conrad used his eagle eyes to spot a column of black smoke rising from the emerald-green canopy of the northern Breechwood Forest, they pushed for the mines as fast as their wings would carry them. Behind the rising smoke, a golden sun sank into the ocean. Behind them, to the east, a gigantic full moon rose over Breechwood Forest. Night was coming fast. When they made it to the mines, the friends circled on warm updrafts high above the mines. What they saw filled their hearts with dread.

Ash and flame leapt from a mountain of dead men, charred beyond recognition. Several yakariian scouts and warriors rummaged through a pile of plate mail and chain armor, trying on breastplates and greaves and gauntlets. Most of the armor was too small for the massive creatures and was tossed carelessly to the side. Every now and again, a piece of armor would be large enough for a yakariian warrior, and a fight would break out amongst them to determine the new owner.

The friends winged down through the late evening sky and perched in the upper branches of a dead ironwood tree. Dani screeched and flapped her wings. "Do you think the dead men were the Iron Guard?"

Derek ruffled his feathers and tightened his grip on the branch. "Looks like it. Who else would have that kind of armor out here?"

Yakariian warriors lumbered about the pebble-strewn beach between the shallow bay and the salt mine's wide mouth. Broad, creosote-soaked ties lay in two tracks from the mine entrance to the shore. A long pier jutted far into the water where the bay was deep enough to allow the flat-bottomed salt barges to tie off. There were several of the barges along the pier, and a knot of yakarii gathered near one of them.

"What do you think they are doing out there?" Conrad asked.

Derek cocked his eagle head and studied the group. He was amazed at the crystal clarity of his vision as a bird of prey. The yakarii were hideous creatures, with skulls like hammerhead sharks, wide mouths filled with serrated teeth, thick, black tusks jutting along their jawlines, and shoulders so broad they would have to turn sideways to fit through most doorways. Derek had seen plenty of yakarii during his years in Zuid Horn. The slightly smaller yakariian scouts, standing only seven feet tall, would come to his father's shop to spend their coin on the thumb-thick arrows favored by their kind. They were disagreeable customers, reeking of sour meat and smoke, but they paid fair coin, and Da never turned them away.

And this was how they repaid him.

"Derek?" Conrad asked again. "What's going on down there?"

"Hard to say," Derek said, "but it looks like they are talking about the barges. If I had to guess, they are getting ready to ship salt. They brought slaves out here for a reason."

A whip crack and a man's howl drew the eagles' attention back to the mouth of the Hagedorn salt mine. A battered clutch of humans pushed a line of salt carts along the path of thick, wooden planks leading from the mine to the pier. Yakariian warriors hounded the humans with black spears and fierce whips. The carts' axles creaked and groaned under the weight of the glistening salt. A terrible tropical humidity weighed on the slaves, only adding to their misery.

Derek scanned the slaves for his parents or Augie or Peter's mother. There was Johan, the cobbler, behind the cart. Other than the shoemaker, Derek didn't recognize anyone. He breathed a quiet sigh of relief that his parents weren't on the beach, under the slave driver's lash.

The yakariian guards roared their irritation at the slaves' plodding pace and let fly with a torrent of blows from their rough clubs. Several people collapsed under the beating. These, the yakarii yanked aside and tossed onto the beach. The slaves staggered in the deep pebbles. Most struggled to even get to their knees. Without warning, the yakarii drew swords from their belts and slaughtered the lot of them. The guards were about to lay into the rest of the slaves when an even larger guard barked and brought some order to the chaos.

Derek and his friends stared in horror. "By the Forge, they are animals! Whatever we are going to do, we need to do it fast," Derek said.

"Agreed," Conrad squawked. "But what are we going to do? If the Iron Guard couldn't free the slaves, what can we do?"
"The Iron Guard took their toll," Derek said. "Look there."

Derek pointed with the tip of his wing to the darkening shadows under the trees lining the beach. The yakarii had lined up their dead there, feet toward the tiny inlet, heads toward the forest. Several wizened yakarii hunched over them, wrapping strips of cloth over the dead warriors' eyes.

"What are they doing?" Dani asked.

"It looks like some kind of burial ritual," Conrad said. "Maybe those yakarii are shamans. That would explain the necklaces and staves."

"Great," Derek piped. "Wizards."

"Don't get too upset about it," Dani said. "Or did you forget that we have a wizard helping us as well?"

"Bah." Derek frowned as well as his eagle beak would allow.

Conrad shuffled on the branch. "So, what are we going to do?" Derek turned his attention back to the salt carts. The slaves had moved the carts over the tracks and down the beach, and they had just arrived at the pier out to the barges. A group of yakariian slave drivers followed at their heels and encouraged the slaves with whips and clubs. The pier swayed under the weight of the laden carts. Many of the yakarii moved to the middle of the pier and spread their arms wide for balance. Farther out on the pier, more than thirty yakarii milled about by the waiting barges. The pier shook and wobbled with the carts' load. Several of the yakarii by the barges windmilled their arms and roared in irritation.

Suddenly, Derek had a vision from the night of the flood, and a plan sprang to life. His beaked bird face broke into a smile, if an eagle can be said to smile at all. "I've got it!" Derek cawed. "But we will have to move quickly." He leapt into the air and flew out over the harbor. "Follow me!"

Conrad and Dani pounded the air with their wings to catch up with Derek. "What is it?" Dani cawed.

"Do you remember about two years ago, when that fleet of merchant cogs from Belvera docked at Ploughman's Wharf?"

"Oh, yeah!" Dani screeched. "They were dragging a dead leviathan behind them. Conrad and I saw them cutting it up to get it out of the water."

"The merchants said it attacked them when they sailed through the Maw. Took down half their fleet," Conrad added.

"That's right," Derek said. "Da and I went down to the wharf. I wanted to see a monster, and that's what it looked like to me, but

Da said it was just a gigantic octopus. I always wondered what it would have looked like when it was alive."

The blue of the bay deepened to a blackened mirror as the light of evening slipped away. A humid heat rose off the water. Derek and the others soared in great circles over the yakarii and the salt barges. Slaves shoveled salt from the carts into open-topped boxes on the barges, while their captors lashed at their backs with barbed whips.

Dani arced sharply so she could fly next to Derek. "Really? That's your plan? You're going to turn into a giant octopus?"

Derek ruffled his feathers. "If a leviathan can sink half a fleet of Belverian cogs, think what one could do to that pier. I'll rip that thing apart. Once the yakarii are in the water, they're done for."

"What do you mean?" Conrad asked.

"Remember the night of the flood?" Derek asked. "Where we met up? Those yakariian scouts were chasing us?"

"That's right!" Conrad cawed. "They hate water."

"And they can't swim," Dani finished for her brother.

"Exactly," Derek said. "This might not get all of the yakarii, but if we can get thirty or forty of them, it will really help our chances in the mines."

Just then, the crack of whips and the rumble of salt carts brought the children's sharp, eagle eyes back to the mouth of the mines. Another group of slaves strained against a line of carts with a pack of yakariian warriors at their backs to prod them onward. Derek scanned the slaves and felt his heart leap into his throat. There was Da behind one of the carts, his bare shoulders darkened with welts. Derek searched the rest of the slaves. Two carts behind Da, Mum labored with another slave to push a load of salt.

"Mum! Da!" he screeched and dove at the yakariian guards.

Behind him, Dani flapped her wings. "Derek, wait! What about the pier?"

"You two take the pier! I have to save my parents!" Derek didn't wait for Dani to respond. He screeched and plunged through the air. Fury raged in his belly. His muscles drew taut, and his vision focused until all he could see was the lead yakariian warrior. The creature looked up just in time to see an eagle's talons tear into his face.

Derek screamed and raked the yakariian warrior's eyes. The beast flailed at Derek, but the bird boy was too quick. Derek buffeted the creature with his wings and found himself wishing he were stronger. He raked and battered the yakariian warrior, but his best efforts had little effect. The yakariian warrior was simply too big, and Derek, in eagle form, was too small.

A flicker from his left caught his attention. Three more yakarii rushed across the beach. "I need to be bigger!" Derek screeched.

A shimmer of heat rippled through Derek. He pounded at the monster, while something inside him twisted and stretched his innards. His limbs lengthened and thickened. He watched the tips of his wings spread into broad, meaty fists, with stout wrists and forearms corded with steely tendons. Derek's shoulders pushed and strained until they would have dwarfed two men Da's size. He roared with delight and felt his beak bubble and wriggle until it opened into a wide maw, filled with teeth that could gnash iron. Although he could not see his face, Derek knew what had happened. How many times had Derek's quick temper made him feel like an ogre? Now, the magic in Gilgameth Tuft's ring unleashed the creature trapped in his heart.

The yakariian warrior before him froze. Not waiting for the creature to recover, Derek grabbed the seven-foot-tall beast and hurled it against the nearest salt cart. The impact sent pure, white salt flying and a dozen slaves, including Derek's parents, scurrying for cover.

"Get away while you can!" Derek roared. "I'll hold them here!" Derek watched his parents and the others flee over the beach. They cast confused looks over their shoulders.

One of the freed slaves stopped and stared at Derek the ogre.

"Augie!" Derek roared.

Augie, Derek's good friend from Gillman's Way, looked in horror at the ogre who somehow knew his name. The boy shrieked and sprinted for the trail leading back to Zuid Horn. Derek grunted. "At least he's away," he said to himself.

Then, the yakarii were on him. Three warriors came at Derek together, their spears drawn and their shields held high. The first one thrust ferociously, and Derek danced to the side. He grasped the spear behind its razor-sharp head and tore it from the warrior's grasp. He twirled it once in a downward arc and batted aside the attacks from the other yakarii. Then, Derek lowered his thick shoulder and rushed them. The warriors braced themselves behind their shields, but Derek's ogre bulk blew them aside as though they were made of paper. The yakarii flew through the air and cracked against the cave wall, where they collapsed in a heap, never to move again.

Derek whirled to face the host of yakariian guards rushing at him from the other carts. Sunlight glittered off the tips of their spears and the keen edges of their swords. "Come on!" he roared. He crouched to meet them and slapped the pebbly beach with the ironwood spear.

Howls of dismay rose from farther down the beach, by the pier. Derek looked over the heads of the charging yakarii and tried to see what the commotion was all about. What he saw made him whoop for joy.

A forest of tentacles writhed in the bay next to the pier. They lashed at the yakarii on the dock and pulled the teetering pier apart, board by rickety board. Black and rubbery, the snake-like leviathan arms were as thick as tree trunks with an underside riddled with pale, puckering suction cups. Three yakarii flailed futilely in the air, caught up in the tentacles. Almost a dozen warriors tried to battle the thing, but their swords could not find purchase on the creature's tough hide. The giant octopus swept the pier with several appendages and toppled almost a score of the yakarii into the frothing water. They flailed about and tried to stay above the surface, but the weight of their armor dragged them down one by one. Any yakarii that managed to cling to bits of the floating pier found themselves wrapped in black coils and dragged to the same watery death as their brethren.

The flash of the full moonlight on steel and the clash of weapons drew Derek's eye to the foot of the pier, where an ogress who looked suspiciously like Wendy battled a clutch of yakarii. Dani the ogress howled with happiness in her new form. The yakarii tried to harass her, but she wielded a tough limb of driftwood as a weapon, and the knot of unconscious warriors at her feet spoke to her effectiveness with the makeshift club. Derek felt a slight twang of regret that he didn't have his table leg with him, but he roared with battle lust nonetheless. His hastily drawn-up plan was working. Soon, the yakariian slavers would be no more, and Derek would be with his parents again.

Derek turned his attention back to the charging yakarii. They were on him in a flash and slashed at him with the jagged edges of crude swords and barbed spears. Several yakariian slave masters had long whips that they uncoiled and used to lash at Derek with stinging cracks. The barbed tips of their whips bit at Derek's tough hide until the skin of his chest and back ran with rivers of red. The pain only fueled his rage, and here, fighting the yakariian slavers who had kidnapped his parents, Derek had a perfect outlet for his fury. He roared and leapt into their midst. He took his spear and swiped at the yakarii with broad strokes. One by one, they fell. Several tripped over their own feet in the deep pebbles in their effort to escape his onslaught.

A cry from deep within the mine announced the arrival of a dozen more yakariian guards. Derek spun to meet them. He crouched low and then sprang at them like a tiger. His spear led the way and impaled the lead warrior full through the chest. Derek howled and yanked his weapon free. With his tremendous ogre arms and the effective range of the spear, Derek could reach his opponents long before they could touch him. He leapt and slashed, felling yakariian warriors left and right. Soon, only a handful of his enemies stood between Derek and his parents. A faint smile cracked through his fearsome visage.

That was when the unraveling began.

The air about Derek shimmered a faint greenish gold. It sparkled and danced. Something about the strange glow made Derek's head swim. The yakariian warriors he was battling stepped back. They looked around to find the cause of the glimmering air, and then they howled and hoisted their weapons over their heads.

Derek rubbed his face. What was going on? He looked at his ogre paws. The flesh wriggled and twitched under the palsied skin. Then, before his very eyes, his hands and wrists and arms shrank until Derek recognized them as his own sixteen-year-old boy body. He spun in the pebbles, trying to find what could have thwarted Gilgameth Tuft's magic. He found his answer in the shade where Breechwood Forest met the beach. Six yakariian shamans chanted in unison. Magic crackled from their taloned fingers and settled over Derek like day-old dust. The yakariian warriors, seeing what their formerly fearsome foe truly was, snickered amongst themselves and lowered their weapons.

"By the Forge!" Derek cursed. He twisted the ring on his finger. "I want to be an ogre!" he shouted, but nothing happened. "I need to be an ogre!"

Derek's fury wrinkled into fear. He tried to pick up the spear he had so easily wielded as an ogre, but Derek could barely manage to get the razor-sharp tip off the ground.

The shamans continued to chant in the forest behind him. Their magic lay over Derek like a wet blanket, extinguishing any hope he had of using magic to escape his fate. A round of yakariian cheers from the beach drew his attention, and Derek risked a quick glance over his shoulder. The battling ogress was gone, and in her place stood Dani, alone amidst a pack of wild yakariian warriors.

"Dani!" Derek screamed. Derek dropped the heavy spear and sprinted as fast as he could to get to her side.

The yakarii hooted and laughed at his desperation. A high-pitched whistling filled the air, and then something wrapped about his ankles. Derek crashed face-first into the beach. He hit the pebbles with a grunt and rolled over as quickly as he could. A heavy, hemp cord with two iron clumps held his lower legs together. Bolas! Derek ripped at the cord until his fingernails tore, but he could not release the tightly wound bindings.

"Derek!" Dani yelled from the shore.

Derek twisted on the beach just in time to see Dani take an ironwood club to the gut. She doubled over, clutching her stomach. The yakarii swarmed on her in a black cloud. Derek swore and tried his magic ring again. "I want to be an ogre! I want to be an ogre!" But the yakariian shamans' magic stymied the ring's best efforts.

A half-dozen yakariian warriors closed on Derek. Their pale, blotchy skin glistened with sweat under the moonlight. Black armor decorated with the teeth of their fallen foes added even more heft to their considerable bulk. While they'd seemed tiny when Derek was in ogre form, they loomed like giants over him now. Derek struggled with the bolas about his ankles and screamed when he couldn't free himself.

"Look at the boy," the yakarii taunted. "So much anger with nothing to back it up." They lowered their spears and closed on him.

A tiny knife lay on the beach next to Derek. He snatched it up and sawed at the tough bola cord. Bit by bit, the cord gave way, but in his heart, Derek knew it was too slow. The yakarii were only steps away and would be there long before he was free. Derek ripped at the cord with the tiny knife. He slipped and gouged his leg.

"Damn the Forge!" he swore, and in his helplessness, the anger turned to despair. He threw the blade into the pebbles.

The first of the yakariian warriors drew near with their spears outstretched. Their reluctance to get too close suggested to Derek that they still feared the ring's magic. They came at him together and closed the circle of steel one step at a time. Derek tried to wriggle away from the threat, but when he twisted away from one spear, he opened himself up to another. A yakarii thrust a hesitant spear at Derek. It entered his side just below the shoulder, and he howled in pain. When the yakarii saw he could be wounded, they flipped their spears around and battered him with the blunt ends of their weapons.

"Don't kill him too quickly," one of them growled. "This one needs to suffer." Then, to the warriors beating Dani, the yakariian warrior shouted, "Bring that one over here. I want them to watch each other die."

Derek's shoulder burned. He tried to get up, but the bolas had a life of their own and refused to relinquish their grasp around his legs. His blood pounded in his head. Blast the shamans! How could he have been so stupid as to trust Gilgameth Tuft and his magic? It was the wizard's fault he was in this mess, and now he and Dani and Conrad were going to die for believing in a wizard.

He didn't care about his own life so much, but Dani and Conrad were another matter. Dani, especially. She came along of her own volition. Once again, like the time she'd brought him water when he was in the stocks, she had come to his aid out of the goodness of her heart. She was about to die for that goodness, and it was Derek's fault. He never should have let her come along.

The circle of yakarii around Derek opened, and they threw Dani next to him in the pebbles. She tumbled over the beach and scurried to her knees. When she saw the blood streaming down his back, she wrapped her arms around his shoulders to protect him.

"Derek! You're bleeding!"

Derek grimaced. "What does it matter? We will be dead soon."

Dani picked up the knife Derek had discarded and held it before her. "Not if I can help it."

Dani pointed the knife at the yakarii, who broke into howls of derision. "Look at the girl," they laughed. "She's funny when she's angry."

She ignored them and crouched at Derek's side. "Get yourself free of those bolas," she whispered. "I'll cover you."

Derek fumbled with the bolas, and with Dani to guard him, he got himself free of the tangle and back on his feet. "Thank you," he muttered.

Dani nodded, her face a grim visage.

One of the yakariian warriors wiped the tears of laughter from its eyes. "Put the knife down, girl, and this will go easier for you."

Dani spat at the beast and crouched lower, the tiny knife in her fist. The yakarii shrugged. "Easy or hard, you're dead either way."

The yakariian warrior raised his spear and roared. The beast reared back, ready to plunge the weapon through Dani's ribs. Derek screamed and reached for her. There was a hissing and a thunk, and the yakarii stumbled forward, a foot of cold steel jutting through its throat. From the back of its neck, six feet of an ironwood spear shaft waved like a cockscomb. How was the thing not dead? The beast dropped its weapon and fumbled feebly at the spear that had come out of nowhere. A spring of dark blood opened beneath the spearhead and ran in smooth rivulets down the yakarii's neck and under its armor. Finally, its yellow eyes rolled back in its head, its thick hands dropped to its side, and it toppled to the beach with a clatter of pebbles.

Everyone froze, not knowing from where the spear had come. There was a clamor, and Derek and the yakarii turned toward the pile of dead, smoldering Iron Guardsmen. Derek's heart leapt for joy. Not all the slaves had fled to the forest when they'd had the chance. A horde of freed slaves, now wielding the discarded weapons of the deceased Iron Guard, cheered the spear toss and rushed the outnumbered yakariian warriors.

There were fewer than a dozen yakarii left standing, and this gave the former captives courage. The yakarii and the slaves came together in a mighty clash. Sparks flew as the fine steel of the fallen Iron Guard's weapons hacked at the inferior yakariian armor. The slaves, far outnumbering the foul beasts, pressed on their foes with a five-to-one advantage. But the yakarii were no easy prey. Born on the field of battle and raised on a steady diet of warfare and violence, these warriors were the epitome of fury unleashed. They relished the odds and felt no fear of death, but rather joy for the opportunity to win glory on the field of battle.

Derek crouched next to Dani and looked for a sword or a spear or a club or anything to use in the fight. Across the beach, a man and a woman battled a hulking yakariian warrior. Derek was surprised to see two slaves taking on such a menacing figure, and his jaw dropped when he realized the couple were his parents! His mother, with her bright, northern eyes, wielded a long-hafted hammer. Derek had never seen Mum fight, had never imagined it, but there she was, howling with rage and raining blow after blow on the yakarii's shield arm.

The yakariian warrior, almost three heads taller than Mum, seemed more concerned with Da, who came at the creature with the signature longsword of the Iron Guard and a steel shield that glittered in the moonlight. Derek watched in amazement as his father worked the blade. While Mum was the very image of Maila — the northern goddess of battle fury — Da worked the yakarii's spear side with the cool mechanics of an artisan. Feinting high and slashing low, Bryton Fulstarter drew yakariian blood from a half-dozen wounds. The creature fell back, realizing it had met its equal in the form of Bryton's skillful swordplay. It brought its shield to bear against Da's keen blade, and that was its undoing.

Mum let fly a devastating blow to the yakarii's exposed left side with her hammer that crumpled the warrior's knee. The beast's leg collapsed with a meaty crunch, and the yakarii toppled to the sand. Mum screamed and finished the creature with a whirling overhand swing of her huge hammer while Da sought their next opponent.

Dani cheered and looked about, her knife ever before her. "We need to help them!"

Derek grunted. "We need weapons first. That pig sticker of yours won't do much against yakariian warriors."

A screech rang out less than a dozen paces away, where a handful of slaves faced off against a single warrior. A yakariian spear had found its target in a man's chest. He tumbled forward and latched onto the spear with a death grip. The yakariian snarled a swamp of curses and tried to yank the spear free from the man's innards, but it was buried deep and would not relent. The thing cursed again and tugged at the spear while the slaves kept up their attacks. They forced the yakarii to abandon the spear and draw the brutal longsword at his side.

Dani elbowed Derek and pointed at the spear. "There's your weapon!" she shouted. "Go get it!" She sprinted over the beach toward the yakariian warrior, whose back was turned toward her as it faced the freed slaves.

"What are you doing?" Derek yelled at Dani, who held up her tiny knife as an answer.

As soon as she was within range, Dani scampered up the beast's back and took a vicious jab at the thing's unarmored neck. The creature howled and reached for Dani, but she was too small and quick for it to get a decent purchase on her. Seizing the opening, one of the slaves slipped in close and drove three feet of Zuid Hornian steel through the beast, then stumbled out of the way before it could collapse on him.

Derek hurried to the abandoned spear and placed a foot on the dead man's chest. "Sorry," he muttered and grabbed the spear. "I really need this." Derek gritted his teeth. He took a breath and tugged the weapon free with a mighty heave.

Just off to his right, a handful of freed slaves squared off against one of the remaining yakariian warriors. Several dead and dying men and women at the warrior's feet attested to the yakarii's fury and skill. In another time, the sight of the towering killing machine would have frozen Derek in his tracks. But after facing Shadizarian pirates and surviving a night of destruction in Zuid Horn, no lone warrior was going to keep Derek Fulstarter from reuniting with his parents.

Derek charged across the pebbly beach with the spear and wedged himself between a pair of freed slaves. The long-shafted weapon, soaked in the blood of a hundred enemies, felt slick and awkward in his hands. Derek slashed at the warrior, but the spear's black-bladed head simply screeched off the warrior's iron leg plates. A second thrust glanced off the yakarii's breastplate and won the warrior's attention. Ignoring the ring of men and women around it, the creature focused on Derek with red, bleary eyes. It opened its shark-toothed maw and roared until Derek felt his chest shake.

Then, faster than Derek would have thought possible, the warrior hurled its tremendous bulk at him and swung with a devastating overhead strike. It was all he could do to get his spear up to defend himself. The yakariian blade snapped the spear in half and sent him sprawling. The thing howled with glee and charged after Derek to finish him off. But in its rush, it left its flanks open. Men and women fell on it from all sides and hacked at the creature until it collapsed under their united assault.

Derek rolled to his feet and snatched up the bottom half of his shattered spear, now a makeshift club. He turned the weapon over in his hand to check its weight. "Perfect," he said with a smirk, and he took a step toward the crowd finishing off the downed warrior.

A crack like thunder broke across the beach, and an emerald aura filled the air. Derek's ears buzzed with a greasy hum, and when he tried to turn his head to look about, he found that he couldn't move. He cursed in his head. He knew exactly what was happening. The shamans at the edge of the forest! How could he have forgotten them and their magic? Curse magic and everything to do with it!

The battle came to a complete stop. Men froze with their spears in the air. Women stood like statues; their swords caught mid-swing. The yakarii, however, were a different story.

Those surviving yakarii buried under freed slaves pushed themselves to their feet and looked about. One of the savage brutes, still burning with battle lust, snatched up the butt of a spear and unleashed his fury on an immobile man. Derek tried to close his eyes to the sight, but whatever magic had settled over them kept his eyes open to the horror.

There was a crunching in the sand next to Derek, and then a hulking figure draped in tattered robes shuffled past, leaning heavily on a worn staff decorated with raven feathers and bleached rat skulls. The yakariian shaman smelled of sage and cinnamon. Several hemp ropes looped over its shoulders. Fat satchels swung from the loops of rope as the shaman ambled past.

"Karak," the thing barked. "Control yourself. The master needs slaves to work the mine."

Karak the yakariian warrior scowled. It gave the poor man one last whack and then turned to join the shaman. "We should kill them all," Karak growled. "Once slaves rise up, there's no trusting them."

The shaman snorted. "Tell the master if you dare. For my part, I say keep these slaves working until we get new ones. We have all of Zuid Horn to raid now that the Iron Guard is in tatters."

Both of the yakarii laughed. The shaman lowered his staff toward the magically held humans. "Get them tied up. My enchantment won't last forever."

Karak grunted and went to work, tying the humans with bits of rope and leather. The shaman tottered from captive to captive. He checked their bindings and muttered incantations to keep the humans magically held.

He hadn't gotten very far when a zipping hiss sliced through the air. A black-shafted arrow punched through the shaman's throat. The savage wizard gagged and grasped at its neck. Thick clots of crimson bubbled through its fingers, and the wizened yakariian shaman toppled forward, lying still. With the shaman dead and its chanting silenced forever, Derek and the other humans on the beach found they could move again.

Derek whirled to find the source of the arrow. Behind them, just to the side of the other yakariian shamans chanting near the forest's edge, Conrad was fitting another arrow to a well-crafted Zuid Hornian short bow. Derek pumped his fist in the air.

"Conrad!" he yelped.

Conrad lifted his chin in greeting and pivoted toward the knot of yakariian shamans whose chanting kept the children from using the magic of Gilgameth Tuft's rings. He drew back on his bow and let fly another black shaft that buried itself deep in a shaman's chest. The creature clutched at the feathered arrow, cast pleading eyes at its fellows, and then dropped dead on its back. The other shamans gasped at an enemy appearing so quickly in their midst. They stumbled in their chants, and Derek felt a warm tingle on his ring finger again.

Meanwhile, Conrad fit another arrow to his bow and drew back. "Their spell is almost broken! Get ready to use your rings!" he shouted and then loosed his third and final arrow, felling another shaman.

The yakariian shamans clutched at the satchels swinging from their robes. They chanted words of magic, but it was too late for them. Conrad tossed his bow aside and charged the creatures. Derek watched as his friend ran with his lean arms in the air, howling and screaming as he closed the gap. From Derek's point of view, it looked as though Conrad were reaching for the full moon, now brilliant over the eastern horizon.

Conrad's flesh twisted and stretched. His nose elongated, pulling his lips forward into two black lines sprouting a needle nest of teeth. Coarse, black hair rose from his widening shoulders and lengthening arms until a fine, sleek coat of fur covered Conrad's new body. A nude tail, fat and obscene, burst from the rear of his trousers and wriggled back and forth. Gleaming nails twisted into talons, crowning every finger and toe. Derek watched in amazement, not understanding his friend's choice.

A wererat? Why would he turn into that?

Conrad the wererat leapt into the shamans. His nails and teeth tore robes and ripped flesh. They fell beneath his fierce onslaught.

"How can you use your rings?" The yakariian shamans squealed. "Our spells should have stopped you!"

Conrad the wererat pounced on the thing's chest. "I didn't use a ring. I *am* a wererat!" Then, he sank his needle teeth into a shaman's neck.

Derek felt his knees go weak as he understood his friend's plight. A wererat! Of course! That would explain what had happened in the ratter's hold of *The Delivery*. Why else would Conrad have been scratching at his forearm all the time? He must have been bitten by a wererat! And tonight was the first full moon since he had been bitten. It all made sense now.

Derek watched his friend wade through the screeching shamans. A yakariian warrior rushed to help them, but its unenchanted weapons had no effect on Conrad's magical hide. Conrad's nails made short work of the beast, and Derek didn't know whether to be repulsed at what had become of his friend or relieved that victory was at hand.

With the yakariian spellcasters taken care of, everything went crazy at once. The humans, formerly frozen, leapt on the remaining yakarii with a vengeance. Swords and spears flew in fierce arcs around the warrior beasts. While the magic held, the yakarii had let their guards down, walking into the midst of the frozen slaves. Now, with the magic suddenly gone, the yakarii found themselves surrounded.

Derek caught a glimpse of his parents battling a mountain of a warrior. The creature was plated in thick slabs of iron over a corset of chain mail. It wielded two massive war hammers and sent curtains of black pebbles flying every time a missed strike pounded the beach. His parents danced in and out of the creature's range. Da kept his gimpy leg to the rear, and Derek could barely tell he had a bad leg at all. His father's blade flashed in the cool light of the moon. The edge of his weapon dripped with black blood.

Mum's eyes burned with battle lust. She swung a long-handled hammer with a heavy, spiked head. The black raven feathers tied to the shaft and the grotesque engravings marked it as yakariian-made. How she could possibly wield the ungainly weapon, Derek couldn't say, but together with Da, they tore the warrior apart, playing their victim from opposite sides. As soon as the thing turned its attention to one of his parents, the other darted in to let their opponent have it.

Derek's chest swelled with pride. He picked up the butt of his shattered spear and loosed his war cry across the battlefield. Dani wasn't far away, so he rushed to her side to help her with a pair of yakariian scouts. Lithe as an alley cat, the street girl dipped and wove through the scattered combatants with her tiny knife, frustrating the yakarii with their slow, heavy weapons.

Dani arranged herself to draw one scout's attention. Derek took full advantage of the distraction, closed in, and leapt on the scout's back. He let the thing have it with a nasty whack from his broken spear. The scout gave a grunt, toppled forward, and was still. Another scout dropped into a crouch and looked about. Seven angry slaves pressed in on it from one side. Not far away, the wererat rose from the shredded remains of the shamans and searched for its next victim.

All over the beach, the freed slaves of the salt mines washed over their yakariian masters. A large yakariian warrior, much larger than the rest, roared, "Retreat! We fight another day!" And then it ran into the woods.

One by one, the yakarii fled the beach. A final scout, braver or more stupid than the rest, lagged before finally hightailing it for the forest. Dani started after it, but Derek stopped her. "Let it go."

She glared at him, and he held his hands up. Derek said, "We need to get everyone out of here."

"But it will bring others."

"I don't think so. Look." Derek pointed across the beach, where Conrad — in wererat form — loped across the pebbles after the yakariian scout. Conrad plunged into the forest. Shortly thereafter, a terrified scream echoed from the shadowy woods.

Dani scrunched up her face. "Was that wererat Conrad?"

Derek looked into her dark eyes. He wanted to tell her the truth about what he had realized about her brother, but all he said was, "Yeah. Those rings are amazing." He cleared his throat. "Don't worry about Conrad. He's got it under control. Let's get these people back to Zuid Horn."

Derek walked to his parents with Dani at his side. Da whooped when he saw Derek. Mum put her hand over her mouth, and then wrapped her arms around him. "Derek!" she whispered. "I can't believe it's you."

Derek buried his face in his parents' embrace. All the fear, all the weight of responsibility, all the dread of not knowing if his parents were alive was finally gone, and the relief came out of him in a flood of tears. He gulped at the air, terrified to let them go. As soon as he did, he knew he would have to tell them about Liza and how he'd failed to keep her safe. He prayed they wouldn't ask about her. Not yet anyway. He buried his face in his parents' arms and wept for himself, for his sister, and for the pain he knew was coming their way.

It was a long time before they let go of one another.

When they finally broke apart, Da looked over Derek's shoulder and smiled. "Dani! Why am I not surprised to see you here?"

"Hello, Mr. Fulstarter. Mrs. Fulstarter."

Derek looked between Dani and his parents. Why weren't they asking about his sisters? That should have been the first thing out of their mouths.

He shook his head, confused, and turned to see his smiling friend, with her short, black hair shimmering in the rising moonlight. Dani's skin glowed like dark silver, and somehow, filthy as she was from the battle, Derek thought she'd never looked better.

He would have kept looking at her, but Mum was busily going over the two of them. "Are you wounded? Did any of those beasts get you?"

Derek squirmed to escape his mother's inspection. "We're fine, Mum. Just a few knicks and bruises. Let's get everyone rounded up so we can get out of here before more yakarii come back."

Da grunted. "Good idea." He looked at Dani and smiled. "Where's Conrad?"

Derek's gut twisted. "I just saw him go into the forest. He'll be here in a bit."

He turned quickly so no one could see his face. His tongue lay in his mouth like jerky, stiff and dry. How could he tell his parents the truth about Conrad? How could he say anything to Dani? Liza's death. Conrad's curse. He should have been happy that his parents were free, but despite the warm, tropical breeze, a chill clutched Derek's heart.

Dani searched the battlefield and kept looking back to the forest where they had seen Conrad run through the underbrush. "Maybe we should go look for him."

Derek saw the worry in her face and realized he needed to tell her the truth. Dani picked up a spear. "I'm going to look for him," she said.

Derek put a hand on her shoulder. "Dani, wait. There's something I need to tell you." Dani looked at his hand on her shoulder, and he dropped it quickly. "I'm sorry, but it's about Conrad," he said.

"What?"

"It's about what you just saw. Do you remember on *The Delivery*, when Conrad was in the ratter's hold?"

Dani screwed up her face. "Yeah?"

Derek took a breath, but before he could say anything, Dani looked past his shoulder and her face lit up. "Conrad! Where have you been?" She pushed past Derek and ran to Conrad in his human form. Dani leapt into her brother's arms.

Derek gave a sigh of relief. He joined his friends and waited for them to stop hugging. Conrad looked over Dani's shoulder and lifted a finger of silence to his lips. His eyes pleaded with Derek and begged him not to let Dani or anyone know about his terrible

secret. Derek placed a hand over his chest and gave a nod. Conrad closed his eyes and held onto his sister.

"Boy!" Da called.

Derek turned to his father. "Yes, Da?"

"I need you."

Derek hurried to Da, who bent to pick up a steel chest plate that had been torn from a fallen Iron Guardsman. "We need to get back to Zuid Horn. Help me get a sword in every hand and a shield on every arm."

"Yes, Da."

"If you see any usable armor, hand that out too."

"Yes, Da."

Having a task from Da made it easy to not talk about Liza. Derek moved as fast as he could. The yakarii had scattered weapons and armor from the dead Iron Guardsmen all over the beach. Derek ran about, finding swords and shields for even the weakest survivors. Once they had everyone outfitted, Derek reported back to his father.

"Well done," Da said. "You did well today."

Derek felt his chest swell with pride. "Thanks." He paused. This was the time. If Derek was going to tell his parents about Liza, it was now or never. "Da?"

"What?"

"There's something I have to tell you."

Da put his hands on his hips. "Go on."

The words were at the back of Derek's throat, thick, like a lump of gravy. *Liza is dead*, he wanted to say. *It's my fault. I couldn't save her.* But his mouth wouldn't work. His face and neck and eyes burned, and then the tears came, and he was sobbing.

Da came close and took Derek into a bear-like hug. "You don't have to say it," Da said.

"What?"

"Liza."

Derek's stomach convulsed. He gulped for air. "It's my fault."

Da moved away from Derek and held him at arm's length. "Why do you say that?"

And between the tears, Derek told Da about what happened the night of the flood — how the house broke apart, how his sisters were kidnapped by the yakarii, how he found Conrad and Dani, and how they tracked the yakarii with his sisters. And with a feeling like he was gutting himself with his own knife, Derek told Da about his plan to rescue his sisters, but how he'd frozen up when it mattered most.

He waited for Da to say something, but the big man simply held his son in silence. Finally, Da kissed the top of Derek's head. "I know," he said. "Your mother and I already know."

Derek stepped away from Da's embrace. Da's eyes were wet. His face was red under his bristling beard. "You know?" Derek said. "How?"

"You know David Weaver, from David's Pottery over on Feasting Lane?"

"Yes?"

"He came to see me and your mother the morning after the flood. He was across the way with his two kids and saw everything."

Derek stared, trying to comprehend. "He saw everything?"

Da nodded. "Your mother and I knew about Liza and Sarah the next morning." Da took a deep breath and wiped his eyes. "It wasn't your fault, Derek. You did everything you could."

"But I froze."

Da shook his head. "What would you have done against a yakariian scout?"

A flash of heat rippled in Derek's chest. He pointed at the field of yakarii dead on the beach. "I can handle myself."

Da held up his hands to stave off Derek's rising anger. "That's not how I meant that. You are a warrior, Derek. I see that now. But what can you do in a situation like that? When the potter told me what happened to you and your sisters, I knew you would take it hard. Who wouldn't? You can't blame yourself, son." Da took a slow breath. "It was hard enough hearing about the girls, and not knowing what happened to you..." Da rubbed his eyes with his big hands. "Mum and I thought we lost you all."

"Da, there's something else. I should probably tell Mum, too."

Mum was nearby, helping a woman with a nasty gash on her leg off the beach. "Hon," Da called. "Come over here for a bit. Derek wants to tell us something."

Mum waved and helped the wounded woman take a seat on a log. Then, she hurried over to Derek and Da. Her long, black hair flashed under the moonlight. The war hammer she used in the fight with the yakarii was slung over her back. She moved like a panther over the beach, and Derek marveled that he had never noticed her strength before, especially now, when it was so obvious.

She gave Derek and Da a tired smile. "What's going on?"

Derek looked at his parents and took a breath. "Sarah's still alive."

Da dropped his hands. "Sarah?"

Derek nodded. "She's still alive, back in Zuid Horn. Wendy is taking care of her."

Mum lifted her face to the sky. "Thank the Forge," she whispered, and drew her fingertips across her forehead and upper chest.

Da looked over Derek into the distance. His mouth hung open, and he breathed heavily. "She's still alive," he said to himself. "We heard she was dead."

And Derek told his parents the rest of the story, about Dani and the spear, their flight from the yakarii, the water and fire elementals, the wizards, finding Niles Crowing and the Magnificent Seven, and finally, their run-in with Gilgameth Tuft, their stay in the Tower of Sorcery and the magic rings. Derek decided not to say anything about his agreement to become Gilgameth Tuft's next apprentice just yet. He knew what his parents thought about wizards, and they had been through enough already.

Da wiped the tears from his eyes and studied Derek. "Incredible. Just incredible. I can't believe who you've become, Derek. A month ago, I thought you wanted to be a cook."

Derek snorted. "No chance of that now."

"You still could be, if you wanted to," Mum said.

Da smiled. "I don't think so. It's clear he has the blood of an adventurer. No point denying it now."

Derek's chest swelled. "But what about you two?"

"Us?" Mum asked.

"Where did you learn how to fight like that?"

Da shrugged. A tiny grin tugged at the corner of his mouth. "I wasn't always a fletcher, you know."

"You weren't?"

"No." Da sighed and gazed over the battlefield. "I was in the Iron Guard for five years, before your mother and I met."

Mum smiled and took Da's hand. Derek felt like someone had slapped him on the back of the head. "The Iron Guard? But what about the shop?"

Da laughed. "When I was your age, I didn't want anything to do with fletching, so I joined the Iron Guard. Did well, too. But one night, I took a nasty arrow to the knee, and my time with the Iron Guard was over. The family business was all I had left."

Derek's throat tightened, and his neck burned. "But then why did you try to force me to stay in the shop?"

Da let out a slow breath and gestured to the dead scattered over the beach. "That's why. I've been there. I've seen friends die. Your mother and I couldn't sleep at night not knowing if you were ever coming back. We love you too much, Derek, just like we love your sisters. Do you know what losing you would do to us?"

Derek's chin trembled. "No."

"It would kill us," Da said. "As much as losing Liza is tearing us apart inside..." He walked over to Mum and wrapped his arms around her. They held one another for several breaths. When they

came away, their eyes were wet again. He went on, "Your mother and I were mad with grief when you were off on *The Delivery*. I nearly killed Crowing when he told me what you were up to, but part of me understood, too." He looked at Dani and Conrad, not far off. "I guess I would have done the same thing." Da turned back to Derek. "I'm proud of you, son."

Derek lowered his eyes. "So, you understand?"

"Of course." Da picked up a shield and a sword from the beach. He slipped the shield over his left arm and turned the steel longsword over in slow circles. "You know, after everything you've been through, what with the Shadizarians, Niles Crowing, the Rat Queen, the flood, and now this," he gestured back to the beach, "I think you've earned a spot with Iron Guard."

"Really?"

Da nodded. "You bet. When I saw the battle lust in your eyes today, you reminded me of your mother."

"I saw it, too," Mum laughed.

Derek looked at her, stunned. "What?"

"You know how Grandma and Grandpa are from north of Bearton?" Mum asked.

Derek shrugged. "Yeah."

"They've all got the battle lust up there," Da said. "People say they go crazy. It's what makes them great warriors." Da slipped his sword through his belt and wrapped an arm around Derek. Mum took Derek by the hand. They led their son away from the beach, toward the trail back to Zuid Horn. "You're a born fighter, boy," Da said. "You've got the battle lust. I'd be crazy to try to stop that. It's who you are."

Derek thought about his temper and the focus he felt every time he was in a fight. "That explains a lot."

"There's no sense denying it. That will only make things worse. What you need is good training to control it."

"The Iron Guard," Derek said, jaw tight. How was he going to get the training he needed to control his temper when he had promised his service to Gilgameth Tuft?

"Exactly. They will need good men now more than ever. When we get back to Zuid Horn, I'll take you to their guild house, if it's still standing. My name is still good there, and I know they would be happy to train my son."

Derek walked next to his parents. He felt an odd tickle at the base of his spine. They really understood him. Derek opened his mouth to say something, to tell his parents he loved them, that he was proud to be their son, and that he would do his best to live up to the family name, but Da held up a hand.

"I know, son. I know. Let's not talk about this anymore until we get back to Zuid Horn. For now, we need to get these people moving."

Mum gave Derek a kiss on the head and went back to help the woman sitting on the log. Da walked away and barked orders as though he had never left the Iron Guard. Derek wiped a bare arm across his nose and hurried after Da, never prouder to be his parents' son.

22

Justice is Served

The *Delivery* docked at Ploughman's Wharf three weeks after it left Zuid Horn. The trip back to the iron city had been slow, as the Shadizarian slaver limped through rough seas without its central mast. But they made it, and the crew was hungry for the pleasures only a port city could provide. It was near midnight, and the decent citizens of Zuid Horn were asleep.

As soon as the gangway was lowered, tired sailors poured onto the pier. The men headed to the noisy taverns lighting up the night along the harbor. Derek leaned on the rail of *The Delivery* with a group of Shadizarians and listened to the disembarking sailors complain about the storm that had crippled their ship. As the sailors walked past a line of gibbets which still held the rotting remains of several minotaurs, a handful of Iron Guardsmen strolled up to the gangplank and waved at Derek and the others gathered along the railing.

The captain of *The Delivery* stood next to Derek at the railing. The first lieutenant, Awwal, stood next to him. "Are you ready for this?"

"Yes," Derek said.

"Are you sure?"

Derek clenched his fist. "Absolutely."

"Well then," the captain said, "let's get it over with." The captain checked his belt, tapped a scroll at his side, and then started for the gangway. "I recognize the lieutenant down there. His name is Hastman Gorzoni. No surprise to see him here." The captain snorted. "Let's go, ladies and gentlemen. It's time to buy some slaves."

The first mate and several of the Shadizarian guards followed the captain down the gangplank. Derek fell in behind, his stomach tight with nerves. Gorzoni and the Iron Guardsmen moved to intercept them. "Captain," the yellow-haired Gorzoni said, "I wasn't expecting to see you. It's an honor."

The captain waved him off. "I wasn't expecting to be back."

Gorzoni jerked a thumb at the sailors heading toward the drinking holes along Ploughman's Wharf. "Sounds like you ran into a storm."

"It's a miracle we are alive, Ra be praised," the captain said. "The waves were like mountains. We lost a quarter of the slaves on the rowing deck."

Gorzoni flashed a quick grin. The yellow of his teeth matched his dirty hair. "That explains why you're back."

"We were only a week out," the captain said, scanning the docks. "I couldn't return to Shadizar without a full hold. Where's the profit in that?"

The Iron Guardsmen laughed. "Profit indeed," Gorzoni said. "Well, your timing is good. The stocks are full tonight. We were expecting a ship of minotaur buyers, but they never showed up. Maybe they got caught up in the same storm you ran into." Gorzoni pointed at *The Delivery's* broken central mast. "Since you are a long-standing customer, I'll give you the first pick."

The captain offered a curt bow, as was the Shadizarian custom. "I am honored you would think so highly of me."

Gorzoni and the other Iron Guardsmen laughed. "Anything to please your king," Gorzoni said. "I trust you have mentioned the work we do for him here?"

"Have no fear," the captain said. "You will be well rewarded for your efforts."

Gorzoni clapped his hands together and rubbed them vigorously. "Well, let me show you what we have." He waved to his men and headed toward the stocks.

The captain turned to his first mate and the other guardsmen. "Let's go." Then, to Derek, he whispered, "Remember to stay back. This could get ugly."

Derek nodded and followed along, doing his best to keep out of sight. As he walked to the stocks, four Shadizarian guards — three men and a woman — came to walk near him. They didn't say anything, but Derek felt better for their presence.

A warm breeze came off the ocean. It smelled of salt and seaweed and fear. Derek was glad to be off *The Delivery*, and he was even more glad to be home. He'd had enough of the ocean, storms, and living on the edge of death. Maybe there were people who yearned for the sea and the high adventure to be found there, but Derek was not one of them. His experience on *The Delivery* had taught him to never trust the sea or the people who crave it. Derek was land-born, and he would do everything in his power to stay there as long as he could.

"Here we are," Gorzoni proclaimed, waving his hand down a line of prisoners locked into the stockades running up and down Ploughman's Wharf. "A fine collection of rats if you ever saw them."

The captain stepped next to Gorzoni and inspected the human wares. He stroked his mustache as he walked up and down the dock. "Good catch," the captain said. "Where did you get them this time?"

Gorzoni pointed to a group of men lying in stocks at the end of the pier. They were clad in tanned hides, an unusual sight in tropical Zuid Horn. Most of the men lay on their backs, snoring loudly. "Them there I found at the Winking Maiden," Gorzoni said.

"A fine establishment if there ever was one. Like to go there myself when the coin is good."

The captain grunted. "Why did you arrest them?"

Gorzoni shrugged. "Does it matter?"

"I suppose not. I'm just curious."

Gorzoni studied the captain for a bit before saying, "Turns out they were running weapons for Valis."

"King Folio's son-in-law?"

"Yep. They were drinking and running their mouths about how Folio is running Shadizar into the ground. You always told me to keep an ear open for anyone bad-mouthing his lordship. So, there you go." Gorzoni delivered a light kick to one of the leather-clad men. The man barely budged. "Do with him as you like," Gorzoni said. "He might know a thing or two about Valis' operation in the west, so I wouldn't rough him up too much."

"Don't worry about that," the captain said. "I know what to do with traitors." He looked down the pier. "So, that's this lot. What about the rest?"

"Most of the rest is the usual," Gorzoni said, strolling down a line of thin and dirty men, women, and children. "Street rats begging on the pier we rounded up, families we scraped out of the Warehouse District." Gorzoni shook his head. "Been doing this for years, but it seems we ain't making a dent cleaning out this latrine. Not sure where all the filth comes from."

"It's the nature of humanity," the captain said. "Rot rises where Ra's light doesn't shine."

Gorzoni gave the captain a sideways glance. "I didn't know you were a religious man."

The captain looked over the prisoners, soon to become slaves. "Ra's grace has shown me the path to righteousness."

Gorzoni and his men burst into laughter. "I'm sure it has. Well, we all have stories to make ourselves feel better. Don't we, boys?" The Iron Guardsmen with Gorzoni continued laughing. "And we have ours. How many years have we been doing this, Captain?"

"Doing what?"

Gorzoni's men kept laughing, but Gorzoni wiped his eyes and looked more closely at the captain. "Feeding you slaves from the stocks. How many years has it been?"

The captain cleared his throat. "A long time."

Gorzoni cocked his head and stared long and hard at the captain. His hand drifted to the hilt of the blue steel longsword at his side. "A long time, yes, but I want you to tell me exactly. How many years have we known each other, Captain? Five? Ten? Fifteen?"

The air chilled. Derek's hand went to the club at his side. Just ahead of him, the captain looked at Gorzoni, then turned to his men. "What's going on here? We've known each other for a long time, Gorzoni. I'm not sure what you're driving at, but unless you want me to report this to King Folio, I suggest we finish this sale and move on to some wine."

Gorzoni slid his sword halfway from its scabbard. The smile was gone from his face, and his eyes were dark and deadly. His Iron Guard brethren stopped laughing and looked about. Gorzoni leveled his gaze on the captain. "I'm not new to this game, Captain. I know when something doesn't smell right, and something about this reeks like bad fish. So, I'll ask one more time. How long?"

The captain put up his hands and smiled. His mustache framed his teeth perfectly. "My friend, you don't want to do this."

Gorzoni pulled his sword free of its scabbard and held it before him. "Actually, I do. Something about you hasn't felt right since you docked. The captain I know isn't a religious man, and you've called upon the sun god twice now. You've never called me 'Gorzoni' before, and your first mate here usually does all the talking." Gorzoni turned the tip of his sword on the first mate. "What do you have to say for yourself?"

The first mate, well out of the range of Gorzoni's sword, glared at the corrupt Iron Guardsman. Drawing his own sword, the first mate said, "I say I've heard enough to know the reports are true. You are a traitor to Zuid Horn and a disgrace to the Iron Guard." Over his shoulder, he shouted, "Master Moonfist, release your spell!"

One of the Shadizarian guardsmen behind the first mate bowed low. "At your command, Captain Gier." Then, he raised his arms and lowered them slowly, muttering words of magic.

The air about them shimmered, and suddenly the Shadizarian crewmen and guards were no longer there. Rather, Captain Gier of the Iron Guard's Eastern District appeared, backed by a unit of the city's finest and most honorable warriors. With them — where the captain and his other officers previously stood — were Niles Crowing and the Magnificent Seven. And surrounding Derek, where four Shadizarian guards had been, were Conrad, Lars, Jenkins, and Dani. Derek grinned at his friends as they drew two feet of Zuid Hornian steel from their belts.

Derek hefted the table leg he had used as a club to liberate *The Delivery*. "Ready?" Derek asked.

Conrad's eyes were as hard as forged steel. "More than you can know."

Wendy the Ogress dropped her gauntlet-clad hands on Derek and Conrad's shoulders. "Not this time, children. You heard Niles."

"But Wendy," Derek pleaded, "we've come so far!"

"And if these criminals get away," Conrad added, "we'll have to do time in the stocks!"

Wendy the Ogress turned her attention to the ring of Iron Guardsmen around Gorzoni. "I don't think so, children. Captain Gier has heard more than enough to pardon you." She picked the boys up and moved them aside as easily as though she were handling toddlers. "Now stay back. If there is blood to be spilled, I don't want any of it to be yours. You've been through enough already."

The ogress rolled like an avalanche over the pier. Gorzoni glared at her and sneered. "Niles Crowing and the Magnificent Seven. I should have known you would be involved in this. Always on the right side of the law, aren't you?"

Niles shrugged and dropped into a loose fighting stance, his deadly rapier held ready before him. "I don't know about being on the right side of the law, but I know where kidnapping children falls. I don't need a law to tell me right from wrong on that account."

Gorzoni raised his shield, a heavy, rectangular affair identifying him as a lieutenant in the Wharf District. The keen edge of his Zuid Hornian steel longsword glinted with sparks of lamplight from nearby taverns.

"Always so sure of yourself, aren't you, Crowing? Always so sure what you're doing is right." Gorzoni twirled his blade over and circled about, keeping an eye on the Magnificent Seven and the Iron Guardsmen surrounding them. "You have these idiots fooled, don't you?" Gorzoni turned quickly to Captain Gier. "Tell me, Captain, has Crowing told you about his time in Shadizar, about how he made his fortune before he came to Zuid Horn?"

Captain Gier glanced at Niles. "What's this about, Crowing?"

Niles shot looks between Captain Gier and Gorzoni. "Don't listen to him, Captain. He's trying to divide us."

Gorzoni laughed like a wheezing hyena. "I don't have to try, pretender. Tell the captain about your time with the Folios." Gorzoni's eyes glittered with malice. His lips pulled back to reveal a nasty nest of sharp teeth. "Tell him about Ra's curse and the Moon Plague." Gorzoni's dark eyes flickered to Derek and his friends. His mouth twisted into a cruel smirk. "What do you think your pretty little friends there will think of you when they hear about your role in bringing the Moon Plague to Zuid Horn?" Gorzoni's gaze settled on Conrad. "Twice now."

Derek looked between Gorzoni and Conrad. "What's he talking about?" Derek asked.

Conrad scratched his arm, where Derek noticed the bite mark his friend had gotten in the ratter's hold. Conrad wouldn't meet Derek's gaze. "I don't know."

Derek pointed to the raw wound on Conrad's arm. "Are you alright?"

Conrad glanced at his arm. "I think so. One of the rats on *The Delivery* bit me. Biggest one I ever seen, but I chased him off."

Derek wanted to know more about the rat, but Captain Gier started in on Gorzoni. "I'll deal with Niles and his story later. For now, Gorzoni, my attention is on you." He straightened himself as tall as he could and pointed his sword at the crooked guardsman. "Hastman Gorzoni, Lieutenant of the Western District, Ploughman's Wharf, I find you guilty of treason. I have heard you confess to working with a foreign agent against our great city and to selling the free citizens of Zuid Horn into slavery. You are under arrest."

Gorzoni shot quick glances at the crooked Iron Guardsmen at his side. Then, he sneered at Captain Gier. "Arrest is it, Captain? I don't think so. You'll need to catch us first."

Captain Gier twirled his blade over twice. Its cold steel flickered in the warm night air. "With a rat like you, it will be a pleasure." The veteran guardsman charged forward and lunged at Gorzoni with an overhead strike that flashed like lightning in the dim light.

Gorzoni stumbled away, but he wasn't fast enough to avoid the tip of Gier's sword. Razor-sharp steel ripped across Gorzoni's chest, but other than hacking through the connecting leather straps of his plate armor, the strike did nothing to Gorzoni. Captain Gier's face twisted in confusion. He kept his silence and delivered a backhanded blow that should have torn open Gorzoni's throat. Again, the captain of the Iron Guard's deadly strike did little more than shave a few thin whiskers off Gorzoni's greasy beard.

Gorzoni cackled. "You're losing your step, Captain," he mocked. "You'll need better steel than that if you're going to catch me." Gorzoni held his shield before him and kept his sword in a ready position over his head. He and his corrupt Iron Guard brothers backed toward the edge of the pier as Captain Gier, Niles Crowing, the Magnificent Seven, and a unit of loyal Iron Guardsmen pressed forward.

Captain Gier advanced warily, a dark scowl written across his face. He hefted the weight of his longsword. "This is good steel from Boettcher's Steel Mill on the Black River. Those strikes should have killed you, Gorzoni. What's going on here?"

Niles Crowing moved to the captain's side. He held his rapier between them and the grinning Gorzoni. "It's the Moon Plague, Captain. Gorzoni's infected. Normal steel will not harm him."

"Moon Plague?"

"Yes — lycanthropy. Gorzoni is a wererat whose inner form takes over when the moon is full."

Captain Gier stared at Niles Crowing. "How do you know this?" Niles sighed. "What Gorzoni said is true. Almost a decade ago, I lived in Shadizar and worked as a mercenary for King Folio. Before I knew it, they had captured my sister and threatened to kill her if I didn't do as they told me. I had to bring this foul creature to Zuid Horn, where I later learned he had been carrying the Moon Plague all along. Their plan was to raise an army of wererats in Zuid Horn's sewers and overrun the city."

Derek's jaw dropped. wererats in the sewers? He had grown up hearing stories about the Rat Queen, but he'd never suspected they were real!

Captain Gier shook his head in confusion. "Why would they do that? Zuid Horn has supplied Shadizar with weapons and armor for centuries."

Niles nodded. "Yes, but it supplied Shadizar's enemies as well. King Folio outfitted his armies with the best steel in the realm. If he could overrun Zuid Horn and deprive his enemies of the same steel..."

"It would be a huge advantage," Captain Gier interrupted.

"Exactly."

Gorzoni and his foul crew backed closer to the edge of the pier. "And Niles Crowing was the lynchpin to get everything rolling."

Captain Gier's face darkened. "You knew this, Crowing, and you did nothing?"

"What could I do?" Niles asked. "They had my sister. But that's why I've been doing everything I've done since I came back to

Zuid Horn. I'm trying to set things right. I've brought down criminal organizations, freed slaves, and now, I have even exposed corruption within the Iron Guard." Niles risked a quick glance at the captain. "At long last, my dark secret is exposed. But now that my shame is revealed, I can move more freely to right the wrongs I've committed. Let me finish this, Gier. We've been friends for years. Please, let me do what's right and finish this."

"But your sister?"

Niles shook his head. "The Shadizarians brought her to Zuid Horn years ago. They infected her with the Moon Plague and gave her to this rat." He gestured to Gorzoni. "He forced her to be his Rat Queen. It will be my pleasure to give this scoundrel what he deserves."

Captain Gier gave Niles a quick nod. "Very well. He is yours, then." To his loyal guardsmen, he barked, "Men, round up the rest of this vile lot. I'll see them in gibbets before sunrise!"

The ring of steel ripping from scabbards sang in the night. Gorzoni peered at the field of blades closing on him. Despite the apparent futility of his predicament, he laughed. "Normal steel won't hurt us, Crowing."

Niles' mouth twisted into a wry smile. "Oh, don't worry. I've thought about that." He paused briefly and held his rapier upright before him. "*Daw alshams!*" he shouted, and his blade burst with a light as bright as the noonday sun.

Gorzoni and his cronies reared back, raising their shields to cover their faces. Several of the cowards squealed when the light touched them. The skin of their faces wriggled as though a thousand worms crawled just under the surface. Then, as Derek and the others watched on in horror, Gorzoni and his allies transformed into man-sized rat creatures beneath their plate mail armor.

Long, greasy snouts burst from their faces. Needle-sharp teeth sprouted from their mouths. Nasty nests of glistening black hair sprouted over their bodies. Beady eyes blinked against the bright light of Niles' sword. The rat-men threw up long, probing fingers in a vain attempt to shield themselves from the light, but it was hopeless. The magic of Niles' rapier found its way through every crevice and exposed the rat-men for all to see.

Derek shook his head slowly. "I didn't think I could be any more surprised."

"I don't feel so good," Conrad whispered so that only Derek could hear. He held his hand up to block the sword light. "I think I'm going to throw up."

Dani studied the glowing sword, her eyes fixated by the light. "Look what magic can do," she whispered. "I never knew."

The captain watched the transformation, impressed. "What's this, Crowing?"

Niles Crowing smirked but kept his gaze focused on Gorzoni. "Magic, sir, that I've searched long and hard to find. It took me years to gather what I needed, but I'm finally ready to avenge my sister."

Gorzoni, now a gigantic rat-man on the pier, hissed and squealed against the magic light. "You'll need more than one sword to bring in me and my crew, Crowing!"

Niles Crowing glared at Gorzoni. "I know." Then, over his shoulder, he shouted, "Now!"

The Magnificent Seven leapt forward, each of them brandishing their weapon of choice. Wendy the Ogress clashed her spiked gauntlets together and roared when blue rays of light burst from her steel mitts. Kassar the Swift slipped from the crowd and into the front ranks, a pair of deadly, glowing daggers in his quick hands. Father Ferrum strode boldly through a narrow gap between the groups, an enchanted mace blazing with the coal-fire of the Forge held high before him. Manny Haccian, towering a full head over the tallest man on Ploughman's Wharf, lumbered forward with a pair of whirling hatchets in his hands. The deadly axes radiated a deep red that matched his ridiculous mane and beard. Alum Aqadh, the Shadizarian lancer, stepped to Manny's side and thumped the butt of his spear on the dock. The long blade flared to life, and the Shadizarian dropped into a fighting stance.

Niles Crowing cast quick glances to his sides. There was a tiny popping sound, and Lenny the Unlucky Leprechaun appeared on Niles' shoulder. The one-legged leprechaun gripped a nasty needle dagger in each fist. Like his companions' weapons, the daggers shimmered with magic. Lenny grinned. "Now?"

Niles' smirk softened into a smile, the kind a starving man gets just before he breaks into a crust of bread. "Yes, now."

The Magnificent Seven moved at once, launching themselves upon the diseased rat-men. Their weapons fell upon armor and shields, and the clash of arms rang over Ploughman's Wharf. Gorzoni and his men fought for their lives and their freedom, and they gave ground sparingly. Derek and his friends watched from the sides as Niles and his crew worked tactical wonders of their own, pressing and releasing the rat-men with their attacks, first driving a section of their defensive line back, then giving way suddenly to draw them out a few at a time, only to close ranks from the sides and deliver death in a wall of flashing steel.

After a few of these clashes, where several of the rat-men fell to the Magnificent Seven and their magical weapons, Gorzoni looked about the pier, his beady eyes darting for an escape route. He glanced over his shoulder, and then a greasy smile rippled over his thin, rat lips. "Push forward!" he commanded his men.

His men obeyed, strengthened by the curse of the Moon Plague. They drove Niles and the others back, step by step. Gorzoni watched his men's advance with hungry eyes, but he did not raise a blade to help them. Instead, the instant a small gap opened between himself and his battling rat-men, he turned and fled the battle, hurling himself off the pier and into the ocean.

Niles, seeing that Gorzoni had fled, pointed behind the remaining rat-men. "Your cowardly leader has left you! Lay down your swords!"

The rat-men leapt back and looked for Gorzoni. When they couldn't find their leader, they hissed and squeaked at one another in their underworld language. Then, as one, they turned and threw themselves over the pier and into the harbor.

Niles and the others hurried to the edge of the pier and looked over the side. Derek quickly joined them and searched the dark waters below. There was only the gentle rise and fall of the sea, slapping against the heavy beams of Ploughman's Wharf. Derek strained his eyes, but there was no sign of the rat-men. Conrad and Dani came up beside him, with Lars and Jenkins close behind.

Derek turned to Niles Crowing. "Can you see them?"

Niles held his glowing sword over the edge of the pier. Its light lit the rippling water below. Some of the light spilled beneath the docks. Conrad got on his belly and dropped his head over the side so he could see under the pier. "Niles! Bring your sword. I think I see something."

Derek and his friends plopped down next to Conrad and peered through the dark mess of cobwebs and flotsam beneath the pier. They were a good twelve feet above the tide water, but the dark was so thick, Derek couldn't make out anything.

"What do you see?" Dani asked.

Conrad pointed into the black beneath the pier, away from the sea and back toward land. "Something was moving back there. It looked like a shadow inside a shadow."

Niles crouched down and thrust his rapier under Ploughman's Wharf. The light showed a stout framework of massive, ironwood beams running in neat rows that paralleled the coastline. Steady waves from the harbor beat in regular time against the braces. Derek peered into the dark, and far to the back, he saw an opening. Thick, iron bars, forged into a gate, lay next to a gaping hole. The light from Niles' sword showed a doorway, framed with crumbling bricks, that led to a black tunnel.

"There!" Derek shouted and pointed. "I see a tunnel!"

Conrad nodded. "That leads to the sewers under Zuid Horn. I'll bet that's where Gorzoni is going."

"To be sure," Niles agreed and stood up. He looked at the Magnificent Seven and then to the children. "And this is where I need to leave you, my friends. Your adventure with us has come to an end."

Derek felt the clench of anger in his gut. "What? After everything we've been through? Why would you leave us behind now?"

A heavy thumping on the dock announced the arrival of Wendy the Ogress. "It's not that we are abandoning you, child. Where we are going isn't safe for children."

Derek snorted and spit. His vision narrowed until all he could see was a white line in front of him. "Isn't safe for children? Are you serious? Niles set us up on a Shadizarian slave ship. We were beaten and tortured. We had to fight for our lives. *Now* you say it's too dangerous?"

Wendy looked as sheepish as an ogress could look. She turned to Niles. "He's got a point, Crowing."

Niles sighed and rubbed his face with his hands. "Derek, you're right. I never should have set you up on *The Delivery* the way I did. But here is the truth — it was the only way I could think of to expose Gorzoni and his foul underlings." Niles pressed his mouth into a tight line. "It was the only way I could avenge my sister."

Derek glared at Niles. The heat of his anger raged through him, but at the mention of Niles' sister, Derek felt the anger bleed out of him like a slow leak. "We could still help you avenge her. Find her if she's still alive, free her if she's captive." When he saw the doubt in Niles' eyes, he pressed harder. "You know we could."

"Derek, we are talking about wererats here, disease and death. There are things living beneath Zuid Horn that drive grown men mad. I can't expose you to that."

"Even though you were willing to trick us to expose Gorzoni?"

The other members of the Magnificent Seven gathered around Derek and his friends, along with Captain Gier and the honorable members of the Iron Guard. Everyone waited to see what Niles would say. Niles looked at each of them in turn, and finally he threw up his hands. "I don't understand why this is my choice. The boy has parents. Shouldn't we ask them?"

At the mention of his parents, Derek felt a wrenching deep in his gut. It had been more than three weeks since he'd seen Mum and Da. There was nothing in the world he wanted more than to see them again. Although he would never say it out loud, he suddenly realized that his longing for his parents outweighed his desire to go after Gorzoni.

Derek was about to say something when Captain Gier stepped forward. "Crowing, aren't these the boys you were telling me about, the ones who broke out of the stockade?"

Niles nodded. "Yes, sir."

"And why were they in the stocks?"

Conrad cleared his throat. "Disturbing the peace, sir. We were fighting in the street on Gillman's Way."

"Fighting, eh?" The captain studied the boys and scratched his black beard. "It would seem to me that before anyone is going on any further adventures, we need to resolve the issue of these boys breaking the law and then running from their punishment."

Derek and his friends dropped their heads and held their breath, awaiting the captain's ruling. The Iron Guard was famous for enforcing the law and strictly adhering to judgments once they were passed. Would Captain Gier grant them clemency?

Captain Gier cleared his throat. "Considering why they slipped their bonds," the captain continued, pointing at Dani, "and the treachery of the corrupted Iron Guard they exposed, I would say they have more than made amends for their crimes."

The boys looked up in relief. "Then, we're free to go?" Derek asked.

"Not so fast," the captain said. "First, we need to take you back to your parents. They will decide how much further you will go on this adventure."

Next to Derek, Lars' shoulders sagged. Captain Gier looked at him quizzically. "What's the matter?"

Lars took a slow breath. "We don't have parents, sir." He looked at Derek. "We're street rats."

The captain studied the boys and Dani. "Is that so?"

Lars nodded, and one of the Iron Guardsmen next to the captain leaned forward and whispered in his ear. The captain listened, shaking his head every now and then. Finally, he turned back to the children. "My lieutenant here has a proposal, and I am willing to support it, if you are."

The children tensed up, not knowing what the captain had in mind.

"As you know, the history of the Iron Guard is long and honorable, with a few notable exceptions." Here, he scowled and glanced over the edge of the pier. "Our guardsmen are trained to be the finest soldiers in the realms. But to become the best in the realms, their training has to start when they are very young." Captain Gier paused meaningfully. "About your age, in fact. Tell me, would you be interested in enrolling as recruits with the Iron Guard? You would have a safe place to sleep and three meals a day. The training would be hard, but in the end, you would be an honored addition to Zuid Horn's finest." He studied the children. "What do you say?"

Derek stood up straight. He remembered when he wanted to be a chef, and it seemed so far away now, compared to living the life of an adventurer. "Yes, sir!"

Niles and the Magnificent Seven chortled at Derek's reaction. The captain waved his hand. "This isn't for you to decide, son. We need to talk to your parents first."

Derek's shoulders slumped. "Really?"

Captain Gier nodded. "Yes. But your friends here, they've been providing for themselves and making their own decisions for years. We need that kind of self-sufficient thinking in the Guard. What do you say?"

Conrad looked at Dani, and then at Lars and Jenkins in turn. Lars and Jenkins were quick to answer.

"Count me in!" Jenkins shouted.

"Me, too," Lars said.

"Wonderful," the captain said, shaking their hands. "We are honored to have you." He turned to Dani and Conrad. "How about you two?"

Brother and sister looked at one another. Dani leaned over and whispered in Conrad's ear. Derek wished he could hear what she was saying. He hoped they would take the offer. Joining the Iron Guard would keep them safe, give them a family to belong to, and pave the way for a future they could have only dreamed of a few weeks earlier.

Conrad listened to his sister, and when she was done, he looked at Captain Gier and sighed. "Thank you, sir. It's a great offer," Conrad started, "and I might take you up on it."

The captain lifted an eyebrow. "But?"

Dani shifted her weight and looked at her feet. "But we've been running from the Iron Guard for all our lives. Sometimes, we get chased just for trying to survive. I don't mean to offend, but some of your men have treated us terribly. They call us 'rats,' lock us up, kick us off the piers when we ask for food." She looked at Lars and Jenkins, whose faces were flaming red. "I don't know that I could forget about that so easily and become the next generation of Iron Guards to harass the street people, just because a twist of fate put me on a different path. What about all my friends I'd be leaving behind? Would I be cleaning them out of the back alleys when my training is finished?"

Lars and Jenkins dropped their eyes. "I hadn't thought about that," Jenkins muttered.

"She's right," Lars added.

Captain Gier rubbed his bearded chin and studied the street children. "There is a hard truth and the honor of friendship in what you say, child. The Iron Guard must right the wrongs your work has uncovered here tonight. What if I were to make you an additional offer?"

"What's that?" Dani asked.

"That you would become the first members of a new unit of Iron Guardsmen, dedicated to protecting the forgotten people of Zuid Horn. You would become their voice and their shield. After basic training, you would work with them to map out Zuid Horn's underworld, root out the criminal elements who prey on the most vulnerable, and make the city safer for everyone in the process." Captain Gier studied the children. "What do you say?"

Conrad and the others came together in a tight circle. Derek wanted desperately to join them, to hear what they had to say, but he knew he didn't have a voice here. He looked at Niles, who gave Derek a simple hand gesture. *Stay calm.*

Derek took a breath and waited. Finally, they broke their circle, and Conrad moved a bit forward. He smiled broadly. "Captain Gier, we accept."

A cheer went up on the docks, and there was a round of hugging and backslapping as the veteran Iron Guardsmen welcomed their newest brothers and sister. When the celebrating was done, Captain Gier turned to Niles.

"That leaves this one," he said, gesturing to Derek. "I know I have no command authority over you, Crowing, but honor would dictate that before you go after Gorzoni, you return this boy to his parents. He has been away from them long enough. After you get him safely home, you and your team can hunt down Gorzoni. We know where he's going, so let's take the time to do this right. I'll head back to the barracks and get a team ready. You're just going on a scouting mission, Crowing. Don't go too deep without a unit of Iron Guardsmen with you. You're not the only one in need of revenge." Niles looked over his shoulder at the harbor. Derek could feel the anticipation seething from the mercenary, but when he turned back, Crowing was smiling. "You're right," Niles agreed. "I need to see Derek back. It is the right thing to do."

Niles and Derek shared a glance. The mercenary flashed Derek a quick wink, and Derek knew enough to keep quiet. Niles smiled and patted Derek on the back. "Well, Derek, shall I take you to your parents? I suspect they will be more than happy to see you."

"I'll say," Derek said. Something was burning his eyes, making them water. After he wiped them clean, he said, "I hope Da isn't mad I disappeared like that. He had that big order to fill."

Niles laughed and pointed in the direction of Derek's house. "Come. Say goodbye to your friends, and then let's get you home. You've got parents to see, and I've got a wererat to hunt down." Niles patted Derek on the back and walked over to chat with Captain Gier.

Derek shuffled to his friends. He went to Dani first because he thought that would be easiest, but when he got there, he had no idea what to say. Dani smiled at his suffering, and then she wrapped him in a warm hug. She smelled of sweat and blood and the sea, but to Derek, it was the best smell in the world.

"Thanks for coming to get me," she said.

Derek pulled her tighter. "Thanks for bringing me a cup of water."

They laughed and broke apart. Derek gave Dani a last smile and then turned to Jenkins and Lars. He offered Jenkins his hand. "Thanks for coming along," Derek said. "This wouldn't have worked without you."

Jenkins took Derek's hand and shook it. "You're not as bad as I thought, Derek. But you better watch out."

Derek cocked his head. "Why's that?"

"Because after my Iron Guard training, I'll finally be able to whoop you."

Derek laughed. "We'll see about that. I'm going to be training too."

The boys laughed and shook hands again. Then, Derek turned to Lars. He offered his hand, but Lars just looked at it. Derek snorted. "Seriously, Lars? After all of this?"

Lars pinched his mouth. The lines around his eyes were tight. "I'm glad we rescued Dani, Fulstarter. And for her, I'd do it again. But this doesn't change nothing between us. I know who you are."

Derek's chest tightened, and his neck tingled. But this time, rather than letting the anger run rampant, Derek took a breath, and the fire faded. "People change, Lars."

"I don't think so."

"Derek!" Niles called from where he was talking to Captain Gier. "Let's go."

Derek and Lars looked at one another one last time, and then Derek quickly turned to Conrad. The boy was scratching his arm, where the rat had bitten him. "Are you going to be okay?" Derek asked.

"Yeah."

"So, the Iron Guard?"

Conrad nodded. "We'll get three meals a day. Never had that before."

Derek laughed. "There you go."

They looked at one another, not sure what to say.

"Derek!" Niles called. "Let's go!"

"Just a bit!" Derek called and turned back to Conrad.

The boys looked at one another. Conrad twisted his mouth, and Derek shifted his feet. Derek wanted to apologize for all the fights they used to have, wanted to say sorry for calling them "street rats" and orphans and more, wanted to say he saw it now — saw the way he used to act but hadn't realized it — wanted to say he was sorry again and again, but the words wouldn't come out.

Conrad watched him and just nodded. "I know," he said. "Thank you."

"Derek!" Niles called. "The sun will be up before we get you home. Let's go!"

"Coming," Derek called. Then, to Conrad, he said, "See you soon?"

Conrad smiled. "Count on it."

23

Derek Finally comes Home to Stay

When Derek and the survivors of the salt mine revolt staggered into Zuid Horn, word of their return spread with the wind. They had been gone for more than two weeks, after all. No one expected them to be alive, much less free men and women, bearing the fine weaponry of the valiant Iron Guard and trophies from their slain yakariian captors. Families celebrated the return of lost members, and neighbors welcomed back their longtime friends with open arms. Derek, Conrad, and Dani were buried under an avalanche of hugs and kisses as word of their heroic rescue efforts were told again and again.

The knot of cheering Zuid Hornians grew as it rolled into the city. Derek paraded next to his father, and when they passed the newly rebuilt archway of a hide tanner's shop, Derek motioned for his father to join him for a short break from the crowd. Resin from the fresh wood stuck to Derek's fingers as he ran his hand over the smoothly planed door frame. The rebuilding of Zuid Horn had begun, and like Zuid Horn's rebirth, Derek realized he was about to start a new phase of his life as well.

He looked at his father. "Da, I have to go."

Da waved at Mr. Innskeep, Augie's father. Mr. Innskeep was gesturing for Da to make his way across the street, where a brewer was opening a keg of ale to celebrate the return of his friends. Da waved back and frowned at his son. "What's this?"

"I have to go."

"Where?"

Derek held up his hand, showing his father the magical ring. "It's like I said at the salt mines. We couldn't have saved you without these magical rings." Derek paused and looked at the ground. "I promised Gilgameth Tuft I would return them after we freed you." He could feel the rising heat of Da's distrust of the wizard. But he had to tell Da the rest of the story — all of it. He took a breath. "I also promised him that Conrad, Dani, and I would return as well. We promised we would stay with him until Niles returned."

"Stay?" Da barked. "He's keeping you hostage? Why would you go back to him?"

"He's not what you think," Derek pleaded. "He wants to find out who did this to Zuid Horn as much as all of us."

"Then why doesn't he use his magic to find out? Why use you and your friends as pawns?"

"He just wants to make sure Niles keeps his word."

"The wizard doesn't need you and your friends to force Crowing to investigate this. You know the mercenary as well as anyone. I'll bet Niles started his investigation before the floodwaters went down."

Derek bit his lip. "But I gave my word that I would return, Da. Doesn't that mean anything?"

"Your word? What's your word to Gilgameth Tuft going to be worth when you're dead?" Da glared at the dark Tower of Sorcery dominating Zuid Horn's skyline. "Never trust a wizard, Derek. I learned that the hard way when I was in the Iron Guard." Da shook his head. "Maybe you'll understand, someday."

Derek dropped his face in shame. After how close they had been at the mines, revealing the full extent of what he had promised the wizard felt like a betrayal. He took a slow breath. "So, I can go? I might be there for a while."

Da turned back to his son. "Why are you asking me? You were going to go anyway."

"I just wanted your blessing."

Da took a slow breath and rubbed his face. "You've always had it. I know I never acted like it, but even when you thought you wanted to be a cook, you had it."

"You can forget about me wanting to be a cook," Derek said.

"Well, you would have been a good one," Da laughed.

"Do you still want me to be a fletcher?"

"I do," Da admitted, "when you're ready. You have other things you need to do now. If I don't let you do them, what kind of father would I be?"

Derek shrugged. "You're doing a good job so far."

Da smiled. "Do you want to know something? When I was your age, my da didn't want me to join the Iron Guard either, but I did it anyway. Turned out to be the best thing I ever did, besides marrying your mother. After I took that arrow to my knee and my adventuring days were done, Da welcomed me back to the shop. Never said anything about it. And here's the funny thing. In the end, it was my connection to the Iron Guard and the rangers that brought in even more business. Da had always made enough to survive, but it wasn't until I left and joined the Iron Guard that our business really took off."

"Was he ever alright with you joining the Guard?"

Da laughed. "Not until long after, when he was an old man. Da was a stubborn old goat, but he was nobody's fool. Besides, I think he liked listening to my stories while we worked." Derek and his father watched the celebration in the street. Mr. Innskeep and the ale master across the way were busy handing out cups. Two fiddles and a tight drum that had survived the flood appeared and brightened the air with a happy tune. Derek glanced up at his father and found him smiling. How long would that smile last, Derek wondered, when Da found out about Derek being Gilgameth Tuft's next apprentice?

Derek straightened himself up. It was time. "Da," he started, but then a happy scream went up.

"Mum!"

Derek leaned out of the doorway to see Wendy the Ogress with Sarah on her shoulders, wading through the crowd. Mum, who had been chatting with the brewer's wife, shouted at the sight of her youngest daughter. "My baby! My baby!" She crashed through the crowd to get to her.

Wendy tenderly took the girl off her shoulders and handed Sarah over to Mum, who covered her with tears and kisses. Wendy the Ogress looked on, with Father Ferrum and Pavaraci Moonfist at her side. Derek waved to Wendy and the others. Pavaraci saw him first and started weaving his way through the crowd toward Derek and Da. Wendy and Ferrum followed him.

Derek watched his friends approaching, noting the smooth confidence that flowed from his adventuring friends. He wanted to know that confidence for himself, especially now, after he had just tasted it. He wondered how long it would be before Gilgameth Tuft let him go on quests as a young wizard. Maybe the master of the Tower would let him adventure with Dani and Conrad occasionally. That would be nice, he thought. But first, he had to come clean with his father.

Da took a couple of steps into the street. "Sarah," he said. "I didn't think I would ever see her again."

"Da, hold on," Derek said.

Bryton Fulstarter stopped. "Let's go see your sister."

"We will. I want to. But first, I need to tell you something."

"Alright."

Derek took a breath. "I haven't told you the whole story about what happened with Gilgameth Tuft," Derek said. A bubble was

building in his chest. He couldn't look Da in the eye. Derek focused on Wendy and the others getting closer instead.

Da put his arm around Derek's shoulders. "Just say it, son. What's going on?"

"When Master Tuft offered us the rings..."

Da scowled. "'*Master* Tuft?'"

Derek ignored the question. "When he offered us the rings, he said the magic came with a price."

Da's arm dropped from Derek's shoulders. "I knew it."

"His current apprentices have almost completed their training. He's looking for a new apprentice, Da. In exchange for the rings, I agreed that it would be me."

It was as if Da had sprung a leak and the life drained out of him in a rush. "His apprentice?"

Derek dropped his face. "I'm sorry, Da. I had to, so I could get the rings. I didn't want to let you down."

Da crossed his arms over his chest. "I can't believe this. I thought you were just going to the tower until Niles figured out who destroyed Zuid Horn. His apprentice? Do you know how long that will take?"

Derek felt his chin quivering. "I'm sorry, Da."

"You rescued us at the price of your freedom? You were already a slave once. Have you learned nothing?"

"Da," Derek cried, the tears welling in his eyes, "I'm sorry!"

Da sighed and shook his curly mane. He scratched his dark beard. "I can't believe this. I have to tell your mother." Da rubbed the back of his head and walked across the street to where Mum was still raining kisses on Sarah.

Derek's chest felt cold and flat. Not only had he let his father down, but he had managed to ruin the reunion with Sarah as well. Could he get nothing right?

Wendy the Ogress, Father Ferrum, and Pavaraci Moonfist broke through the noisy crowd to meet up with Derek. Somehow, they missed the tears in Derek's eyes and took turns picking him up with big, bear hugs.

"Look at you!" Father Ferrum said. "We thought you were gone forever, yet here you are, a hero again!"

"Here I am," Derek said, his voice flat.

Conrad and Dani appeared from behind Wendy. They jumped on her and started talking to the ogress at the same time. Wendy laughed and tried to unravel their tales of the salt mines. Derek was happy for his friends. They had a home now with the Iron Guard, something they'd never had before. He hoped he could see them again once his apprenticeship to Gilgameth Tuft was over.

Derek was about to head over to Dani and Conrad when Pavaraci Moonfist pulled him aside. "Derek, I can't say how happy I am to see you and the others alive and well, but there is something I need to tell you."

The wizard's eyes, which were usually sparkling from a secret joke, were serious. Derek felt a clench in his stomach. "What's the matter? Did someone die?"

Pavaraci shook his head. "No. Well, yes. Someone died, but there's more."

Derek's head spun. "What are you trying to say?"

"It's Niles. He is missing."

"Missing?"

"Yes. He's been missing for several days now."

"What happened?"

"He was on the trail of the people who destroyed Zuid Horn. One of his leads took him below the city."

"To the sewers?"

Pavaraci nodded. "Yes. That's where he learned that Lydia had died."

"His sister? The Rat Queen?"

"Don't let Niles hear you call her that, but yes, the Rat Queen."

"She died? How?"

"In the flood. The waters that did all of this..." He gestured to the destruction of Zuid Horn. "Most of it left through the sewers. The tunnels are practically choked with the dead."

"By the Forge. What happened to Niles?"

"When he found his sister's body, after everything he had done to free her from Gorzoni, he went mad. He raced out of the sewers, and we haven't seen him since."

Derek pushed past Pavaraci and started down the street. "What are we waiting for? We have to find him!"

Pavaraci grabbed Derek by the elbow. "Wait, wait. It's not going to be that easy. The last we saw, he was raving about getting revenge on the people who killed his sister."

"Did you ever find out who caused the explosions in the foundries that started this whole mess?"

"Not quite. Niles kept most of the information to himself. He is so blazing secretive — one of his more irritating qualities. And now he's mad with grief, hunting down a pack of killers without the Seven to watch his flanks." Pavaraci shook his head. "I've never seen him like this."

"By the Forge," Derek swore. "Niles needs me more than ever. Now what do I do?"

"What do you mean?" the Elf asked.

Derek took a breath and explained everything to Pavaraci, from the rings to the apprenticeship.

"Well," the wizard said, "that's a surprise. I didn't know you were interested in magic."

"I wasn't, but Gilgameth Tuft must have seen something in me. Anyway, now I have to go to the Tower of Sorcery just when Niles needs me most." Derek ran his fingers through his hair.

"Do your parents know about your deal with Gilgameth Tuft?"

"Are you kidding? I thought my da was going to explode when I told him I had to go back to the tower. When he found out about the apprenticeship..." Derek rolled his eyes.

"It sounds like you don't have much of a choice here."

"But what about Niles?"

Pavaraci waved his hand. "You leave Niles to the Seven. We'll find him. And don't worry. If we need you, we will come get you."

"But what if Gilgameth Tuft doesn't let me out of the tower?"

"The truth is, you won't be out of the tower for years, Derek. That's how a wizard's apprenticeship works."

"What? *Years?*"

"I'm afraid so. Learning to control magic is even harder than learning swordplay. No one learns it overnight." Pavaraci chewed the inside of his cheek. "Well, there are ways to make it seem faster, but the price is steep, too steep for anyone who wants to hold onto who they are inside here." He patted his chest.

Derek's shoulders slumped. What had he gotten himself into? His heart wanted to go after Niles, but he had made a deal to get the rings. When he looked over the street at the reunited families celebrating and the neighbors welcoming back dear friends, he knew what he had to do. Derek would go to the Tower of Sorcery and keep his word to become the next apprentice. It was a sacrifice, to be sure, but that's what heroes did. They made sacrifices to keep others safe, and that's what Derek was — a hero.

A gasp went up from the crowd around them, and the celebration in the streets came to an abrupt halt. Derek stood on his toes for a better view. Heads scampered right and left, but he was still too short to see into the crowd. He hopped over to Wendy, Dani, and Conrad.

"Wendy, what is it?" Derek asked.

"Wizards," she said with a frown.

The last of the crowd skittered away to reveal three black-robed wizards — two men and a wizard — who strode directly to Derek, Dani, and Conrad. Derek recognized them from the night of the flood. Wendy put out her gigantic paws and pulled the children behind her. She growled at the pale-skinned wizards. Derek poked

his head out from behind her. "We just got back to Zuid Horn. We were on our way to the tower."

Naomi regarded Derek over her uplifted nose. "Your lies mean nothing to me. I am here for the master's rings." She stretched out her hand to Derek and the others. "Give them to me. Now."

The children yanked the rings off their fingers and gave them to the woman. "Can I say goodbye to my parents before we go to the tower?" Derek asked.

"Why?" the wizard scoffed. "You're not going to the tower."

Derek froze. "I'm not?"

"No," she said with a snort.

"But Gilgameth Tuft made me promise to be his next apprentice." The crowd around them gasped, and Derek felt his chest puff up a little.

The wizard sniffed in disdain. "You? I think not. The master traded the use of his rings with the promise that one of you would become his next apprentice. He has chosen," she pointed at Dani, "this one."

It was as if the ground had dropped from beneath Derek's feet. "Dani?"

"Me?" Dani asked. Her eyes were wide. Was that fear in her eyes or excitement?

"You," Naomi said simply. "I am to accompany you to the Tower of Sorcery, where your training is to begin immediately."

The crowd around them stepped back, amazed that one of their numbers — a girl known to be a street rat — could be so instantly elevated to the highest level of power in Zuid Horn.

The back of Derek's neck began to tingle. "I don't understand. I was supposed to be the next apprentice."

"On what grounds did you decide that?"

The edges of Derek's vision swam with fuzz. His chin trembled. "'On what grounds?' Are you serious?"

"Quite."

He could feel the crowd watching him, could almost hear their snickering that Dani, not Derek, would be Gilgameth Tuft's next apprentice. His face and neck burned with shame. Derek tried to check his rising temper. Dani's voice in his head warned him to stop, but the anger had its talons in his heart now, and it forced the truth from his lips.

"Who rescued her from Shadizarian slavers? Me! Who fought pirates and slavers with a table leg? Me!" His voice kept rising until it was almost a shout. His face and neck were on fire with rage. He swept his arm wide at the Zuid Hornians freed from the salt mines. "Whose plan freed these people? Mine! Every time we ran into a problem, who solved it? Me! How could I not be the next apprentice?" His hand drifted to the makeshift club tucked in his belt.

The wizard shook her head slowly, her eyes narrow slits. "Watch yourself, boy, or your next mistake could be your last."

Derek's breath came in quick pants. His lips pressed so tight they were going numb.

The wizard continued. "The master never said you would be the next apprentice. He only said that he needed a new apprentice. It was arrogance to assume it was you."

"But he said he's been watching me for a long time."

"The master watches many people for many reasons. Don't assume you are special."

Derek's fists were knots of wood. Through the fog of his rage, Dani's dim form came to him, her voice like a trickle of cool water down a cracked throat. "Derek, please. Let me do this."

He whirled on her, angry that she was getting this credit he knew he deserved, angry that she was the one paying the price for the rings. Wasn't that his responsibility? Wasn't he supposed to be the hero, not her? But there was something else there too, something that wiggled like a worm through the anger when he heard Dani's voice. When that something raised its head, he saw it was fear.

His chest shook. "Dani, don't," he pleaded. "After everything I've done to keep you safe, why would you throw it away like this?"

Dani cocked her head. "'Throw it away?'"

He threw a gesture toward Naomi with her pale skin and haunted eyes. "Look at her, Dani! What do you think is going to happen to you if you do this?"

Dani took a deep breath. "I don't have to follow the same path she did. There are good wizards in the realm as well. What about Pavaraci?"

Derek glanced at the Elven wizard, who nodded slowly. "It's true, Derek. Dani can choose her own path."

"Magic has a price, Dani," Derek said, turning back to his friend. "A price! You've seen what price the healers pay. What do you think wizards have to do for their magic? Are you willing to pay? I can't let you do that!"

Dani stepped close to Derek, so close that they were toe to toe. Her eyes were sad, but at the same time, they were full of something Derek had never seen before — not from anyone outside of his family, anyway. She took his face in her hands and looked him full in the eye.

"Why don't you let *me* decide if I'm willing to pay the price?"

A bubble rose in Derek's throat. His chin trembled, and then the bubble burst with a flood of tears and truth. "I'm scared, Dani. I can't lose you," he whispered so no one could hear. "Not after all this. Not after losing Peter. Not after losing Liza." He closed his eyes and wept. She pulled him close, and Derek breathed in the scent of her. Sun, sand, sea, and sweat. This was the Dani he had come to love, and now he was going to lose her. "I can't do it, Dani. I can't let you go."

"Have you considered that maybe this is the price, Derek? This is the price we need to pay to save Zuid Horn?" Derek shook his head, and she continued. "You are a hero, Derek," she whispered. "I've known it since we met. You are always willing to put yourself on the line, to risk everything for someone else. You saved me, and I will always be grateful. And, you saved these people. Zuid Horn is going to need heroes now more than ever. Be a hero for Zuid Horn, Derek. Please, if you love me, then respect my chance to be a hero, too."

"Love you..." Derek repeated, and he realized it was true.

Dani pulled him close again and held him tight. "Please."

"You're going whether I agree or not, aren't you?"

"Yes."

The tears came again, but they were different this time, tinged with bittersweetness and longing. "Will I ever see you again?"

Dani pulled away and took his head in her hands. She pressed her lips against his and kissed him lightly. "I hope so," she said with a sad smile. "For both of our sakes."

She let him go, and his fingers trailed after her. She walked over to Conrad, hugged him, and whispered in his ear. Conrad nodded, and when they came apart, their eyes were wet. Then Dani went to the wizard. "I'm ready," she said.

The wizard nodded, and without another word, she turned and led Dani and the other two wizards through the onlookers. The crowd filled in behind them.

Conrad came to stand at his side. "That was tough," he said.

"I'll say."

"Did you ever notice that you have a bad temper?"

Derek snorted. "Up yours."

Conrad laughed, and Derek felt his heart lighten a little. They watched the crowd of citizens and freed slaves return to their celebration, raising cups of ale and singing songs. Together, they looked at the Tower of High Sorcery, Dani's new home. When would they see her again? Derek's eyes blurred, and he dropped his gaze from the tower into the dark of an alley across the street. Something moved in the shadows, and Derek's body tensed. Was that a yakariian scout? He rubbed his eyes with the back of his

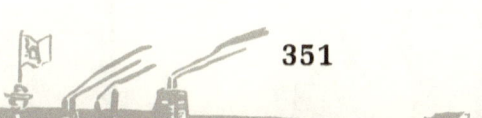

wrist. When he looked again, the alley was empty. He let out slow breath. "You okay?" Conrad asked.

"Yeah. Just seeing things, I guess."

A breeze came gently through the streets, bringing the scent of rot and gray silt left over from the flood.

"By The Hammer, that reeks," Conrad said, covering his nose.

"Yeah," Derek replied with a deep breath, "but I smell hope there, too."

Conrad looked at Derek with a raised brow. "Hope smells like a latrine?"

"You never know," Derek said.

They laughed again. Conrad scratched his arm, where the white scar of a bite mark marred his deeply tanned skin. Conrad caught Derek staring at the scar and tucked it behind his back.

Derek ran his fingers through his hair. "We've got a lot to do, my friend. We have to help the Seven find Niles. Zuid Horn needs to prepare for an attack from the yakarii. But I'm not worried," he went on. "In fact, I've never felt better. We can do this. As scary as the past month has been, it all feels right somehow." He glanced at the Tower of Sorcery in the distance. "Even if it hurts."

Conrad grunted. "I know."

Derek pointed at Conrad's arm. "And we've got to find a way to take care of that."

Conrad sighed. "If there was a way, Niles would have found it for his sister."

"Niles isn't us, though, is he? We'll find a way."

Da came up behind the boys and put his arms around them. "Well, this has been quite the day, hasn't it?"

"I'll say," Derek said. Then, thinking of the way he lost his temper in front of everyone, he muttered, "So you saw all of that?"

"I did."

"How embarrassing..."

Da shrugged. "You'll get over it. Everyone makes mistakes. As the saying goes, it's how you recover from your mistakes that shows who you are."

"I suppose."

"I'm still not happy about Tuft taking one of you kids as an apprentice, but something tells me Dani is the right choice."

Derek's first instinct was to argue, but then he paused and admitted, "Yeah, maybe you're right."

"You'll be fine, boys. We'll all be fine. Trust me on that. But for tonight, enough of adventure. Let's go see your mother and your sister. We need to be together now."

Derek breathed a sigh of relief. "Let's go."

"And you," Da said to Conrad, "are coming with us. You're part of the family now."

Conrad beamed, and they all turned toward Mum and Sarah. Da led the way, his smile broad beneath his bristling beard. "I can't wait to get home. What's left of it anyway. I want to sleep in my own bed tonight."

Derek sighed. A broad smile broke across his face. "I couldn't agree with you more."

24

It All Comes Together

It was well after midnight when Niles and the Magnificent Seven escorted Derek past the taverns lining the wharf, down the dark streets of Zuid Horn, up back allies stuffed with heaps of trash, and through the artisan neighborhoods. Finally, they came to Gillman's Way.

Apart from a few oil lamps placed high upon cast-iron posts, the street was completely dark. Derek expected this, of course. Gillman's Way was home to a wealthier crowd. Not nobles, by a long shot, but much better off than most of Zuid Horn. A unit of Iron Guardsmen marched up the street. Niles stepped forward to greet them, exchanged a few words, and shook hands with their captain. He stepped back to watch them march away.

Once they were around a corner, Niles waved Derek and the others over. "Well," Niles said, "here we are." He pointed down Gillman's Way to Derek's house.

Derek walked to the middle of the street. From where he stood, he could see a candle's dim light shining through the window of Da's shop. "Just like every night," Derek whispered.

"What's that?" Niles asked.

"Nothing," Derek said.

Derek, Niles Crowing, and the Magnificent Seven stood and looked at the Fulstarter shop. It was two stories tall with living quarters on the second floor, like most houses on Gillman's Way. His grandfather had built this house, and one day, it would be Derek's. Something inside Derek felt warm with that thought, but something else also felt sad. He was pondering this conflict when Niles said, "Do you want us to go in with you?"

Derek shook his head. "No. I think it would be better if I went in alone."

Niles laughed. His eyes glittered in the lamplight. "Why's that?"

"When my father finds out why I was gone, he's not going to be happy."

Niles frowned. "I can see why you'd think that, but you might be surprised."

"You don't know my da the way I do."

"Maybe not," Niles said with a smile, "but there may be things I know that you don't."

Derek eyed Niles. "Like what?"

Niles laughed again and patted Derek on the back. "Maybe another time. For now, what do you say about going after Gorzoni?"

"Me?"

"Why not? You and your friends. Something tells me no one knows the tunnels under this city like your friends do. Captain Gier said your friends' first mission would be protecting the people of the street from threats. What greater threat is out there right now than Gorzoni and the wererats?"

"I suppose," Derek said, "if you can get them away from their Iron Guard training." Derek's shoulders slumped. "But what about me? I've never been in the sewers before. I'd be useless."

"I've seen you fight," Niles said with a chuckle. "It's Gorzoni who needs to be afraid."

"I'll say," laughed Wendy the Ogress. "You wield a pretty mean club."

Thanks," Derek said, "but he's a wererat. I'd need an enchanted weapon to deal with him."

Niles smirked. "Well, let's just see what happens."

"What's that supposed to mean?"

"Never mind for now." Niles glanced up and down the street. "Look, I need to get going if I'm going to catch up to Gorzoni." He looked Derek straight in the eye. "What do you say? I will send Kassar or Pavaraci in the next couple of days."

Pavaraci Moonfist smiled. "I'll be happy to get out of the sewers by then."

Derek's gaze went between Niles and the shop. A deep part of him wanted to continue his adventure with Niles, but he also knew that his father needed his help. The deeper part of him grumbled, and before he knew it, he said, "I'll do it."

Niles patted him on the back. "I knew you would! Excellent. You've got the blood of an adventurer in you, like I always told your da." He gestured for to the Magnificent Seven to come closer. "Alright, friends. This is where we see Derek off and head after Gorzoni."

Derek grabbed Niles by the arm. "What if we just went now? I'm afraid that if I go home, Da isn't going to let me out again for the rest of my life!"

Niles laughed. "I doubt that, my friend. Don't you worry. We'll be back for you when the time is right." Then, to the Seven, he said, "Say your goodbyes, and we'll be on our way."

One by one, the Magnificent Seven offered Derek handshakes and words of encouragement. Wendy the Ogress picked him up, burying Derek in a crushing embrace of cool, flabby flesh and the reek of ammonia. Derek sighed in the stink, knowing he would miss it, at least for a while.

"Come, child," the ogress said. "I will walk you home and catch up with the others afterwards." Derek gave Niles and the others one last wave and headed down Gillman's Way with Wendy. When they came to his house, Wendy stopped and picked Derek up for one last hug. "You be good," she said.

"Me? I'm always good." Wendy the Ogress glared at him, but there was a sparkle in her deep, brown eyes. "Well," Derek admitted, "I'm mostly good."

Wendy grunted. "That's the truth." She looked back down the street, where Niles and the others had disappeared. "It sounds like I'll see you again in a few days."

"It does."

"Be safe until then."

"I will."

After a final pat on Derek's head, which almost buckled his knees, Wendy turned and headed down Gillman's Way, her bulk jiggling from under her armor. "Tell your da I said hello."

"I will," Derek called quietly, and then he moved to the front door. He was just about to knock when something Wendy had said made him stop. Derek turned to catch her, but the street was already empty. Somehow, Wendy the Ogress, as massive as she was, had slipped silently into the night.

"How does she know Da?" Derek wondered aloud.

He shrugged and knocked quietly on the front door. He was about to knock a second time when he heard the shuffle of drying arrow shafts on a wooden table, followed by heavy steps on the other side of the door. The latch clicked and slid to the side, and then the door opened. Da loomed over him. Derek's breath caught in his throat, tangled in a web of relief, anxiety, and fear.

Dark rings hung under Da's eyes. A tattered canvas work shirt and a pair of dirty breeches stretched to cover his broad shoulders and meaty thighs. His dark hair and beard were snarled messes. He squinted into the dark street, and when his eyes adjusted to the low light, Da gasped like a fish gulping for air. He clutched at the door frame and swayed uneasily.

"Derek," he barely managed to whisper. Then he lunged forward and caught the boy up in his arms. He crushed Derek in a hug that made Wendy seem like a child. Still clutching his boy tightly, Bryton Fulstarter shouted over his shoulder, "Mum! Girls! Derek is back!"

There was a squeal and a rush of feet down the loft's ladder. Da carried Derek inside and turned him over to his sisters and mother, who lavished him with attention and tears. This went on for a long while. His mother kept looking him over for scrapes and bruises, lifting his shirt and turning him around, refusing to believe him when he insisted that he was fine. Her eyes filled with tears when she saw the ten white scars from the row master's whip, and Derek had to promise all over again that he was alright.

Liza brought Derek a bowl of that evening's stew — braised lamb and leeks. Derek closed his eyes and sniffed. "Home," he whispered.

Sara dragged a stool over for him to sit on while he ate and recounted his adventure. Derek kept expecting his father to fly into a rage when we told them about the plans they made with Niles Crowing to free the slaves on *The Delivery* and expose the corrupt underbelly of the Iron Guard, but he never said so much as a word.

By the time Derek wrapped up his tale, dawn's gray fingers were reaching across the sky. Banging shutters from nearby shops announced the coming of a new business day. The smell of charcoal lighting and coffee brewing on the neighbors' cooking fires wafted through the windows. Liza and Sara kept drifting off, until Mum insisted they go to bed for a little sleep before the day started. His sisters and mother gave him another kiss, and then they climbed the ladder to the loft.

That left Derek and his father alone for the first time that night. "So," Da said, "your adventure has come to an end."

"I thought you would be mad."

Da looked at Derek. "About what?"

"We just got that big order, remember? You needed me, and I disappeared."

Da took a deep breath and leaned back on his bench. "Well, when I came down to the wharf, I was pretty angry. But after you disappeared that night, all the madness left me."

"How did you find out?"

"About you being gone?" Da asked. "Niles told me."

Derek chewed his lip, not sure if he should ask his next question, but needing to know just the same. "You weren't mad at him?"

"Of course, but I've known Niles for a long time. I know how he is."

"You do?"

"Yes. I knew him from some years ago, back when he first came to Zuid Horn. We used to chum around together."

Derek stared at his father. "'Chum around?'"

Da laughed. "You don't believe me?"

"No, it's just that you two are nothing alike."

Da shrugged. "Maybe that's why we like one another. Anyway, when he explained about Gorzoni and rescuing the slaves, I was still mad at him for putting you at risk, but I understood why he did it. And I had to trust him when he said he would keep you safe. I owe him that much, after all the times he's saved my life."

Derek froze. "Wait. What?"

Da waved his hands to cut Derek off. "Never mind, not now. I'll tell you about it another time. For now, let's just say Niles and I have known about Gorzoni's crooked ways for a while, and that I would do anything to save his sister."

Now Derek was totally baffled. "Wait, how do you know all these things about Niles? I thought I was going to have to explain everything, yet you already know."

Da laughed again and trundled Derek toward the loft and the sleeping skins. "Not tonight, Derek. That's a tale for another time. I need to open the shop now, and you need to rest. I've got a full day of work planned for you. We still have that big order to fill, and now we are three weeks behind. Think you can handle that?"

"Maybe we could hire Peter and Augie on to help? They said they would help, last time I saw them."

Da shrugged. "We'll see. You boys spend more time getting into trouble than getting things done when you're together. And I don't want to worry about Peter flirting with Liza. It's too much for an

old man like me." Da pointed to the ladder. "Up you go, now. Get some sleep. We have a lot of work to do. You ready to help?"

Derek crawled up to the sleeping loft. He hadn't realized how tired his eyes were. "Yes, sir. I'll be down after a little nap. Is that okay?" Derek looked over the edge of the loft to see Da watching him. There was a spark in his father's eyes that hadn't been there when he first opened the door. "I think that will be just fine." Da smiled at Derek, and the happiness came from deep in his eyes. "I'm glad you're home."

"Me too, Da. I can't think of any place I'd rather be." It was out of his mouth before he knew it, and the warmth in his chest told him it was true.

Derek crept past his sleeping mother and sisters and lay down on his blankets. He closed his eyes, and as his breathing slowed, he swore he felt the rise and fall of the ocean beneath him as he drifted off to sleep.

ACKNOWEDGEMENTS

One of my great joys in life is bringing people together to create a product. The creation of this book was one of those joys. I could not have completed this story without inspiration from several important people:

To Derek Belter and Scott B. Conrad, who were better friends to me than they could ever know.

To Nancee Beal, whose dedication to our shared craft inspired me to write and write and write. I miss working with you!

To John Hickman, my perennial first reader. I often wrote with the image of you reading my stories with a pipe and glass of red close at hand.

To my dear friends Thomas Baxter, Bill Ringelstetter, Kevin Strattan, Jimmy Hauck, Mikey Boulware, Scotty Annon, Dave Thunstrum, and Chuck Everette, who destroyed my favorite fantasy city in one night of gaming and in the process inspired years of therapeutic writing (leading to this book).

To Kim Suhr, my writing teacher and primary editor. I am a better writer because of you, and I look forward to more lessons under your tutelage.

To Charlie Blue, James Wicke, and Katie "Splinter" Read, my student beta readers. Thank you for providing honest feedback from my intended audience.

To Anna Bauer-Baxter, Thomas Baxter, Bill Ringelstetter, Kevin Strattan, Cara Pennington, Patrick O'Connor, and Tanja Read. Thank you for being my adult beta readers and giving me the feedback I needed to tighten the story.

To Steve Langenecker and Chris Keefe, my art teachers. Thank you for encouraging me with my drawings, and thank you for your patience as I continue to insist on only drawing in ink.

To Eric Anderson, for being my perpetual cheerleader. Thanks for the push! Huggzzz!

To Scott Curty, my good buddy and a hell of a photographer. Thank you for photographing my artwork. Now, can you help me find a use for all this homemade maple syrup?

To Shannon Ishizaki, Jayden Shambeau, Jenna Zerbel, and the team at Ten16 Press. Thank you for taking a chance on me and helping me bring this one to the finish line.

To the Core Four, for bringing the love of storytelling to the next generation. Gavin Curty and Ben Ferguson, continue looking to the morning star for guidance.

To my sweet boys, Hunter and Reese. May the story of your lives reveal the heroes I see in your hearts.

To my siblings, Dave, Amy, and Sarah. I will always have your backs.

To my parents, Peggy and Jim, who have always supported me with patience and love.

And finally, to my beautiful wife, my biggest fan, and the love of my life, Michelle Weber. As always, everything for you.

Michael Weber teaches high school-level history, writing, and film in Wales, Wisconsin. An avid believer in the power of storytelling, Michael emphasizes the importance of students becoming the protagonists of their own tales. When not writing fiction or drawing accompanying artwork, Michael is busy being a husband, dad, beekeeper, and chicken wrangler. Visit Michael on his Instagram page @mr.weberdoesstuff

www.ingramcontent.com/pod-product-compliance
Lightning Source LLC
Chambersburg PA
CBHW030555020726
47494CB00005B/1629